ONCE UPON a *Devilishly Enchanting* KISS

#1 The Whickertons in Love

BY BREE WOLF

WOLF PUBLISHING

Once Upon a Devilishly Enchanting Kiss by Bree Wolf

Published by WOLF Publishing UG

Copyright © 2020 Bree Wolf
Text by Bree Wolf
Cover Art by Victoria Cooper
Hard Cover ISBN: 978-3-98536-006-2
Paperback ISBN: 978-3-98536-000-0
Ebook ISBN: 978-3-98536-001-7

WOLF Publishing - This is us:

Two sisters, two personalities.. But only one big love!

Diving into a world of dreams..
  ...Romance, heartfelt emotions, lovable and witty characters, some humor, and some mystery! Because we want it all! Historical Romance at its best!

Visit our website to learn all about us, our authors and books!

Sign up to our mailing list to receive first hand information on new releases, freebies and promotions as well as exclusive giveaways and sneak-peeks!

WWW.WOLF-PUBLISHING.COM

Also by Bree Wolf

The Whickertons in Love

The WHICKERTONS IN LOVE is a new series by USA Today bestselling author BREE WOLF set in Regency-era England, portraying the at times turbulent ways the six Whickerton siblings search for love. If you enjoy wicked viscounts, brooding lords as well as head-strong ladies, fierce in their affections and daring in their search for their perfect match, then this new series is perfect for you!

#1 Once Upon a Devilishly Enchanting Kiss

#2 Once Upon a Temptingly Ruinous Kiss

#3 Once Upon an Irritatingly Magical Kiss

#4 Once Upon a Devastatingly Sweet Kiss

#5 Once Upon an Achingly Beautiful Kiss

#6 Once Upon an Accidentally Bewitching Kiss

Prequel to the series: Once Upon A Kiss Gone Horribly Wrong

ONCE UPON a *Devilishly Enchanting* KISS

Prologue

London, England 1800 (or a variation thereof)

"Anne, you look as though you're about to faint," Lady Louisa Beaumont, second eldest daughter to the Earl of Whickerton, commented upon seeing her cousin's whitish, pale face and her huge, round eyes staring at the crowded ballroom as though facing a firing squad. "This is your first ball, not your execution." Chuckling, Louisa squeezed Anne's hand reassuringly. "You'll be fine."

Whether or not Anne believed her was unclear as she continued to eye her surroundings with wary caution, her shoulders tense and her steps all but steady.

Turning her head to look at her younger sister—by only one year, mind you—Louisa whispered over her shoulder, "She looks worse than you did, dearest Leo." A sisterly snicker followed.

For a short moment, Leonora all but ignored Louisa's comment. Then she remarked in a mere observational tone, "I comported myself in a perfectly appropriate fashion."

Louisa nodded, unable to keep a grin from stealing onto her face. "Yes, you did, and you looked awfully uncomfortable the entire time."

Leonora sighed and then looked past Louisa at their cousin. "Do not look at all those you do not know," she advised. "Seek out those you are acquainted with and remind yourself that you're not alone." She moved to Anne's other side and took ahold of her hand. "We are here."

For a moment, Anne closed her eyes and inhaled a deep breath. Then she nodded, a hesitant smile coming to her lips as she looked at her two cousins affectionately. "Thank you for being here for me."

"What are cousins for?" Leonora smiled warmly.

"To tease each other mercilessly?" Louisa asked mockingly as she gently patted Anne's hand.

"Not today!" Leonora stated, a warning tone in her voice and a rather authoritative look in her blue eyes.

Louisa nodded. "Very well." She let her gaze sweep the crowded ballroom. "On the lookout for acquaintan—" Louisa flinched when Tobias Hawke all but materialized out of nowhere in front of them, his chocolate-brown eyes fixed on Anne as he held out his hand to her. "Care for a dance?"

Sighing, Anne seemed to relax on the spot, and her hand slipped into his without thought.

When Anne's childhood friend pulled her onto the dance floor, a few whispered words left his lips and that endearing half-smile of his once more curled up the corners of his mouth.

Louisa moved closer to her sister, both watching the two of them stand up for the next dance. "There's a couple in the making," she remarked with absolute certainty. "Mark my words; this is Anne's first and last Season."

"You cannot know that," Leonora objected, a slight frown upon her face as she regarded the young couple. "They've been friends for years and—"

"That is precisely what I mean," Louisa interrupted her sister, wondering how to explain to Leonora the magic that could exist between two people; not that Louisa herself had ever felt it. Since her own debut two years ago, she had frequented balls and picnics, concerts and plays, hoping to find the one man who would melt her heart.

All she had found had been disappointed hopes.

At least so far.

Still, Louisa understood well the smile she often saw on their parents' faces when they caught each other's eye across a crowded room. After over thirty years of marriage and six children born to them, Lord and Lady Whickerton were still as smitten with each other as on the day they had first met, at least according to Grandma Edie. Of course, Louisa and her siblings had not been born at the time so could not speak from experience.

But they all believed Grandma Edie; the woman had never been known to be wrong.

Ever.

Younger than Louisa by no more than a year, Leonora, however, had never been able to grasp the effect love could have upon one's life. She had a very rational way of looking at the world, even when it came to emotions. She was not cold or unfeeling, not at all; she possessed a truly watchful eye—not unlike Grandma Edie's—and knew how to spot the first sparks of love or the pangs of heartbreak. Still, for Leo, it was hard to calculate with something as unreliable as emotions. Yet, she was fascinated by them, perhaps even more so because they could not be added up like two and two.

Louisa, though, was the opposite in every way.

Like fire and water, day and night, the two sisters could not be more different. Where Leonora was rational and calculated, Louisa was passionate and spontaneous. She followed her heart, loved to feel the sun upon her skin and the sensation of twirling in the open air until her head spun. Balls meant delightful company, dancing until dawn and people she cared for sharing in her joy. They also allowed her to mingle with eligible gentlemen, whispering of a match not unlike her parents'.

That had been Louisa's dream ever since...

...ever since she could remember.

A man who would set her world on fire with a single look.

A man who—

"Lord Barrington is looking at you," Leonora remarked with no more than a slight suggestion in her voice; indeed, for her, it was merely an observation. Nothing more, and nothing less. Or was it? Louisa had to admit that sometimes she was not certain what hid behind Leonora's dark blue eyes.

At her sister's words, Louisa stilled, then carefully glanced in the direction Leonora indicated. Of course, Louisa had taken note of him the second they had stepped into the ballroom.

Of course, she had.

She always did.

Tall, with raven-black hair and devilishly dark eyes, Phineas Hawke, Viscount Barrington, was an imposing man. Often, one could find a bit of a wicked grin upon his face and hear a daringly teasing remark fall from his lips.

Elder brother to Mr. Tobias Hawke, Anne's childhood friend, Louisa had known him for years; however, they had never spent much time in each other's company. Lately, though, she had felt his gaze linger upon her.

As it did now.

Louisa inhaled a slow breath as his dark gaze swept over her face before seeking hers with bold curiosity. Something in her stomach began to flutter, excitedly, teasingly, deliciously.

"Do you welcome his interest?" Leonora asked curiously beside her as she brushed a dark curl behind her ear as though it was obstructing her view, hindering an accurate observation.

Louisa sighed, then forced her gaze from Lord Barrington's. "What interest?" she asked, displeased with her sister's watchful attention. "He's merely looking in our direction."

Leonora's gaze narrowed before she turned to observe the man in question more thoroughly.

Louisa wanted to sink into a hole in the ground. "Do not stare at him!" she hissed at her sister, urging her over to the side where two large refreshment tables were set up.

"Then you *do* care for his attention," Leonora concluded, her blue eyes settling on Louisa before they narrowed once more. "What bothers you? Your interest in him? Or the fact that I observed it?"

Louisa sighed loudly, "Both. Neither." She shook her head. "Would you mind seeing to Grandma Edie for a little bit so Jules can have a chance at dancing? The woman will end up an old maid with our dear grandmother glued to her side."

Leonora nodded and hurried away to where their beloved grandmother sat on the fringes of the ballroom with their eldest sister Juliet —or Jules as their family called her. While Grandma Edie still possessed as sharp a mind as ever, her body was slowly failing her.

While Lord and Lady Whickerton had been blessed with six children, five of them were girls, which was a bit of a curiosity among the *ton*. Indeed, most believed that after welcoming a son, Troy, as their first-born, they had sought to provide a spare after procuring the heir without any difficulties at all. However, five girls had followed and even today Louisa sometimes saw a bit of a pitying glance from an old matron here and there.

Of course—as usual!—people could not be more wrong.

Carefully, Louisa glanced over her shoulder back at Lord Barrington to find him in conversation with another gentleman. A small stab of disappointment settled in her heart that surprised Louisa. Never had she thought of herself as dependent upon a man's attention; nevertheless, the temptingly dark look in Lord Barrington's gaze had never failed to stir her heart. Truth be told, she wished she were better acquainted with him. Perhaps Anne would help her in the matter.

At present, though, Anne was following her childhood friend out of the ballroom, a wide grin upon her face as he whispered something in her ear. Louisa smiled, seeing her prediction all but confirmed. If only she could say with the same certainty how the man's elder brother thought of her.

Gathering her courage, Louisa sidled across the ballroom, doing her utmost to appear inconspicuous. She smiled left and right, exchanged a word with an acquaintance here and there and accepted a glass of punch, her hands grateful to have something to occupy them.

And then, she had reached her destination, her feet coming to stand no more than an arm's length from where Lord Barrington was conversing with a friend. With her back to him and his to her, Louisa hung on every word as she pretended to observe the dancers.

"How is life treating you these days, Barrington?" the other gentleman inquired, the tone in his voice suggesting the answer to his question was not of great interest to him.

"As expected," Lord Barrington replied. "And yourself?"

The man sighed before he shuffled on his feet, turning back toward the dancers.

"Is something wrong, Lockton?" Lord Barrington asked, and Louisa noticed him shift from one foot onto the other out of the corner of her eye. She wished she could turn and look at him more directly; that, however, would reveal her interest, and at present she was not quite ready to do so.

"Are you looking for someone?" Lord Barrington asked his friend, a hint of exasperation in his voice as the man failed to answer.

"A moment ago, she was across the ballroom..."

Lord Barrington chuckled, a teasing, slightly dark sound that snaked its way down Louisa's spine. "It is about a woman then? Who pray tell caught your eye?"

Lord Lockton sighed, "The Lady Louisa."

Louisa stilled. He couldn't possibly be talking about her, could he? Nevertheless, only moments ago, she *had been* across the ballroom...

"Lord Whickerton's daughter?" Lord Barrington asked to clarify.

"The very one," the other man confirmed, warmth in his voice. "She is remarkable, is she not?"

Louisa could barely keep herself from turning to look upon the gentleman's face, who held her in such high esteem. His voice did not sound familiar, and she had only just caught his name. Could she have made such an impression on someone she did not even know?

"Are you acquainted with her?" Lord Lockton inquired then.

Lord Barrington inhaled a slow breath. "A little," he replied, his voice somewhat tense as though he wished to say more but did not dare.

Louisa felt a cold chill sneak down her spine. and her hands tensed upon the glass of punch she had all but forgotten.

The other man seemed to have noticed Lord Barrington's reservations as well, for he asked, "Do you object to the lady?"

Again, Lord Barrington sighed, his shoulders rising and falling in a shrug. "I know you to be a man of many intellectual interests, which is why," he sighed yet again, "I must advise you place your attentions elsewhere, yes."

Louisa's jaw clenched harder and harder until it felt as though it would break clear off.

"Although she is a beautiful woman," Lord Barrington continued, "her mind deserves less adoration." He cleared his throat and leaned toward the other man, his voice dropping to a whisper. "To be frank, she is a pretty head with nothing inside. I wouldn't be surprised if she didn't know how to read."

"I had no idea," the other man exclaimed in astonishment as Louisa felt her insides twist and turn painfully. Tears shot to her eyes, and her jaw felt as though it would splinter at any moment. The delicious flutter in her stomach had turned to a block of ice, and without another thought, Louisa fled the scene.

Her feet carried her out of the ballroom and into a deserted hallway where she sank down in a puddle of misery, the glass of punch still clutched in her hands. Fortunately, no one came upon her there, giving her a much-needed moment to collect herself.

Still, the words she had overheard would forever be burnt into her memory for Lord Barrington had spoken the truth.

As much as it pained her to admit it—even if only to herself—Louisa did not know how to read. She could write her name, but not much more than that. Never had she been able to make sense of letters and words and their meaning.

Still, to this day, no one knew.

No one had ever suspected.

Until now.

Until Lord Barrington.

How had he discovered her secret? Or had it merely been a lucky guess?

Whatever it had been, it had shattered Louisa's delicate, little world. Somehow, she had found a way to stand tall even without the skills that everyone took for granted. She had developed ways to distract others where reading and writing were concerned. Somehow, she had always found a way. She was clever and ingenious and prided herself on her quick wit.

Still, deep down, Louisa had always thought of herself as inferior. In every other regard, she and her siblings were simply different. Different in many ways. Each had their own special talent. Each possessed a unique way of looking at the world. Each used their mind in different ways.

In this one regard, however, Louisa was inferior. She had always known it, and now Lord Barrington's words had confirmed what she had always known to be true.

Never would she forgive him for this off-hand remark.

Never.

Never again would she be able to look at him and not remember this crushing feeling of loss and disappointment.

To be considered wanting.

To not be worthy of another.

To be inferior.

Chapter One

A PARTICULAR WOMAN

Windmere Park, England, December 1801 (or a variation thereof)

About one and a half years later

Snow had draped a thick blanket over the world, perfectly fitting for Lord Archibald's annual Christmas house party. Now, there would not only be singing, parlor games and mistletoe kisses, but also outdoor activities, such as ice-skating and sleigh rides.

Phineas Hawke, Viscount Barrington, had never much cared for these seasonal affairs. He had often remained in London and amused himself with like-minded gentlemen, who preferred card games to parlor games and did not mind losing the occasional coin.

This year, though, was different.

This year, Phineas had decided to attend Lord Archibald's house party for one very particular reason.

Or rather because of one very particular woman.

"How are you, Phin?" Anne Thatcher, his younger brother's childhood friend, asked as she and her two cousins, accompanied by their elderly grandmother, alighted from their carriage.

As far as Phineas knew, the Whickertons attended Lord

Archibald's house party every year without fail. Why only the two sisters and their grandmother—aside from their cousin Anne—disembarked from the single carriage standing by the front stoop, he did not know.

Beside him, Phineas felt his brother tense. It would seem Tobias had been persuaded to attend for very much the same reason as Phineas himself.

The reason was a woman.

Fortunately, not the same woman who had moved Phineas. As different as he and his brother were, they had always been loyal to a fault.

Tobias greeted the dowager Lady Whickerton with a formal bow. "I'm delighted you are in attendance as well." His gaze moved to Anne and lingered, and he seemed to have all but forgotten what to say. Then, however, he abruptly redirected his attention back to the old lady eyeing him with amused curiosity. "Do you remember my brother, Lady Whickerton?"

To Phineas' delight, the old woman chuckled devilishly. "Of course, the wicked one." Her watchful eyes seized him up. "Have you acquired manners since last we met?"

Phineas had to admit he rather liked the dowager. "I thought I had," he laughed, "though, I'm afraid I might have misplaced them once again. I'll inform you immediately should I succeed in locating them."

The old lady chortled, her pale eyes lighting up with glee. "A wicked one, indeed." Then she turned toward the front hall, leaning heavily upon her walking stick. "Give me a head start, ladies," she told the three young women. "I'm certain you'll catch up with me at the landing."

Phineas had to admit that the dowager possessed the kind of humor he appreciated most; a spark of which he often saw in Lady Louisa. If only she had not come to loathe the very sight of him.

His gaze moved to her, took note of the dark glare in those enchanting green eyes and then moved on to settle on Anne. "*Little Annie*," he greeted her, finding villainous delight in the way his dear brother tensed beside him. Merely friends, most certainly! "How long has it been? Ten? Twenty years? I must say I hardly recognized you."

Shaking her head at him, Anne smiled that sweet, dazzling smile that had no doubt been complicit in stealing his brother's heart. "How are you, Phin?" she asked, ignoring his lacking manners.

Grinning rather mischievously at the woman Tobias loved with an ardent fervor—judging from the way his eyes had narrowed into slits— Phineas teased, "I am utterly fine now that you're here, Annie. I must say I missed you dearly."

Tobias looked ready to murder him.

Phineas wanted to chuckle for his brother had yet to confirm his intentions to wed his lovely friend. In fact, Tobias had gone to great lengths to prove that they were merely that, *friends*.

It had been a long time since Phineas had heard such nonsense!

Anne shook her head at him, smiling. "Are you ever serious, Phin? A man of your age should have learned to comport himself, should he not?"

Phineas frowned. "Are you calling me old?"

"No, simply immature."

He laughed, "That, I can live with."

Out of the corner of his eye, Phineas glanced at Lady Louisa. Her strawberry blond curls glistened warmly in the bright winter sun. Her dark green eyes, though, seemed to be on the brink of shooting lightning bolts...his way, no less.

Not that he was surprised!

Still, Phineas could not say why Lady Louisa had come to dislike... or rather loathe him, to speak quite truthfully. She simply had.

Whenever he set foot into a room, she made a point of spinning on her heel and disappearing. Whenever he joined her conversational circle, she would make up an excuse and leave. Whenever their eyes happened to meet—be it at a ball or a garden party—Phineas could not help but think that she wished he would be swallowed up by the earth.

And it bothered him.

It had *been* bothering him.

With a gaze that whispered of her current desire to strangle him, most likely with her bare hands, Lady Louisa regarded him through narrowed eyes. "I had not realized that you would accompany your brother to this house party. I'd heard you had decided to remain in Town."

Regarding her, Phineas could not help but smirk for he both loved and hated the way she glared at him. It spoke of a passionate nature, which to him was quite alluring; however, he would have preferred to see her passion directed toward more pleasurable emotions. "Did you now?" he teased her, enjoying the way her chest rose and fell as she fought to remain calm. It seemed the only time she did *not* run from him was when he challenged her, teased her, baited her. "Well, my dearest Lulu," her nostrils flared at his nickname for her, "I must say you sound displeased to see me. Have I done anything to wrong you?" He clearly had; if only he knew what it was.

Still, the lady remained as tight-lipped on the matter as always.

That, though, was the only matter she refused to comment on.

"Do not call me that!" Lady Louisa fumed, outrage darkening her enticingly green eyes as she took a step toward him. "I've told you so before, and I'm saying it again. I am not a poodle, and you're not to call me that! Is that clear?" Without waiting for an answer, she spun on her heel and rushed inside, her dark-haired sister following in her wake.

Phineas sighed, looking after her. If only she would not always run from him!

"Was that truly necessary?" Anne said reproachfully. "You used to be such a charming boy."

Phineas chuckled, "What can I say? Your cousin brings out the best side of me." Indeed, he had never felt more alive than when those dark green eyes looked into his, stirring his heart into a most unfamiliar rhythm.

"You truly ought to apologize, *Lord Barrington*," Anne told him sternly.

Phineas feigned a sigh, then rushed off, only too glad to have an excuse to seek out Lady Louisa yet again. He caught up with her and her sister as they stepped off the last stair onto the landing on the first floor.

As though sensing his approach, Lady Louisa glanced over her shoulder, and the moment she beheld him, her eyes narrowed into slits and she spun to face him like a warrior ready for battle. "Are you following us?"

Phineas grinned at her as he strode closer, stepping onto the landing and forcing her to lift her chin to maintain eye contact. He towered over her, and he could see that she hated it; still, she would not yield.

Phineas admired that about her. "Your cousin sent me," he told her in hushed tones, completely ignoring her sister who stood only a few steps away, watching them with curiosity.

Lady Louisa's lips thinned. "She wouldn't," she snarled. "She knows how much I detest you."

Phineas could not prevent a stab of pain jerking through him at her words. "She bade me apologize to you," he told her, leaning closer, curious to see if she would retreat.

She did not.

"Apologize?" she asked, drawing in a slow breath. Still, the pulse in her neck hammered wildly. "For what then?" she challenged with a daring gleam in her eyes.

Phineas grinned and moved closer another inch; he could feel her breath against his lips. "That, she did not say," he teased, noting the way she fought the outrage that bubbled under her skin. "Perhaps you care to enlighten me?"

Her jaw clenched, and for a moment, she simply looked at him, the expression in her eyes almost contemplative. "I'd appreciate it," she bit out then, taking a step back, her chin still raised proudly, "if you did not address me in the future."

Before she could rush off, Phineas reached out and the tips of his fingers brushed her arm.

Lady Louisa flinched and drew in a sharp breath before once more schooling her features into a mixture of bored indifference and right-eous indignation.

"Would you have stayed away," Phineas asked, his eyes searching hers, "had you known I would attend this house party?"

Holding his gaze, she paused. "Do not for a moment believe that your comings and goings have any influence upon how I spend my time." Her eyes narrowed once more. "I detest you, yes; but I would never allow you to ruin this holiday season for me." Her brows shot up in challenge. Then she gave him a feigned smile, nodded her head to him and bid him a good day before hastening down the corridor, her sister on her heels.

"Until later, Lulu," Phineas called after her, unable to keep his lips sealed.

As expected, her shoulders tensed, but she kept walking, successfully fighting the urge to turn back around and rip his head off.

Phineas smiled. Oh, how he loved ruffling her feathers!

Chapter Two

A FOOLISH WAGER

Needing a moment to herself, Louisa decided against joining the other guests downstairs, but rather remained on the first floor. After all, she longed neither for entertainment nor refreshments, but for solitude instead. *That man* had once more gotten under her skin, and she hated herself for this inexplicable weakness of hers where he was concerned.

With a shake of her head, Louisa marched down the corridor, away from the large staircase leading to the ground floor and toward the back of the house. She passed door after door, her eyes seeing nothing of the paintings hung upon the walls or the vases filled with hot-house flowers set on side tables here and there. No, instead, her eyes continued to conjure *that man*'s smirking visage—much to Louisa's displeasure!

Now and then, another guest passed her after leaving their chamber to head downstairs and mingle with the others. Louisa, however, proceeded to march up and down the corridor, now and then turning a corner and heading down a thus far unfamiliar hallway. Where she was going, she did not know nor care.

At least not until an annoyingly familiar voice called her name.

Or rather that vexingly inappropriate and completely infuriating nickname that dratted man had reserved only for her! Oh, what an honor!

Flinching at the sound of his voice, Louisa drew to an abrupt halt, her hands balling into fists as she listened to his approaching footsteps. She wanted to run, to flee—to scratch his eyes out!—but her body seemed to disagree for it behaved in a rather mutinous fashion, refusing to comply in any acceptable way.

"My dearest Lulu." Stepping around her, Phineas Hawke smirked down at her. "How wonderful to find you here. How are you?" A mocking frown descended upon his features. "You look a bit flushed. Is everything all right?"

Glaring at him, Louisa willed herself not to respond—after all, her parents had taught her better. Still, never in her life had she faced a more trying moment, had she? At least, she could not recall one. Her heart burnt, and her mind spun as her stomach churned with anger. Louisa knew she was about to explode...and then suddenly and rather unexpectedly, her body did move.

The paralysis fell from her and she found herself stepping away, her hand moving to reach for a handle, then pushing open a door. Without thought, Louisa slipped through it, ignoring the man staring at her and...belatedly realized that she had stepped out onto a balcony.

Snowflakes drifted down and settled in her hair. One even landed on the tip of her nose. An icy wind blew, and she wrapped her arms around herself, beginning to shiver, her woolen dress no match for nature's wintry breath.

"Would you care for a coat?" that familiar voice asked in an equally familiar, mocking tone. As Louisa turned to glare at Phineas Hawk, she found him standing in the doorway, a bemused smile upon his lips as his dark gaze swept over her. "Your lips are turning blue," he observed, a wicked gleam coming to his eyes. "Shall I warm you?"

Gritting her teeth, Louisa fought hard to subdue the renewed urge to claw his eyes out, to fling herself at him with outstretched hands and... She did not dare finish even the thought for it would prove that there was quite another side to her, one unfit for a lady. Her parents would be displeased if they knew!

Watching her carefully, Phineas Hawk waited. When she remained silent, though, he took a step forward, following her out onto the balcony. Snow settled into his raven-black hair, softening the dark edges of his appearance. For a moment, Louisa looked at him and saw not her enemy, but someone she had liked once. She watched as a snowflake landed on his left temple, melted upon touching his warm skin and then slowly snaked its way down.

And then his hand settled upon her arm, and Louisa flinched. Her gaze dragged down to meet his, and she found his eyes looking into hers without even the slightest bit of amusement or mockery. "You should come inside," he whispered, his hand on her arm remaining where it was as he took another step closer. "You're shivering. You'll catch cold." He moved sideways, his free hand gesturing to the open door behind him. "Come."

For a split second, Louisa almost believed him, believed that there was a kind and caring side to him. She wanted to. She wanted to very badly, but she had learned her lesson and she would not forget.

Unwrapping her arms from around herself, Louisa all but shoved Phineas Hawk out of her way. Then she stormed back inside, welcoming the warm air upon her chilled skin. Her feet kept walking, her eyes fixed on the other end of the corridor. Unfortunately, she managed to take no more than a step or two before *that man* once more stepped into her path.

Huffing out in annoyed breath, Louisa glared up at him. "What is it that you want? Why are you here?" Again, she crossed her arms and lifted her brows in a challenging manner. "Say what you wish so we can each go our separate ways."

A moment passed before that familiar, mocking grin once more appeared upon his face as though he were capable of an altogether different emotion. "Do not pretend you're not happy to see me," he teased, moving closer, undoubtedly aware of how much his presence annoyed her. "After all, is that not why you're here? No doubt, you found out that I would attend this year's house party, and so you thought to yourself—"

Louisa scoffed, "Do not for a second believe that I am here because of you. I am here *in spite of* you. My family always attends this house party," she regarded him with a pointed stare, "you, however, do not."

A most annoying chuckle left his lips. "Do they? If that is true, then I cannot help but wonder where they are." He made a show of turning his head left and right as though trying to spot them. "I doubt one can overlook them; after all, there are so many of you." He frowned, a bit of a quizzical look coming to his face. "How many sisters do you have?"

"Five," Louisa huffed out before she could stop herself. "Don't pretend to care!"

"Ah, yes, and one brother, is that not so?"

Louisa glared at him. "What do you want from me? A prize for remembering that I have a brother? Applause, perhaps?"

His grin broadened in a very unsettling way. "That won't be necessary." He moved closer, and Louisa had to fight the instinct to retreat lest he think he could intimidate her. "I'd settle for a kiss."

Her eyes bulged. They felt as though they wanted to jump out of her head. "You're mad! Completely and utterly mad!" Oddly enough, outrage was not all she felt in that moment.

The man had the nerve to reach out, his fingers grasping the tip of a loose strand dancing down from her temple. He twirled the curl between the pads of his thumb and forefinger, his dark gaze never leaving hers, once again daring her to retreat. "Are you truly offended? Or are you trying *not* to be intrigued?" Again, he flashed that grin at her.

Trying her best not to explode, Louisa ignored the tantalizing flutter in her belly, slapped his hand away and raised her chin. "You are insufferable!" Then she made to storm past him, but didn't get far because he once more stepped into her path. "What are you doing? What is it you want from me?"

His chest rose and fell with a slow breath as he continued to gaze at her, the look in his dark eyes hinting at emotions Louisa did not dare dwell on. "If only I knew," he mumbled under his breath, and his feet brought him closer yet again as though he were being pulled toward her by an invisible force.

For a terrifying moment, Louisa thought he would reach for her— Her! Not a curl of her hair! Then, however, he stilled, blinked and that annoying grin was back on his face. "So, no kiss?"

Louisa gritted her teeth. "No, no kiss," she forced out, a surprisingly poignant spark of disappointment settling in her heart as the words dropped from her lips. "Now, get out of my way!" She moved to step around him, but he swiftly blocked her path.

Louisa wanted to slap him! No, strike that! She wanted to punch him!

"I'll let you pass if you answer a few questions," he told her with a wink as though he had suggested something utterly indecent. "Deal?"

Louisa frowned. "How many questions?"

An approving smile came to his lips. "A valid point! I like...it."

Louisa had the strangest feeling that he had wanted to say *you* instead of *it. I like you.* What a foolish thought! "One, then."

"Five!"

Louisa laughed. "Two."

"Four." His grin grew deeper. That dratted man seemed to be enjoying this far too much! "Very well, let's meet in the middle and say three."

"Fine," Louisa relented, feeling herself tense at the thought of what he might ask of her. "What then?"

Putting a hand to his chin, Phineas Hawke put on a great show of pretending to consider all possible questions. "Let's see." He frowned as though in thought.

"Today!" Louisa insisted, wondering if she should simply try to shove him out of her way. Perhaps if he did not see her coming, she would get away with it.

"Ah!" the man exclaimed, his forefinger raised as though he had just had an epiphany. "Why is your family not here with you?" His voice sounded surprisingly caring, and the look in his eyes no longer held mischief. "At least, not all of your family."

Louisa sighed. "Because they caught a cold," she told him honestly, suddenly feeling too exhausted to continue this strange game of theirs. "My youngest sisters, Chris and Harry, came down with a fever two weeks ago. They are better now, but are still feeling a bit weak. After them, the cold made its way through the family, bringing down my eldest sister Jules as well as my brother Troy."

"And your parents?"

"My father caught it as well," she replied in a heavy voice, taken off guard by how much she missed having her whole family here with her. At Christmas, no less. "My mother did not. But she was concerned and so she sent us away."

"She did not leave herself?" he asked gently as his hand once more reached out and almost tenderly tugged on that errant curl. "She stayed to tend to them?"

Louisa nodded. "They'll be fine. Mother said they would all be fine." She swallowed, her voice thickening. "But Grandma Edie is old, and the elderly sometimes..." Her voice trailed off as she forced the thought back into oblivion. A life without her beloved grandmother was unimaginable!

"Do you miss them?" As his fingers toyed with her hair, his knuckles brushed against the line of her jaw, sending an odd chill down her spine.

Louisa shook herself, finally taking a step back. "You've already asked your three questions. Now, let me pass."

Phineas Hawke chuckled. "I asked one. The others were only to encourage you to continue with your answer." He leaned closer. "I still have two left."

Louisa swallowed, wondering why she suddenly felt so vulnerable. "No, we're done. Let me pass." Her hands trembled, and she could feel tears pricking the backs of her eyes. What on earth was wrong with her? She could not break down now! Not in front of *him*!

To her utter surprise, Phineas Hawke nodded, then moved to step aside, allowing her to pass. "Very well."

For a moment, Louisa was too dumbfounded to move, her eyes fixed upon his face. "Why are you simply giving in?"

A small smile curled up his lips, one not tinged with mockery. "Do you want me to fight for you?"

A reply formed on Louisa's tongue quick as lightning, and she struggled to hold it back before he could hear it. After all, the one word that lingered, that refused to back down without a fight was not *No*.

It should be *No*.

It had to be *No*.

And yet, it was not.

Tearing her gaze from his, Louisa marched down the corridor past countless doors and around corners until she no longer knew where she was. Deep down, she could not help but think that she was running away.

Away from the warm glow in his eyes.

Away from the foolish desire to have him...care for her.

Away from the thought that he did not.

Louisa knew he did not. He could not, she reminded herself, once more forcing her mind to recall that one moment almost two years ago. That one moment that had changed everything.

No, he could not care for her.

Ever.

She ought to remember that.

❧

A sly smile stole onto Anne's face as her blue eyes moved from Leonora to Louisa. "Indeed, if I didn't know any better, I'd say...*you* liked him."

Louisa felt as though someone had punched her in the stomach. "You must be mad!" she retorted later that same afternoon, outraged that anyone dare suggest she could have feelings for this...this miscreant, this reprobate, this... "I hate that man. No, *hate* is not a strong enough word. I loathe that man." Or didn't she?

No, she did! And that was final!

Judging from the smile that refused to leave Anne's lips, her cousin did not believe her, though. "Why? What on earth has he ever done to you?"

Louisa's jaw tensed as she felt her cousin's as well as her sister's eyes on her as they stood out in the hall near the drawing room. Indeed, what *had* he done? Nothing she could share with them for they both remained in the dark about Louisa's humiliating flaw.

"It cannot simply be because he calls you Lulu," Anne reasoned quite correctly. Yes, it was not merely that name, but what it represented. Louisa hated that nickname because it told her loud and clear

21

that Phineas Hawke thought of her as a simpleton, a pretty head—as he had said—pretty, but empty.

"I agree," Leonora threw in. Louisa wanted to slap her. "Even taking your effervescent character into account, I cannot imagine that anyone would be riled in such a way by a simple dislike to a nickname."

Anne grinned at her. "Indeed. Therefore, I assume that you do like him for your reaction is as telling as mine." As the last words left her mouth, Anne tensed and swallowed hard.

Charging forward, Louisa grasped for the straw Anne had carelessly held out to her. "I was right!" she exclaimed, returning her thoughts to the matter they had been discussing before Anne's inquiry into Louisa's feelings toward Phineas Hawke. "You *do* like him." And by *him*, she meant the miscreant's younger brother, Tobias Hawke, of course.

"Perhaps," Anne croaked, looking almost as uncomfortable as Louisa had felt a moment earlier.

"Would you stop saying that?" Louisa huffed out. For the past months, she had been trying to convince Anne that Tobias Hawke was not simply her *childhood friend* or even her *best friend*, but the man she loved, the man she ought to marry. "Why can't you simply admit that you care for him? He clearly adores you. Why are you so afraid to kiss him?"

A hint of alarm came to Anne's face as she looked up and down the corridor. "Why are you so certain he's the one for me?" she asked quietly.

"Very well." Louisa threw up her hands and inhaled a calming breath. "I admit I'm growing tired of this discussion. So, how about this?" Her gaze settled on Anne's. "You kiss Tobias under some mistletoe, and," she held up her right forefinger, "if I'm right, if he actually is the one for you and you end up marrying him, then I promise I'll kiss... that man." Louisa's jaw tightened. Had she truly just said that? Where on earth had those words come from?

"You'll kiss Phin?" Anne asked, clearly astonished and unfortunately not hard of hearing.

"Yes," Louisa ground out, regretting her thoughtless outburst already. Perhaps her head was empty after all. It was a painful thought.

"Under some mistletoe?"

Louisa shrugged, fighting to keep up the pretense that she had not just made the biggest mistake of her life. "I don't care. Wherever you like."

Anne and Leonora exchanged shocked glances. "You heard her say it, too, didn't you?"

Leonora nodded. "Are you serious?" she asked Louisa. "Why would you agree to kiss someone you detest?"

Louisa sighed, "Because I want to see her happy." She glanced at her cousin, who had always been like another sister to her. Anne's mother had passed away when she had been young and her father had followed his wife to the grave only a few years back, at which point Anne had come to live with the Whickerton family. "And I'm convinced she'll never be happy with another. As I'm unable to convince her of it, I suppose this is the only way to get her to agree." She held out her hand to Anne. "Do we have a deal?"

Louisa prayed that Anne would not allow a great man like Tobias Hawke to slip through her fingers because she was afraid to risk their friendship. After all, was love not friendship mixed with passion?

"You'd do that for me?" Anne asked, her eyes wide and searching.

"Of course," Louisa told her warmly. "I may not appear as the most compassionate person, but I want to see you matched with the man who holds your heart." She sighed, wondering if she herself would ever find a man who would look at her the way Tobias looked at Anne. How could her cousin not see that the man loved her? "If you believe nothing else, can you at least believe that?"

Tears pooled in Anne's eyes, and she grasped Louisa's hand. "Deal."

Louisa hoped fervently that she would not come to regret this. Kissing Phineas Hawke? That could only end in disaster. He would no doubt tease her about it endlessly. Still, for Anne's happiness, Louisa would shoulder worse.

Unfortunately, it was Anne's and Tobias's mistletoe kiss that ended in disaster!

Chapter Three

A MOMENT IN THE SNOW

Phineas bowed his head after witnessing his brother kissing the girl he loved under some mistletoe. Indeed, it had not gone well. In fact, it could not possibly have gone worse.

The second Lady Louisa had spirited Tobias away outside the library, Phineas had known that she was up to something. Clearly, whatever it was had to have had something to do with Anne. It seemed Lady Louisa, too, had taken note of the longing glances and shy smiles exchanged between the two of them and had decided to help them along.

Unfortunately, her plan had backfired. Tobias was now more than ever convinced that Anne only considered him a friend. Her reluctance to kiss him had proved that beyond the shadow of a doubt. At least, as far as Tobias was concerned.

Phineas, on the other hand, had seen Anne tremble not with reluctance, but with nerves. If he was not at all mistaken—and he rarely was—then she had been as nervous about the kiss as Tobias himself, afraid to reach for more and lose what they had.

In the end, it took all of Phineas' powers of persuasion to wrest a promise from his brother that he would speak to Anne again the next day. Alone and away from prying eyes.

And by *speak*, Phineas meant *kiss*. He could only hope his brother had gotten the message. On occasion, Tobias proved a bit daft. At least, where love was concerned.

Rounding a corner, Phineas walked across the foyer and toward the stairs, to his surprise ready to retire rather early compared to what he was used to. Indeed, contrary to general opinion, matchmaking was hard work especially when one had to deal with two utterly reluctant parties. Perhaps he simply ought to bow out and leave this up to fate!

Still, Phineas knew he would never forgive himself if Tobias lost the woman he loved because of some kind of misunderstanding. Because that was what it was, was it not? Why was it so hard for those two lovebirds to realize how they felt? Or rather how the other felt? Was it not obvious?

Phineas thought it was.

"Should we not wait for her?" came Anne's voice from down the corridor.

Phineas pulled to a halt, then ducked into a small alcove as footsteps drew nearer.

"It is dark out by now, and besides, she should not be out on her own, should she?"

"She promised to stay on the terrace and Grandma Edie promised to keep an eye on her from the drawing room window," Lady Leonora remarked, a hint of exhaustion weighing down her voice. "You know Louisa. There is no changing her mind, and my toes feel as though they've fallen off."

Anne chuckled slightly as they walked past the alcove. "Mine as well."

Waiting until all sounds of their footsteps had ceased, Phineas then stepped back out into the corridor, deciding to peek into the library before he stepped outside. Indeed, the thought of Lady Louisa out there by herself drew him like a moth to a flame. It was the strangest sensation, one he could not seem to shake. Still, if Lady Louisa's grandmother was keeping an eye on her, he would rather know in advance. In truth, he had thought the old lady had already gone to sleep.

To his surprise, Phineas did find the dowager seated in a lush armchair by the softly crackling fire in the drawing room, a thick blanket wrapped around her legs. However, the old woman's eyes were closed tightly and soft snores drifted from her lips as her chest rose and fell with the gentle breaths of slumber.

Phineas grinned. He could not have planned it better if he had tried!

Careful not to make a sound, he slipped out through the side door, quickly pulling on the thick coat he had retrieved before heading over from the foyer. Indeed, Fortune seemed to smile upon him!

The wind blew harshly, and Phineas quickly drew the warm piece of clothing around himself, momentarily stunned that Lady Louisa had decided to remain in this freezing hell a moment longer than necessary. His skin stung with the cold, which quickly began to spread along his limbs. Still, the moment his gaze fell on a cloaked figure on the edge of the terrace, every discomfort ceased to matter.

In the dim light of the crescent moon, Phineas slowly made his way over the snow-covered terrace, fresh flakes dancing in the cold air like dancers twirling to music. He heard a soft crunch whenever his feet sank into the snow, feeling oddly reminded of snow ball fights he had fought with Tobias when they had been children. That had been long ago, and yet, the thought chased a smile onto his face.

"I said I was fine. There is no need for you to—" Spinning around, Lady Louisa broke off when her eyes fell on him, clearly having expected anyone *but* him. She wore a long, dark cloak over her gown, the hood pulled down into her face. Only here and there did a blond curl peek out, its light color in stark contrast to the surrounding dark.

"So I heard," Phineas replied as he stepped closer. In this dim light, he could not tell if her dark green eyes were shooting fire or not, and he rather disliked that.

"What do you want?" she demanded with narrowed eyes as well as a chilling cold in her voice that would put winter's efforts to shame. "Have you not annoyed me enough for one day?"

Phineas laughed, watching her wrap her arms around herself under the cloak. He wondered if it was for warmth or comfort. Did he truly unsettle her so? "It might surprise you, but it is not my goal in life to annoy you." He chuckled, unable to help himself. "It is merely an amusing byproduct."

Her shoulders tensed, and she shifted her posture in a way that spoke of displeasure, if not anger. Knowing Lady Louisa, it was probably anger for whether he could see it or not, Phineas was certain that *now* her eyes *were* shooting fire at him.

"If you will not leave," she snarled with barely contained outrage, "then I will." Whirling around in her haste to leave his side, Lady Louisa lost her footing on the iced-over terrace. Her arms flew out and her eyes went wide as she flailed helplessly.

Phineas had never been one quick in his reactions; however, before he knew what was happening, he had closed the small distance remaining between them and pulled her into his arms, surprisingly steady on his feet himself.

Her hands grasped his arms, holding on tightly as she closed her eyes and rested her head against his shoulder, exhaling a deep breath. "Thank you," she mumbled, those two words screaming loudly of the deep shock that had stunned her into forgetting *who* she was speaking to. Otherwise, she never would have thanked him!

Not in a thousand years!

Phineas rather liked it. He liked holding her in his arms even more. She felt warm and tempting, and despite the cold air, the smell of summer seemed to linger upon her curls. He looked down into her face, her eyes still closed, and without thought, his arms tightened upon her, wishing to prolong the moment.

Phineas knew it to be a mistake even before her eyes flew open and she grew rigid in his arms.

"Release me!" Lady Louisa snapped a bit breathlessly, shoving against him. Clearly in need of some distance between them, she staggered a few careful steps backwards. Once she had found her footing, she brushed her hands over her gown rather distractedly, her gaze not meeting his. "Is there anything in particular you came out here to say?"

Phineas smiled as her eyes continued to avoid his. "I did, yes." Disliking the distance between them, he moved closer, noting the way she tensed, but held her ground. "I could not help but notice how spectacularly your endeavor to unite our two lovebirds failed tonight."

At his words, Lady Louisa's head snapped up and she glared at him, her upper lip quivering with anger. "What?" She swallowed then, unable to argue that it *had* indeed failed. "Well, at least, I'm trying to help them. That is more than can be said for you."

Ignoring her jibe at him, Phineas kept his eyes fixed on her, delighting in the way she fought to draw breath while holding his gaze. "That kiss could not have gone worse, could it?" he asked conversationally, inching closer.

Lady Louisa swallowed before her gaze darted to his mouth. Realizing where her attention had strayed, though, she jerked it back up, her cheeks blazing a deep shade of red. Or was that from the cold?

Phineas chuckled in absolute delight. "Perhaps they'd be more successful without onlookers to spoil the fun." Smiling at her, he deliberately moved his gaze down to trace the curve of her lips before once more meeting her eyes. "Would you not agree?"

Although she seemed a bit flustered, Lady Louisa met his gaze without flinching. "I suppose so," she replied, a somewhat devilish curl to her lips that he found deeply intriguing. "*I've* always thought so."

The smirk upon Phineas' face died a quick death as something that —shockingly enough!—felt like red-hot jealousy shot through him at the insinuation of her in another man's arms.

Lady Louisa, however, grinned with delight. "Do you not agree? A man of your reputation must have an opinion on this matter."

Setting his jaw, Phineas stalked closer, not bothering to hide his intention for she seemed very much aware of it. Still, when he failed to slow his steps, a hint of alarm widened her eyes despite the fact that her chin rose in proud defiance. "Care to test that theory?" he asked as he leaned in closer until he could feel her breath upon his skin.

The pulse in her neck hammered wildly, and yet, Lady Louisa remained outwardly calm. Yes, her cheeks shone in a charming red and her hands were balled into fists in front of her. Still, she did not flinch or retreat, but held her ground, a teasing smile curving those enchanting lips of hers. "I would love to," she whispered, surprising him.

An answering grin spread over his face. "You would?" Phineas whispered, inching closer. Temptation burnt in his veins; still, he could not shake the feeling that this was too good to be true.

Unfortunately, the next moment proved him right. "Certainly,"

Lady Louisa replied. "With anyone but you."

Phineas had all but seen her words coming; yet, they still felt like a punch to the stomach. "Is that so?" he growled, fighting the urge to simply pull her into his arms. Perhaps a kiss would change her mind. A good kiss, not the disastrous kind Tobias and Anne had shared.

"It is." Her dark green eyes remained locked on his, a daring gleam in them. "Now, if you don't mind, I'd like to go back inside. I'm beginning to grow cold." She made to step past him, but his arm shot out to stop her. "Let me pass!" she growled, those wide eyes of hers narrowing into slits.

"We should work together," Phineas heard himself suggest, realizing that he was speaking without thought, his only intention to keep her here...

...with him.

A frown creased her forehead. "Work together? What do you mean?"

"To unite our two lovebirds, of course."

Her lips thinned, and she shook her head. "I work alone." She walked past him.

"Alone you failed," Phineas called after her. "Tobias is more determined than ever to remain friends. How does *Little Annie* feel about their kiss?"

Stopping in her tracks, Lady Louisa turned to glare at him. "It is nothing more but a momentary setback," she hissed at him. "One that shall be rectified shortly."

"What do you have in mind?" Phineas called after her as she reached to open the door to the drawing room.

"That is nothing to concern yourself with, Lord Barrington," she snapped, not even bothering to look back at him. "Good night."

"Good night, Lulu!" A wide grin came to Phineas' face when she shut the door behind her with a loud bang, a clear indication that he had gotten to her. She was far from immune to him; however, he wished she would respond in a somewhat different fashion.

"Patience," Phineas mumbled to himself, rubbing his hands against the cold. "Good things will come to those who wait." He certainly hoped that was true.

Chapter Four

ON THE STAIRS

Sleep had never been something to elude Louisa. Her first night at Windmere Park, though, proved troublesome. The bed was perfectly fine. The mattress was soft and warm, and the linens felt smooth and comfortable against her skin. A fire burnt in the grate, giving the room a soothing glow. Still, sleep would not come.

What did come and refused to leave were thoughts of Phineas Hawke.

Unfortunately, these thoughts did not focus upon his utterly annoying personality. They did not point out his tendency to mock her, tease her, even ridicule her. No, indeed, they continued to draw forth the dark shade of his eyes as they had looked into hers. They painted vivid images of how close they had stood together in the snow, his warm breath tickling her skin. They forced her to recall how tempted she had been to kiss him. Had *he* truly intended to kiss her? Or had it only been a tease?

When morning finally dawned, Louisa was exhausted. Her eyelids felt heavy as lead, and her limbs complied only with great reluctance. Still, she managed to heave herself out of bed and dress for breakfast. What finally managed to lift her spirits was that apparently Anne and

Tobias had met in the library that morning and...there had been another kiss.

And judging from the glow upon Anne's face, it had gone significantly better! Who knew what else could have happened—perhaps a betrothal!—if Lord Gillingham, a most persistent suitor of Anne, had not interfered in that very promising moment.

"You look tired," Leonora remarked as they headed down the corridor to see to Grandma Edie. "Go on head downstairs. We shall see to grandmother."

Anne nodded in agreement. "See you at breakfast."

Louisa cast them a grateful smile; however, as she was making her way down the stairs to the ground floor, her luck ran out for none other but the man who had haunted her night walked across the entrance hall in that very moment.

Seeing him, Louisa reacted on instinct, pausing in her step, her breath lodging in her throat as she did her best not to move. Perhaps if she remained completely still, he would not see her. *Don't be such a ninny!* A voice in the back of her head chided.

Louisa almost flinched. Indeed, what was she doing? She was not one to hide, one to avoid others simply because she disliked them. Never had she done so, and she would not start today. Gritting her teeth, Louisa took another step down.

Curse that man, but he turned and looked in her direction in that moment.

Louisa groaned as he immediately changed direction and walked over, positioning himself by the foot of the stairs, one elbow resting leisurely upon the banister as he looked up at her. "You look well rested, Lulu," he remarked with that annoyingly smug grin upon his face. "Did you dream of me?"

Doing her utmost to ignore the flutter that came to her heart, Louisa continued down the stairs, her chin raised and a most haughty expression upon her face. "You are a vile creature, *Lord Barrington*, and I will not stoop so low as to deign your question with a reply. Good day!" She made to step around him.

Quick as lightning, Phineas Hawke moved to block her path,

forcing her to remain on the bottommost step. "Have you already spoken with Anne this morning?"

Louisa paused, her gaze moving to search his face. "Why?" He looked even more smug than he usually did; Louisa could not help but wonder why.

Phineas Hawke laughed, leaning in as though they were confidantes, exchanging secrets. "I can see that she told you."

Frowning at him, Louisa crossed her arms over her chest, once again feeling the need to place a bit of a barrier between them. "Well, I assume your brother told you." A question swung in her voice, and she was rather surprised that her nemesis deciphered it without a moment's hesitation.

"It was I who urged Tobias to seek out a more secluded spot for their kiss," he remarked with a wide grin, those dark eyes of his not veering from hers. "No wonder it was by far more successful than...the previous one." His brows arched up in a teasing manner

Louisa wanted to slap him! "Are you saying your brother has asked for her hand?" she inquired with a challenging glare, knowing it not to be so.

The smile upon his face vaned a little. "Not yet."

"Has he declared his intention to do so?" While Anne had certainly been delighted with their kiss, she had still seemed uncertain about her childhood friend's feelings toward her as well as his intentions that might or might not be inspired by them.

One corner of his mouth twitched upward before he shook his head. "He has not. Yet, I believe it is only a matter of time before he does."

"If he has not, then you have no reason to consider your *advice* a success, *Lord Barrington*. Good day." Louisa moved to the other end of the stair to walk past him, but he mirrored her step, once again blocking her path.

"I apologize," he said instantly, the look upon his face, though, was far from contrite.

Louisa huffed out an annoyed breath, then stepped back over to the other side...almost simultaneously with him. "What are you doing?"

He chuckled. "I'm trying to let you pass."

"Are you?" she demanded.

He grinned at her. "What are you suggesting? That I intend to keep you trapped here?"

"I wouldn't put it past you." She gave him a pointed stare. "This staircase is by far wide enough for two people to pass each other comfortably. Pick a side."

A mock frown came to his face, a perfect match for that teasing grin of his. "You mean like, good or bad?"

Fighting to hold on to her composure, Louisa exhaled slowly. "Left or right."

Phineas Hawke nodded as though he had only just now understood her meaning. "Left, then."

"Very well," Louisa replied and stepped to her left, which, of course, was his right, and should have allowed them both to proceed onward.

Unfortunately, it did not.

Finding her path once more blocked, Louisa glared at him. "What are you doing? You said *left*!"

"Oh, your left or my left?" he asked, sounding baffled, his eyes still glowing with mirth. "When I said *left*, I meant your left, which is why I moved to the right."

Louisa gritted her teeth. "Very well. Then my left, understood? You move to the right?"

He nodded, and yet, she could not shake the feeling that the same thing would happen again.

And it did.

Louisa was about to explode when she noticed a deeply unsettling smile come to his lips. It was different from all those other ones that teased or portrayed smugness. Indeed, it was one that whispered of intention, like the silence before the storm.

His eyes settled upon hers more firmly as he leaned forward. "Let's try something else," he mumbled then, a moment before his hands seized her waist.

Louisa drew in a sharp breath at the feel of his hands upon her, holding her tightly. She fought to voice her displeasure—truth or not!

—when he suddenly lifted her off her feet. Her hands flew up, grasping his upper arms as he slowly turned around and then gently set her back down on the floor.

Staring up at him, her heart beating rapidly, Louisa tried to breathe. She could still feel his hands upon her as they lingered where they lay. She knew she ought to snap at him, pull away or demand he release her.

But her voice failed her.

"Are you all right?" Phineas Hawke asked in a strangely tender voice. "You look a bit pale. Perhaps you should eat."

Reminding herself where she was and who she was with, Louisa finally managed to pull away, pushing his hands off her. "Don't you ever dare touch me again!" she hissed in a whisper as a small group of guests, chatting and laughing, stepped into the foyer, crossing it on their way to the breakfast parlor.

Phineas Hawke flashed another one of those familiar, teasing grins at her. "Are you saying you do not approve of my solution to our little problem?"

"Leave me alone!" Louisa snapped, then spun around and marched off. "And don't you dare follow me!" The beat of her heart still rang like a horse's gallop in her ears as she made her way across the foyer on trembling legs. Oh, what was it about him that unsettled her so? Why could she not simply chide him for his rude behavior and not feel any of...of...this? It seemed she loathed him and longed for him with almost equal measure, and the latter was dreadfully inconvenient.

Before Louisa stepped through the archway leading out of the foyer, she glanced over her shoulder and belatedly realized that instead of going upstairs, that miscreant was heading down a corridor toward the back of the house. Indeed, he had never intended to ascend to the first floor, had he?

All this had been a game to him.

Nothing more.

Chapter Five

A MISCREANT BY THE NAME OF PHINEAS HAWKE

Louisa's ankle hurt. It truly hurt, throbbing as though a living thing had taken up residence there and was now fighting to get out. At the very least, she had sprained it with her daring stunt to ensure Anne was not kissed by the wrong man!

Still, her cousin's happiness was worth it.

"You're quite a menace, my dear Lulu," that miscreant remarked with a wide grin as they stood near the frozen lake in the snow. Of course, he had been standing on the bank! Of course, he had seen her fling herself across the ice...and land rather crumpled upon the ground. Of course!

Many guests had strapped on a pair of skates and proceeded onto the ice while others amused themselves with a snowball fight or a sleigh ride near the maze, a labyrinth formed by tall-growing hedges. Warm beverages were served by footmen hurrying back and to from the house. Jolliness hung in the air, mingling with the icy wind and steam wafting upward from mugs filled to the rim with hot chocolate or cider.

Glaring at Phineas Hawke for no longer than a heartbeat, Louisa gritted her teeth and chose to ignore him. As hard as it was not to bite his head off, she would simply have to rise above. With her gaze fixed on Tobias, she stated, "I know you care for her. Why then do you stand idly by and allow another to steal kisses?"

Indeed, Tobias looked miserable, almost resigned at her reference to Lord Gillingham's pursuit of Anne; yet, something jealous, wild and deeply primitive sparked in his dark brown eyes. "What ought I have done? I was too far away."

Louisa wanted to slap him! "Not this morning in the library," she challenged. Indeed, only moments after the two lovebirds had shared another kiss, Lord Gillingham had come upon them. Blast the man! He had almost succeeded in maneuvering Anne under a sprig of mistletoe only moments later. "*I* interfered and prevented the worst as I did again just now." She gestured toward the other side of the frozen lake where another sprig of mistletoe dangled from an overhanging branch. "However, I won't be able to keep Lord Gillingham away from her indefinitely." Without thought, Louisa took a step toward him and flinched as fresh pain shot through her ankle. She sucked in a sharp breath and gritted her teeth, determined to get her point across. "You need—"

"Are you hurt?" Phineas Hawke asked as he reached out and grasped her hand. The nerve of that man! His gaze dropped to her right foot as he moved closer.

Glaring at him, Louisa jerked her hand away. "I'm fine," she snapped with as much venom as she could. "I'd appreciate it if you didn't touch me, *Lord Barrington*." Indeed, he kept touching her far too often!

The miscreant had the nerve to look hurt at her icy tone. Hell would freeze over before Louisa allowed herself to believe that an actual, human heart beat inside his chest.

"Why?" Tobias asked, eying her curiously. "Not that I'm not grateful for your interference, but why?"

Suddenly feeling exhausted, Louisa sighed, "Because I want to see her happy," she told him, noting the way the corners of his mouth quirked upward as though in agreement, "and because I believe you're the one to achieve it." She held his gaze, praying he was hearing her. "She loves you, and I feel deeply confident in my conclusion that you love her as well. Is that not so?"

Tobias blinked, a look of utter surprise coming to his face; yet, no words left his lips. Still, his gaze briefly moved to the house where Anne and Leonora had retired after Louisa's rather unexpected and perhaps somewhat extreme rescue act.

Louisa sighed, shaking her head at him. "Apparently, you're as blind as she is." She moved another step toward him, hoping that her words were finding their way through that thick skull of his. Unfortunately, her efforts sent another jolt of pain through her ankle. "How can you not see it?" she demanded before she cleared her throat. "Be that as it may, if you no longer think of her as *Little Annie*, then you need to act. Fast."

Standing behind her shoulder, Phineas Hawke scoffed, "That's precisely what I said."

Louisa turned to stare at him. "You did?" The thought that he truly cared for his brother seemed utterly foreign. Did he possess a functional heart after all? How else would he have—?

"Believe me," the dratted man replied, wiggling his brows in that deeply infuriating way, "it came as quite a shock to me as well that we actually agree on something." He moved closer; his gaze fixed on hers. "A grave sign, indeed, for it surely prophesies the end of the world as we know it." Then he did what he always did; he laughed.

Rolling her eyes at him, Louisa turned back to Tobias, cringing at yet another painful step. "Well?" she dared him. "What do you intend to do?"

Instead of answering her question, he looked down at her aching foot. "You should have a doctor look at your ankle."

"Don't try to distract me," Louisa snapped, gritting her teeth against the pain. "You—"

"I'm not trying to distract you," Tobias interrupted her, his gaze insistent. "However, I do believe you're in significant pain. You should—"

"He's right," exclaimed Phineas behind her, and before Louisa could object, the man swept her into his arms and started marching up the path toward the house.

For a short moment, Louisa was so dumbstruck that she could not move, could not speak, could do nothing but hang in his arms like a lump, unable to believe that this was truly happening. No one in their right mind would...

But then again, Phineas Hawke was anything but in his right mind, was he? He never had been.

"Put me down, you miscreant!" Louisa hissed at him, her hands shoving against his chest. "How dare you? Put me down this instant!"

His dark gaze shifted down to meet hers and a low rumbling chuckle spilled from his lips. He did not slow down, though, and his hold on her did not lessen in the least. His strong arms hugged her to his chest, warm and alive and determined. His eyes were almost black as they lingered upon her face, something wicked lurking in their depths that made Louisa's heart beat wildly in her chest.

Swallowing, Louisa willed herself to ignore that teasing shiver that snaked down her back and smacked the miscreant upon his shoulder... again and again. "Put me down! Now!" Her voice rose with each step he took, his lips sealed for once, his failure to reply grating on her nerves.

"You cannot simply pick me up and carry me around!" Louisa snarled, giving him another hard slap upon his shoulder. Indeed, her inability to free herself from his hold on her was deeply unsettling. No matter what she had said, it was unmistakably clear that he *could pick her up and carry her around!*

A deep chuckle rose from his throat. "You *are* a menace," he repeated his earlier words to her, his dark gaze locked upon hers as he marched up the small snow-covered slope toward the house. To Louisa's utter shock, pride rang in his voice!

Her gaze narrowed as she regarded him. "You say that as though..."

His arms around her tightened. "Before you accuse me of anything else," he laughed in that teasing way of his, "I assure you it *was* meant as a compliment."

"I'd appreciate if you didn't," Louisa snapped before her insides turned completely liquid at the odd sensation of him regarding her favorably. Why on earth would he pay her a compliment?

"Pick you up or give you a compliment?" he asked, his voice baiting. No doubt, he was only waiting for her to fly into a fury once more. None of this made any sense!

"Both!" Louisa replied pointedly. "Now, put me down!"

Grinning at her, Phineas Hawke shook his head. "You risked life and limb to prevent Gillingham from kissing Anne, why?" A thoughtful expression came to his face as he regarded her.

"Because he's the wrong man for her."

"And my brother is?"

"In my opinion, yes," she told him, wondering why he was asking her these questions. "I thought you agreed?"

"I do." He nodded. "I'm not questioning your motivation, merely your method." Again, that grin stole back onto his face.

"My method?" Louisa demanded as outrage once more triumphed over temptation.

"You got hurt," Phineas Hawke pointed out with a glance at her sprained ankle before she could gather her wits for another well-aimed insult. Not that he did not deserve it!

"I—"

"You got hurt!" He stopped in his tracks, his gaze hard as he looked down at her. "Whatever your motivation, you ought to have gone about it a different way." His nostrils flared. "What were you thinking flinging yourself at them at such speed? You could have broken something or worse!"

For a moment, Louisa was speechless. Never had she seen him like this. If she did not know any better, she would swear tooth and nail that he...that he had been afraid for her. But that could not be, could it?

Of course not! That proud voice deep down exclaimed with vehemence. *The man thinks you a brainless ninny!*

"That is none of your concern!" Louisa fired back.

Again, his nostrils flared. "Don't you ever do such a thing again!"

"You cannot tell me what to d—"

He jerked her more tightly against his chest. "I can, and I will!" He inhaled a slow breath, his lips pressed into a thin line, before he strode onward, his gaze now fixed at the house instead of her. "Don't you ever do this again!"

Louisa could not help the unsettling feeling that Phineas Hawke had been afraid for her, that his words—as harsh and condescending as they had been!—had come from a good place. "Let go of me!"

"No!"

"Now!"

"No!"

"You vile blackguard! You..." Louisa barely noticed her surroundings change. She did not see the entrance hall nor the stairs he climbed with no effort at all. All her attention was focused on feeding the fire of her anger because if she did not...

There was something deeply enchanting, something warm and tempting unfurling in her belly. Something that urged her to stop resisting, to simply lean into him and rest her head upon his shoulder.

Her teeth gritted together as Louisa shoved against his chest once more, not even considering what would happen if he did in fact release his hold upon her. "You foul-mouthed oaf! Put me down this instant!"

To their right, a door was flung open and Anne and Leonora appeared in its frame, open-mouthed and wide-eyed, staring at them. "What is going on?" Anne asked, glancing from Louisa to the caveman who refused to release her.

"Miss Thatcher, Lady Leonora," the miscreant greeted them with one of those infuriating smiles upon his lips. Still, he kept walking until he paused for a short moment outside a door.

Her door.

Louisa froze in surprise before he had even pushed it open, wondering how he knew.

The moment passed quickly, though, and Louisa immediately continued to struggle in his arms as he strode inside, not wanting him to get the impression that she was in any way surrendering.

"What happened?" her sister asked from the door where she and Anne stood watching them.

"He won't put me down!" Louisa thundered. "This poor excuse for a man won't—"

"She twisted her ankle with that little stunt of hers," Phineas Hawke interrupted her. "I asked to send for a doctor." *He had?* "But I suggest you cool her ankle until he arrives."

While Leonora immediately darted off, Anne remained where she was, observing them curiously and with no small amount of amusement. Louisa wanted to sink into a hole in the ground!

With no other place available to release her anger, Louisa once more shoved against the man's chest, seeking to free herself. Unfortunately, what she had failed to notice was that they had reached her bed and Phineas Hawke was about to set her down upon it. He was leaning forward when she shoved against him, promptly upending his balance.

A gasp escaped Louisa's lips as they fell onto the bed together, his body half atop hers. He barely managed to break his fall, his right hand sinking into the pillow beside her head, his mouth dangerously close to her own.

His breath fanned over her lips, and Louisa found her eyes snap up to meet his. Dark and dangerous, they shimmered in the bright light streaming in from the window as a devilish smile drew up his lips.

Louisa's heart stopped as she stared up at him before it raced off in a wild gallop, stealing her breath as well as her voice, leaving her nothing to defend herself with. Nothing to demand he get up immediately.

Indeed, instead of rising to his feet, Phineas Hawke stayed where he was, his gaze locked upon hers. "If you wanted me in your bed," he whispered against her lips, that insufferable, teasing note still in his voice, "all you had to do is ask."

Chapter Six

WICKED TO THE BONE

Her lips were so close; all Phineas had to do was dip his head ever so slightly and steal a kiss.

But he did not.

Blast it! Why didn't he?

He wanted to; there was no denying that. The moment he had swept her into his arms, Phineas had known that he wanted her. He had suspected a certain partiality on his part for a while. She drew his thoughts even when she was nowhere around. And now that they were under the same roof, Phineas could barely take a step without wondering where she was. He felt a certain annoyance at this rather unexpected obsession; still, the deep longing he felt for her was rather pleasant, and he could not help but wonder what it would feel like to kiss a woman who occupied his thoughts so completely.

However, his little *Lulu* was far from amenable.

Indeed, she had fought him tooth and nail every step of the way, shrieking like a banshee and hurling insults at his head. Still, Phineas could not help but think that if she had truly meant to free herself, she could have.

After all, his little *Lulu* was far from weak. He still remembered the determination in her sparkling green eyes when she had shot across the lake, coming to Anne's rescue. She possessed strength and an iron will, did she not?

Holding her gaze, Phineas noted the way her chest rose and fell with each shuddering breath. It came faster than he would have thought, and he wondered if somewhere deep down, she was as tempted as he was...but did not dare admit to it.

Perhaps he ought to take a page out of Lord Gillingham's book and maneuver his *Lulu* under some mistletoe as well.

In fact, earlier that morning Phineas had found himself under one such piece of greenery when he had come to the aid of a young woman. She had swayed dangerously upon her feet from lack of food as she had confided to him. Why some women ate like sparrows was beyond Phineas!

Still, the peck he had given her had been nothing but a formality. He had felt nothing while the mere *thought* of kissing Louisa set his blood on fire. Indeed, it was a thought worth considering! After all, it was Christmas! Why should he not make use of it?

Her dark green eyes flashed. "Get off me!" she hissed then, a slight tremble dancing down her limbs before her expression hardened once more. "Or I swear I will end you!"

Phineas chuckled. Although he would have loved to kiss her— under some mistletoe or anywhere, really!—he could not deny that he admired her dauntless spirit. In truth, he wanted her to *want* to kiss him as well. "Charming as always," he whispered as he rose to his feet, "dear Lulu."

Her gaze narrowed, shooting daggers at him.

Ignoring her, Phineas glanced at her ankle, remembering the pain she had to be in. "For once," he told her, his voice not teasing in the slightest now, "take care of yourself." Then, before she could hurl another insult at his head, he turned, smiled at Anne on his way out and disappeared down the corridor.

Still, no matter how many steps he put between himself and her, his thoughts continued to linger. They remained fixed on the few precious moments when she had been in his arms. As though she had left an imprint upon him, Phineas could almost feel her when he bent his arms, her warmth, the soft weight of her, the rapid beating of her heart.

Heat shot to Phineas' face, and he wondered at his own youthful musings until he realized that he was idly standing in the hall, still dressed in his heavy winter coat. Chuckling at his own absentmindedness, he strode back out into the chilling air, intent to clear his head. He marched through the snow without any thought for direction for an hour or perhaps even two—he could have been walking in circles for all he knew.

As Fate would have it, though, he stumbled upon none other but Anne.

Little Annie with her cheeks flushed and her blue eyes aglow.

"Are you looking for someone?"

Turning to look at him, she shivered, her teeth briefly digging into her lower lip. "I might be."

Phineas could not help but grin. "Am I right to assume that you're looking for my brother?"

Anne swallowed. "Perhaps."

Phineas laughed, grasping her by the shoulders, his gaze imploring as it settled upon hers. "You're as bad as he is, dear Annie," he told her with a smirk, remembering Lady Louisa's earlier words. "I'll go and fetch him for you, but you have to promise me that you won't let him get away."

Striding through the snow once more, Phineas wondered what his Lulu might have said to her, for although Anne seemed as nervous as ever, there was a determined glow in her gaze he had not seen before. He could only hope that she remained true to her word and would not let his blockhead of a brother get away.

"Anne is looking for you," he told Tobias as he found him walking rather aimlessly among the trees, lost in thought...not unlike he himself had been moments earlier. Perhaps a sickness was going around. A chuckle left his lips at the thought.

As expected, Tobias proved a bit hesitant, but finally asked, "Where is she?"

"Near the maze," Phineas told him with some relief. "You should go and find her." He looked at his brother imploringly. "And you should hurry."

Tobias tensed. "Why?"

Glad that his brother had finally decided to give him his full attention, Phineas grinned and leaned leisurely against a tall tree trunk. "Because I saw Lord Gillingham move toward her when I stepped away, and we all know what *his* intentions are, do we not?" There, that ought to do it!

As though a shot had been fired, Tobias tore through the underbrush toward the house and the maze beyond, single-minded purpose now burning in his eyes.

Phineas closed his eyes, praying that by the end of this day, all would be as it should be. That Tobias and Anne would be betrothed. That they would be happy, looking forward to a shared future.

Phineas wanted that for his brother as well as for Anne. Still, for the first time, he wondered if he might be wanting it for himself as well. A deep sigh left his lips as his thoughts were almost inevitably drawn back to the woman who hated him like no other.

Why could it not be simple for him as well? Why could he not simply walk up to her, steal a kiss and ask for her hand? The thought jarred him back into a straight-backed position. Did he want her as his bride?

Rubbing his ice-cold hands over his face, Phineas inhaled a deep breath, then turned his feet around and headed back toward the house as though drawn by an invisible force. More than anything, he wanted to seek her out, but knew he would not be welcome.

Why did she hate him thus? The thought had been on his mind many times before; however, he had never dared ask it, not in earnest, worried that he had indeed done something to earn her wrath, something unforgivable.

More than once, he circled the house, his feet unerringly returning to the prints he had left the round before. What was he to do? Honesty was generally considered a wise choice; nevertheless, Phineas could not shake the feeling that even if he were to ask his Lulu openly, she would not answer him. Never had she accused him of anything specific but had always hurled nondescript insults and curses at his head.

He feared she would not be forthcoming, and then what? What was he to do?

As Phineas trudged back into the house, he glimpsed many of the guests still out by the lake, steaming mugs of tea or chocolate offered by footmen with laden trays. Not in the least tempted, he stepped into the entrance hall, only to come to a jarring halt when his brother's voice echoed to his ears.

Sighing, Phineas closed his eyes, praying that Tobias had not done anything remarkably stupid. Honestly, how hard could it be to match two people so obviously in love?

Fortunately, as he stepped into the drawing room, Phineas found not only his brother standing near the fireplace, but Anne by his side, both of them grinning from ear to ear like the two love-sick pups they were.

"Have you heard?" Lady Leonora asked as she looked over her shoulder at him, her face aglow with joy.

Phineas shook his head, striding forward. "I have not; fortunately for me, though, I know how to add two and two." He met his brother's gaze. "Please, tell me it's four, and you've finally asked this poor girl to marry you."

While Tobias did his best to frown at his brother, the two cousins laughed heartily, their joy infectious. Anne beamed up at her freshly minted fiancé, and it did not take long for Tobias to grin at her with the same silly expression and forget to be irritated with his elder brother.

Phineas shook his head at them. "How did you manage?" he asked his brother, remembering that Lord Gillingham had to have stood in Tobias' path to claiming Anne's hand. "I hope no one is dead...or missing something...vital."

Tobias rolled his eyes at him; still, a bit of a satisfied and even triumphant smile teased his lips. "I'm not you, dear Brother. If you insist, I'll tell you the whole story."

"There is no need. I'm perfectly satisfied knowing the ending." He turned to look at Lady Leonora. "Does your sister already know?"

The lady shook her head. "She's asleep. I shall tell her as soon as she awakens." Then she turned back to the happy couple and grasped Anne's hand. "If you don't mind, I would like to hear the whole story."

"Certainly," Anne beamed, and Phineas took that opportunity to slink from the room. He could not recall having made up his mind to visit Lady Louisa; his feet carried him to her door all the same. Asleep or not, he had to see her.

After a quick knock, he waited until a faint voice called for him to enter. To his surprise, it was the dowager countess who sat in a large armchair by Louisa's bed, watching over its sleeping occupant. "The wicked one," she greeted him with a matching smile.

Phineas chuckled, "You have not forgotten." He closed the door behind himself and stepped closer.

"How could I?" the old woman chortled. "You're a man after my own heart if I may be so bold." Her gaze drifted to her sleeping grand-daughter in the bed before it returned to him. "Not unlike my late husband, I might add."

Phineas inhaled a slow breath, holding the old woman's gaze as her words sank deeper. "Is that so?"

Smirking, she nodded. Then she cleared her throat and set aside the blanket that had lain draped over her legs. "Now that you're here, I think I might go and stretch my legs." She pushed herself to her feet and reached for her cane. "Will you keep an eye on her?" She glanced at Louisa.

Phineas stilled, his gaze moving from the grandmother to the granddaughter and back again, a slight frown coming to his face. Still, he could not help but say, "I'll keep both on her if you like."

Patting his arm, the dowager countess walked past him to the door. "Wicked to the bone," she chuckled yet again.

Phineas turned to look after her, confused. "You're not jesting," he mumbled. "You don't mind leaving me alo—"

The dowager looked at him from over her shoulder. "There's nothing wrong with wicked, my boy," she told him, that mischievous gleam once again flashing in her pale eyes.

Phineas grinned. "Countless mothers would disagree, terrified their daughters might end up in a compromising situation with a known rake." He wiggled his brows at the dowager.

The old woman laughed. "I suppose that's true."

Silence lingered for a moment; however, when the dowager did not respond to the question hidden in Phineas' remark, he finally asked, "Then how come you're not?"

The dowager glanced at her sleeping granddaughter, then shrugged. "I'm not her mother."

Phineas felt slightly exasperated, but laughed nonetheless.

Sighing, the old woman stepped toward him, her wrinkled hand patting his arm. "Wicked or not," she told him smiling, "I know you will not do anything to harm her."

"I thank you for your trust," Phineas replied before a frown creased his forehead, "but how can you know that? How can you be certain?"

A rather indulgent smile came to the dowager's face as she once more patted his arm. "Because you care for her," she whispered as though not wishing to be overheard. Then she turned and left, closing the door behind her.

Phineas laughed softly, unwilling to admit to anyone—least of all, himself—that the dowager's words had unsettled him in any way. After all, Louisa was merely an acquaintance. He had known her family for years and the sole reason he had come to her chamber was to...to...

Inhaling a slow breath, Phineas moved his gaze from the far window to the sleeping woman in the bed. Her chest rose and fell...*almost* evenly. Her hands...had curled into fists at her sides. Had they already been clenched like this when he had entered?

Curious, Phineas rounded the bed and moved closer, his eyes fixed upon Lady Louisa's face. Indeed, her lips seemed to thin and her nostrils almost flared.

Phineas laughed, then leaned down, moving his face over hers. "Do you want me to kiss you awake?"

Her eyes flew open instantly, and she sucked in a sharp breath as she found him hovering above her.

Phineas grinned. "Works every time," he teased, reaching for a golden curl and twirling it around his finger. He knew he was a beast for lingering, but he had to admit he loved seeing her on edge.

Her jaw tensed as his right hand sank into the mattress beside her head, bracing himself while the other continued to play with her hair. "How often do you threaten to kiss women awake?" she hissed, glaring at him in that enchanting way of hers.

"Oh, at least two or three times a day," Phineas replied with a smirk. "I like to keep busy."

She huffed out an annoyed breath, and he felt the soft puff of air brush over his lips like a caress. Phineas almost kissed her right there and then.

"Will you move?" she snapped as her right hand rose to press against his chest while the muscles in her neck tightened as she prepared to lift her head.

Phineas stayed where he was. "I'd rather not," he whispered, and his gaze briefly dropped to her lips. "But feel free to sit up." The thought of her lips closing in on his was a tantalizing one indeed.

"Get up!" Lady Louisa hissed, a slight flush darkening her cheeks.

In the end, it was neither her anger nor her mortification that made Phineas comply, but rather the slight tremble in her voice. It held something vulnerable, and as much as he liked to tease her, he would not hurt her.

Never.

Pushing herself up into a seated position, Lady Louisa looked around the room before her gaze came to linger upon her grandmother's empty chair. "I cannot believe she left me alone with you." She glared at him and her arms crossed over her chest.

Phineas sank into the vacated chair. "Your grandmother seems to be an excellent judge of character," he told her with a grin. "Otherwise, she wouldn't have left—"

"She's planning something," Lady Louisa hissed under her breath, her eyes closing as she shook her head.

Phineas leaned forward in his chair, elbows resting on his legs. "Planning what?"

As though she had only just taken note of his presence, Lady Louisa's eyes widened in alarm. For a moment, she stared at him before her lips thinned once more. "What do you want?"

Leaning back once more, Phineas sighed. "I came to tell you the good news."

"Good news?"

"We are to be family," he told her with satisfaction. "Tobias finally worked up the nerve to ask for *Little Annie*'s hand. They're downstairs in the drawing room, celebrating."

Utter joy came to Lady Louisa's face, and for a precious moment, she closed her eyes, exhaling a deep breath.

Phineas watched her. He saw deep emotions etched into her face: joy, warmth, love. A passionate heart beat in her chest, perfectly complementing her iron will and rock-hard determination.

"Why are you here?" she asked then, all warmth and joy fleeing from her face as she regarded him with suspicion. "Why did you come?"

"To tell you."

Her frown deepened. "Why?"

Phineas shrugged, unable to put into words the need to see her. "You worked as tirelessly as I to see this happen." He shrugged yet again, trying his best to keep any sense of disapproval out of his voice. Indeed, he had overstepped earlier, but he had been afraid for her. Never would he forget the moment he had seen her sailing through the air with nothing to cushion her landing. "I thought you should know. I thought...I thought you'd want to know."

Her green eyes lingered upon his, and for once, they held no disdain or contempt, no disapproval or displeasure. She was simply looking at him as though they had only just met, and her mind was not yet made up about his character. "Thank you," she whispered then, a hint of incredulity in her voice as though she herself could not believe what had prompted him to seek her out.

As though she could not believe she was thanking *him* of all people.

Rising to his feet, Phineas strode over. "You're welcome," he replied in the same hushed voice, his eyes unable to move from hers.

And then she blinked, and that precious moment slipped away, replaced by one Phineas knew well and had experienced many times. "You may leave now," Lady Louisa muttered, busying herself with straightening her bedclothes.

Phineas sighed, "How is your ankle?"

She paused, and her eyes met his. "It's fine. It's...it's only a sprain."

"Was it worth it?"

One corner of her mouth curled into a tentative smile; her eyes, however, lit up like a bonfire. "It was," she said nodding.

Phineas smiled at her. Then he took a step closer to the bed, enjoying the apprehensive way she was watching him. "No regrets?"

Lady Louisa frowned. "None." Her gaze narrowed further as he took another step nearer. "What are you doing?"

"Nothing," Phineas replied with a distracted shrug, then in a bold move sat down next to her on the bed.

The lady inhaled a sharp breath, her body leaning away from him as her mouth opened in protest.

Phineas, though, cut her off. "Would you do the same for your sisters?" he asked, his gaze now fully-focused on hers, the words leaving his lips nothing more than a distraction.

"Of course," she replied instinctively, her eyes still wide and searching. "What are you—?"

And then Phineas grasped her hand, pulled it gently into his own...and felt her body turn to ice in utter shock.

Her muscles tensed, and she held herself rigid as though suddenly unable to move. Her dark green eyes stared into his before they briefly dropped to her hand resting in his, his fingers gently wrapped around hers, warming at least that small part of her.

"Good night," Phineas whispered, hopelessly tempted, but willing himself to rise his feet nonetheless. "I hope you'll feel better soon." Now standing, he bowed low over her hand and placed a tender kiss upon her skin. Then he lifted his head, and once more their gazes collided in that powerful way that had him reeling. He felt off balance, uncertain by this odd change in their communication, and so he grinned at her as he had a thousand times, the grin that never failed to enrage her. Why on earth could he not help himself?

Indeed, it *did* break the spell.

Lady Louisa came back to life. She jerked her hand from his, the look in her eyes screaming her outrage. "How dare you?" she snarled, her chest rising and falling rapidly.

But not with indignation.

Phineas would bet anything he possessed.

Smirking at her, he stepped away and moved to the door. With his hand on the handle he paused, then looked over his shoulder at her. "If you're not satisfied, I could give you a real kiss." His grin broadened. Oh, what he would not give for her to ask him to stay! To ask him to kiss her! "It'd be my pleasure."

As always, her eyes narrowed, and she glared at him with the familiar fire, her composure reclaimed. "Not mine, I can assure you."

"Are you certain?" he dared her.

"Deadly so," she snarled, crossing her arms over her chest and all but glaring him into oblivion.

Phineas shrugged. "Perhaps one day." He was about to leave when he saw the expression upon her face still, freeze as though even now she knew somehow that he spoke the truth. That one day she would wish for him to kiss her.

He could only hope so.

Chapter Seven

A KISS THAT WAS TO HOLD NO MEANING

Barrington House, England, Spring 1802

A few months later

Louisa watched as Anne and Tobias whispered to one another, their eyes aglow and the smiles upon their faces utterly bewitching. Anne's hand would every so often find its way to her new husband's face, gently tucking a stray curl of his dark hair behind his ear, the tips of her fingers brushing against his skin. Tobias' eyes would find hers then, his breath almost stuttering to a halt at the feel of her touch. Longing rested in his dark brown eyes as they lingered upon hers, and he moved closer, whispering words into her ear that made Anne blush and giggle.

Louisa sighed as her eyes swept the terrace of Barrington House.

Early bloomers bestowed first colors upon the green gardens while the terrace had been filled with greenhouse flowers in honor of this happy occasion. Wedding guests mingled in the drawing room as well as outside in the early warmth of spring. The sun shone gently, and the soft trilling of birds could be heard in-between conversations here and there.

"You look glum," Jules commented as she came to stand beside Louisa. "Are you all right?"

Again, Louisa sighed, meeting her eldest sister's moss-green eyes. Her dark hair had been pulled into a simple chignon and she wore an equally simple gown with no adornments. Indeed, it seemed as though Jules had no intention of catching a gentleman's eye. Ever. "I'm perfectly fine," Louisa told her with a half-hearted smile. "Perhaps a bit...envious."

An understanding smile touched Jules' soft features. "They remind me of Mother and Father," Jules replied in a whisper, and two sets of eyes moved to the other end of the terrace where their parents stood side by side, gazing out into the gardens, their hands linked, their heads turned to one another. "I pray that they shall always be as happy."

Louisa nodded.

"Your time will come," Jules counseled, gently squeezing Louisa's hand. "Are you impatient?"

Was she? Louisa wondered. Or had she simply given up hope?

Indeed, she had danced and flirted for more than one Season, trying to find her other half, a man who would set her blood on fire, but who was also—she glanced at Anne and Tobias—her best friend, someone she trusted without hesitation. Did such a man exist for her? Could he ever, considering the secret she kept? The secret she had never shared with another soul?

Looking at her sister, Louisa smiled. "Are *you*?" she asked instead of answering Jules' question. After all, her eldest sister was already considered on the shelf by most of society. If she waited any longer...

Her sister swallowed, her gaze dropping for the briefest of moments. "Not everyone is cut out for marriage. I do delight in tending to my family. Perhaps that is my path. Perhaps I need to be open to—"

"You need to get out from under Grandma Edie's thumb," Louisa laughed, shaking her head. "The woman monopolizes your time. Perhaps—"

"She needs me," Jules protested, glancing at their grandmother soundly snoring in an armchair by the pianoforte in the drawing room.

"There are others who could tend to her," Louisa suggested, noting the tense expression upon Jules' face.

Her sister shook her head. "It's not the same as family. I could never leave her."

"I'm not saying you should, and besides, *we* are her family, too," Louisa countered. "Nevertheless, I fail to see why you need to remain glued to her side at every ball, why you cannot even dance one dance, why you've never even shared words with a gentleman without her sending you off on another errand the next second." Her brows rose challengingly. "If you like, I'll speak to her. You're the eldest and certainly the most maternal of us, but you're not alone. We all can see to Grandmother. We are all her family."

Jules smiled at her warmly. "You have a kind heart, Lou, and I thank you for your consideration. But there is no need. I know how to tend to her best of all, and I do not mind." She squeezed Louisa's hand. "Truly." Still, a hint of sadness lingered in her eyes, and Louisa wondered if her sister genuinely believed what she said.

A shadow fell over them from the side and a deep voice asked, "Have you seen our dear newly-weds?"

Turning to their elder brother, the sisters stilled. "What do you mean?" asked Louisa before her gaze moved to the spot where...Anne and Tobias had been only moments earlier but were no more.

Troy's brows rose as she looked back at him. "So, it is not my eyesight that is at fault here, is it?" he asked with a sigh, his pale blue gaze sweeping the terrace and the grounds beyond. "Where could they be?"

"Perhaps this was all a bit too overwhelming to them," Jules suggested with a worried frown. "Perhaps all they need is a moment of rest."

Louisa suppressed a chuckle at her eldest sister's innocent words. She glanced at her brother and saw the same restraint upon his face as he cleared his throat, trying not to laugh. "We should find them," he stated evenly. "Some of the guests are beginning to wonder where they are."

Louisa nodded. "I'll go. I know this place better than you do."

Indeed, in the weeks leading up to Anne's wedding, Louisa and

Leonora—along with their mother and grandmother, of course—had spent a lot of time here together, planning the festive celebration. It was a beautiful house, elegant and tastefully furnished, with a sweeping staircase and a vast library. Anne favored it while Louisa had always steered well clear of it. Tall windows and vaulted ceilings created a warm atmosphere for the sun seemed to make the inside of the stately manor glow whenever it set upon the hill to the west.

Anne loved her new home, and Louisa had to admit that she, too, had come to like it. Or would have if it weren't for the annoying miscreant lingering within. Although Phineas Hawke had never been known to spend much time at his country estate, he now seemed rarely absent, always nearby, always finding her in the most unexpected of moments, teasing her, annoying her in ways that made Louisa wonder what he was about. Why that sudden interest in her? Was he determined to torment her? To get her to admit loud and clear what he already knew or at least suspected?

Pushing Phineas Hawke from her mind, Louisa rushed inside, her feet carrying her down familiar corridors. She opened doors here and there, peeking inside, before hurrying onward.

"Ah! There you are!" she exclaimed as she stumbled into yet another room in the west wing and spotted the newlyweds in each other's arms, barely aware of her entrance.

Tobias' jaw tightened as he turned to look at her, his hands reluctantly releasing his new wife before he took a step back. Anne looked equally displeased with Louisa's sudden appearance. "What are you doing here?" she demanded as her hands flew over her gown, trying to smooth the wrinkles her husband's wandering hands had left behind.

Louisa chuckled, "Looking for you. After all, it is your wedding day, and you cannot simply disappear without it being noted."

Anne sighed and cast her new husband a meaningful look. Relenting, Tobias nodded. "Very well. We'll return to share in the festivities." He offered Anne his arm.

Stepping closer, Louisa tucked a loose curl back behind Anne's ear. "I think that is advisable," she said grinning, a warm feeling suddenly swelling in her chest. "I do love to see you two so happy." Her gaze moved from Anne to Tobias. "You must admit you're quite fortunate to have me as your family. After all, without my assistance, I doubt we'd be here today celebrating your union."

Tobias laughed, "Are you fishing for a compliment, *dear cousin?*"

A deep smile came to her face for Louisa had come to care for and admire Tobias greatly. He was a decent and caring young man, and he doted upon Anne as she deserved. "A thank-you will do, *dearest Tobias.*"

A half-grin upon his face, her new cousin gave her a formal bow. "I'm offering you my deepest gratitude for your wisdom in urging us to recognize the bond between us." He smiled at his wife, who hung on his arm with a dream-like expression upon her face. "Your determination and selfless sacrifice shall never be forgotten."

Although endearing, Louisa could not help but feel reminded of Tobias' miscreant brother. "I must say that is a very unbecoming quality," she told him with a slight crinkling of her nose. "You sound just like your awful brother."

At her words, Anne's eyes widened a little before a bit of a mischievous smile touched upon her lips. "That reminds me," she said, meeting Louisa's gaze. "You have yet to fulfill your end of our bargain."

A cold shiver danced down Louisa's back as her thoughts were drawn back to the unfortunate moment at Lord Archibald's house party when she had thoughtlessly offered to kiss the miscreant brother if only Anne would give Tobias a chance. Louisa had been desperate, afraid Anne would throw away her chance at happiness for fear of losing her childhood friend.

In the end, Louisa had been proved right; unfortunately, that also meant...

"Will you forfeit?" Anne dared her with a wicked twinkle in her eye.

Louisa's jaw tensed as the moment Phineas Hawke had deposited her on her bed unbidden crowded her thoughts. She could almost feel his breath upon her lips, his hand upon her shoulder and remembered the shiver that had gone through her as his dark eyes had looked down into hers. Why was it that despite her aversion to the man there were moments when...when...?

"Never." The word left her lips without thought, and yet, Louisa knew she would never run from a challenge. She was not one to give up, to cower in fear, to turn her back and run. No, she had always stood tall and proud...except when it came to her flaw.

Again, she heard the miscreant's words echo in her ear as they did so often. *She is a pretty head with nothing inside. I wouldn't be surprised if she didn't know how to read.*

Anger burnt in her heart, alive and strong, as it had that first day upon hearing his opinion of her. No, she would not give him or anyone else reason to think less of her. She had given her word, and she would see it through.

Louisa met her cousin's gaze head-on when she suddenly heard approaching footsteps. A moment later, the door flew open and none other than Phineas Hawke marched inside. "What are you all doing in here?"

Gritting her teeth, Louisa glared at Anne. "You did this on purpose!" As determined as she was not to back down as terrifying was the thought that the moment to prove herself had come so quickly.

So unexpectedly.

Still, there was nothing to be done about it. And so, Louisa huffed out a deep breath, gathered her courage and spun to face her greatest challenge.

As Fate would have it, the man looked devilishly handsome in his formal attire with his dark, unruly hair and his almost black eyes sparking with mischief. The teasing smile upon his lips was directed at her alone as he watched her approach with open fascination as well as a hint of confusion. Louisa could all but see a teasing remark form upon his lips; however, he never had the chance to speak it.

"Don't read anything into this," she told him with a meaningful look before her hands seized his face and she pulled him down into a kiss.

It was not Louisa's first kiss, and yet...somehow it was.

A shock wave went through her the second their lips touched, almost knocking her off her feet. Sensations, unfamiliar and intoxicating, pulsed under her skin, and she struggled to remind herself that this kiss meant nothing.

That it held no meaning.

That it was merely a way to uphold her word.

That—

And then she felt his hands seize her waist, urging her closer into his embrace as his lips moved against hers, deepening her kiss.

A kiss that meant nothing.

A kiss that *was* to mean nothing.

A kiss she ought to break before—

Shoving him away, Louisa freed herself from his embrace, her pulse thudding wildly in her veins as she all but stumbled backward. "I told you not to read anything into this," she snapped at him, ignoring the dark, possessive look in his eyes. She spun to face her cousin, willing her features back under control, relieved that this matter had finally been resolved. "There," she said to a wide-eyed Anne. "Satisfied?"

Anne was about to respond when Louisa felt a hand grasp her arm from behind, spinning her back around with a swiftness that stole her breath. And then she was in Phineas' arms again, his hands on her waist, locking her in his embrace. His eyes were dark and insistent as he looked down at her, urgency in his gaze. "Far from it," he answered the question she had directed at Anne, a sinfully tempting smile curling up the corners of his mouth.

Then he dipped his head and his lips claimed hers once more.

And she let him.

She did not stop him. She did not struggle or protest in any other way. She completely and utterly failed in making it unmistakably clear that she despised kissing *him* of all people.

She should have.

But she did not.

For it would have been a lie.

The truth was that his touch made her feel utterly alive. He was the wrong man, but his response to her was right in every way. The deep longing in his eyes, eyes that seemed to see only her, eyes that held hers as though no force on this earth could persuade them to look away. The insistence in his embrace, the determination to keep her close, to not let her slip away. The passion in the way he kissed her, all-consuming and overwhelming, whispering of a need that echoed within herself. Something she had wished for, hoped for...

...but never thought to feel in the arms of her greatest enemy. That was what he was to her, was he not? The man who thought her inferior to others, to everyone.

To him.

Resistance built within her, and Louisa lifted her hands in a feeble attempt to break away, to protect herself, to replace vulnerability with strength. Still, her attempt was half-hearted at best for the magic of the moment still held her in its grasp.

Indeed, this was not her first kiss; unfortunately, none of her previous kisses could compare to this one.

Right here.

Right now.

With the wrong man.

The world fell away, and Louisa belatedly realized that this was no longer *his* kiss, but theirs, for she was kissing him back with equal enthusiasm, her fingers curling into his lapels, pulling him closer.

His left hand moved to grasp her chin, angling it upward so he could deepen their kiss. She felt his fingers trail over her skin, along her jaw and down her neck, before his hand slipped to the back of her head, preventing her from pulling away.

Never had she felt such sensations, such an overwhelming need for another...and it terrified her.

Dimly, Louisa heard a door close. It was no more than a soft *click*. To Louisa, however, it felt like a bucket of cold water was dumped upon her head.

She froze, suddenly remembering where she was, what had just happened, that they were not alone...

...that she was still in Phineas Hawke's embrace.

Something inside her snapped in that moment and sudden strength gathered in her arms. Her hands moved back to his chest, her palms flat, and then she shoved against him with all her might, finally breaking his hold on her. "Stop!"

Chapter Eight

A LOATHSOME CREATURE

P hineas had felt her tense. He had sensed the shift in her mood and was not surprised—although reluctant—when she demanded, he release her.

His arms fell away, and he took a step back, his breathing as fast as her own as he stared at her.

Her eyes were wide, the darkest shade of green he had ever seen. They held shock and remnants of passion, but also no small measure of regret.

Phineas' jaw tightened. "Are you all right?" he asked gently, still confused about what had just happened here. Never in a thousand years would he have expected her to kiss him like this.

Or at all.

A quiver trailed up her jaw before Louisa clamped her lips shut, her eyes narrowing accusingly. "You had no right," she all but stuttered, and he could see how frayed her nerves were. She was shaken. Their kiss had upended her world as much as it had upended his.

At a loss, Phineas did what he always did. He grinned at her. "I had no right?" he demanded, a playful note in his voice. "*You* kissed *me,* or have you forgotten?"

She all but flinched as though he had struck her. "I told you not to read anything into it."

Phineas laughed, "How could I not? Out of nowhere you walk up to me and—"

"It was a wager!" she exclaimed, her body tense as she spun away from him and headed toward the door. "Nothing more."

Unwilling to let her get away this easily, Phineas followed in her wake, his hand once more reaching out to stop her, to bring her back to him. "What are you talking about?" he demanded as he spun her back around, his hands settling upon her upper arms, holding her tightly despite her attempts to break free. "Stop squirming and answer my question!"

Gritting her teeth, Louisa stilled, then looked up to meet his gaze, something deeply vulnerable in hers. "In order to gain Anne's cooperation," she forced out, alarm in the way she tried to angle herself away from him, "I promised her that if she and your brother were ever to wed, I would..." She paused, her eyes falling from his for a moment. "I would kiss you." Her jaw moved. "I had to offer something outrageous to—"

Phineas felt his hands tighten on her. "Outrageous?" He leaned closer, holding her gaze, noting the way her eyes widened ever so slightly. "So, kissing me is outrageous?" Slowly, his hands slid to her back, urging her closer as she drew in a shuddering breath. "And here I thought your kiss was fueled by passion. It felt as though it was." He leaned down to her, aware of the pulse in her neck quickening. "You cannot deny that you felt something."

Why he asked her that, Phineas did not know. He could see clear as day that she regretted what had happened. That she had not *wanted* to feel something.

The truth, though, was that she had, and he wanted her to admit it.

Her shoulders tensed, and her hands once more lifted to press against his chest. "Let go of me," she ordered in a hard tone; still, that slight quiver remained.

"Answer my question," Phineas countered, holding her gaze to better gauge her reaction. "Why would you offer to kiss me? Why is kissing me so outrageous?"

Louisa stilled, regarding him carefully. "Those are two questions."

Phineas grinned at her. He had always enjoyed the twisted pathways of her mind. "If you prefer to stay here with me all day, then..." His voice trailed off as he let his gaze drop to her lips, still so temptingly close.

Clearly annoyed, she huffed out a breath. "If you must know, I find you a loathsome creature and, therefore, you were the perfect way to prove to Anne how serious I was about her and your brother." As she spoke, her nerves seemed to steady, and her gaze became harder, daring, challenging. "There," she finished, her green gaze locked on his as though she too was gauging his reaction. "Satisfied?"

Phineas laughed, surprised that she would repeat the question that had all but made him jerk her back into his arms. "Are you daring me to kiss you again?" he asked, smirking at her.

A shuddering breath left her lips, and for a short moment, she seemed truly tempted. Then, unfortunately, her gaze darkened, and he felt her body tense, once more leaning away from him. "Release me," she ordered in a tone that told him she meant it.

Sighing, Phineas complied, his hands dropping from her arms. "No matter how hard you try to convince yourself that our kiss didn't touch you, I'll never believe it."

Her jaw hardened as she glared at him. "It was a wager. Nothing more." She took a step back. "Stay away from me." For a moment, her gaze held his. Then she spun around and rushed from the room. Phineas could not shake the feeling that she was fleeing...perhaps afraid of what would happen if she stayed.

Sighing, he rubbed his hands over his face, still rattled by their kiss. A part of him could not help but doubt that it had happened; however, Louisa's scent still lingered in the air, honeysuckle and sunshine. She was like a force of nature, strong and unyielding, and Phineas had always liked that about her.

Unable not to, Phineas returned to the terrace, wondering if Louisa would be there. His gaze swept the guests as they laughed and chatted, enjoying the happy occasion. Even his brother and Anne had returned, standing in a small circle of family and friends, the joy upon both their faces palpable.

A twinge of envy seized Phineas' heart, and he frowned. Never had he thought of himself as a family man, one longing for marriage and children. Still, seeing Tobias and Anne together—lending a hand even in uniting them—had changed something for Phineas.

Oddly enough, whenever the notion of marriage crossed his mind these days, an image of Louisa drifted before his eyes. Admittedly, he hardly knew her, and yet, there was something about her that felt familiar...

...as though he did know her.

...as though he had known her long ago.

It was an odd notion, and yet, he could not seem to shake it.

The problem was that Louisa had come to loathe him according to her own words. *You're a loathsome creature*, had she not precisely said that? The question that remained, the same as before, was why?

Glimpsing her across the terrace where she stood off by herself, her gaze directed out into the gardens of his ancestral home, Phineas wondered if there was any way he could ask her for the reason to which she would actually provide an answer.

A part of him doubted it very much. Why, then, was she so tight-lipped? It was quite unlike her; after all, she did not hide her dislike of him, merely its reason.

"It is a beautiful day, is it not?"

Turning at the soft voice speaking out from behind him, Phineas found himself looking at the young woman who had swayed in his arms at the Archibald house party last Christmas. Fortunately, today, she seemed to have eaten for she was much steadier on her feet. "It is indeed."

Moving to stand beside him, she cast him a warm smile before her gaze traveled over the awakening garden stretching out toward the horizon. "This place, too, is beautiful. Perfect for a wedding."

Phineas nodded, wondering why she had sought him out. "You do not feel light-headed?" he asked with a smirk.

A tinge of red came to her cheeks, but she laughed quickly. "No, not at all." She straightened as though to prove her words. "My feet are firmly planted upon the ground."

"I'm glad to hear it," Phineas told her. "Miss...?"

"Mortensen," the young woman supplied helpfully. "Miss Mortensen." She glanced away before once more meeting his gaze, a hint of shyness in the way she looked at him. "I'm glad to see Anne so happily settled."

Phineas barely heard what she was saying for he had caught sight of Lord Hastings moving closer to Louisa out of the corner of his eye. "You are acquainted?" he asked absentmindedly.

"We are," Miss Mortensen replied. "We've known each other since childhood, and both had our coming out the year before last."

"I see," Phineas mumbled, his body tensing as he watched Louisa smile at Lord Hastings who had sidled up beside her, a wide grin upon his face. "If you'll excuse me..." He muttered in the direction of Miss Mortensen and then stepped away without another look. He knew he was being rude; however, something inside him objected to the sight before his eyes.

Indeed, over the course of the past year, he had seen Louisa dance and chat with many a gentleman. He had not been particularly fond of the sight, but never had it made his stomach churn as it did now. Something had changed.

Today.

A few moments ago.

"Hastings," he exclaimed as he stepped up to them. Instantly, Louisa's eyes narrowed, snapping to glare at him as though he were the devil incarnate. "Your mother appears unwell. Perhaps you should see to her."

The man's smile slid off his face, alarm marking his features. "Thank you, Barrington," he said, then bowed to his companion. "Lady Louisa."

Anger still marked her features, but she managed to grant the man a kind smile before he walked off in search of his mother. The moment he had left, Louisa rounded upon Phineas. "How dare you?"

He chuckled, "Why so angry?"

Her lips thinned, and he could sense more unflattering words upon her tongue. Still, she held herself back, her gaze briefly glancing around the terrace, taking in the many people in attendance.

The many people within earshot.

Phineas inhaled a calming breath, then moved closer as much as he dared without inciting her anger yet again. "What did I do to make you hate me, Lulu?" He cursed himself for uttering that nickname for he knew she despised it. He himself had become utterly fond of it, though, for it seemed intimate in a way nothing else ever had. It was his name for her, one that only he used.

No one else.

"Do not call me that!" she hissed under her breath, her face tense before she cast a feigned smile at an acquaintance walking past.

"Then answer my question," Phineas replied in the same hushed tone. He did not wish to blackmail her; nevertheless, he was growing almost desperate to receive an answer.

Her lips thinned, and her nostrils flared as she glared at him. "You're a despicable person!"

"You've said so before," Phineas replied evenly. "Care to explain how you've come to that conclusion?"

Scoffing, Louisa shook her head at him as though the reason should be obvious. Then she turned and made to walk away, mumbling something unintelligible under her breath.

More insults, no doubt.

Without thought, Phineas reached out to hold her back, his hand once more settling upon her arm. "You can hate me all you like," he snarled, his gaze now as hard as her own as he looked down upon her, "but you cannot deny that you enjoyed our kiss."

Red crept up her cheeks, and yet, her nostrils flared as though she wished to throw herself at him and claw his eyes out.

Phineas smirked upon seeing her so torn.

Her teeth gritted together, and again, she made to leave, but stopped when he refused to release her. "Let go!" she hissed quietly.

Phineas lowered his head another fraction down toward hers. His eyes remained locked on hers, only now he could make out the small golden flecks dancing in her emerald eyes. They shone like little sparks, whispering of the passion that lived in her heart. If only she would express it in a different, more appealing manner. "You stole a kiss," he whispered, delighting in the way she drew in an unsteady breath, "be assured that I shall return the favor." He grinned at her, wanting nothing more in this moment than to see her eyes flare once more.

She was beautiful in her anger, and he hated releasing her when she jerked on her arm, threatening to cause a scene. His hand fell away though, and she huffed out an annoyed breath. Then she turned and strode away, her shoulders tense.

Her eyes, fortunately, still held the same fire Phineas had always seen in them whenever they fell upon him. A fire she seemed to have reserved for him.

No one else.

It was a small mercy.

But not enough.

Phineas wanted more.

Chapter Nine

THE FREEDOM TO CHOOSE

"Unbelievable!" Louisa moaned as she and Leonora walked down the pavement, their family's London townhouse coming into view. "I can honestly say I've never been more bored in my life."

"Huh?" With her nose still stuck in her precious notebook, Leonora walked without sight, her attention wholly focused on the notes she had taken during the dreadful lecture to which she had dragged Louisa.

Not even if her life depended upon it could Louisa now name the title, or the field, or the stuffy, old man whose lecture had threatened to send her into a deep slumber.

Unfortunately, it had not. Louisa had remained awake from the beginning until its equally dull end. It had been torture, and no matter Leonora's promises, she would never again agree to accompany her sister to such an event.

The thing barely deserved the word. No, strike that. It did not deserve the word. Not in the least.

Leonora clearly disagreed for she had been rapt with attention the whole time, her blue eyes sparkling with enthusiasm and fascination. Likely, she had been severely disappointed when the lecture had finally come to an end.

"You did not like it?" Leonora asked without looking up, her eyes still glued to the page.

Louisa laughed. "Truly? What could possibly have given you that idea?" she asked, sarcasm dripping from every word.

Too distracted by her notes, Leonora failed to identify her sister's tone of voice. "Well, first, I heard you moan again and again as though you were in agony. Second—"

"I was!" Louisa insisted, rolling her eyes at her sister, which, of course, she failed to notice as well. "It was torture."

"U-hu," was all Leonora could manage by means of a reply as her feet carried her onward.

Louisa sighed, feeling a slight pang of regret. "I admit a part of me wishes I had something I felt equally passionate about." Perhaps that was why she had agreed to go with Leonora; in the hopes that she might find something else to fill her life besides endless balls as well as their meaningless nattering. Her own life often seemed empty compared to the depth Leonora's possessed.

Most women considered marriage their greatest goal in life, their sight set on snaring a husband with title, fortune and reputation to raise their own position. They desired to be wives, and, of course, mothers and thought little else to be of equal importance.

Of course, society at large agreed.

Louisa sighed, glancing at her sister, once again feeling envious of Leonora's mind, her curiosity, her ambition and tenacity. Perhaps the fact that their parents had never pressured them to find a desirable match according to society's standards, that they had always encouraged them to follow their hearts instead made Louisa feel even worse. She knew that she was fortunate to be granted such freedom by her parents, and yet, she did not know what to do with it.

It seemed like an unforgivable waste!

"Leonora?" Louisa said with a slight chuckle in her voice as she stopped by the steps leading up to their front door.

Her sister, on the other hand, continued walking, her nose still stuck in her book. "Huh?"

Louisa laughed., "Where are you going? Is there another lecture that calls to you?"

Leonora stopped and finally her head rose, her eyes abandoning their focus. She looked up and her head turned as her gaze swept over her surroundings for the first time since leaving the lecture hall. "Oh," she breathed, and a tinge of red came to her cheeks as she turned to look at her sister. "I suppose I was a bit distracted."

Laughing, Louisa shook her head. "A bit? That, my dear sister, is the understatement of the century."

Arm in arm, the two sisters climbed the front steps to their home and then walked through the front door. "Will you come with me again next week?" Leonora asked as they handed their bonnets and gloves to a footman.

Louisa rolled her eyes, slightly annoyed that her sister had not even heard her objections. "Not even if you paid me."

Leonora frowned before her gaze once more fell upon her note-book. "If you'll excuse me," she mumbled, already heading for the large staircase that led to her chamber on the upper floor, "I need to review my notes." And with that, she was gone, lost in a world all her own.

Louisa sighed, then flinched when something small came darting into the hall from the back of the house. It moved fast, crossing the hall in a few large bounds before it disappeared into the drawing room. "Harry!" Louisa called out, torn between annoyance and amusement that her youngest sister's most recently rescued charge had yet again gotten away.

In the next moment, Harriet—or Harry!—came crashing through the very same door, her face flushed. "Have you seen Sir Lancelot?" she asked, panting.

Louisa paused, frowning at her. "You call your rabbit Sir Lancelot?"

"Where is he?" red-haired Harry demanded, her green eyes wide as they searched their surroundings. The cluster of freckles upon her nose moved as she crinkled it as though trying to sniff out her errant pet. "Here, Sir Lancelot. Here! Here!"

"He's not a dog," Louisa observed with a frown as she followed in her sister's wake. Even though, Harriet had turned eighteen only a fortnight ago, she often behaved like a girl much younger in years. "And he went in there." She indicated the drawing room.

"Did you find him?" In strode the Whickerton's second youngest daughter Christina—or Chris!—the golden curls dancing artfully down her back in stark contrast to Harry's wild, fiery-red mane. "Where is he?" She glanced at Sarah, their former neighbor and Chris' best friend.

"In here!" Harry exclaimed, waving the others forward before she darted into the drawing room.

The other two girls followed as did Louisa, curious to see what had happened in her absence. As childish as her two youngest sisters still were—granted, Harry far more than Chris!—their day seemed to have passed in a more entertaining manner than Louisa's. Perhaps she was doing something wrong!

"Close the door!" Harry called as they all stepped over the threshold. "Or he'll escape again!"

Chris slammed the door shut with a vehemence that made the paintings on the walls rattle. "He's over there!" Her finger pointed to the settee, and they saw a bushy, white tail disappear underneath.

Leaning back against the closed door, Louisa watched with amusement as her youngest sister scrambled after Sir Lancelot, who seemed rather disinclined to allow himself to be caught.

"Since when does Harry have a rabbit?" Sarah asked with a smile, clearly as amused as Louisa to see Harry darting over and around furniture to reclaim the little creature.

Chris sighed, "She found it in the country on our way back from Anne's wedding." A chuckle escaped her when Harry tripped on her hem and landed hard on the floor. She would not be detained long, though, and was up on her feet only a moment later.

Sarah laughed, "I assume it was injured," the young girl observed with the knowledge of one who had known Harriet for years.

Until recently, Sarah and her family, Lord and Lady Hartmore, had called the townhouse next door their own. Due to Lord Hartmore's unfortunate gambling habits, though, they had been forced to sell it and move into a smaller residence. It had broken Chris' and Sarah's hearts to no longer live next door to one another, sneaking through a gap in the tall hedge standing on the border between their two houses whenever the occasion called for it.

And it had called for it quite often.

"Of course, it was," Louisa replied. "Else even Harry would not have been able to catch it." Which was evident considering her current misfortune.

"It was a beautiful wedding, was it not?" Sarah remarked rather dreamily. "I have never seen Anne this happy. She was radiant."

Louisa smiled. "Love does that."

Sighing longingly, Sarah nodded. Then she paused, her gaze darting to Louisa before once more slipping away.

"Is something wrong?"

Sarah shook her head. "I was...I was merely wondering if...if you're acquainted with Lord Barrington." The color in her cheeks darkened a little.

Louisa would have smiled at her innocent portrayal of young affection if Sarah had not set her sights on the one man Louisa loathed with every fiber of her being. Now, more than ever. "Unfortunately."

"He is quite handsome, is he not?" Sarah beamed, her thoughts too taken with the miscreant for her to notice the disapproving tone in Louisa's voice. "Is he...?" She looked shyly at Chris before her gaze returned to Louisa. "Are you betrothed to him?"

Louisa's jaw dropped to the ground as she stared at Sarah in shock, unable to form a coherent thought.

Chris shrugged. "I wasn't quite certain. You never speak of him, and yet..." Her voice trailed off; still, Louisa had not missed its meaningful tone.

Sarah tensed. "I mean, I...I saw you speaking to one another and I merely wondered if—"

"We're not!" Louisa exclaimed as outrage replaced paralysis. "And we never shall be. The man is—" She stopped, noting the flustered expression upon Sarah's face as well as the curious one on Chris'. "If you want him, he's all yours." She took a step closer, her gaze intent as it held the girl's. "But be mindful for he is not who he might seem to be." There, she had uttered a warning. More she could not do without being forced to explain herself.

Bidding Sarah a good day, Louisa slunk from the room, careful not to let Sir Lancelot escape, and headed upstairs, feeling suddenly in need of solitude.

Ever since Phineas Hawke had somehow come by her secret—or was he truly merely suspecting?—Louisa felt reminded of her flaw more than ever. Of course, every day brought its challenges, from calling cards over letters to interesting snippets in the paper; still, Louisa had managed. She had developed a way to distract those around her, feigning fatigue or annoyance or disinterest or anything that might appear reasonable to have another read instead of herself.

And so far, no one had taken note.

At least not as far as she knew.

No one except for Phineas Hawke.

Her nemesis.

Closing the door to her chamber behind her, Louisa sighed and sank into the beautiful armchair by the window, her gaze drifting to the gardens beyond, its greens growing in intensity, here and there interspersed by blossoming flowers. It was a calming sight; today, though, it failed to soothe Louisa's battered nerves.

Always had she worried that one day, she would not be able to uphold this ruse that had become her life. That one day there would be no more excuses or distractions. That one day she would be found out.

After all, all the memorizing in the world could only do so much. It certainly could help her recite poems, allowing her to pretend she had read them herself when in truth she had merely been listening carefully upon hearing them, quickly repeating their lines to herself, trying to hold on to them before they could slip away.

Always had Jules read to them as children. As the eldest, it had brought her such joy to entertain her younger siblings. Carefully, Louisa had worked to uphold that tradition, remarking upon how dear these memories were to her and that they all ought to hold on to a piece of their childhood. And thus, Jules read to them even today, at five-and-twenty years of age, all of them curled up in one of their chambers, all five sisters silent and listening except for one.

Louisa's mind knew how to remember, how to retain information almost indefinitely and reproduce it upon request. That was not a problem, and Louisa felt almost at peace when the topic of discussion strayed to literature or ancient cultures or anything safely belonging to the past. She might not enjoy each topic for its own sake but cherished them because they made her feel safe.

News in the paper or leaflets about museums and operas posed a threat, of course, and Louisa always prayed that they would not find her unawares, forcing her to react without knowledge of the subject she was asked to remark upon.

Closing her eyes, Louisa tried her best to ignore the nagging voice that echoed in her mind so often these days. *She is a pretty head with nothing inside. I wouldn't be surprised if she didn't know how to read.*

But failed yet again.

Unbidden, Phineas Hawke's face loomed before her mind's eye, smirking at her, his eyes laughing as he looked down upon her. Although she could never detect a sense of superiority in his gaze, he made her feel small and insignificant. She felt vulnerable under his scrutinizing eyes, which never failed to make her anger spark anew.

Pushing to her feet, Louisa gritted her teeth to hold back the frustrated growl that threatened to rise from her throat. "That loathsome man!" she hissed under her breath, unable to ban that teasing look of his from her mind. He enjoyed mocking her, did he not? He enjoyed seeing her squirm, was that not true? Why else would he always seek her out? Always linger nearby, watching her?

Because he was, wasn't he?

Louisa swallowed hard as she recalled one moment the day of Anne's wedding. She had tried to shove it away, ignored it with all her might, and yet, it kept knocking on the door to her consciousness.

No, not knocking.

Pounding.

He had returned her kiss most passionately. Most eagerly. His hands insistent upon her back, holding her close. The memory still made her shiver, and she bit her lower lip, angry with herself for allowing that miscreant to affect her so.

You stole a kiss. Be assured that I shall return the favor.

The thought of kissing Phineas Hawke again, of having him kiss *her* again stole the air from her lungs and sent a jolt of awareness through her body. Never had she felt anything remotely like it, and it was deeply unsettling.

Pinching her eyes shut, Louisa shook her head as though sheer willpower could hold at bay the temptation he presented. "No. No. No. No." Why did this have to happen? Why did he make her feel like...like this? Why him of all people?

Hanging her head, Louisa buried her face in her hands, feeling exhausted. Life itself was exhausting enough without adding Phineas Hawke to the mix, and now she couldn't help but worry what would happen the next time they laid eyes upon each other.

The problem was *worry* was not the only word that came to mind when her thoughts drifted to Phineas Hawke.

Chapter Ten

QUESTIONS & ANSWERS

"Why don't you go and talk to her?" Phineas heard his brother's voice beside him as they stood on the fringes of the dance floor in Lord Hastings' lavish townhouse. "Nicely, I mean," Tobias clarified in a warning tone that made Phineas turn his gaze from the arriving Whickertons and look at his brother with a deepening frown. "Don't pretend you don't know what I mean," Tobias chided him. "You have a way of riling her that will not get you what you want."

Phineas inhaled a slow breath, willing his features not to betray the excitement he felt at seeing Louisa here tonight after a fortnight of not even catching a glimpse of her. "What I want?" he asked lightly. "And what do you suppose I want?"

Tobias crossed his arms, a challenging smirk coming to his face. "That indeed is an incredibly good question. What *do* you want, Phin? And don't bother pretending." His brows rose. "I saw the way you kissed her."

The reminder of their kiss at his brother's wedding not long ago sent a jolt of longing through every fiber of his being. "She kissed me," he pointed out, willing his gaze not to stray from his brother and seek her out again.

Tobias smiled at him rather indulgently. "Her kiss was no more than the payment of a wager. Yours, however—"

"You knew?" Phineas demanded, suddenly furious. "You knew and you didn't tell me?"

Casting a glance at his young wife, who had gone to greet her cousins, Tobias took a step closer to his brother. "Don't you dare pretend you're angry with me, Brother. If you want to be angry with someone, be angry with yourself."

"You had no right—"

"Truly?" Tobias interrupted, his outspoken behavior rather uncharacteristic. "After you meddled in my life to your heart's delight, you now object when I do the same?"

Phineas heaved a deep sigh. "I only did what I did because I wanted to help. I hope you can believe that. I knew you loved Anne—heck, every fool with eyes knew you loved Anne!—and I merely thought to help you along, to ensure you would not lose her." He shook his head. "Do you truly hold that against me?"

A slow smile stole onto his brother's face that made Phineas a bit uneasy. "What makes you think my reason differs from yours?"

Phineas stilled, for once no lighthearted remark upon his lips. "You..."

His brother sighed, "You care for her, do you not?"

Overwhelmed by this sudden turn in their conversation, the depth of it unfamiliar to him, Phineas laughed, "You jest, dear Brother. I assure you I—"

Tobias held up a hand. "Fine. Deny it all you want, but don't be surprised when someone else snatches her up one of these days, and she'll be lost to you." His brother's dark brown gaze held his, his words echoing the very ones Phineas had spoken to him not long ago. "For once in your life, be serious, Phin, and ask yourself what it is you want." He glanced over his shoulder to where Anne was hugging Louisa. "And if it is her you want," he continued, his gaze once more seeking Phineas', "then don't be a fool. Believe me, I know what I'm talking about." He chuckled, then patted Phineas on the back and headed over to join his wife.

Running a hand through his hair, Phineas leaned back against a marble column, his heart beating in an odd rhythm as his gaze strayed to the golden-haired fury, who loved nothing more than to glare at him. Again, he wondered what reason she could have to detest him so, and he realized once again that it bothered him.

It bothered him a lot.

His jaw tensed as he watched her, watched her laugh and smile, her dark green eyes vibrant and full of passion. She was magnificent, proud and daring, but also kind and loyal to a fault. He remembered her efforts—which had by far exceeded his own—to unite Anne and Tobias despite their own objections, and she had been right. She had fought for them, sacrificed her own well-being to see someone she loved happy. She was a rare woman, and the thought that another would one day call her wife turned his stomach.

As though on cue, Lord Hastings approached her, his manners impeccable and his smile a mile wide. They exchanged a few words before he held out his hand to her, no doubt asking for the next dance.

Phineas tensed, his teeth gritting together as he watched them stand up together. Of course, he had seen her dance before. He had seen her chat and laugh with gentlemen countless times over the course of the previous two years; now, seeing her like this felt different.

It felt wrong.

How had this happened? Had it been their kiss?

To this day, Phineas could not shake the overwhelming need that seized him every time his thoughts drifted back to that day, that moment. Something had changed when she had been in his arms, and whether he liked it or not, he now thought of her as...his.

Could his brother be right? Had he come to care for her? Beyond anything he had ever felt before? For anyone? For any woman?

As he followed Louisa and Lord Hastings with his gaze, he took note of another woman lingering nearby, her eyes seeking his with unerring intention. Phineas blinked, remembering the soft smile upon her young face.

Miss Mortensen—if he remembered correctly.

That morning at Windmere Park, after cornering Louisa on the stairs, Phineas had walked rather distractedly around the house and then found himself under a sprig of mistletoe with her. He had given her a quick peck on the lips and then escorted her to the breakfast parlor. As far as he was concerned, that had been it.

Lately, however, he seemed to be seeing Miss Mortensen everywhere, always nearby, always watching him. It would seem the young woman had taken a fancy to him, perhaps hoping for him to approach her.

Not wishing to encourage her, Phineas turned away, his thoughts instantly drawn back to the problem he was facing. Perhaps he had been approaching it from a wrong direction. Perhaps Louisa was not the woman he ought to speak to for he felt certain she would not be forthcoming. Perhaps he ought to speak to someone who knew her well.

A sister perhaps.

His gaze moved to settle upon Lady Leonora, her dark hair in stark contrast to Louisa's glowing appearance. She stood with her younger sister Lady Christina, no doubt offering some counsel before she was asked onto the dance floor, leaving her elder sister behind.

Seeing his chance, Phineas approached her. "Good evening."

Her dark eyes settled upon his, a calculating frown coming to her kind face. "Good evening, Lord Barrington."

He chuckled, "Your sister always calls me by my name. She only ever uses my title when she wants to insult me."

The lady's eyes briefly dropped from his. "I apologize, my lord, and assure you that my sister..." She broke off, unable to give that sentence a truthful ending and refusing to lie all the same.

Phineas appreciated that. "Do you know why?" he asked without preamble. "Why she seems to loathe me like no other? I admit," he chuckled uneasily, "I do not know what I might have done."

Lady Leonora heaved a deep sigh, her gaze becoming distant as though she was searching her mind for an answer to his question. Then she looked up and met his eyes. "I'm afraid I do not," she replied, a hint of disappointment in her voice. "In fact, I've wondered about it myself. It is odd, is it not? Strong emotions deserve a valid reason." She shook her head in that rational way of hers, disappointed that her observations did not add up.

Phineas once more cast a glance at Louisa as she allowed Lord

Hastings to guide her across the dance floor. "Do you think," he began carefully, feeling a little unsettled to be uttering this question, "that you could find out?"

Lady Leonora's eyes narrowed slightly as she watched him, not unlike a scientist observing a new specimen; Phineas almost squirmed under her scrutinizing gaze. "Do you care for her?" she asked bluntly, open curiosity upon her face.

Again, Phineas felt the urge to squirm, to turn away, to deny what her words suggested.

Her head cocked sideways a little, her curious eyes sweeping over his face. "Indeed, your interest in knowing the reason suggests that she means something to you, that you find her reaction to you bothersome."

Phineas chuckled, trying to hide the fact that she was right. "Who would enjoy being loathed by another?"

Her seeing blue eyes remained locked on his face for a long moment as though she paid attention rather to his thoughts than his words. Then she nodded, a gentle smile coming to her face. "I promise, I shall speak to her; however, knowing my sister, I cannot promise that she will answer me anymore than she answers you."

Phineas cast her a grateful smile. "I thank you for your efforts," he told her honestly, for once not feeling the need to jest or say something to make light of his words. There was something deeply honest in her eyes that compelled him to speak what was on his mind without concern to have it ridiculed or twisted in some way or used against him. It had been a long time since he had felt this at ease in another's company.

Chapter Eleven

WORDS OF NO CONSEQUENCE

Louisa did her utmost to ignore the man standing on the edge of the dance floor, his dark, almost black gaze lingering upon her. She could feel it, like a touch upon her skin, as though his fingertips were gently grazing the line of her neck. A shiver went down her back, and she forced her eyes to settle on the man who held her in his arms. "You're a marvelous dancer, Lord Hastings," she exclaimed with more enthusiasm than she had intended.

Lord Hastings beamed at her. "I'm delighted to hear it," he replied, new eagerness coming to his gaze. "However, your own proficiency far exceeds mine."

Louisa smiled at him gratefully, unable to keep her eyes from darting over his shoulder in the next instant, once more settling upon the man with the most infuriating smile she had ever seen.

To her utter shock, she found him standing with her own sister, their heads bent to one another as words left their lips. Louisa's heart jerked at the sight, a cold shiver now replacing the tantalizing memory of his searing gaze. What was going on? Never had she seen the two of them converse. Who had sought out whom, she wondered, wishing she could hear what they were discussing.

For a shocking moment, the thought that Phineas Hawke might

have taken an interest in her sister crossed her mind. It made her feel ill, and she felt the sudden urge to run to her sister and chase him away. Never in a thousand years would she allow that man to fool tender-hearted Leonora into believing that a true and live heart beat in his chest. For she, like no other, knew that it was not the case, that it could not be.

Fortunately, the music drifted away, its last notes lingering upon the air as the dancers slowed their movements and then stopped. Lord Hastings once more complemented her before offering her his arm.

Accepting, Louisa allowed him to guide her off the dance floor, her gaze unerringly returning to her sister, surprised as well as relieved to find her alone once again. "Pardon me, my lord," she addressed the man by her side. "I'm afraid I must see to my sister. She seems unwell."

Lord Hastings mumbled something that might have been concern, his gaze obliging, before Louisa hurried away, leaving him behind without another thought. She reached her sister's side in record time, trying to catch her breath, doing her utmost to appear nonchalant. After all, it would not do to let Leonora see her thus. Her sister's mind was already most curious, her eyes always watchful, and she would no doubt see that something had deeply unsettled Louisa.

Curse that man!

"Do you not also wish to dance?" Louisa exclaimed with a joyful smile as she sidled up to her sister. "You must be utterly bored to be standing here all evening." Although Louisa could not help but feel annoyed with this charade, she felt that it was necessary to better hide her true intention.

Leonora returned her smile, her blue eyes lingering in a strange way though. "Oh, I assure you I am far from bored," she replied, an odd tone in her voice. "In fact, I find it most fascinating to be observing all the comings and goings, to try to judge by the look of a face what kind of heart beats in that person's chest. It is a study in psychology, is it not? Livelier than a lecture, but equally interesting." Her gaze once more swept the crowded ballroom before she glanced at Louisa. "Would you not agree?"

Louisa could not help but feel a slight tingle snake its way down her spine, warning her that her sister had an ulterior motive, that her eyes were more watchful than usual. "And what have you discovered?" she asked, almost bursting with curiosity to find out what Leonora and Phineas had been speaking about.

A slight chuckle rumbled in Leonora's throat before she turned toward her sister, her blue eyes open and seeing. "Is that truly what you wish to know?" Her eyebrows rose challengingly. "In fact, what I have observed is your own reaction to seeing me here, in this very spot, speaking to the very man you cannot bear lay eyes upon without muttering insults. Then," she continued with her observation, "you hurried over here as though the devil himself were behind you." Leonora smiled up at her. "And now you attempt to draw me into a conversation when it is most obvious that there is a question burning on your mind. Would you not rather ask it?"

In utter shock, Louisa stared at her sister. Never in her life had she known Leonora to be this observant when it came to those around her. Certainly, her sister had always been taken with the sciences; however, she had never known that Leonora's interest stretched to observing the nature of human behavior. What else had her sister gleaned in the past months?

For a second, Louisa was tempted to pretend that she had no clue what Leonora was referring to; unfortunately, one look into her sister's eyes told her that it would be a futile attempt. And so, she huffed out an annoyed breath, rolled her eyes for good measure, and said on an exhausted sigh, "Very well. If you must know, I was simply wondering what on earth you and that man were speaking about." She swallowed hard, inexplicably nervous suddenly. "After all, you have nothing in common. So naturally, I am puzzled." She shrugged. "Can you blame me?" There, no one could have possibly conjured a better denial out of thin air! Louisa was strangely proud of herself.

A soft grin came to Leonora's face as she watched Louisa, her head shaking from side to side in a rather endearing gesture. "You are undeniably the most stubborn woman I have ever met," Leonora commented with a chuckle, warmth shining in her deep blue eyes, "and I do mean this as a compliment."

Louisa felt her nerves settle, her heartbeat resuming at a more normal pace. "How sweet of you to notice," she laughed, reaching out and squeezing her sister's hand affectionately. "Well?"

Leonora inhaled a deep breath, her eyes briefly darting across the ballroom, not lingering anywhere, but rather as though looking for someone. "Well," she finally said when her gaze returned to meet Louisa's, "we were speaking about you, dear sister."

"Me?" Louisa barely noted the shrillness in her voice as she stared at her sister in disbelief. "Why on earth would you...?" Her eyes narrowed, a dark thought taking on shape in her mind. "What did he say about me?" Fear slowly crept up her spine; what if he had told Leonora about her...her secret?

Her sister's brows drew down slightly. "Are you all right? You suddenly seem tense." Leonora took a step closer, her soft hand coming to rest upon Louisa's arm, giving it a gentle squeeze. "Do you honestly believe that he said something to your disadvantage? In fact, he did not. He merely asked a question."

A deep breath swept from Louisa's lungs, and she almost crumpled to the floor in relief. "What question?"

"The question you seem to be determined not to answer, no matter who asks it," Leonora stated, pausing for a moment, her eyes still lingering upon Louisa's face. "He wished to know why you dislike him so, something—I admit—I have wondered myself many times." A questioning look came to her eyes.

Louisa felt her shoulders draw back, her chin lift, her hands ball into fists as though she were a warrior, readying herself for battle. "As though he doesn't know," she all but snapped, regretting deeply that her sister was the recipient of these words. "He is a most horrible creature, and he does not deserve an explanation. If he does not know, if he does not even remember what he said, then..." Suddenly, tears choked her voice. Louisa cursed herself for showing such weakness, but the thought that the words that had all but destroyed her had not even left an imprint on his mind was crippling.

Leonora's gaze softened, her eyes searching Louisa's face yet again. "What did he say?"

Louisa swallowed hard, then shook her head. "It does not matter. It was a long time ago, and I've moved past it."

"That is not true," Leonora replied, her hands gentle, but drawing Louisa closer, nonetheless. "If it were so, the mere sight of him would not unsettle you as it does. Please, tell me what happened. Unburden your heart, and I promise if it is your wish, I shall never speak of it to anyone. I shall not tell him. I swear."

Louisa smiled at her sister, welcoming her kindness and her affection, knowing that she was fortunate to have someone who cared so deeply about her, who knew her so well. If only she dared confide in Leonora and tell her everything. How would her sister react if she knew? Leonora of all people was someone who cherished knowledge, the written word and all the wisdom it had brought her as well as all it promised. How would she react if she found out that her sister could not even read? Would she feel compassion and offer her help? Or would she feel pity, shocked to learn that Louisa had not even mastered something so simple, something that lay at the base of all knowledge?

"The words he said were of no consequence," Louisa explained, cursing herself for not having the courage to at least admit to the flaw that plagued her daily. "He was rude and disrespectful. It was the way he spoke, not the words he said. I now know that he is not a man I wish to be acquainted with. Please, leave it at that."

Sadness stood in Leonora's eyes as well as a hint of disbelief; nonetheless, she nodded her head in acquiescence. "If that is your wish," she said gently. "Nevertheless, should you ever change your mind, please know that I will always have an open ear for you."

"I know." Smiling at her beloved sister, Louisa reminded herself that despite her flaw, she was a most fortunate woman. She could call so much her own, a dear family, sisters to share her life with and the freedom to choose her own path. A lot to be grateful for, Louisa reminded herself, determined to never again forget the good over the bad.

Chapter Twelve

A MOMENT IN AN ALCOVE

Ball for ball, Phineas found himself watching the crowd, his gaze sweeping over face after face, looking for *her*. No one else seemed to matter. All that mattered was her. When had this happened? How had this obsession taken root in his blood? Had it been their kiss?

Exhaling a deep breath, Phineas leaned back against a marble column, his thoughts drawn back to that one moment when Louisa had been in his arms. It certainly was a moment he could not forget. It lingered in his mind often, and, yet again, for what seemed like the thousandth time, he found himself wondering when he ought to repay her for the kiss she had stolen. Indeed, the thought brought a deep smile to his face.

And then his gaze snapped up and his eyes unerringly settled upon her.

Arm in arm with her sister, Louisa walked into the ballroom, surrounded by the rest of her large family, parents and siblings as well as her dear grandmother, the woman who referred to him as "the wicked one." The thought made Phineas chuckle. Indeed, he liked the dowager countess for she possessed a dark streak of humor, one not unlike his own, one he had seen in Louisa as well. Phineas could not help but think that her grandmother would not object if he were to...

Phineas stilled as his thoughts cleared, and he finally realized—with no small amount of shock—in what direction they had been going. Was he courting Louisa? Or rather, did he want to? Indeed, she had been foremost on his mind these past few weeks, months even. He had attended a Christmas house party because of her. He had remained in the country at Barrington House simply because she, too, had been there. He had been acting quite unlike himself...and all for her. What did this mean?

Indeed, the answer that lingered somewhere just out of reach brought with it a somewhat terrifying note, and Phineas did not dare dwell on it.

The muscles in his jaw tensed when he saw Louisa accept Lord Hastings' arm and stand up with him for a minuet. The two younger Whickerton sisters followed onto the dance floor; only the eldest remained behind, faithfully keeping the dowager countess company.

Crossing his arms, Phineas remained with his shoulder rested against the column, his eyes fixed on Louisa as she smiled and laughed. His insides twisted and turned in answer, and he cursed himself for allowing her to affect him thus.

Phineas shook his head, hoping to clear his mind and banish the thoughts of her, but it would not work. His eyes did not dare stray from her for too long, drawn back as though they were two magnets, unable to deny each other. If only she felt the same pull!

Huffing out an annoyed breath, Phineas pushed off the marble column, not knowing what to do with his arms. He felt like a fool, dancing from one foot onto the other, without a purpose. And then out of the corner of his eye he caught sight of another's gaze directed at him. For a moment, he tensed wondering if someone had taken note of his strange mannerisms. Were people already laughing about him behind his back? He certainly deserved it.

Daring to look, Phineas was surprised when he found none other than Miss Mortensen looking back at him. A small blush came to her face as their eyes collided, and she instantly dropped her gaze. Still, a moment later, he found her walking in his direction, moving ever closer despite the hint of shyness lingering in her eyes.

Willing a polite expression upon his face, Phineas greeted her kindly. "It is a most marvelous night, is it not?" He offered her no more than a simple pleasantry, for he had nothing else to say.

Miss Mortensen nodded enthusiastically. "It is almost magical; would you not agree? The music is divine, and I can think of nothing I'd rather do but dance the night away."

Phineas understood perfectly that she wanted him to ask her onto the dance floor; nothing was further from his mind though. His gaze barely met hers as he kept his eyes fixed on Louisa. The second the dance ended and Lord Hastings hastened back to his mother—bless the old lady!—Phineas mumbled a quick apology to Miss Mortensen and then rushed after Louisa.

Unaware that he was following her, Louisa left the ballroom and proceeded onward toward what Phineas presumed to be the ladies' powder room. She did not rush, but walked leisurely, giving him a chance to catch up.

Like a hunter, Phineas kept his gaze fixed on her, long strides carrying him closer. With each step, the hustle bustle around them receded. Voices grew dimmer, and he no longer sensed a crowd around him. On his way, he nodded to an acquaintance every now and then, barely turning his head, oddly worried that he might lose sight of her. And then she slipped around a corner and was gone.

Instantly, Phineas quickened his steps, grateful that the corridor lay deserted. He rounded the corner and found her no more than a few steps ahead of him, still walking at a leisurely pace. A roguish grin came to his face as he wondered—just for a moment—if she would have walked faster had she known he was in pursuit.

Phineas had almost reached her when he spotted the door to the ladies' powder room beginning to open. Voices, chatting excitedly, drifted out into the corridor.

Stilling for no more than a second, Phineas acted quickly.

In two long strides, he had caught up to Louisa, seized her arm and pulled her over to the side toward a darkened alcove.

A startled gasp escaped her, her eyes going wide as he spun her around to face him. "What on—?" Her voice broke off the second her eyes fell on his face. Her features tensed, a snarl coming to her lips before she dug in her heels, resisting him as he had expected her to. "What do you want?"

Phineas glanced over her head, pulling her closer, and whispered, "Do you want them to find us together?"

Louisa stilled her struggles and quickly glanced over her shoulder at the first lady now exiting the powder room, her head turned back toward her friend, her voice ringing loudly down the corridor.

A muttered curse escaped Louisa's lips before their roles all but became reversed for she was now the one to seize his arm and pull him into the darkened alcove.

Phineas chuckled under his breath as they squeezed into the small space, stood pressed to the wall face to face, praying not to be discovered as the two ladies slowly made their way down the corridor and back toward the ballroom. Their chattering voices nicely masked the muttered curses Louisa could not seem to suppress. "Do you mind?" she hissed under her breath, looking up at him through narrowed eyes. "You're standing too close."

"Am I?" Phineas whispered, feeling her shiver as his breath fanned over the delicate skin on her neck. His hands settled on her waist, and he moved even closer, pressing her against the wall.

"Yes!" she hissed next to his ear, her palms flattening on his chest, trying to urge him backwards. Then she lifted her chin and gazed over his shoulder. "They're gone," she whispered, relief loud and clear in her voice. "Move!"

Remaining where he was, Phineas chuckled. "They might come back," he teased. "Or others might happen by."

Louisa huffed out an annoyed breath, then her hands tensed upon his chest and she shoved against him. When half an arm's length separated them, her chin rose and she met his eyes, her own shooting daggers. "Why are you doing this?" she demanded, open accusation in her dark green eyes.

Phineas chuckled, reaching out to toy with one of her blonde curls. "Oh, dearest Lulu, there are countless reasons."

Gritting her teeth, she slapped his hand away, then made to step past him. "I detest you."

Caught up in this delightful amusement, Phineas was most unwilling to allow her to rush off so soon. Once more, he caught her around the waist and pulled her back, stepping in her path. "Tell me why," he said, surprising even himself.

With her lips in a snarl, she glared up at him. "Tell you what? Why you are the most annoying man to ever walk this earth? Why—?"

"Why you detest me," Phineas interrupted, the need to know suddenly boiling in his veins. With his gaze locked on hers, he once more urged her backwards until her back was against the wall. "I will not let you leave, unless you tell me."

For a moment, all thoughts seemed to flee her head. She was staring up at him with wide open eyes, her chest rising and falling rapidly, whispering of the turmoil in her heart. If only he knew what it was!

"Let me go," Louisa demanded, anger swinging in her voice, mixing with a hint of panic. "Now!"

Slowly, Phineas shook his head, his gaze never leaving hers. He breathed in deeply, savoring that unique scent of her: sunshine and honeysuckle.

Her jaw clenched. "I'll scream," she threatened in a feeble voice.

Phineas chuckled, then moved, his head lowering toward hers. "Do so," he whispered. "I dare you."

Glaring up at him, she breathed in deeply, once, twice. "You're bluffing," she muttered, a touch of uncertainty in her voice. "Your reputation, too, would suffer if we were found together like this. You cannot want this anymore than I do."

Slowly sliding his hands further onto the small of her back, Phineas felt her shiver. "Dear Lulu," he whispered, the words falling onto her lips, "you have no idea what it is I want." He held her gaze a moment longer before he let it briefly drop to her mouth.

Louisa inhaled a sharp breath. "I'll scream," she threatened yet again, the pulse in her neck hammering wildly.

A slow grin spread over Phineas' face. "Go ahead," he replied, wondering if she meant what she said. "I assure you I have ways of silencing you."

Clearly understanding the innuendo behind his words—for now her own gaze darted lower if only for a split second—she tensed, her hands upon his chest trying to hold him at bay...a feeble attempt at best. "You wouldn't."

"You know me better than that, Lulu," he teased, pushing closer still. "Answer me, and I shall release you. Fail to answer, and..." His voice trailed off, his brows quirking upward, making it unmistakably clear what he intended.

Her lips thinned. "Why do you even care? You—"

"I do," he assured her, his head lowering another inch toward hers.

"I don't believe you."

"I can see that," Phineas replied, close enough now that he could feel her breath mingling with his own. Yet, she did not pull away nor try to stop his approach.

"I detest you," she whispered breathlessly as though to remind herself of what she ought to feel.

"Why?" Phineas pressed, one hand abandoning its place upon her waist and reaching upward. Gently, he grasped her chin simply because he liked to hold on to her, to feel her skin against his own.

"Don't pretend you don't know," she whispered, her breath quickening with each heartbeat. Her dark green eyes stared up into his, not even a hint of fear in them.

"I don't."

"I don't believe you."

"Tell me," he urged, and his lips brushed against hers ever so softly. He felt it like a clap of thunder. A jolt shot through him, and a deep yearning settled in his bones.

"Nev—"

Before Louisa could finish that one word, Phineas dipped his head, closing the last small distance between them. His lips claimed hers, and all restraint fell from him.

From them both, as it seemed, for Louisa's fingers suddenly curled into his lapels, pulling him closer. Her mouth opened beneath his, and she responded to his kiss as passionately as he had always hoped was her nature.

Her hands snaked upward, and he felt the tips of her fingers brushing against his skin. They moved farther up, along his neck before disappearing in his hair, tugging him ever closer.

Phineas' heart soared at her willing response, his longing for her intensifying with each stroke of her tongue against his, each tentative, and yet, utterly bold touch. She was breathtaking in the truest sense of the word, and he could not imagine ever wanting to kiss another.

And then she suddenly stilled, her body growing rigid. Her hands fell from his hair and returned to his chest, her palms flattened against him. She did not shove him this time, but he could feel her resistance grow until she finally wrenched her lips from his. Panting, she stared up at him. "Release me. Now."

Reluctantly, Phineas did as she had asked. He took a small step backwards, careful not to allow the distance between them to grow too much. "Will you still deny the passion between us?" he demanded, offering her a meaningful grin, delighting in the way she glared at him. Why did he? A part of him wondered. Why could he not simply tell her how she made him feel?

Her lips thinned, and her eyes grew hard as she lifted her chin and straightened her shoulders. "Do not for a second believe that you know me," she hissed, her shoulders trembling—with passion or anger, he did not know. "You know nothing about me." She took a step sideways, away from him, closer to the corridor and her way out. "Do not ever come near me again, do you hear?"

The moment she made to turn and hurry away, Phineas grabbed her arm. He pulled her back against him, his head lowered to hers. "Then tell me what I wish to know," he told her, his gaze searching hers, wondering for the thousandth time what he could have done. "It is your choice. A few simple words, and you shall be rid of me." Of course, Phineas did not mean to uphold his end of the bargain. Never would he stay away. He could not. The mere thought was absurd, ridiculous. He needed her; as shocking as that was, he needed her.

Instead of lashing out at him, instead of calling him every insulting name she had used before on numerous occasions, Louisa remained silent, not a word leaving her lips. Her green eyes were fixed upon his, contemplating, and a touch of defeat, of exhaustion sparked in their depths. Still, she would not give in. A part of her clearly wanted to, though, was as tired as he was of this animosity between them.

"Why can you not simply tell me?" Phineas whispered gently. "What did I do that you cannot forgive?"

Her jaw hardened then, and he was certain that she would yell at him now, perhaps even slap him.

But she did not.

A shadow seemed to fall over her face, something dark and sad and anguished. She looked vulnerable suddenly, and Phineas felt the unexpected urge to comfort her, to shield her from the ugliness of the world. Before he could, Louisa took a step back, her lips still pressed into a tight line, unrelenting. "Stay away," she demanded once again before turning on her heel and slipping out of the alcove, leaving him behind with more questions than before.

Chapter Thirteen
UNWANTED SUITORS

The sun shone brightly, and laughter echoed to Louisa's ears as her younger sisters and their friend Sarah chased Sir Lancelot through the gardens. Somehow the rabbit had gotten away again as it had on numerous occasions. How he always managed to do so was beyond Louisa. Usually her younger sister Harriet had an almost magical touch when it came to animals. Sir Lancelot, however, proved immune to her powers.

"Where is he?" Harry called; her eyes squinted against the sun as she peered under a rosebush. "He was here a minute ago."

"He could not have gotten far," Chris remarked, her golden curls shining brightly in the afternoon sun, a stark contrast to Harry's fiery red tresses. "At least, he cannot slip out of the gardens." She sighed, clearly annoyed that her sister's errant pet had gotten loose again.

Seated on an old oak bench, Louisa laughed, shaking her head at her youngest sister. "Why would you assume that?" she asked, glancing at Sarah seated beside her. Their former neighbor had given up on chasing Sir Lancelot only a few minutes ago, now catching her breath and watching with amusement as he continued to slip through her friends' fingers. "If *we* managed to squeeze ourselves through the gap in the hedge and sneak over to our neighbors," she grinned at Sarah, noting a hint of sadness coming to the young girl's face, "then surely Sir Lancelot will have no problem. Would you not agree?"

Sarah nodded. "Quite frankly," she whispered for only Louisa to hear, "more than one of Harry's pets has found its way into our garden over the years. My mother was less than amused; still, it always made me feel like one of you." She heaved a deep sigh and gazed toward the hedge, no doubt thinking of the house beyond she had once called home. "Do you know who lives there now?"

Louisa gently patted her hand. "That I cannot say. All I know is that a gentleman has purchased it. Who he is remains unclear as he has yet to arrive. Only workers have been coming and going these past few weeks."

Sarah heaved another deep sigh, "I wonder what changes he is having made. I wonder if any part of our old home will remain."

In that moment, Harry tripped over Sir Lancelot when he suddenly changed direction and was now dashing back in the opposite direction. As Harry landed face-first in the grass, Chris barely managed to pull up short before stepping onto her sister. "Are you all right?" she asked panting, holding out a hand to help Harriet back onto her feet.

Dauntless as ever, Harriet ignored her sister and was up and once more running after Sir Lancelot in a matter of seconds, her gown stained green and dirt under her fingernails. "Come here, Sir Lancelot! Come here to Mama!" She called sweetly, the softness of her voice in stark contrast to the wild nature Louisa knew her to possess.

"May I ask you a question?" Sarah spoke out beside Louisa, once more drawing her attention away from the chase through the gardens.

"Of course."

A small smile flitted across Sarah's face. For another long moment, she remained silent, her mouth opening and closing once or twice before she had sorted her thoughts. "What do you look for in a suitor? My mother urges me to look for a *suitable match*; however, that is not something the heart notices, is it?"

Louisa sighed, determinedly pushing away all thoughts of Phineas Hawke. Why they had returned to him of all people and in this moment no less was beyond her. "I suppose that depends on what your mother means by *suitable*. Knowing your mother," Louisa stated with a confirming look at Sarah's face, "I assume she speaks of title and fortune."

With her head slightly bowed, Sarah nodded. "Of course, I understand her reasoning, especially given our reduced circumstances." She swallowed hard, and a tinge of red came to her cheeks. "I do not wish to disappoint her, but I have noticed that my heart is urging me down a different path. I cannot see myself marrying any of the gentlemen she has thus far pointed out to me. Is that wrong?"

Louisa hesitated, knowing that Sarah's parents were not like her own. They had other expectations when it came to whom their youngest daughter was to marry. "I do not believe it to be wrong," Louisa told her sister's dearest friend. "I myself wish for a gentleman who will sweep me off my feet," she admitted smiling, once again determinedly pushing all thoughts of Phineas Hawke away. "I do believe all young women dream of a great love, just as most mothers feel the need to ensure their daughters' future in a more reasonable manner. It is the way of the world." She looked at Sarah for a moment, then said, "There is a gentleman who has caught your attention, is there not?"

Sarah blushed profusely. "Is it that obvious?"

Louisa chuckled, "I'm afraid so. Has he shown an interest in you?"

Sarah heaved another deep sigh. "I'm afraid he barely knows I exist," she answered, deep regret darkening her lovely features. "I have spoken to him once or twice, and he's always kind to me, but..."

"Give it time," Louisa counseled carefully, getting the feeling that Sarah was not yet ready to reveal who that gentleman was. "Don't appear too eager. Try to catch his attention, but then wait until he comes to you. Some gentlemen do like a bit of a chase." The last sentence tumbled from her lips without thought, and Louisa could not help but wonder where it had come from. Yet, the moment she did wonder, she knew it to be a mistake for it conjured an image of none other than Phineas Hawke.

Curse that man!

Bidding Sarah farewell, Louisa rose from the bench and headed back toward the house. It seemed the more they spoke of suitors, the more a certain someone lingered in her thoughts. Even if she could not prevent him from seeking her out, she could—and should—do her utmost to banish him from her thoughts.

Still, this was easier said than done, for after their last encounter it seemed she could think of little else. It had been shocking, to say the least; not only his behavior, the way he had seized her, but also the way she had responded to him. Like before, at Anne's wedding, she had found herself helpless, unable to resist. What was it that made him so irresistible to her? Was it the wickedness in his eyes? Or the dazzling smile upon his lips?

"Are you all right, dear?"

Pausing in her step halfway down the corridor toward the front hall, Louisa turned and found her mother standing in the doorway to the library. Her blonde curls shone in the afternoon sun, and her pale blue eyes glowed warmly as she smiled at her daughter. "You look sad somehow," her mother observed, stepping out into the corridor, her eyes sweeping over her daughter's face as she came to stand in front of her. She reached out a gentle hand and tucked a loose curl behind Louisa's ear. "What happened? You have been acting strangely for at least a fortnight. Is there something you wish to talk about?"

Louisa heaved a deep sigh, wishing she dared share all that rested upon her heart with her beloved mother. Still, a part of her shrank back from the mere thought, afraid of how her mother's eyes would look upon her if she knew. "I simply have a lot on my mind," she replied with a soft smile.

"Anything you can share?" her mother asked, something knowing resting in her pale eyes as though she could read Louisa's thoughts or at least the direction in which they lingered.

"Oh, it is nothing," Louisa remarked, determined to hold onto her secret. However, when she saw her mother's face darken, the clear wish to know, to help visible in her kind eyes, Louisa knew she could not leave her with nothing. "I find myself pursued by a most persistent... suitor." Not that Phineas Hawke was her suitor, of course not. Still, without going into further detail, it was the closest reference Louisa could think of.

Her mother frowned. "Persistent?" She took a step closer, her hand reaching out to settle upon Louisa's arm. "In what way? Has he over-stepped—?"

"Not at all," Louisa rushed to assure her mother, only in that moment realizing that indeed he had. If her mother knew what intimacies she had shared with Phineas, what would she think of her? Would she be disappointed? "He merely seeks me out at every opportunity."

Her mother nodded slowly. "And you do not enjoy his company?"

"Of course not. How could I? He is so...so..."

A soft smile curled up her mother's lips, and her hand brushed gently up and down Louisa's arm. "Sweetheart, I must say it sounds as though you *do* like him."

Startled, Louisa stared at her mother. "Why would you say that? The mere thought of him makes me angry. Whenever I see him, I want to claw his eyes out. As soon as he opens his mouth, I want to slap him. He is so infuriating." Gritting her teeth as a wave of anger rushed into every fiber of her being, Louisa tried to remain calm, inhaling a slow breath, one after the other.

When she once again opened her eyes, she found a rather indulgent look upon her mother's face. "You know," her mother began gently, a faraway look coming to her eyes as she spoke, "when I first met your father, I could not stand the sight of him." She blinked, and her eyes returned to look upon her daughter.

Louisa frowned. "But...we always thought that..." She shook her head to clear it. "Mother, you always spoke as though it had been love at first sight. What are you saying?"

Her mother laughed, pulling Louisa into her arms. "Sweetheart, one does not exclude the other. Still, I admit it took me some time to realize that the reason he angered me so with a simple look, a simple word was because I cared for him." The corners of her mouth curled upward, a mischievous smile coming to her lips. "Love and hate are both strong emotions. If we truly hate, it usually means that someone has hurt us deeply, and you cannot be hurt by someone who means nothing to you. Not in such a profound way." She took a step back, her eyes settling upon Louisa's, her hands resting gently upon her shoulders. "Search your heart, Lou. Ask yourself how you truly feel, and do not be afraid to answer yourself honestly. What you find might be shocking, but there's nothing worse than living a life of lies, especially the ones you tell yourself." She brushed a gentle hand over Louisa's face, then stepped back into the library. "I shall see you at supper." And with the last smile, she closed the door.

Utterly shocked, Louisa stood and stared at the closed door, her mother's words echoing in her mind. Could she be right? The thought was outrageous, and instinctively Louisa shied away from it.

Do not be afraid to answer yourself honestly, her mother's words instantly surfaced, a chiding tone attached to them.

Burying her face in her hands, Louisa wished she could trade lives with Sarah. Was it not so much easier to attract a bit of an elusive suitor instead of repelling one most persistent? Perhaps what she ought to do for now was focus on someone else's problem. Perhaps at least for a little while, Louisa could allow herself to ignore Phineas Hawke and the problem he presented. Perhaps for now she could focus her energy, her thoughts on assisting Sarah.

Perhaps.

Chapter Fourteen

A FEW PENNED LINES

Standing in the corner of the ballroom, Phineas watched Louisa as she smiled and laughed, chatting with gentlemen left and right. Occasionally, she would glance over her shoulder, her eyes meeting his, and glare at him as though her heart burned with hatred. Never in his life had he met a woman who could destroy another with a single look. Louisa, however, had honed this skill to perfection, it would seem, for Phineas felt his heart clench every time their eyes met.

His temper was on a bit of a short leash these days, and Phineas felt tempted more than once to simply stride across the ballroom, seize her and drag her away, demanding an explanation. Unfortunately, that would not only cause a scene, but also a scandal. Neither he nor she could afford one, and Phineas knew that Louisa would never forgive him for humiliating her thus. But what else could he do?

In that moment, his gaze fell on Lady Leonora. She stood a bit off to the side with her sister Lady Christina as well as another young lady Phineas had met on several occasions. It was Miss Mortensen, twirling a finger in her blonde curls.

Straightening, Phineas made up his mind, his feet carrying him over to the other side of the large, domed chamber in a matter of strides. "Good evening, Lady Leonora," he bowed his head to her and then to her companions. "Lady Christina. Miss Mortensen."

Lady Christina smiled politely at him while her friend blushed and then mumbled a quick greeting. Phineas, though, had already turned his attention to Lady Leonora. "Would you grant me a moment of your time?" he asked with a sideways glance at her sister and Miss Mortensen. "It is about my brother and your cousin."

Lady Leonora frowned. "Anne?" Then she nodded, muttered a quick apology to the other two before following him to a more deserted corner of the room. "What about Anne? Has something happened? Is she well?"

Phineas shook his head. "I apologize for the deception, but I wish to speak to you about your sister."

A look of understanding came to the young woman's features, and she nodded. "I see," she replied, her blue eyes hesitant for a moment. "I'm afraid there is nothing I can tell you."

Sensing that she was not being completely straightforward, Phineas stepped closer. He could not help the thought that Louisa had indeed confided in her sister and that her sister now viewed him in the same light. What on earth had he done? "You spoke to her?"

Lady Leonora nodded.

After unsuccessfully waiting for a reply, Phineas asked, "Why can you not tell me? Do I not at least deserve to know what I have done? I assure you I do not have the slightest inkling what it could be." A sense of hopelessness settled in his bones, a feeling he had never experienced before. Louisa affected him in the most unexpected ways.

Lady Leonora's features softened a little. For a moment, she seemed to consider his words, to consider *him* before she sighed, her lips parting. "I assure you I do not know. I did ask my sister, but she refused to answer me. All she said was that you knew. She said you ought to know. From her words, I understood that it must've been something you said." Her gaze narrowed thoughtfully as she looked up at him. "Can you truly not recall an instance where you might have spoken to her in a less than appropriate manner?"

Racking his mind, Phineas quickly went through all the moments they had shared, no matter how short or seemingly insignificant. In truth, until a year ago, they had rarely spoken. He had noticed her here and there but had been too preoccupied elsewhere to allow his thoughts to linger. "I cannot fathom what it could be," he told her, shaking his head in defeat. "Did she honestly say nothing that would give you an idea? Nothing at all?"

"I'm afraid not," Lady Leonora replied, disappointment resting in her own blue eyes. "My sister can be quite secretive. I've long since wondered if there might be something she's keeping from me, from all of us." She shrugged. "Although I admit, I do not know what it could be. Yet, sometimes, there is a moment when she looks at me and I feel as though...she wishes to say something, to confide in me. But then her jaw hardens, and the moment passes."

Concern settled in Phineas' heart. "Thank you for your open words," he said to Lady Leonora, suspecting that if Louisa knew how her sister had spoken to him, she would be furious.

Her gaze rose and settled upon his. "Do not make me regret it. I am trusting you because I cannot help but conclude that you care for her. All evidence points to it. Therefore, it is illogical to assume that you would hurt her." For a moment, she simply looked at him, a hint of a warning in her blue eyes. "However, even hypotheses based on solid evidence have been known to be wrong. I sincerely hope that this is not one of those cases."

Phineas nodded to her, hoping she could see the sincerity in his eyes. "I promise you it is not."

In that moment, a footman appeared beside him, handing him a small envelope. Excusing himself, he stepped away to open it. Only a few short lines were written on the card within.

P—

Meet me in the library when the clock strikes ten.
I must speak to you.

L—

· · ·

Phineas' breath lodged in his throat, and he felt a rather familiar, tantalizing tingle dance across his skin. The mere thought of her, the thought that she might have given in, unable to deny herself any longer, brought deepest longing to his heart. Did she feel torn? Clearly, she hated the very sight of him because of something he had said at some point in the past; yet, whenever she was in his arms, he could sense that another part of her yearned for him as much as he yearned for her. Was she at war with herself? Had for this one time, the other side won out?

A clock chimed somewhere in the house, the sound muffled and dim. To Phineas' ears, though, it felt like a clap of thunder. Ten o'clock had come, and without another thought, he rushed from the ballroom, afraid that she might leave before he got there.

His feet carried him down the corridor, his eyes searching for the right door. He opened a wrong one by mistake, cursed, and hurried onward. His heart thudded wildly in his chest, pounding against his rib cage.

And then he found it, the door he had been looking for. He all but threw himself against the polished wood, pushing it open and surging across the threshold in a single stride. He closed the door quickly, his eyes searching the dim room before they fell on a shadowy figure, standing by the window. "Lulu?" he whispered, his feet carrying him closer. He wanted to rush to her, to pull her into his arms; however, even before she turned around to face him, his feet drew to a halt, and he knew that something was wrong.

Very wrong.

For the woman standing by the window was not Louisa.

"Miss Mortensen?" Phineas asked, confused and deeply disappointed. His gaze swept over her golden curls, took note of the slight blush coming to her cheeks, and noticed her eyes widening ever so slightly as she looked upon him. "What are you doing here?" The card that had brought him to this very spot was still in his hands, and his gaze dropped down to linger upon it, wondering. "Did you write this?" he asked, accusation seeping into his words. After all, had she not sought him out again and again, always lingering nearby? After his failure to respond, had she resorted to trickery?

Miss Mortensen's face paled, her steps unsteady as she came toward him. "I did not," she whispered breathlessly. "I received one myself." She lifted her right hand, and there, held securely between thumb and the tips of her other fingers, Phineas spotted a card exactly like his own.

A deep frown came to his face, and he crossed the distance between them, snatching the card from her hands. His eyes fell to the words written there, and his teeth ground together in anger and frustration.

S—

Meet me in the library when the clock strikes ten.
　I must speak to you.

L—

Reflexively, Phineas' hand closed over the card, crumpling it up into a little ball. Anger boiled in his veins, and his head snapped up, his eyes hard as they fell on Miss Mortensen. "You say you received this?"

Looking a bit fearful, she nodded. "A footman delivered it."

Raking a frustrated hand through his hair, Phineas wheeled around, his gaze wild as he began to pace, trying to make sense of what had happened. Why would Louisa send each of them such a card, urging them to meet here, alone? What was she planning?

"Does yours say the same as mine?" Miss Mortensen asked, her voice feeble and confused. "I suspected mine was sent by Louisa. She has been most kind to me as of late, lending the ear of an elder sister as my own is too far for me to speak to...on these matters."

Her words cut Phineas deeply for they seemed to support the idea that Louisa had sent both cards, seeking to play matchmaker. Did she think to free herself from him by connecting him to Miss

Mortensen? Did she truly detest him so deeply that she would go to such lengths?

"I wonder why she sen—" Miss Mortensen's voice broke off, and her eyes widened when footsteps echoed closer from outside in the corridor. Someone was heading toward them.

Phineas could have groaned. If they were indeed discovered here alone together, the scandal would be enormous. They would be forced to wed. Had this been Louisa's plan? Still, there was no time to think about this now. It would have to wait for them to sort out later.

In three large strides, Phineas stood in front of Miss Mortensen. He grabbed her by the shoulders, his gaze locking on hers. "I shall leave through the window," he whispered urgently. "Close it behind me, then feign a headache if anyone enters. I was never here. Do you understand?"

Swallowing hard, her eyes still as round as plates, Miss Mortensen nodded, her ability to speak momentarily lost.

"Good." And without another word, Phineas hasted to the window. He threw it open and looked down into the shadowy garden.

From the dark shapes beneath, he suspected that a bush of some kind had been planted under the window. Hopefully, it would break his fall.

Sitting on the window ledge, he swung his legs over, then lowered himself as far down as he could before dropping the last stretch. He landed in a springy thicket, felt a branch jab his right thigh and sighed in relief that it was not a thorn bush. Quickly, he scrambled to his feet, brushed his hands down his clothing, righting it, before he strode away into the dark.

When he was a good distance away, near the corner of the house, he glanced back over his shoulder and saw a dim outline of a woman closing the window. Then she vanished from sight, and Phineas hoped that she would keep her wits about her if someone were to enter the library. Perhaps he ought to hasten back inside and ensure that whoever it was did not mean her harm. After all, the footsteps they had heard could easily belong to another gentleman seeking an empty room.

Phineas would do as he saw fit, and then he would head home and once more consider the events of this night from every possible angle. Had Louisa truly sent each of them such a note? Or was this some kind of misunderstanding? Phineas fervently hoped that it was. "She better have a good explanation," he gritted out, his pulse still thudding wildly in his neck.

Chapter Fifteen

BURDENS

It was a beautiful day. Birds twittered outside her window, and the sun streamed in, warming her chamber and casting a warm glow over everything. Louisa had slept like a log and felt utterly refreshed as she rose that morning. A soft melody drifted from her lips as she hummed under her breath, dressing and then leaving her chamber to seek out her family downstairs for breakfast.

As she entered the parlor, warm smiles greeted her. Her father sat at one end of the table and her mother at the other with her siblings in between. "Good morning, Lou," her father said to her smiling. His dark brown eyes were the same color as his rather cropped hair, an odd match to his full beard, giving him the impression of a woodsman rather than an aristocrat. Yet, her father had never put much stock in what other people thought. He held out a hand to her, and when she took it, he gave it a gentle squeeze. "You look as though you had sweet dreams. Do I need to be worried?" A deep chuckle rumbled in his throat before he winked at her as he often did.

Louisa laughed, "Always." Then she strolled farther down the table and seated herself next to Leonora. Across from her, Harry and Chris were in a bit of a heated conversation about Sir Lancelot. Apparently, he had once more gotten away and found his way into Chris' bedchamber, building himself a little nest out of her favorite books, ripping pages out of some and dirtying others in the process.

"You cannot truly intend to keep him," Chris complained, shaking her head at her younger sister. "He does not belong in the city. You should return him to the country where you can still visit him."

Harry crossed her arms over her chest, a deeply defiant look coming to her green eyes. "How can you say that? Sir Lancelot's family. He would miss us terribly."

Chris laughed, "Do you genuinely believe that? Then why do you think he always runs off? Perhaps it is his way of telling you that he wants to leave."

The discussion between the two sisters continued, and Louisa turned away when her mother addressed her. "Your father is right, my dear. You do look as though you've had sweet dreams." A suggestive smile curled up her mother's lips, her light blue gaze questioning as it held Louisa. Unlike her father's down-to-earth nature, her mother shone like a light, her pale eyes a perfect match to her white, creamy skin and light golden curls. "Anyone in particular?"

Louisa rolled her eyes at her mother, trying her best to mask the way her mother's words unsettled her. Indeed, what had she dreamed last night? She could not recall; however, she had woken with a big smile upon her face and a dizzying warmth lingering in her heart. "Where's Grandma Edie?" she asked, hoping to steer the conversation back to a safer topic. "I hope she is well." Reaching for a cup of tea, Louisa averted her gaze, relieved to have something else to focus her attention on.

"Oh, she's quite well," her mother replied, the tone in her voice suggesting that she knew perfectly well what Louisa was doing. "She's still in bed. You know how she likes to sleep in."

Louisa chuckled. Indeed, Grandma Edie often proclaimed that now that she was an old woman, she could get away with anything, and she often tested that theory.

"Another dead," her father suddenly exclaimed in a grave tone. His brows were furrowed as he glanced down at the paper lying on the table next to his plate. He momentarily leaned closer, his eyes squinting ever so slightly that Louisa wondered if a pair of spectacles might benefit him.

"What do you mean, Father?" Troy inquired, casting a doubtful look at his two youngest sisters, concern in his gaze. He was no doubt worried about whether such a topic might be suitable for their ears. Louisa almost laughed, knowing better than her older brother just how inquisitive Harry and Chris were. No doubt, they knew more than Troy would ever even consider in his dreams.

"Shot in Hyde Park," their father replied, glancing up at his son. "It looks like a duel yet again."

Troy frowned. "That is...what? The third in only half a year?"

Their father nodded. "It seems the young men of today have little to do that could be considered productive." He shook his head. "Such a waste! And all because of hot-headed thoughtlessness!"

"Here, read this," Leonora mumbled to Louisa, pulling a letter out of her pocket and handing it to her. "It might amuse you." Her light blue eyes so much like their mother's lingered for a moment, a hint of scientific curiosity mixed with sisterly concern visible there.

Louisa froze. It was a perfectly natural request, one any of her sisters could have complied with without thought or hesitation. But not Louisa. Her gaze fell to the letter, her heart picking up speed, panic slowly creeping up into every region of her body. The breath lodged in her throat, and she wished a hole would open in the earth and swallow her without delay.

This was nothing new. Louisa knew this feeling of panic and shame well. It was her constant companion. And so, she inhaled a deep breath, willing herself not to submit to its devastating lure, but to remain calm and not allow her family to see how such a simple request unsettled her.

Feigning a yawn, Louisa took a sip from her tea. "It is too early in the morning for letters," she groaned, her eyes now half-lidded as though her night had been far from restful. "What does it say, Leo? Who's it from?"

Leonora shrugged and then unfolded the letter. "It's from Anne," she replied, not the slightest hint of suspicion in her voice.

Louisa breathed a sigh of relief.

"She writes that Lord Barrington seems to be in a bad temper as of late," Leonora half-read, half-remembered as her eyes flitted over the parchment. It seemed so simple, so easy, so effortless.

Louisa envied her.

"She wonders what happened," Leonora continued, still none the wiser. "It seems he has locked himself in his study, barely comes out, and when he does, he is in a most foul mood."

Louisa frowned, shifting her attention from her sister's reaction to the contents of the letter. "Why would she write that? What are we supposed to do about it?" Again, she reached for her cup, for a reason to avert her eyes, because she worried to see her sister roll her eyes at her. Not that Leonora was the kind of woman who often rolled her eyes at people. Still, after their last conversation about Phineas Hawke and why she hated him so, Leonora had been most observant. No doubt her curiosity had been piqued. Louisa's reaction puzzled her, and now she sought to solve the riddle.

That was Leonora.

This time, fortunately, Leonora seemed to have no hidden agenda. Her voice remained calm and interested, but free of any innuendo Louisa would have expected. "She begs us to come visit," her sister continued once more. "She wonders if a little diversion would do him good." She lifted her eyes off the parchment and looked around the table.

Chris and Harry, who had finally stopped arguing about Sir Lancelot, nodded eagerly. "I'd love to go visit," Chris replied with a wide smile upon her face.

"Me as well," Harry agreed, their earlier argument all but forgotten.

Louisa shook her head. "Well, if you are all going," she replied, willing her tone to remain light, "then I don't need to. Honestly, I do not feel like visiting today. I'd rather stay by myself and enjoy the sunshine."

This time, Leonora's gaze did hold something deeper, and Louisa wondered what it was her sister might be thinking in that moment. "Very well," Leonora said to her two younger sisters. "Anne bids us visit as soon as we are able. Do the two of you have anywhere to be after breakfast?"

Both sisters shook their heads.

And thus after breakfast, Leonora, Chris and Harriet left the house to visit with Anne while their parents stepped outside into the gardens for their morning stroll, arm in arm. Their brother Troy left to peruse the morning paper in the library while Jules declared her intention to see to Grandma Edie.

With everyone leaving the table, Louisa remained behind, with no rush to go anywhere. Her thoughts were still occupied with her latest lie, for that was what it was: a lie. She had lied to her family yet again, pretended to hide the truth. A part of Louisa felt relief while another wept for the secret that kept them apart. Her heart felt heavy as she rose from the table and slowly trudged upstairs, her limbs heavy as lead. The delight and joy she had felt earlier that morning were gone. The sunshine and the soft bird songs failed to lighten her spirits. All seemed gloomy and dark and deserted.

Standing at her bedroom window, Louisa looked down into the gardens and watched her parents stroll down the small path past the rose bushes. They were a beautiful sight, two people as one, whispered words passing between them, meaningful smiles cast back and forth. Occasionally, they would stop and then simply stand there in the middle of the path for a moment or two, gazing into each other's eyes. Sometimes, her father would lift a hand and gently brush a curl behind her mother's ear, his fingers tracing along the line of her jaw before he gave her chin a little pinch. It was a ritual, something utterly endearing, something her parents had been doing for many years, perhaps forever, and it always made Louisa yearn to find something so meaningful and precious for herself.

But, how could she? Even her own family did not know who she truly was. Never would she be able to speak to a husband about her secret. No doubt, he would instantly regret marrying her. But without honesty, without truthfulness, could there ever be such a bond?

Turning from the window, Louisa proceeded to pace her chamber, her thoughts hopelessly entangled, drifting back and forth between her secret and—of course—Phineas Hawke. Ever since his off-hand remark, he had been connected to that part of her. She could no longer think of her flaw without thinking of him. Neither could she think of him without thinking of her flaw. It was a vicious circle, and he a constant reminder. And yet, a part of her longed to see him again, wished she had gone with her sisters.

Curse that man!

Annoyed with him as much as herself, Louisa strode from the room, hoping to find a distraction elsewhere. She ventured downstairs and headed across the hall toward the back of the house. For a moment, she thought she would head into the gardens, but then remembered that her parents were there, and she did not wish to disturb them. So, she turned sharply and headed back, walking down the corridor that led past the library. It was a corridor Louisa avoided. It made no sense, of course. Yet, the proximity of the library always unsettled her. It, too, was a constant reminder.

Inhaling a deep breath, she quickened her step and made to walk past. However, as she drew closer, she noticed that the door was ajar, and voices echoed to her ears. She recognized her brother's voice immediately. That of the other man momentarily confused her though.

Curious despite her apprehension, Louisa slowed, then stopped outside the door. She inched closer, straining to listen.

"I saw the way you looked at her," the other man stated, open reproach in his voice. Still, there was something compassionate about the way he spoke. "I know how you feel, but there is no point."

A loud thud echoed to Louisa's ears as though someone had slammed a fist upon a sturdy surface. "Don't you think I know that?" her brother roared, anger darkening his voice in a way she had never heard before. "Do you think I chose this?"

"Of course not," the other man replied, the kindness in his voice sounding familiar. "I never meant to suggest that you did." Footsteps could be heard as someone moved closer toward the windows. "There is a masquerade tonight at Hamilton House. Perhaps you should go. Perhaps it will be a distraction."

"You know that is not me, Lockhart," her brother replied, a hint of reproach in his voice. "I thought you knew me better than that."

Lockhart? Louisa frowned. Indeed, the name was most familiar; however, the man had not come by for some time. As far as she knew, he had taken a tour of the continent.

It seemed he had returned.

As Louisa turned her attention back toward the door, the sound of muffled footsteps drifted to her ears from behind. Her heart slammed to a halt, and her shoulders snapped back. Inhaling a deep breath, wondering who had come upon her, she slowly turned around.

To her utter relief, it was Grandma Edie, who hobbled toward her, resting heavily on her cane. "I thought you knew better than to listen at open doors," her grandmother chuckled quietly, a gleam of mischief in her eyes. "Although I do admit, listening at closed doors is far less efficient."

Walking the remaining few steps toward her, Louisa smiled. "How much did you hear?"

Her grandmother grinned. "Not nearly as much as you, I suppose." Her gaze narrowed as she watched Louisa, something playful lurking in those perceptive eyes of hers. A short snicker followed, and she shook her head, her eyes sweeping over Louisa's face. "I can practically see the thoughts forming in your head, Lou."

Indeed, Grandma Edie was right for Louisa found most intriguing thoughts beginning to bloom in her head. Lockhart, her brother's oldest friend, had spoken of a masquerade. He had urged her brother to attend, calling it a distraction, something—it would seem—her brother needed as much as she did. Fortunately, Troy had stated quite vehemently that he had no intention of going.

A slow smile spread over Louisa's face. Perhaps another Whickerton should attend then. For heaven knew, she could use a distraction!

"You be careful," her grandmother warned, lifting a chiding finger. Her usually warm and cheerful gaze had hardened, and Louisa could see concern resting upon her face. Still, her grandmother did not forbid her. She clearly understood what was going on in Louisa's head, but she did not tell her to forget about this idea. Louisa suspected that her grandmother—better than anyone—understood how Louisa felt. Always had she thought Grandma Edie to be a kindred spirit. And now, she was proven right.

Louisa squeezed her grandmother's hand affectionately. "I promise," she vowed, holding her grandma's gaze for a moment longer before she spun on her heel and hurried back the way she had come.

A lot needed to be done, planned, prepared if she were to sneak out of the house tonight and attend a secret masquerade, hoping at least for one night to forget all the troubles of her life, to be free for a few precious hours and unburdened of everything that had been weighing upon her shoulders as of late.

Louisa could hardly wait.

Chapter Sixteen
OUT INTO THE NIGHT

The house was dark and quiet when Louisa carefully opened the door of her bedchamber and peeked out into the corridor. For a heartbeat or two, she simply stood there, waiting, her eyes sweeping up and down the hall. When nothing moved, and no sound could be heard, she stepped out, quietly closing the door behind her.

Silent footsteps carried her past her sisters' doors and down the stairs, her heart beating wildly in her chest. She pulled the cloak she wore tighter around her shoulders, pulling the hood deeper into her face, which was covered by a simple black mask, all she had been able to procure on such short notice.

Louisa crossed the front hall, trying to remain in the shadows in case someone was lingering nearby. She headed toward the back of the house, reasoning it would be simpler if she slipped out the servants' exit. Quiet footsteps carried her down the hall, and she was about to turn the corner when an unexpected sound reached her ears.

Louisa froze, her eyes wide as she stared ahead, unable to move.

In the next instant, Leonora rounded the corner, her eyelids half-closed, and fatigue resting upon her face. She looked pale and almost half-asleep, her notebook clutched to her chest. No doubt, she had been up in the library once again, researching one topic or another, forgetting about time, about food, about sleep, about everything.

Quickly, Louisa reached up and pulled the mask from her face; unfortunately, she had tied the knot too well and it wouldn't loosen. She merely succeeded in pulling it lower down her face. She quickly righted it.

Leonora stopped in her tracks, her eyes widening before they swept over her sister. "Lou?" she exclaimed, a startled sound leaving her lips. She glanced around the darkened corridor, her brows drawing down into a frown. "What are you doing here? Why are you still up?"

Louisa decided that attack was the best way to defend in that moment, to distract her sister before she became too suspicious. "Why are you still up?" she asked, trying to keep her tone light as though she did not have a care in the world. "Did you fall asleep again, pouring over some book?"

A soft snicker drifted from Leonora's lips. Then she shrugged. "I did not notice how late it had gotten," she replied by way of an explanation. "I awoke, and it was dark."

Louisa smiled at her sister, pulling the hood a little farther into her face, trying to hide the mask. "Then you should head to bed," she told her sister, stepping around her and putting a hand on her shoulder, urging her back toward the stairs. "You look asleep on your feet, Leo. You truly need sleep. You need to take better care of yourself."

Leonora nodded, another wide yawn opening her mouth. She took a step forward in the direction Louisa urged her, then another, and Louisa's heart lightened.

Louisa was about to turn around, her eyes sweeping sideways, searching for the door that would lead to freedom. But then, her sister suddenly stopped in her tracks. She whirled around, a deep frown upon her face. "What are *you* doing up?" she repeated, stepping closer, the look in her eyes no longer fatigued, but curious, suspicious even. "And what is this on your face?" She reached up a hand, and before Louisa could move or say anything, Leonora pulled away the hood, revealing the black mask hiding half of Louisa's face. "What is this? Why are you wearing a mask?" Her gaze narrowed, and her jaw set, deep suspicion coming to her voice. "Where are you going?"

Louisa exhaled a slow breath, her spirits falling from up high. Failure loomed over her, and the promise of a carefree evening slowly slipped away. "It is nothing," she told Leonora, pulling the hood back up onto her head. "Please, can you forget you saw me here tonight? I promise I shall take care of myself, but I need this. Please, understand."

Confusion darkening her eyes, Leonora shook her head. "Understand what? Where are you going?"

The corners of Louisa's mouth quirked upward. "To a masquerade," she replied, knowing she would never get away without at least providing a few answers. "Isn't it obvious?"

Shock whitened Leonora's face. "A masquerade?" she gasped, her hands tightening on the notebook still clutched to her chest. "You cannot be serious! Do you truly intend to leave the house in the dark of night all by yourself? You must be mad!" She shook her head vehemently. "No, you cannot. You simply cannot."

Louisa felt her lips thin and her chin rise. She inhaled a deep breath, and met her sister's gaze, her hand reaching out to grasp Leonora's upper arms. "Please, Leo," she whispered, looking at her sister imploringly. "I need this. I need an evening away from...from all of this."

"From what? What is going on?"

"I cannot explain," Louisa told her sister, hoping against hope that for once Leonora would rely on her heart and not her head. "Please, pretend you did not see me. Let me go. Please."

Leonora stared at her. "I cannot do that," she whispered. "What if something happens to you? You cannot go by yourself. Can you not ask Troy—"

Louisa laughed darkly. "He would never, and you know it. Please, Leo, this is my only chance. Please, trust me. I know what I'm doing."

Leonora heaved a deep sigh, doubt and concern clearly etched into her face. Still, Louisa could see a spark of compassion and understanding in her sister's pale blue eyes. "Lou, I wish... But..."

Louisa grasped her sister's arms tighter, her gaze even more imploring now than it ever had been in her life. "Leo, please!"

Her sister inhaled a slow breath, her gaze holding Louisa's for a long moment. Then she nodded. "Very well." Louisa exhaled a deep breath, relief sweeping through her body. "But I will go with you."

Louisa's head snapped up, her eyes widening. "What? No!" she stammered. "You cannot."

"If you can, I can," Leonora replied, a touch of nervousness in her voice; nevertheless, her eyes shone with determination. "Do not for a second think you can talk me out of this. I will not let you leave this house by yourself. If you absolutely must go—for a reason you cannot tell me, mind you—then you have no choice but to take me with you." One eyebrow arched upward. "Which will it be, dear sister?"

Louisa hesitated, wondering if there was any way she could persuade Leonora to remain behind. "Fine," she finally exclaimed, reminding herself that time was ticking by and she was wasting precious moments. "Then head upstairs, find your cloak and a mask of some kind. I'll wait here for you."

Shaking her head, Leonora chuckled. "I'm not a fool," she told Louisa with a pointed look. "I've known you long enough to know that when I come back downstairs, you will be gone." She jerked her chin toward the front hall. "You go."

Sighing, Louisa accepted her fate. With an eye roll cast at her sister, she whirled around and then headed back upstairs to retrieve a cloak for Leonora as well as a mask. Fortunately, last All Hallows' Eve had inspired them to fashion quite a few and in vastly different designs.

"Have you always been this insistent?" Louisa asked her sister as she returned, handing over the cloak and mask. "I think I liked you better with your nose stuck in a book."

Leonora smiled at her, draping the cloak over her shoulders and fastening it in the front. "I might get lost in a book now and then," she admitted, donning her mask and then pulling the hood over her head, "but I am not inattentive." Her brows rose, emphasizing her point. "I might seem to be, but I do like observing others, trying to understand their motivations, their intentions, even trying to predict what they might do next. It's all very fascinating to me."

Louisa moaned, "For one night, do you think you can forget your sciences and not look at the world with an analytic eye, but simply have fun and enjoy yourself?"

Heading to the back of the house and the servants' entrance, the two sisters stepped out into the night. "Is that what this is about?" Leonora whispered as she gazed around at their darkened surroundings. The wind whistled through the trees, and the stars shone brightly on the black canvas above. Distant noises drifted to their ears, and the air after dark somehow smelled quite different than it did when the sun was shining. "Having fun?"

Louisa chuckled, "I assume that is an entirely foreign concept to you, is it not?"

"I *have* fun," Leonora huffed out as they quietly sneaked out onto the pavement running by their house. "I simply have fun...in different ways." She shrugged, unable to explain it any further. "So, where are we headed? It's not far, is it?" Pulling the cloak tighter around herself, Leonora let her gaze sweep their surroundings, deep worry drawing down her brows.

"Hamilton House."

"That's where the masquerade is?"

Louisa nodded, feeling her skin begin to tingle with anticipation. Distracted by Leonora's interference, Louisa had all but forgotten to think about what the night might hold. Now, however, breathing in the fresh night air, she felt her spirits soar, her thoughts drawn to all the possibilities and abandoning all the worries of the day.

Fortunately, Hamilton House was not far away, and it took them no more than ten minutes to arrive at the place. All the while, Leonora clutched her notebook tightly against her chest, wide eyes cast nervously about.

"I cannot believe you brought that thing!" Louisa muttered, casting an annoyed look at her sister. "We're going to a masquerade after all!"

"I...I simply forgot I was holding it," Leonora stammered, her eyes once more sweeping from side to side, across the street and back. "I like holding things."

Turning the next corner, Hamilton House loomed tall, proud and dark in front of them. It seemed to glitter in the night, lights dancing in its windows, music and voices echoing outside. Carriages pulled to a halt in front of its front steps, and masked people alighted from them, chatting happily as they made their way to the door.

Leonora suddenly clutched Louisa's arm. "Do we need an invitation?"

Louisa frowned, annoyed with herself that she had not contemplated this obstacle. "I'm not certain." She stood for a moment and watched more people arrive, wishing she could see farther up to the door where the Hamilton butler greeted his master's guests. Then another carriage pulled up, and a group of young ladies disembarked. Their voices echoed through the night as they walked arm in arm, laughing and chatting, their masks sparkling in vivid colors, reflecting the moonlight. "Let's join them," Louisa exclaimed, grabbing her sister's arm and pulling her forward.

Leonora followed rather reluctantly, but Louisa would not give her a chance to object. In a few steps, they reached the small group of ladies and quickly fell into step beside them. Before they knew it, they were swept up the few steps to the front door and inside the entrance hall. They relinquished their cloaks, trying their best to move along with the rest of the group as they proceeded farther into the house, toward the ballroom, from which a cacophony of sounds echoed to the ears.

The large, domed chamber was darker than Louisa would have expected, than she was used to from other balls she had attended. Candles glowed everywhere, casting eerie shadows over the dancers in the center of the room. The air smelled like Jasmine, and Louisa spotted the night bloomer in various decorations placed all over the room. A large table laden with food and drink had been set up in one corner, whereas, the orchestra played in another, its soft music soothing her excited nerves.

"What now?" Leonora's dim voice spoke out from behind her, almost swallowed up by the sounds dancing around them. Her face looked tense, and her eyes were wide as she watched the people around her.

Everything seemed rather normal and familiar. It was a ball after all, with dancing and conversation. And yet, everything was just the slightest bit different. The lights, the sounds, the way people conversed, the way they looked at one another. Touches lingered just a little bit too long. Gazes held, overwhelming in their intensity. Secrets seemed to hover in the air as well as the forbidden. Now and then, Louisa felt as though she might have recognized someone, but never quite knew if she was correct. Hidden behind their masks, people acted differently, their usual comportment forgotten on this one evening where one had the chance to be someone one was not.

It was exactly what Louisa wanted.

What she needed.

At least for one night.

"I want to dance," she exclaimed, taking a step forward. A hand on her arm held her back, though. She turned around to look at her sister.

Leonora's eyes were still wide. "I'm not certain this is a good idea." She glanced from side to side. "I think we should head home."

"I thought you wanted to take some notes," Louisa reminded her, hoping that playing on her sister's curiosity would gain her a few hours. "Look around; is this not fascinating?"

Leonora swallowed, her face tense as she looked around herself. If Louisa was not at all mistaken, she thought to glimpse a spark of curiosity in her sister's guarded eyes. Nevertheless, Leonora seemed disinclined to indulge herself for one evening, no matter how curious she was. "I still think we should go home," she replied, her eyes back on her sister. "I do not believe this to be wise."

Louisa huffed out a deep breath, wishing she had been more careful and not stumbled over her sister on her way out. "Fine!" Exasperation rang in her voice as she spoke. "If you wish to return home, then do so. I, for one, intend to stay."

Once again, Leonora's hand grasped Louisa's arm. "I'm not leaving you here alone."

"Then stay," Louisa told her sister with a shrug, freeing her arm. "It is your choice as it was mine to come here tonight."

Leonora's mouth opened, and Louisa could all but see more words of objection forming on her sister's tongue. However, before she could utter any, Louisa simply shook her head and took a step back. "There's nothing you can say that will make me change my mind." She cast her sister a quick smile, then spun around and within moments found herself swallowed up by the crowd.

Lights and sounds whirled around her, soothing and intoxicating all at once. It was like a wave that carried her to a distant shore, and she moved with it without thought.

If only for tonight.

Chapter Seventeen

A FAVOR TO ASK

S tanding in front of the tall mirror in his bedchamber, Phineas placed the simple black mask upon his face. He had done so many times before as he was no stranger to masquerades. He enjoyed the opportunity to mingle among people, who for a change behaved in a rather honest and straightforward fashion. They said what came to mind and did what they liked. Phineas had always appreciated this kind of honesty. Tonight, regrettably, he did not feel the usual hum of anticipation.

Tonight, something was different, and he contemplated whether he even ought to go.

A knock sounded on his door in that moment, and after he bid him to enter, his butler stepped inside, handing him a sealed envelope. Frowning, Phineas nodded to the man, then broke the seal and pulled out the parchment. Who would write to him this late in the day? Who would write to him at all? Never had he been one to inspire letters, notes perhaps, but not letters.

His gaze fell to the parchment, and he began to read.

To the Wicked One,

. . .

Phineas chuckled at the salutation, knowing instantly who had sent this letter. Still, the question remained, why?

I do apologize for disturbing you this late; however, I do have a favor to ask.

Two of my granddaughters sneaked out of the house tonight, intent on attending the masquerade at Hamilton House. Since you make a habit of attending such events, I am certain that you shall be present at this one as well.

How on earth did the woman know that? Phineas wondered. It seemed the ailing dowager countess was well-informed.

Therefore, I beg you to keep an eye on them. While bold, I fear that Lulu—as you call her—might find herself in a situation outside of her expertise. She deserves a night of freedom, but as her grandmother I cannot in good conscience sit back and merely wait and hope.

Thank you.

GE

Phineas chuckled, knowing that the dowager countess was known to her family as well as those strongly associated with it as Grandma Edie.

Still, his amusement faded quickly when he pictured Louisa and likely her sister Leonora alone at a masquerade. Knowing from personal experience how the anonymity of such an event tended to lower inhibitions, Phineas felt his chest tighten. Indeed, a most unusual emotion settled where his heart beat rather rapidly against his rib cage. Was it concern? It could be for he felt the sudden urge to leave, to rush out and head to the masquerade without delay.

Dropping the letter, Phineas hastened from the room. His legs moved with purpose, and he quickly reached the stairs.

"Where are you headed?" Tobias asked as he and his wife Anne began to climb the stairs from the lower floor. "You look like a highwayman!" On his arm, Anne laughed, giving her beloved husband a friendly slap. "Oh, do not tease him." She chided him before turning to Phineas. "You look dashing!"

Phineas smiled at her, but quickly hastened past them. "Have a nice evening."

"Where are you headed?" his brother asked once more.

"To a masquerade," Phineas called over his shoulder as he turned to slip his arms into his coat held out to him by a footman.

Tobias rolled his eyes at him from halfway up the stairs. "That I can see," he replied. "But where?"

"Hamilton House," Phineas replied, walking out the door and sighing in relief as it closed behind him. He did not have the time nor was he of the mind to discuss his comings and goings with his brother. Indeed, he felt rushed, something pricking the back of his head, sending cold shivers down his back as he imagined the Whickerton sisters at the masquerade, swarmed by masked strangers, most of whom were most likely deep in their cups. Phineas knew how such an event could turn out only too well for he himself had attended more than he could count.

As his carriage rolled down the darkened street, Phineas sat on the bench, his fingers drumming impatiently upon his legs. He kept looking out the window, marking their progress by the houses they passed, all but counting every turn of the wheel. When the carriage finally drew to a halt, he threw open the door before his footman had any chance to do so and hastened up the steps to the front door three at a time.

Only then did he realize that he had forgotten his invitation. Nevertheless, thanks to his rather infamous reputation, the Hamilton butler was easily convinced to allow him inside.

Stepping into the hall, Phineas stilled. His gaze swept the scene, and although he had attended many a masquerade before, now he saw it through different eyes. He did not see the exhilaration, the freedom and the opportunity to enjoy himself and break free from daily restrictions. What he saw instead was danger lurking in shadowy corners. He saw cloaked men chasing after masked ladies, and an ice-cold shiver ran down his spine at the thought of the Whickerton sisters amidst this crowd.

Pushing onward into the ballroom, Phineas swept his gaze over the crowd, his eyes lingering on mask after mask. How was he to find her? It was a sea of anonymity, hiding her perfectly. Still, he kept looking, unable not to, his body tensing with each moment that passed. He saw elaborate masks with feathers and pearls. He saw gowns cut lower than would ever be considered decent. He saw young women swaying on their feet, their movements unsteady, their eyes glassy. What on earth had inspired Louisa to come here this night? He knew her to be adventurous. This, however, was reckless. It was dangerous, and anger began to burn in his veins. What had she been thinking?

Tearing through the room, Phineas was close to ripping masks off people's faces when he suddenly stopped and stared at a young woman in a simple gown, a black mask not unlike his own hiding her face. Her silhouette struck him as familiar. There was something about her, about the way she moved, the way she smiled that called to him. He looked closer and saw the familiar curve of her lips, the adventurous flash of her eyes, the strawberry blonde curls dancing down her back.

Instantly, his heart seemed to pause in his chest as though seeking to draw his attention, to confirm what deep down he already knew.

It was her!

And then the gentleman she was dancing with pulled her into his arms, and Phineas almost doubled over in shock. For a disbelieving moment, he simply stood and stared, watching as the man held her close, leaning down to whisper something in her ear. A strained smile appeared on her face as she lifted her hands, trying to urge him back, a flicker of unease coming to her eyes.

It was that moment of vulnerability more than anything else that propelled Phineas forward. In only a few long strides, he had crossed the room, all but elbowing dancers aside on his way. His hand shot out and grabbed the man by the arm, jerking him away from her.

While the man muttered a rather unintelligible sound of annoyance, Louisa's head snapped up, her eyes coming to linger upon him, narrowing when she no doubt recognized who he was.

"Leave!" Phineas hissed at the other man, glaring at him in a way that made him stumble backwards, almost tripping over his feet. With a last look at Louisa, the masked man then turned and vanished in the crowd.

"What are you doing here?" Louisa demanded, rounding on him, her eyes no longer vulnerable but shooting daggers instead.

Turning to face her, Phineas felt his clenched hands shake with barely suppressed anger. "What am *I* doing here?" He snarled into her face. "What are *you* doing here? Are you mad, attending this masquerade? Do you have any idea what happens at these—?"

"Do not speak to me as though I am a child," she hissed back at him, her arms crossed over her chest. "I know very well what this is, and I am here because I want to be. I am not a fool!"

Phineas scoffed, "You could fool me."

Louisa's gaze narrowed, and her lips thinned. "Then why don't you leave?" she demanded, her voice harsh. "You are not my brother. You're not responsible for me. It is not your duty to ensure no harm comes to me or my reputation." Her brows arced upward, a clear challenge in the way she looked at him. "Leave! Now!" Without waiting for his reply, she turned on her heel and moved back into the crowd.

Aghast at her reckless behavior, Phineas surged after her. His hand found her arm and spun her back around. "I may not be your brother," he snarled, his voice deadly calm, "but I am here to ensure that no harm comes to you or your reputation." His gaze held hers, his own all but daring her to look away.

Louisa inhaled a slow breath, her wide green eyes not veering from his. "How did you even know I was here?" Her gaze narrowed, and a dark suspicion sparked in her eyes. "Did you follow me?"

A dark chuckle rumbled in Phineas' throat, "Believe me; I have better things to do than to follow you." Darkness clung to his voice, and Phineas wondered where it had come from. "I am here, because your grandmother sent me."

Louisa froze. "My...my grandmother?" She slowly shook her head. "No, she wouldn't."

His hands tensed upon her arms, urging her closer to him as he lowered his head to hers. "She did," he whispered, feeling her rapid breaths brush against his lips. "She sent me a letter and asked me to come here and look out for you." His gaze narrowed, and now he was the one to shake his head. "What were you thinking? Do you have no regard for your safety?"

Her jaw tensed, and Phineas could see that his words had hit a mark. "I know what I'm doing," she insisted, trying and failing to free herself from his tight grip.

"Do you now?" he demanded. "I must say, you did not seem to have everything under control when that *miscreant*," she all but flinched at the word, her eyes going wide and staring up into his, "pawed at you. In fact, you looked frightened."

For once, Louisa did not argue. Her eyes remained wide, and her chest rose and fell rapidly as she looked up at him, the shadow of what had happened passing over her face. Indeed, she *had* been frightened, and she knew it.

"You should not have come here by yourself," Phineas told her, his voice gentler now. "You should—"

"I'm not by myself," she suddenly exclaimed, her shoulders tensing once more as she tried to step away from him.

Phineas frowned, ready to argue, to demand an explanation when he belatedly remembered the dowager's letter. Indeed, it had not only spoken of Louisa, but of one of her sisters as well. How could he have forgotten? "Leonora?" he asked, not bothering with formalities. "Is she the one who accompanied you here?"

Louisa's eyes hardened, and she lifted her chin. "She is," she replied, the expression upon her face more at ease now that she was collecting her thoughts.

Holding her gaze, Phineas asked, "And, where is she?"

A sudden jolt went through Louisa, and he could feel her flinch as she all but rocked back on her heels, his hands upon her arms steadying her. Her eyes remained on his, but they grew wider once again before they fell away, and she turned to sweep them over their surroundings. "She was... She was right there," she mumbled, her gaze directed toward the wall near the arched entry. "She stood there... taking notes. She was curious, and..."

"And where is she now?" Phineas asked, feeling a dark sense of unease crawl over his skin. "You don't know, do you?"

Slowly she turned, her wide green eyes finding his, and what he found there no longer made him angry or upset or furious. Fear stood in her eyes and shivered over her skin. Suddenly, she looked vulnerable, close to a panic, pale in the dim light of the shrouded room. "I do not." Her voice was no more than a whisper, and it seared Phineas all the way to his bones.

Chapter Eighteen

BEHIND A MASK

The magic of the night instantly fell away when Louisa realized that she did not have a clue where her sister could be. Only moments ago, Leonora had been standing by the arched entry, her eyes wide as they had swept the many dancers, her fingers tense upon the pencil she had used to scribble notes into her little book. She had been there; Louisa was certain of it. Again and again, she had found herself looking toward the entry, toward where Leonora had been. Their eyes had met over the crowd now and then, and she had seen a small smile come to Leonora's face in these moments. At least on some level, her sister had been able to understand why Louisa had needed to come here tonight.

Not with her head, but with her heart.

And now she was gone. "Where is she?" Louisa gasped as naked fear slowly snaked its way down her spine, sending cold chills into every region of her body. "She has to be here!"

"I'm certain she is," Phineas Hawke exclaimed as he, too, slowly turned in a circle, his tall stature allowing him to see above the heads of the people surrounding them. "What is she wearing? What kind of mask?"

Louisa frowned, cursing her memory for not remembering; after all, had she not gone to fetch it herself? "I don't remember," she whispered frantically, her pulse thudding wildly in her neck. "I don't remember. How can I not remember?" She spun on her heel and sought Phineas' eyes. "How did you find *me*? My grandmother couldn't have given you details. She never saw me leave. She never saw what I was wearing. She never knew—"

His hand gently settled upon her shoulder, cutting off the words. "I'd know you anywhere," he whispered almost tenderly, his dark eyes looking deep into hers.

A new shiver danced over Louisa's skin. Only this one did not feel cold or unpleasant or frightening. Well, perhaps a little frightening because it seemed to steal the breath from her lungs and trip up the pulse in her veins.

Louisa swallowed, her head spinning, and she all but swayed on her feet. Suddenly, she felt exhausted, overwhelmed and frighteningly close to tears. She no longer had the strength to fight, to argue, to worry. "I only want to find my sister," she whispered, suddenly grateful that he had come.

Phineas nodded, his right hand reaching out and settling upon her shoulder once more. It felt warm and comforting, and for a short, utterly brief, fleeting moment, Louisa wished he would draw her into his arms and hold her.

But he did not. "Let us look for her," he said instead, his hand slipping into hers and pulling her along.

Together, they went about the large room searching the dancers, every shadowy corner they could find, but came up empty. "Do you think she would've left the ballroom?" he asked her, a muscle in his jaw twitching with nervous agitation.

Closing her eyes, Louisa inhaled a deep breath, trying her best not to panic. "I don't know. I don't think so. Perhaps if she..." Only too vividly did Louisa remember how absent-minded her sister could be sometimes. "There's no telling what she might do once her curiosity is piqued." She looked up at him with wide eyes, feeling tears pooling in their corners. "Where could she be?"

Phineas' teeth gritted together, but he squeezed her hand reassuringly. "We shall find her," he spoke vehemently, almost defiantly, as though daring fate to root for a different outcome. "Come."

Together, they rushed back into the entry hall where fewer people lingered. The sounds grew dimmer, and Louisa could all but hear her own heart beating loudly in her ears. Her eyes swept over a corridor leading off to the side before she turned and glanced down another. "Which one? How do we know?"

Suddenly, Phineas tugged on her hand. "There!"

Before she could turn to look in the direction he had indicated, he pulled her forward and, stumbling over her own feet, Louisa followed. They strode no more than a few steps down a corridor leading off to the back of the house when she spotted Leonora heading toward them like a shadow separating itself from the darkness lingering around it. "Leo!" Louisa exclaimed, releasing Phineas' hand and rushing forward. She wished for nothing else but to embrace her sister and know that all would be well now.

But then her eyes fell on Leonora's pale face, upon her tousled hair as well as her ripped sleeve, revealing white skin marked by darkening bruises.

Louisa froze in her step, staring at her sister as she hobbled toward her, her right shoe missing...as was her mask. "Oh, no." It was no more than a breathy gasp, but it was enough to make her realize what her night of freedom had done to her sister.

Tears pooled in her eyes as her feet suddenly surged forward, no longer able to keep still. Her hands found her sister's face, brushing aside loose curls before trying and failing to mend the deep tear in her sleeve. "What happened? What—?" Words failed her, and her heart broke into a thousand pieces as she watched her sister slowly crumble to her feet.

Together, the two of them sank down to the floor, Leonora sobbing helplessly, her hands clutching Louisa's arms. Louisa stared past her sister's head as it rested against her shoulder, not knowing what to do, terrified to move, to speak. Was this truly happening?

And then warm hands settled upon her shoulders, a strong presence drawing near, soothing and calming. "Who did this to you?" Phineas asked, his question directed at Leonora while his gaze sought

Louisa's. His tone was calm, but the look in his eyes was nothing short of murderous. "Tell me his name."

Staring up at him, her sobs quieting, Leonora shook her head. "I don't know. He wore a mask. He... He..." Tears streamed down her face, and the breath caught in her throat before new sobs wracked her body.

Louisa did not know what to do. Her mind, her heart seemed frozen, unable to think, even unable to feel. And so, she allowed Phineas to take charge, to decide and tell them what to do. From the mere fact that she would never under normal circumstances have allowed him to dictate her actions, she knew how deeply shaken she was.

"Let me take her," Phineas said, urging Louisa to release her sister. "Here, put your arm around my shoulder." Gently, he lifted Leonora into his arms, then stood and met Louisa's gaze. "Come."

Louisa nodded, and then followed him back into the entrance hall and out the door. Silently, they walked down the few steps and then stepped into his carriage, which was waiting only a few paces away by the curb.

All but dropping onto the bench, Louisa watched as Phineas settled Leonora next to her. Her sister's eyes were staring into nothing, wide and unseeing. Her sobs had died down, and suddenly it seemed as though she was no longer there, her body an empty shell.

"She's in shock," Phineas told her gently, his jaw tense, but his eyes held compassion as well as anguish as he looked from her sister to her. "I'll take you home, but that is all I can do." He swallowed hard, the muscle in his jaw twitching once again, whispering of the helplessness he, too, felt. "She will need you," he told her then, his hand suddenly reaching out and grasping hers. "If she tells you who...who did this to her," he paused, his lips thinning dangerously, "you'll tell me. Promise me."

Staring at him, Louisa nodded, grateful beyond words that he was here, that he was taking care of her, that he was taking care of Leonora. Oh, what had she done? "I'm so sorry," she whispered into the sudden stillness. "I didn't mean for this to happen. I never thought..." Tears spilled over and slipped under her mask. She felt their cool wetness against her heated skin, and anger began to burn in her heart.

More than anything, Louisa wanted to rip the mask from her face for it no longer represented a night of freedom, but only the foolish thoughts of a foolish girl. Her need to forget, to distract herself had put Leonora in danger. Louisa did not dare think about what had happened to her sister tonight, but from the ghostlike expression upon Leonora's face she knew that it was nothing her sister would ever forget.

"I will speak to your father," Phineas said as the carriage swayed slightly on the cobbled street. "I will explain—"

"No." Leonora's eyes blinked, her voice no more than a whisper, but still strangely strong and determined. She pushed herself up in her seat, one hand reaching to brush a damp curl from her forehead. Then she blinked and lifted her head to look at Phineas. "Say nothing. Nothing happened." A shadow fell over her face, but her jaw hardened in determination as she forced it back. "There is no need to worry Father."

Louisa did not know what to say. Her gaze drifted to Phineas, who looked equally confused. "But he needs to kno—" Phineas began; Leonora, though, cut him off, her lips set in a hard line and her head shaking vehemently.

"No." It was all she said. One word. But it was enough, for the look upon her face told them all they needed to know. She had made up her mind, and sharing what had happened this night with their father would go against her wishes.

"But—"

Louisa squeezed Phineas' hand, stopping his words, knowing there was no point. Her fingers felt warm as they lay settled snugly in his large hand, and suddenly, she dreaded the moment he would release her.

His gaze moved to hers, lingered there, and she could see beyond the shadow of a doubt the thoughts that ran through his head. She saw doubt and anger and the need to object, the desire to do something, the longing to make it better, to help. Louisa understood all these emotions for they reflected her own. Still, one look at her sister's fallen face told her that right here and now there was nothing they could do.

When the carriage finally pulled to a halt outside their home, Phineas helped them both alight. The night air felt ice-cold to Louisa, prickling her skin. She pulled her cloak tighter around her and then helped Leonora do the same.

Glancing up and down the street, Phineas rushed them toward the back entrance. "I do not like this," he whispered to Louisa as she opened the servants' entrance. "I should speak to your father. He needs to know what happened tonight." His gaze was imploring, and even though Louisa felt ill at the thought of breaking her father's heart, she would have done so without a moment's hesitation...if only Leonora had not begged her to remain silent on the matter.

As her sister stepped inside, her footsteps hollow on the floors, Louisa turned back to Phineas. "I shall speak to her," she promised him as much as herself. "Perhaps..."

Holding her gaze, Phineas nodded. He inhaled a deep breath, and for a moment, she thought he would say something. Then, however, he took a step back and then another, the night slowly swallowing him up as though he had never been there.

Quietly, Louisa closed the door, then hurried after her sister.

Once again, Leonora's gaze was distant, empty. She moved slowly, almost like a ghost hovering in the air. Her feet seemed to barely touch the floor, her movements fluid, and yet, reminding Louisa of a puppeteer they had seen once, the way he had moved his puppets, their arms and legs controlled by strings.

Fortunately, no one came upon them as they made their way upstairs. Without hesitation, without pausing, without stopping to look at Louisa, Leonora headed to her chamber, opened the door and stepped inside. Louisa followed, completely at a loss. What was she to do now? How could she possibly help her sister?

"I'm fine," Leonora said quietly as she turned around, her pale blue eyes finally looking at Louisa. "Go to sleep, and I shall do the same."

For a long moment, Louisa stared at her sister. "What happened tonight?" A part of her did not wish to know, but another knew that she had to.

Leonora's features tensed, and her arms rose to wrap around herself. "Nothing," she replied breathlessly, her jaw clenched.

Louisa did not know what it was. Perhaps it was the pain in her sister's eyes, the anguish and terror. Perhaps it was the vulnerability her movements betrayed. Perhaps it was that one simple word that spoke more to how deeply her sister had been wounded than tears and cries ever could.

Whatever it was, Louisa suddenly grew angry.

A red, hot ball of fire burned in her belly, its flames slowly snaking their way through her veins into every region of her body, fueling her words and chasing away the passivity she had felt before. "That is not true," she all but snapped, taking a step toward Leonora. "Why are you lying to me? Tell me what happened." With a huff, she ripped the mask from her face, tossing it across the room, wishing it had never come to hide her face.

For a moment, Leonora's eyes closed, and Louisa felt certain that her sister would finally break down and share with her the horrors of this night. Nevertheless, when her eyes opened once more, Louisa saw there was no vulnerability there, but defiance. Leonora's gaze hardened, and the hands she held clasped upon her arms tightened, her knuckles standing out white. "Do not speak to me like this," she said in a quiet voice. "You of all people have no right to speak to me like this."

Her sister's words felt like a stab through the heart, and Louisa almost crumbled to the floor, fresh tears shooting to her eyes. "Leo, please. Let me help you." Of course, if she had not been so foolish, so stubborn, so selfish, none of this would have happened. Her sister was right to blame her!

"I have my secrets," Leonora said calmly, her blue eyes locked upon Louisa's, open accusation in them, "and you have yours. Do not demand of me what you are not willing to give of yourself." She swallowed, sudden fatigue falling over her face. "It has been a long night, and I'm tired now. Please, leave me be and go to sleep." Without another word, Leonora turned away, her fingers moving to unfasten the cloak upon her shoulders.

Torn about what to do, Louisa finally took a step back, knowing that no matter what Leonora truly needed she would not accept help tonight. Not from Louisa.

With a heavy heart, Louisa left and returned to her own chamber. She, too, unfastened her cloak, then slipped out of her dress, her fingers moving without thought as her mind lingered on the painful memories she had gained that night. When she finally slid into bed, her eyes once more brimmed with tears before they rolled down, soaking her pillow. What had she done? Oh, dear heavens, what had she done?

Chapter Nineteen

CALLING ON FRIENDS

S leep would not come the night of the masquerade, and Phineas continued to pace the length of his bedchamber until dawn finally broke. Again and again, he relived the moment he had arrived at Hamilton House, the moment he had seen Louisa pulled into another's arms, the moment she had glared up at him and then the moment when she had realized that her sister was missing. The naked fear in her eyes had almost brought him to his knees, and his hands still trembled as he recalled it.

Raking a jerky hand through his hair, Phineas once more spun around when he reached the end of his chamber, his legs carrying him back down the way he had come. "Why did I not hurry more?" he moaned, remembering how Leonora had staggered toward them out of the darkened corridor. Never would he forget the paleness of her skin, the way her eyes suddenly seemed different, horrors reflected there that he never wished to know about. And yet, he did, for a murderous fury burned in his veins and he longed to rush out into the night and seek out the blackguard who had dared harm her.

As he spun around once more, his gaze fell on the dowager's letter. Indeed, she had asked him to look after her granddaughters, and he had failed her. Guilt burned a hole through his heart, and he wished more than ever that he could go back and do it over, protect them from all the evil in this world.

But he could not.

It was simply not possible. Neither could he do anything else. Leonora had all but asked him to keep this night a secret. It had been clear that she did not wish to speak about it. She did not even want her parents to know. Of course, regarding her reputation, it would be best if this night were forgotten as though it had never happened. Any rumors would damage her prospects.

However...

Bracing his hands against the cold windowpane, Phineas stared out at the rising sun. His eyes, though, did not see a golden morning, but were instead drawn back to an image of Leonora. She had seemed like a ghost, merely a shell of the woman she had once been. What to him had been even more shocking had been the change in Louisa. Gone had been the defiant look in her eyes, the daggers always shooting toward him. She had not been herself, and he had seen how terrified she had been, how her heart had broken at the sight of her sister's misery. Would she be able to help Leonora? Phineas wondered, fearing that it might not be so, at least not for a good long while.

Although Phineas itched to seek out Louisa and speak to her, he did not. He waited as the days passed without even the slightest glimpse of her. The family came and went, attended balls and picnics, but Louisa and her sister remained indoors, never once leaving the house.

Standing with his back to the door, Phineas gazed out the drawing room windows. These days, he did not know what to do with himself. Energy hummed in his veins, and yet, there was nothing to be done. If only he could speak to Louisa!

The door behind him quietly slid open, and his sister-in-law's voice drifted to his ears. "No, it is utterly strange," she said, stepping into the room. "I have not seen them in a fortnight. It appears the world swallowed them whole. It is indeed very strange."

"Did you call on them?" Tobias asked his wife, closing the door behind him. "Perhaps they are simply under the weather."

Phineas tensed, reminding himself that, of course, Anne and Tobias had taken note of the sisters' odd behavior. How could they not?

Anne sighed. "I did," she replied, seating herself somewhere where Phineas could not see her. "Jules told me that they were indisposed."

Tobias scoffed, settling near his wife. "What does that mean?"

"Apparently, Leonora has gotten lost in another science project," Anne replied with a chuckle. "Of course, that is nothing new; still, I've never known her to vanish so completely."

"And Louisa?" Tobias asked.

At the mention of her name, Phineas felt a jolt go through him. His hands clenched and unclenched, and he felt a sudden need to run from the room and...

And what?

"That is even stranger," Anne said, a hint of incredulity in her voice, "for no one quite knows. Jules said that she is in an awful mood and has been for days. She barely leaves her room, barely eats or sleeps." A heavy sigh left her lips. "Something is wrong, Tobias. Very wrong. And I'm worried."

As am I, thought Phineas.

"Phin," came his brother's voice, and Phineas flinched. "Have you heard anything?"

Willing his face not to betray the thoughts currently running through his head, Phineas slowly turned around to face his brother and sister-in-law. "Nothing," he said with a nonchalant shrug of his shoulders.

Tobias' gaze narrowed. "Are you certain?" his brother asked, his dark brown eyes lingering, a contemplative note in them. "You must admit you've been rather close with Louisa as of late."

Phineas frowned at his brother. "What makes you say that?"

The hint of a teasing smile curled up Tobias's lips. "Am I wrong?" he asked without answering Phineas' question.

Anne suddenly surged to her feet. "I'll call on them right now," she stated vehemently, the tone in her voice brooking no argument. "I've waited long enough, and I cannot wait a minute longer. Something is very wrong."

Tobias nodded, then rose to his feet. "I shall accompany you, dear."

Phineas tensed, torn about how to proceed. Of course, he, too, wanted nothing more than to see Louisa, to speak to her. But would he be able to if he accompanied his brother and sister-in-law? Was there any point in visiting them?

In the end, it did not matter. Phineas had spent the past fortnight worrying and wondering and he could take no more of it. At least, this was a chance, a chance for him to see how the sisters fared. And so, he joined Anne and Tobias on the short walk over to the Whickertons' townhouse. They were shown into the garden, where most of the Whickertons sat on the terrace, enjoying a spot of tea. Even the dowager was present, the look in her eyes less jubilant than Phineas remembered, and he could not help but wonder whether she knew what had happened.

"Oh, no, Leonora is still busy as ever," Lady Juliet, the eldest Whickerton sister, told them. Still, a hint of unease rested in her eyes. "She refuses to leave her room and mumbled something about her notebook and her notes..." She shook her head, confusion coming to her gaze. "I don't quite recall what exactly she said." She gave a short, slightly forced sounding laugh. "But then again, I rarely do."

"But is it not odd," Anne asked as she and Tobias were seated, "how the two of them retreated from everything? They have never even been out of the house, have they?"

As the conversation continued to circle around the sisters' odd behavior, Phineas crossed the terrace and then stepped out into the garden where the two youngest Whickerton sisters, Lady Christina and Lady Harriet—as far as he recalled—were playing with a rabbit. "Good day, Lord Barrington," the golden-haired girl greeted him with a wide smile. "Would you care to meet Sir Lancelot?"

Phineas frowned. "Sir Lancelot? Am I right to assume that you are referring to the rabbit?"

Lady Harriet nodded eagerly, her fiery-red curls dancing up and down. "He is such an adorable creature," she beamed, her green eyes glowing in the warm afternoon sun. "Would you care to hold him?"

In fact, it seemed that Sir Lancelot would prefer to be set free as he continued to squirm in Lady Harriet's arms. The girl, however, continued to hug him to her chest, gently stroking his long ears.

"Well, actually..." Before Phineas could decline the offer, his mind provided him with a rather unusual idea. Still, considering that he felt rather desperate now, Phineas was willing to try anything.

With a careful smile, he stepped toward the girl, then held out his hands to receive the animal. "I hope he's friendly," he remarked, a skeptical look directed at the squirming rabbit.

"Oh, he is very friendly. You have nothing to worry about."

Feeling the soft weight of the rabbit settling in his arms, Phineas glanced upward at the house. Behind a window, someone moved, like a shadow falling over him for a second before disappearing once more. Was that Louisa? He wondered, knowing he could not leave this house without seeing her.

The moment Lady Harriet turned to look over her shoulder and smiled at Lady Christina, Phineas dropped Sir Lancelot. "Ouch!" he exclaimed, shaking his hand, his gaze narrowed. "He bit me."

Sir Lancelot instantly darted away, taking this chance presented to him. He disappeared into the bushes, and Lady Harriet's eyes grew wide as she watched him dash away. "Oh, no! Sir Lancelot!" she called, not a single thought for Phineas' imaginary bite. "Chris, help me catch him!" Instantly, both sisters darted away—Lady Christina a bit reluctantly—their voices alternately calling for the rabbit as well as for more help from the terrace.

Phineas stepped back as the terrace slowly emptied, more and more Whickertons swarming onto the lawn until only the dowager countess remained.

Ducking behind a tree, Phineas circled back around, careful to move quietly and swiftly so as not to draw anyone's attention as they flitted around the garden, trying their best to corner the poor little rabbit. Part of Phineas hoped that Sir Lancelot would get away!

"Her door is the second one on the right," the dowager countess told him with knowing eyes the moment he stepped onto the terrace.

For a moment, Phineas looked at her, saw the sadness and concern in her gaze, and then nodded before hurrying into the house. He climbed the stairs two at a time, hoping that his absence would not soon be noticed. Large strides quickly ate up the distance, and in no time at all, he found himself outside the second door on the right. For a moment, he paused, wondering if he ought to knock. However, he knew that Louisa would never allow him in. No doubt, she had reverted to her old, defiant self, determined to keep him out. It was who she was, but he would not have it today.

Pushing down the handle, Phineas stepped over the threshold, then closed the door in his back. His eyes found her instantly. She stood by the window, her back to him, but slowly turned the moment the door clicked shut.

"Phineas?" Disbelief echoed in her voice as she stared at him; it lasted only for a moment though. "What are you doing here?" she demanded, her eyes narrowing. "You have no right to be here! Leave! What if someone finds you here?"

Having expected no less, Phineas merely shrugged, then stepped into the room. Still, he could not deny that hearing his given name fall from her tongue pleased him. "I came to see how you were," he told her honestly, raking his eyes over her face, taking note of the dark circles under her eyes and the remnants of tears upon her cheeks. "How is your sister?"

Louisa flinched as though he had slapped her, her body jerking and her arms flying up to wrap around herself, her fingers all but digging into her flesh. "That is none of your concern," she hissed, shaking like a leaf. "Get out!"

Holding her gaze, Phineas slowly shook his head, his feet carrying him ever closer. "Not until you talk to me."

Louisa looked as though she wished to shrink back, the look in her eyes painful. "There's nothing to say."

Two more steps and Phineas stood before her, inhaling a slow breath as his eyes lingered. A thousand questions raced through his head, all he wished to ask, all he wished to know. In the end, he asked the one question that had been on his mind for days. "What were you doing at the masquerade in the first place? Alone, with only your sister to accompany you? How could you not have known this was madness?"

The moment the words left his lips, Phineas knew them to be a mistake. In truth, he had not meant to say them, had not meant to lay blame at her feet. They sprang from a deep desire, a deep wish to undo what had happened, knowing that it was impossible.

Hope often was irrational, though, was it not?

Chapter Twenty

DESPERATE WORDS

Staring at Phineas, Louisa felt new tears forming in her eyes, slowly gathering substance, growing larger and larger until they finally spilled over and slowly snaked their way down her face. And still she stared, unable to speak, his words, their meaning echoing within her.

Of course, he was right, she knew him to be. It was her fault. If she had not...

"How is your sister?" Phineas asked gently, a hint of regret in his eyes now. No doubt, he saw how his words had shaken her. For a reason she could not name, he knew her well. Was her face so easy to read? She wondered. Or was it something else?

I'd know you anywhere. Was that not what he had said to her at the masquerade? *I'd know you anywhere.*

The words washed over her like a caress, and her skin began to tingle. The thought that he would recognize her no matter how much she disguised herself was oddly...appealing? Heartwarming? It was, was it not? As much as Louisa wished it weren't so, it was. Why he affected her thus she could not say, but she knew it to be true.

"I don't know," Louisa finally said, knowing that he would not leave if she did not answer him. "She remains locked in her room, pretending to work on something or other—I don't know. I never know." Another tear spilled over, and she felt it slowly run down her cheek. "She refuses to speak to me. Of course, she does." A large lump settled in her throat, cutting off words she needed to say, but didn't even dare think.

Heaving a deep sigh, Phineas ran a hand over his face, his thumb and forefinger drawing down to pinch the bridge of his nose. "Perhaps we should speak to your father or your mother..." His voice trailed off as he looked at her.

Louisa shook her head. "I cannot do that," she told him, her fingers beginning to ache from digging them into the flesh of her arms. "She asked me not to say anything, and I will not betray her." A heavy sob escaped the tightness of her throat, startling Louisa as much as Phineas. Overwhelmed, she shrank back, lifting a hand to keep him away.

His gaze softened, grew anguished, as he stepped toward her, nonetheless. "You cannot continue like this," he told her. "It is destroying you."

Through a curtain of tears, Louisa looked up at him. "And what if it is?" she demanded as misery flooded her heart, threatening to crush it. "Do I not deserve it? Is all this not my fault? It was my decision. I wanted to go, and I would not let her dissuade me." She threw her arms in the air as rivers of tears ran down her face. "It is my fault. I did this to her. Me."

For a long moment, they simply stared at one another as though frozen in time, unblinking, unmoving. And then, Phineas was suddenly right in front of her, his hands on her arms, drawing her against him. How her head ended up on his shoulder Louisa did not know, but neither did she care. He gathered her in his arms and held her as she cried. Her fingers curled into the lapels of his jacket, holding on, wishing he would never let her go. Somehow, she felt safe with him. Somehow, his presence soothed her aching heart. Somehow, it was he who knew exactly what to say.

For he said nothing.

Nothing at all.

Phineas simply stood there, his arms wrapped around her, one hand gently brushing a curl behind her ear, the tips of his fingers grazing her skin. She felt his heartbeat beneath her ear, his chest rising and falling with each breath, strangely attuned to her own.

For how long they stood like this, Louisa did not know. But slowly her sobs eased. Her breathing calmed. Her mind cleared, and suddenly, finding herself in his arms startled her, as though she had not noticed his presence until this very moment.

Drawing in a sharp breath, Louisa jerked out of his embrace, her eyes wide, unable to meet his. "You need to go." Her feet retreated until her back was up against the cold windowpane.

"I will not," Phineas said stubbornly. His dark gaze lingered upon her. She could feel it as though he had reached out and touched her. "Talk to me."

Balling her hands into fists, Louisa felt her fingernails digging into her palms. Her gaze rose slowly, moving off the floor and climbing higher until she found his almost black eyes looking into hers. A shiver went through her. It was a most intimate moment, for she felt as though he could see deep within her, see how selfish she had been, how she had only thought of herself. "There is nothing to say," she told him with a shrug. She tried her best to remain calm, but deep inside despair still lingered. Never would she forget the pain and anguish in her sister's eyes, knowing that she was the one who had put it there. "Nothing I say will change anything so there's no reason to speak at all. Leave. I assure you I am fine or as fine as I'll ever be."

Again, he simply stood there, his gaze not veering from hers. "You look like a mere shadow of yourself," Phineas said suddenly, a hint of reproach in his voice. "You're not yourself, and neither is your sister."

At the hint of condescension in his tone, Louisa felt anger flare to life. A part of her was well aware that he had not meant what he had said as criticism; however, she felt herself reach out and hold on to the burning flame of outrage, slowly growing bigger within her heart, for the simple fact was that anger was much easier to bear than despair. "How would you know that?" she snapped at him. "You don't know me. You know nothing about me. We are not friends. We are...nothing to each other."

His jaw hardened, and something menacing came to his dark gaze.

He inhaled a slow breath as though trying to calm himself before moving a step closer. "Whether you want to admit it or not," he whispered with a deadly calm, "I know you. I can see perfectly well how the night of the masquerade destroyed you, and I'm telling you now that I will not allow you to retreat from the world and simply sulk in your misery." He shook his head, emphasizing his determination. "The Louisa I know would not cower. She would stand tall and find a way to deal with what happened. Always have you been strong. Always have you done the impossible. And never did you allow anyone or anything to intimidate you. That is who you need to be right now. That is who your sister needs to help her through this."

Shocked by his words, Louisa stared at him, the words he had said to her the night of the masquerade once more echoed in her mind. *I'd know you anywhere.* Was it true? Did he truly know her so well? How was this possible? Never had they spent more than a few fleeting moments with each other, except of course when he had been teasing her, when she had lashed out at him, when they had been fighting.

Fatigue suddenly settled in Louisa's bones. All these thoughts and feelings were weighing heavily upon her. She had not had a good night's sleep in a long time, and suddenly, the lack of sleep seemed to catch up with her. Her arms and legs felt heavy as lead, and she began to sway on her feet. "Please, simply leave. There is nothing you can do." She swallowed hard as fresh tears began to prick the backs of her eyes. "There's nothing I can do."

For a moment, Phineas' lips thinned as he watched her. Then he shot forward, his hands grasping her upper arms, pulling her against him. "Tell me why!" he all but snarled into her face. "Tell me why! Why did you go to the masquerade? Why was it so incredibly important to you? You knew the dangers. You are an intelligent woman. You knew what could happen. What was so important that you disregarded everything? Tell me!" His hands on her shoulders tightened, and he gave her a quick shake. "Tell me or I swear I shall march downstairs and tell your parents everything!"

Chapter Twenty-One

A REVELATION

Phineas watched the blood drain from Louisa's face. His words had shocked her, rocked her to her bones, as he knew they would, as he had hoped they would. The way she had hung in his arms had frightened him more than anything he had ever known. She had not been herself anymore, and he did not know how to wake her up, how to reawaken the old Louisa, the woman he knew and respected and admired...and cared for.

For that was the truth of it, was it not? He cared for her. Her pain was now his, and he found that he could not bear it.

"You wouldn't!" she hissed, and he felt her straightening. Her shoulders drew back, and the muscles in her arms tensed. "You wouldn't!"

Phineas cast her a mischievous grin, knowing from countless experiences how much it infuriated her. "Try me," he dared her, leaning closer, watching her watch him, seeing her trying to gauge if he truly meant what he said.

A muscle in her jaw twitched, and she pressed her lips into a thin line. Anger stood in her eyes, scorching hot. Her chest rose and fell with a long, deep breath and then her chin flew up and she jerked backwards, freeing herself from his grasp. "I knew you could not be trusted," she hissed, accusation vibrating in her voice. "I always knew.

You do not know the meaning of honor and trust. You're a blackguard! A scoundrel! A miscreant! And I loathe the day our paths crossed!"

Phineas swallowed hard at her accusing words, realizing with no small amount of shock how deeply they wounded him. He had thought himself immune to a few simple words, knowing that they were simply spoken in anger. But he was not. Still, he needed to stay focused and say what needed to be said. "Is that so?" he dared her, giving her another wicked grin, another teasing gleam coming to his eyes. "I was not the one to drag my sister to a masquerade and then leave her there alone!" Staring down at her, he moved closer. "I was not the one to think only of myself!" Another step, and he felt her skirts brush against his legs. "I am not the one hiding in my chambers while my sister suffers alone!"

Her jaw trembled, and tears glistened in her eyes. Still, her chin remained raised and no matter how much he crowded her, she did not retreat. "You're right," she spat to his utter surprise, loathing and disgust thickening her voice; surprisingly, they were not directed at him, though. "I did all those things. I failed my sister. I am failing her now." Tears streamed down her face, and yet, she held his gaze, admitting to her faults with her head held high. "There? Are you happy now? It was my fault. I made the mistake, not her, and yet, she is the one paying for it. I don't even know what happened to her because she refuses to talk to me. Of course, she does. It is my fault after all." The tone in her voice grew shrill, a hint of panic and despair sneaking into her eyes. "I wanted one night," she exclaimed with a shake of her head, her eyes strangely distant as though she could not believe how one small decision had led to something so horrible. "One night of freedom. One night of not thinking about this. One night of not feeling small and insignificant and inferior to everyone around me." Her gaze snapped back to him, her jaw clenched. "I wanted one night without thinking of you. One night without remembering the words you said." She shook her head, fresh tears spilling over. "I never meant for this to happen. I did not even want her to come with me. But she insisted, and I..." She closed her eyes, once again looking defeated. "I let her come. I should've argued harder. I should've stayed home. I should not have risked her." She blinked, and her eyes rose to meet his. "All this pain," she whispered, her voice choked with tears, "and only because I'm too dumb to read."

Phineas stilled, staring at her, as the words slowly sank in. He blinked at her as they circled around in his mind, free of logic and sense and reason. "Pardon?"

Seeing his reaction, Louisa froze, her eyes going wide and her jaw dropping. "B-But y-you know," she stammered, shaking her head in disbelief. "Y-You know."

Still doubting his ears, Phineas slowly shook his head. "How could I know? How could I—?" Breaking off, he tried to sort through the mess in his head, rubbing his hands over his face. Still, when he dropped them once more, Louisa still looked as shocked and terrified as a moment earlier. "You cannot read?" It was a simple question, and yet, it seemed utterly wrong. How was this possible? She was such a strong and intelligent woman. Always had her quick wit impressed him. For heaven's sake, he teased her the way he did because he enjoyed the sharp twists and turns of her mind, the way she responded, quick and unimpressed. How was this possible?

As he stepped toward her, Louisa flinched and all but fled from the windows. In a few quick steps, she had reached the door, her hand settling on the handle, when she suddenly paused. With her eyes wide and her mouth open, she looked over her shoulder back at him, her body trembling. Then she turned, her back suddenly pressed against the door, and stared at him. "Leave."

It was a desperate plea, and Phineas understood in that moment that she could not bear his presence. For some reason, she had believed that he knew and realizing now that he did not had shocked her, had pulled out the ground from under her. Her instinct was to flee from him, to seek safety elsewhere, sanctuary, a place where she felt calm and reassured. However, that place was here.

This was her bedchamber, and he was the intruder.

"I'll leave," Phineas told her, certain that if he were to push her even a little farther, she might break. As he walked closer, she moved from the door, seemingly desperate to maintain a certain distance between them. "I shall leave...for now. The last word on this issue has not yet been spoken." He held her gaze for a long moment, needing her to hear him. Then he stepped to the door and opened it. "Please know that if you need anything—"

"Leave," she interrupted, still backing away, her delicate frame trembling, shaking like a leaf tossed about by a strong wind.

Phineas nodded, then stepped from the room, closing the door behind him.

For a long moment, he simply stood there, listening to his own heartbeat, strangely faint, and yet, utterly unrestrained, wild even. He felt torn, a part of him urging him back inside, remembering the desperation in her eyes, the exhaustion and the pain. She needed him. She needed...someone. Yet, he had promised not to say a word, had he not? Of course, he had not meant what he had said. Never would he betray her confidence. Still, was he simply to leave?

A faint rustling of skirts drifted to his ears, and Phineas snapped to attention. His eyes flew sideways, and he caught a faint flutter of pale-yellow skirts vanish around the corner. Instantly, his heart tensed. Had someone been there? Could someone have overheard what they had spoken about? Did anyone in her family know?

Following down the corridor, Phineas headed back downstairs. Slowly, he approached the wide French doors leading out onto the terrace. Excited voices drifted inside on a warm summer's breeze, a stark contrast to the chill that still lingered in his bones.

Phineas was far from able to pretend in this moment. The thought of forcing a smile onto his face and a joyful tone into his voice was too much to bear. And so, he stood back, hiding behind the curtains, no more than peeking around the corner at the happy family seated outside. Anne and Tobias were still there, laughing as Lady Christina and Lady Harriet were still chasing after the rabbit. His gaze swept over their faces, and he wondered if any of them now knew the truth.

Yellow skirts?

Indeed, none of the sisters nor Anne wore yellow. It had been none of them. Then who? Who had been outside Louisa's door? And what had she heard? The thought sent a cold chill through Phineas, for he knew beyond the shadow of a doubt that Louisa had never shared her secret with anyone. Why then had she thought he knew? It did not make any sense. None at all.

"I shall speak to her again," he whispered quietly to himself before turning around and walking away, "but not today."

Louisa needed time, and honestly so did he. Perhaps in a few days, he would seek her out again and then perhaps she would have calmed down, and they would be able to talk.

As he left the Whickertons' townhouse without even a word of farewell, a small voice whispered in his head, reminding him that he and Louisa had never been able to talk. Never had she spoken to him. Always had she kept herself at a distance, offering him no more than harsh words, insults and accusations.

Of course, he had baited her, teased her, riled her. A small smile tickled his lips at the memory of their many heated arguments. Always had Phineas enjoyed them, realizing in this moment how much he missed her.

The woman she had been.

The woman she was deep down.

Now, that woman lay buried under guilt and shame and despair. Would she ever rise again? Phineas could only hope so, for he would miss her dearly if she did not. Still, knowing Louisa as he did—no matter what she had said—Phineas was certain that her fate was now tied to her sister's. Only if Leonora found a way to overcome what had happened the night of the masquerade would Louisa recover. Was there a way for him to help them?

Phineas heaved a deep sigh. What could he possibly do? He of all people? Indeed, Louisa would never let him. She had almost thrown him out of the house. "Then I shall claw my way back in," Phineas muttered, casting one last glance over his shoulder at the tall, imposing townhouse before his feet carried him around the corner.

Chapter Twenty-Two

DARE TO TRUST

L ouisa could barely keep herself on her feet. Her limbs, every inch of her, was trembling so badly, she felt certain she would trip if she were to take another step. Her heart hammered in her chest almost painfully as though it wished to break through her rib cage and escape, find a place to hide somewhere warm and safe and soothing. Thoughts whirled in her head, and when Louisa closed her eyes, waves of dizziness washed over her.

Her hands moved without thought. They clenched and unclenched. Her fingers tugged on her hair, brushing a curl behind her ear, which instantly swung forward again, refusing to stay where she had directed it. Her hands flew over her face, covering her eyes, before they lowered and brushed over her skirts. Still, every movement seemed without purpose. There was no reason for it. It was simply a distraction, something to focus on because if she did not, her thoughts unerringly returned to the shocked look upon Phineas' face. "He did not know," she whispered to the empty room, shock of her own freezing her limbs, a cold that was painful and devastating. "He did not know."

How was this possible? Louisa had been so certain he had known after what he had said about her. Had he truly simply guessed? Had he simply wanted to be hurtful and said whatever had popped into his mind in that moment? Why had he said what he had in the first place? Why had he spoken of her with such disregard and then continued to seek her out?

Sinking into the armchair by the window, Louisa hung her head, her mind and heart hopelessly overwhelmed. Nothing made sense. What was she to do now?

For a long time, Louisa simply sat there, her eyes staring out at the blue sky, watching feathery, white clouds drift lazily westward with the soft summer's breeze. Then joyful laughter drew her attention, and she shifted her gaze down to the terrace. Still, seated in her chair, she could not see the people she knew were down there. A moment later, though, Chris and Harry charged into her field of vision as they hurried down into the gardens, chasing after a fluffy, white ball of fur. Back and forth, up and down, they went, laughter bubbling from their lips. Then someone else joined them, her golden hair shining in the bright afternoon sun, a perfect match to her lovely yellow skirts. It was Sarah, unable to stay away, her gaze moving over to the house beyond the hedge, the house she had once called home.

It seemed that misery was everywhere. Where had all the joy gone? Never had Louisa felt so crushed and hopeless. Always, despite everything, had she looked at life with a happy heart. Now, however, everything was different.

A soft knock sounded at her door, jarring her from her thoughts. "It's me, dearest," called Grandma Edie's voice through the closed door. "May I come in?"

Brushing the last remnants of tears from her eyes, Louisa cleared her throat, praying that her grandmother would not see with one glance what lived in her heart. "Of course," she called, once more running her hands over her skirts, trying to smooth them.

Leaning heavily upon her walking stick, Grandma Edie hobbled into the room, giving the door a swift push to see it fall closed behind her. Her pale eyes were watchful as always as she slowly moved closer, then sank into the armchair opposite Louisa's. "You look like hell, Sweetheart," her grandmother chuckled, a soothing warmth in her eyes. "Will you tell me what happened?"

Louisa stilled, detecting an odd note in her grandmother's voice. Indeed, she seemed most curious, barely able to hide her interest in Louisa's answer. "You knew he would come to see me," she said rather accusingly. "You knew he had been here all this time, didn't you?"

Her grandmother chortled, "Of course, I did. After all, I'm the one who sent him to you."

Louisa felt her jaw drop. "Why would you do that? Have you no sense for propriety? What would have happened if—"

"Oh, balderdash!" Grandma Edie exclaimed, rolling her eyes most dramatically. "There are more important things in life than propriety. Far more important things." Setting her walking stick aside, she folded her hands. "He is one to ruffle your feathers, is he not?"

Louisa dropped her gaze, not wishing her grandmother to know just how much Phineas *ruffled her feathers*. "He is a most infuriating man," she finally said before lifting her gaze once more. "But you do know that, do you not? You know how much he upsets me. As my grandmother, should you not seek to keep such people away from me?"

Grandma Edie laughed, "Oh, Sweetheart, you do not need me for that. You are strong and brave and perfectly capable of taking care of yourself. Still, even the strongest among us need someone to lean on occasionally."

Louisa gaped at her grandmother. "And you thought that someone could be him? What a ridiculous notion!"

"Why?" her grandmother inquired, her pale eyes flaring with challenge. "I admit, he has a quite unusual way about him." Again, she chuckled, and Louisa could not help but think that her grandmother liked Phineas' rather ungentlemanly side very much. "Still, beyond all else, he is a most loyal and devoted man, would you not agree?" Her brows rose, daring Louisa to contradict her.

Almost squirming in her seat, Louisa felt the sudden urge to drop her gaze. "Do you truly think so?" she asked, aware that she was stalling for time.

Seeing through her ruse, Grandma Edie grinned at her. "I certainly do," she assured her. "Why else would I have sent him after you the night of the masquerade?"

The question felt like an arrow shot through Louisa's heart, and from one second to the next, her body was once more flooded by emotions she feared she could no longer bear. Tears shot to her eyes, and her hands began to tremble.

Watching her, her grandmother inhaled a deep breath, her eyes clouding, a shadow falling over her face. "Something happened," she said, and it was not a question.

Gritting her teeth, Louisa nodded. "Why didn't you stop us? Why didn't you stop *me?*" Her hands clenched together, her fingernails digging into her flesh.

Leaning forward, her grandmother reached out a weathered hand and gently placed it upon Louisa's clenched ones. "I know you're hurting," she said gently, an echo of Louisa's pain visible in her pale eyes. "Still, you need to make your own decisions, the good and the bad. It is a life lesson, sometimes harshly taught, but always invaluable."

Louisa closed her eyes, and fresh tears squeezed out, running down her cheeks and dripping down onto her hands. As much as she wanted to scream and argue, Louisa knew that her grandmother was right. Indeed, the night of the masquerade had been a valuable life lesson. Unfortunately, it had been Leonora who had paid the price.

How Grandma Edie knew everything she did, Louisa did not know. Still, strangely, it had always been thus. "You're angry with him," her grandmother whispered, her thin fingers closing more tightly around Louisa's hands. "Why?"

Slowly, Louisa's eyes opened, and she lifted them to look upon her grandmother, surprised that for once it seemed she did not know. "I was a fool," Louisa whispered, cursing herself for blurting out her secret. After all, Phineas had not known, and now she of all people had been the one to tell him. "I said something, told him something, something no one knows, something I never wanted anyone to know."

Grandma Edie nodded, but did not ask what it was. "What are you afraid of, Child?"

Louisa's mouth opened and closed. Once. Twice. The words were there, but she was afraid to utter them. They were terrifying, soul-crushing and deeply unsettling because for the past two years Louisa had hated Phineas Hawke with a burning passion. She had told herself day after day that he was a loathsome creature, not worth her time, that she would be better off not knowing him. She still told herself all these things, but somehow something had changed.

She no longer believed them.

"What if...?" Louisa stammered, uncertain how to put into words what worried her so. Deep down, she knew, and yet, it took enormous courage to admit it to herself. "What if...what I told him will make him...walk away," she blinked, feeling a lone tear collect in the corner of her right eye, "and never come back?"

Indeed, the thought of Phineas not seeking her out anymore brought an odd tightening to her chest. Where once she would have rejoiced, Louisa now knew that somehow, he had found a way to make her care for him. It was a shocking revelation, and if she had been standing, she would have no doubt rocked back on her feet.

Watching her granddaughter intensely, Grandma Edie then shook her head, an amused glimmer in her eyes, and began to laugh. "Oh, my sweet child, you could dump a bucket of mud over his head at the next ball, and he would still remain firmly by your side." Once again, she patted Louisa's hand. "Do you not know that?"

Unable to respond, Louisa merely stared at her grandmother. Her emotions were hopelessly entangled, her thoughts torn between lingering on the horrors of the night of the masquerade and the shock of accidentally revealing her secret to Phineas. What was she to do now about either situation?

Sighing, Grandma Edie reached for her walking stick, then slowly pushed to her feet, swaying for a moment before finding her balance. Her pale eyes looked down at Louisa, kind, and yet, challenging. "Let him help you," she urged her granddaughter. "You'll find the dark moments of this world look much brighter when someone holds your hand. Not even you can deny that Phineas Hawke wants to be that person for you. Why do you think he came here today? Why do you think he went after you the night of the masquerade? Why do you think he's been lingering nearby all this time?" She smiled warmly down at Louisa. "Dare to trust him, and I have no doubt that he will surprise you." Then she brushed a gentle hand over Louisa's head, turned toward the door and then slowly left the room.

Staring into nothing, Louisa remained where she was for the rest of the day. Again, and again, the moment she had accidentally told Phineas she could not read replayed in her mind. Certainly, he had been shocked. Who would not have been? But how did he think of her now? Would he truly remain? And even if he did, would he still look at her the same way he had before?

It was that thought that terrified Louisa the most for she knew she could not bear to have him look at her and have him see someone unworthy, someone inferior. Even if he were never to say it to her face, but only thought it, she would not be able to look him in the eye ever again.

Ought she truly give him a chance? Or would it be wiser to cut all ties and spare herself the moment of disappointment that would surely come? For if not even she could not think of herself in a through-and-through favorable light, how could he?

Chapter Twenty-Three
A MOST WELCOME INVITATION

With the season at its end and everyone retiring to the country, Phineas felt restless. Once again, he had taken to pacing. No matter where he was, the study, the library, the drawing room, any room would do. He paced and he paced and he paced, annoying himself with the simple fact that he could not stop, his mind as active as his feet.

Louisa's revelation kept coursing through his head. He had a thousand questions to ask her, and yet, he did not doubt that she would refuse him. Always had she kept to herself, and he could not help but wonder whether her family even knew. He doubted it. He doubted it very much. Had she shared her secret with anyone at all?

Always had Louisa seemed full of life and laughter, her courage boundless. With the greatest ease, she had always been able to approach others, to speak freely, to laugh and smile and make others laugh and smile. She was honest and daring, and Phineas had always admired that about her. How many times had he watched her?

Phineas shook his head, unable to recall.

Still, he could not have been very observant for how else could it be explained that he had not noticed her inability to read? For a moment, he wondered if it was even true. Then, he recalled the paleness of her face, the way all blood seemed to have drained from it in utter shock as she had spoken without thought, revealing something to him she had always hidden. Indeed, it had to be the truth. Still, how was it possible?

Always had he thought her one of the most clever and quick-witted people of his acquaintance. And she was, wasn't she? Indeed, reading was simply a skill one could learn. It did not, though, speak to one's intelligence. Nevertheless, judging from the look upon Louisa's face, Phineas realized that she believed it did.

A sharp pain pierced his heart at the thought of her thinking so lowly of herself. Never would he have thought it possible considering the way she always carried herself proudly, the way she had always unflinchingly met his daring gaze. Louisa, cowering in a corner? It was unthinkable.

Belatedly, Phineas realized that the door to the drawing room had swung open. He turned and found his brother standing in the doorway, a curious look upon his face as he watched him. "Are you all right?" Tobias asked, stepping closer, his eyes fixed upon Phineas. "You seem out of sorts, not like yourself." A tense chuckle drifted from his lips. "I must say, I am strangely worried about you. I never have been before, at least not like this." He stopped in front of Phineas, the expression upon his face sobering. "What is it?"

Utterly tempted to confide in his brother, Phineas searched his mind. He could have used some advice, some counsel, knowing that his brother would understand. Nevertheless, he knew he could not betray Louisa's confidence. Of course, she had not made him promise not to reveal her secret to another; yet, Phineas could not in good conscience do so without her permission.

So instead, he shrugged. "It's nothing," he replied, then instantly turned away and strode over to the window, not wanting his brother to see the—no doubt—guilty expression upon his face. "I am merely at loose ends now that the season is over."

"I see," Tobias replied, the tone in his voice betraying that he did not believe a word Phineas had uttered. "What happened the other day?" he inquired, slow footsteps carrying him closer until he came to stand beside Phineas. He inhaled a slow breath, then turned to look upon his brother. "When we went to visit the Whickertons'? You vanished inside and then left without a word. Why?"

Phineas forced a chuckle from his lips. "I admit, it was rather rude, but I was bored. So, I left."

A muscle twitched in Tobias' cheek. "Is that so? For I could've sworn I saw you standing at one of the upstairs windows...with Louisa." His gaze widened daringly as he looked at Phineas.

Gritting his teeth, Phineas turned to look at his brother. "What are you saying?" he asked, a tense tone in his voice.

His brother stilled, a hint of caution coming to his gaze. "Something happened, didn't it? Between the two of you?"

Phineas turned away, crossing the room in large strides. "That is none of your business."

"I'm afraid I must disagree," Tobias stated calmly as the brothers looked at one another from across the room. "She is my wife's beloved cousin; that makes her family." He held Phineas' gaze, slowly walking closer. "I want your promise that you will treat her with the utmost respect."

Phineas inhaled a slow breath, anger warring with respect within him. Indeed, his brother meant well, looking out for Louisa. Still, the underlying suggestion that he, Phineas, would do anything to harm her, to treat her ill angered him. "I assure you," Phineas gritted out through clenched teeth, "I shall treat her with the utmost respect. There? Is that enough for you?"

Slowly, Tobias' head bobbed up and down, his gaze still watchful. "Is this merely a game to you," he asked curiously, "or do you genuinely care for her?"

The question, rather abrupt and unexpected, sent a jolt through Phineas, one that almost made him rock back on his feet. He knew not how to reply. Fortunately, though, the door to the drawing room once more swung open in that moment, and Anne entered. "Ah, there you are," she exclaimed as her eyes fell upon her husband. "I've been looking for you everywhere." She paused then, her gaze going back and forth between her husband and her brother-in-law, a contemplative glitter coming to her eyes. "Is everything all right?"

Putting a smile upon his face, Tobias turned to his wife. "Yes, dear.

Everything is all right," he assured her with a sideways glance at Phineas. "What did you wish to speak to me about?" He strode toward her and drew her hand into his. It was such a simple, uncomplicated gesture, whispering of deep trust and intimacy, that Phineas could not help but envy his brother's relationship with his wife.

"Well, I simply meant to let you know," Anne began, her gaze briefly straying to Phineas, "that I've made all the arrangements."

Tobias nodded knowingly. "Wonderful."

Phineas frowned. "What arrangements?"

With a smile, Anne turned to him, something oddly expectant in her gaze. "We've been invited to visit Whickerton Grove," she told him, her eyes lingering upon his in a most inquisitive way. "Would you like to accompany us? We'll leave in a fortnight."

Deep down, Phineas knew what Anne was doing. Likely, it had been her and Tobias's plan all along. No doubt they had noticed something passing between him and Louisa. Had his brother not commented on the like before? It seemed that after he, Phineas, and Louisa had meddled in their relationship, it was now his brother's and sister-in-law's turn to repay them in equal kind.

Phineas would have laughed if the situation at present had not been so tense. Nevertheless, he could not deny that the thought of visiting Whickerton Grove appealed to him. It certainly would give him a chance to see Louisa, to speak to her and perhaps with any luck at all find out more. Perhaps over time, he could wear her down, and she would confide in him. That was what he wanted, was it not? To be her confidant?

Phineas met Anne's gaze, giving her a little smile. "I believe I would like that, yes," he told her, trying not to sound too enthusiastic. "After all, there's little left to be done here in London. Perhaps a trip to the country would be most diverting. I shall see that my things are packed on the day." Nodding to his brother and sister-in-law, Phineas strode off, thinking it best not to remain in their presence for too long. Still, the moment he walked past Anne, he could not fail to notice the small smile upon her lips spreading into a wide grin. It would seem he had played right into her hands.

Phineas did not care though if he got to see Louisa.

Chapter Twenty-Four

WHICKERTON GROVE

Happy laughter drifted across the grounds as Louisa slowly strolled down the small gravel path into the gardens. Not far off, she could hear Chris and Harry as well as their friend Sarah chatting and laughing, hidden from her eyes somewhere beyond bushes and trees and hedges. The vastness of Whickerton Grove always amazed Louisa after months in London. Everything was so far and wide, seemingly endless. The horizon whispered of places far away, beckoning her forward, and yet, she knew no matter how far she would walk she would never reach its end.

The jubilant effervescence in her sisters' voices spoke of the same joy and delight to finally be out in the country again. Harry loved everything green and wild and boundless. Every day brought new creatures to tend to, to observe and learn about. Chris blossomed under the warm sun, her cheeks flushed with the fresh air as she and Sarah ventured off to the small pond nearby. Sarah, too, seemed more at ease here, her thoughts distracted from the losses her family had suffered so recently. Indeed, here at Whickerton Grove, time seemed to have stood still, preserving happiness and the ease of childhood days.

Unfortunately, its magic did not extend to Leonora.

Weeks had passed since the night of the masquerade, and still dark shadows rested upon Leonora's face whenever Louisa's eyes fell upon her. She rarely left her bedchamber, all but locking herself away, mumbling something of a new project. Yet, she never offered details, and Louisa wondered if her sister was truly working on something, even if only to distract herself, to banish at least for a short while the demons that lingered.

Turning the corner, Louisa spotted her eldest sister Jules heading toward her. Their eyes met, and Louisa intuitively knew that there was something on Jules's mind. "Is there anything I can help you with?" she asked her sister once they met near the small fountain.

Jules heaved a deep sigh, concern darkening her eyes. "I was about to ask you the same question," she told Louisa, reaching for her arm and pulling it through the crook of hers. Then the sisters proceeded down the path at a leisurely pace. "I worry about Leonora," Jules said after a while, her gaze drifting sideways to Louisa. "And about you as well." She stopped and turned to look at Louisa more fully. "What happened?"

Louisa shrugged, contemplating what to tell her sister. Then she turned and continued onward, Jules hurrying to catch up with her. "I'm not certain," Louisa told her honestly as they drew near to the pond.

A small grove stood nearby, shielding a lone bench facing the still waters. Fortunately, their younger sisters had moved on, and the pond lay deserted.

"Are you truly only concerned as I am?" Jules asked her as they stopped by the bench. "Or do you know more about what plagues her?" She reached out a hand and placed it upon Louisa's arm, urging her to turn and face her. "You've always been so close. I cannot believe that you know nothing." Her moss-green eyes searched Louisa's. "Please, talk to me."

Sinking onto the bench, Louisa closed her eyes, feeling as though everyone these days was urging her to talk to them. Where had all the secrets come from? How had life turned so complicated? Had it not been simple once? Or had that merely been the innocence of childhood?

Jules seated herself beside her, then reached out a hand and gently placed it upon Louisa's. Only then did Louisa realize that her own was balled into a fist. "You clearly know something," Jules whispered gently. "Please let me help you, you and Leonora."

Louisa looked up at her older sister. "I cannot tell you all that happened," she whispered, unable to stop herself as the need to share this with another rose stronger than ever before. "I promised Leo, but I feel I might go mad if I do not speak of this."

Jules nodded encouragingly, her hand gently squeezing Louisa's. "I give you my word I shall not speak of this to anyone."

Louisa inhaled a deep breath, her shoulders rising and falling with it. "A few weeks past, Leonora and I sneaked out of the house after dark." She felt Jules's hand tense upon her own; however, her sister remained silent. "It was my idea. I felt restless and trapped and..." She shook her head, unable to explain without going into details, without revealing her secret; and Louisa was not yet ready for that. "Leonora came upon me when I was about to leave the house. She refused to let me go on my own and insisted on accompanying me. I should've stopped her. I should've..." Guilt assailed Louisa anew, and she hung her head.

Again, Jules gently squeezed her hand. "Where did you go?" she asked on a breezy whisper, apprehension only too clear in her voice.

Swallowing hard, Louisa looked up and found her sister's face oddly blurred, realizing only now that tears had begun to form in her eyes. "To a masquerade."

Jules's jaw dropped and her eyes widened. "A masquerade?" she gasped, a look of horror coming to her face. "Why would you do that? Do you not know how dangerous—?"

"I wasn't thinking!" Louisa exclaimed on a sob, her fingers no doubt digging painfully into her sister's arm. "I didn't think. I should have. I failed Leonora in the worst way, and now I don't know what to do." Angrily, she wiped the tears from her face. "There's nothing I can do to help her. She won't even speak to me."

Jules frowned. "What happened that night?" she asked, the look upon her face though told Louisa that her sister did not truly wish to know.

Straightening, Louisa met her sister's gaze, reminding herself that she needed to try to be strong if she were to help Leonora eventually.

"I don't know," she admitted. "We were...We were separated, and I don't know what happened to her during that time."

For a moment, Jules closed her eyes. "Do you think we should speak to Mother and Father?"

Louisa shook her head, meeting her sister's eyes. "We cannot. Leo wouldn't want us to." She pulled back her shoulders and sat up straighter. "But I promise I shall speak to her again. I shall do what I must to find out what happened and to help her."

Jules nodded, still the look in her eyes was far from confident. "Perhaps she simply needs time."

Louisa wished with all her heart that it were that simple. "I do not think time will heal her." She heaved a deep sigh. "I don't know what will."

Rising to her feet, Jules brushed her hands down her skirts. "I shall try and speak to her as well," she told Louisa with a small smile, "without mentioning that you've spoken to me. I promise." Then she lifted her gaze and looked back down the path they had come. "I must go and see to Grandmother. Will you come with me?"

Louisa pushed to her feet, thinking that perhaps a little time with her family would set her mind more at ease and help her find the right words when next she would speak to Leonora. She was about to agree when her gaze fell on a lone man striding down the path toward them. Her eyes widened, and her heart all but paused in her chest. "What is *he* doing here?"

Jules turned her head and squinted her eyes against the sun. "Lord Barrington, is it?" she asked, then nodded as he moved closer, his face now quite recognizable. "I suppose he must've arrived with Anne and Tobias." She turned back to look at Louisa, and a slight frown came to her face.

"Was he invited?" Louisa demanded, her voice tense even to her own ears. "Or did he invite himself?"

"That I cannot say," her sister replied, concern once more darkening her eyes. "Are you all right? You look...flustered suddenly."

Forcing a smile onto her face, Louisa nodded. "I'm merely surprised. That is all."

After squeezing Louisa's hand gently, Jules then retreated down the path. Louisa watched her walk away, greet Phineas kindly and then head back up to the house.

The moment her sister disappeared from sight, Louisa felt an odd shiver dance down her back. She could not say if it was anticipation or dread. Indeed, a part of her rejoiced at seeing Phineas. He was still seeking her out, but why? How would he treat her now that he knew her secret?

It was a thought that deeply unsettled Louisa, perhaps even more so because somewhere deep down she had come to care for him. More than anything, she wanted him to think well of her, and the thought that he might not—that he likely did not—felt utterly crippling.

Her feet retreated a step and then another. Before Louisa knew that she had decided on anything at all, she felt herself whirl around, her feet carrying her away from him. She slipped into the grove, moved quickly past tall standing trees and vanished into the thicket. Only too well did she remember this place from her childhood days. Countless, precious memories drifted back into her mind as her eyes swept over old forts, now helplessly overgrown, as well as rotting ropes, dangling down from the tall branches above like snakes. Oh, how she had loved this place as a child!

Now, however, she did not pause, not for a second doubting that Phineas would pursue her. She needed to get away and find a place to collect her thoughts. But what was she to do now that he was here? She could not escape him forever. Perhaps it would be wise to simply stop and get it over with, hear him out and meet his disdain with a brave face. Surely, there could be no other reason he wished to speak with her.

When she reached the small clearing surrounded by bushes and brambles and tall trees where long ago they had played at knights and dragons, Louisa stopped. She lifted her head and squared her shoulders, then turned around, determined to face him.

Chapter Twenty-Five

A LONELY CLEARING

Nodding a greeting to the two youngest Whickerton sisters as well as their friend, Phineas strode onward not wishing to be detained by idle chitchat. Still, he frowned and once more looked over his shoulder before he rounded the next corner, wondering where he had seen the sisters' friend before. A second or two passed before sudden realization hit him, and he knew the sisters' friend to be none other but Miss Mortensen, the young woman who had developed a bit of a fancy for him.

Indeed, he had seen them in each other's company before. Still, he could not deny that he was displeased finding Miss Mortensen at Whickerton Grove for he found it rather tiresome to try and avoid her attentions.

By the time he rounded the hedge though, all thoughts of Miss Mortensen fled his mind. His eyes settled on Louisa with deadly precision even from such a distance. He could barely make out her face as she sat with her eldest sister on a lone stone bench under a grove of trees. A small pond glistened in the sun near them, and the beauty of the world around them struck him for it stood in such stark contrast to the misery he knew to be lingering upon the two sisters. Had Louisa confided in Juliet?

Impatiently, Phineas quickened his step, now almost desperate to be near her, to look into her eyes once more, to hear her speak even if she were to lash out at him, which he supposed she definitely would. It was who she was, and Phineas would not have her any other way. He enjoyed their quick-witted battles; to him they spoke of the passion they shared: one they might even feel for one another.

As expected, Louisa seemed more than a bit reluctant to meet him. The shock of her revelation still stood clear as day on her face. While Juliet rose and headed back up the gravel path, Louisa seemed to retreat, step after step carrying her farther away.

"Good day, Lord Barrington," Lady Juliet greeted him with a kind smile. "I assume Anne invited you to join us here."

Phineas smiled at her. "You assume right, Lady Juliet. I hope you do not mind."

"Of course not," she assured him; still, something inscrutable lingered in her gaze, and Phineas suspected that she knew more than she let on. "If you'll excuse me, I have to see to my grandmother." And with that, she walked away, soon disappearing around the large hedge.

Phineas' gaze swung back to Louisa, barely catching a glimpse of her as she disappeared into the grove. Indeed, she was running from him. In truth, it was most unlike her and told him just how deeply her secret and his knowledge of it rattled her. Did she honestly believe that he now thought less of her?

To him, it was an impossible thought.

Once again quickening his steps, Phineas pursued her, knowing that he could not allow her to slip away. They needed to speak to each other, to address what had happened for her sake as well as his own.

The warm sun fell away as thick branches overhead shielded him from its glowing heat. He stepped over roots and around brambles that grew onto a soft, once well-trodden path leading through the tall growing trees. He spotted the remnants of an old fort and smiled at the thought of Louisa and her siblings playing here as children.

On and on, he strode, hearing the faint rustling of another moving not too far ahead. Then the soft sounds ceased, and Phineas wondered if she had hidden herself or was awaiting him with open eyes.

Stepping around yet another wild growing bush, Phineas left the dense trees behind and moved out into a small clearing filled with sunshine. And there, in its center, stood Louisa.

Her chin was raised, and her shoulders drawn back. Her gaze looked defiant even from this distance, and Phineas knew that after all the guilt and grief she had suffered so recently, a spark of courage had once more ignited. It gave him hope.

"Why are you here?" Louisa demanded the second he stepped close enough. Her hands which were balled into fists opened when she saw him glance down at them. She forced them to hang loose at her sides, willing to appear unburdened and unconcerned. Still, only moments later, her arms once more rose as though of their own accord and crossed over her chest. A defiant and resistant gesture if ever there was one!

"I came to speak to you," Phineas told her honestly as he slowly moved closer, step-by-step. "I told you I would not walk away, did I not?" In truth, he could not quite recall what he had said. All he knew was that the thought of not seeking her out was one he could not bear.

"I have no desire to speak to you," she told him icily, and for a moment, Phineas felt reminded of the many moments she had hurled insults at his face. There was something deeply familiar and comforting about the situation. "I'd appreciate it if you left. After all, I do not recall inviting you nor do I believe did my family." Her tone was still cold, but Phineas got the distinct impression that the ice in her voice was forced. Did she not feel it? But merely used it to drive him away? If so, she could not have made a worse choice.

Phineas smiled at her. He could not help it since the way she reacted to him only reinforced his feeling of old familiarity. "Call me every vile name in the book if you must," he told her with a smirk, "but I shall not leave. I came to speak to you," holding her gaze, he moved closer until he stood no more than an arm's length away, "and speak to you I shall."

Looking up at him, Louisa barely blinked. Her jaw hardened, almost stone-like if it weren't for the one slight twitch in her cheek. "What is there to talk about?" A challenge rested in her eyes, and Phineas wondered what she was hoping he would do.

Alone with her, here in this clearing, far away from everybody else,

Phineas understood that this was his chance to finally receive some answers. "I understand very well that you never meant to reveal to me what you did the other day," he said gently, doing his best not to rile her for right here in this moment he did not want passion, but honesty instead. "Why you thought I already knew is beyond me. Still, it has not escaped my notice—how could it have?—that you've despised me for far longer." He sidled closer another step. "Why?"

Defiance still blazed in her eyes. Nevertheless, her chest rose and fell with rapid breaths and she was chewing rather nervously on her bottom lip.

"Louisa, please," Phineas all but begged.

Her brows drew down, and she stared at him, defiance replaced by incredulity. "You called me Louisa," she whispered almost breathlessly.

Phineas nodded. "I did."

A soft breeze traveled across the clearing, gathering up her golden curls as they gleamed in the sunshine and twirling them around her face. Her eyes still held his, suddenly so still and watchful as though she were looking upon him for the first time. "Two years ago," she told him softly, her voice distant and rather unexpectedly free of accusation, "I attended a ball. You were there as well." Her wide, green eyes lingered upon his face as though expecting him to remember from these few words alone. "You spoke to a friend. That friend—Lord Lockton, I believe, was his name—he expressed...a certain partiality toward me." She paused, looking up at him and waiting.

Oddly enough, Phineas felt a mild echo of what she had said. He could not quite recall the moment, but it sounded familiar, frighteningly familiar, for it chased goosebumps up and down his arms. What had he done?

Her gaze dropped from his for a split second before she once more looked up at him, the softness in her gaze weakening. "You dissuaded him from pursuing me," Louisa continued, accusation once more tainting her words. "You told him that I was nothing but a pretty head, that you believed I could not even read."

As though winter had suddenly descended, Phineas felt locked in a block of ice. Every inch of him grew cold when suddenly, the fog cleared, and he recalled the moment she had just described with perfect clarity. A groan slipped from his lips for he finally understood why she had hated him these past two years. How could he have been such a fool to utter these words? Of course, he had not meant them. But how could she have known?

Louisa's lips thinned, and her fingers dug deeper into her arms, a clear sign of how deeply he had hurt her. "You did not think me good enough for your friend," she told him, her voice stronger now, no longer distant and far away. Her chin rose, and steel returned to her green eyes. "You put him on his guard because you thought me inferior to him. He never addressed me. He never spoke to me or asked me to dance. You did that!" Her hands fell from her arms once more balling into fists as she glared at him. "And then you sought me out again and again, baiting me, riling me, insulting me. Was it fun to torment me? Were you hoping I would slip up, and my secret would be revealed to the whole world?" Gritting her teeth, she shook her head, disgust curling up her lip. "You have no idea how deeply I loathe you." The words left her lips in a snarl, and yet, a tear glistened in the corner of her eye.

Contemplating his own stupidity, Phineas rubbed his hands over his face, wishing he could undo what had led them down this path. For it lay at the root of everything, did it not?

"Let me explain." He reached for her, but she stepped back.

"Do not touch me!" she snapped, and the tear spilled over and snaked down her cheek. As though angry at it for revealing her vulnerability in a moment when she needed to be strong, Louisa brushed it away with an angry huff. "Leave for there's nothing left to say!" She whirled around and made to hurry away.

Ignoring all tender emotions toward her, Phineas grasped her by the arm and jerked her back, knowing that he needed to be more forceful to make her listen to him. "You're wrong!" he growled into her face, noting the way she struggled against his grip, no sign of fear in her eyes though. He liked that about her. "Listen, and I will release you," he told her, "but not a moment before."

Ignoring him, Louisa shoved against his chest. "What else is there to say? You chose your friend over me," a dark chuckle rumbled in her throat, "something that I—in all truthfulness—cannot even hold against you. Nevertheless—"

"He was not my friend, and you have no idea why I said what I said!"

She stilled then, and her eyes narrowed. "Why then?" she demanded, her hands upon his chest once more, curling into fists. "What reason could you possibly have had? What could possibly excuse what you said?"

"I said what I said because I wanted you for myself!" The words fell from his tongue without thought, shocking them both.

Silence lingered as they breathed in and out, their gazes locked. "What?" Her voice was barely audible as she stared up at him, her cheeks suddenly pale.

Phineas swallowed. Never in his life had he allowed himself to be so vulnerable. "I said what I said," he forced out through gritted teeth, knowing that if he did not speak now, he would not get another chance, "because I did not want him to pursue you. His interest in you caught me off guard, and I grasped for the first words that came into my mind to dissuade him." He closed his eyes and breathed out deeply. "I know it was foolish and disrespectful, but it was an impulse. Nothing more."

When he opened his eyes once more, her own still looked into his with the same disbelief as before. "Are you saying...you care for me?" If possible, the incredulity in her voice even grew.

Phineas snorted, "Is that truly so hard to believe?" he demanded, his hands tensing on her arms, holding her close. "Why else do you think I tease you so?" He jerked her closer, lowering his head to hers, his gaze insistent as it held hers. "Darn it, I've missed you these past few weeks!" His words were no more than a groan full of longing, and before he knew what he was doing, his head had swooped down, and his mouth closed over hers.

Chapter Twenty-Six

A MESS OF THINGS

All strength, all anger, all pain had fallen from Louisa the moment Phineas had uttered these words, *Because I wanted you for myself!*

Treacherously, her heart seemed to dance in her chest, alternately thudding rapidly, wildly even, and then stumbling along as though it did not know how to continue. She felt his own beat in a similar rhythm—if one could call it that—as her hands unclenched, her palms settling upon his chest.

His words warmed her, and yet, they chased goosebumps all over her skin. Her mind spun, and her heart did not know what to feel. And then he was kissing her, and the tumult in her heart grew a thousandfold.

Still, the confusion only lasted for a second or two before a rather unexpected and utterly overwhelming longing surged through her being, silencing everything else. It swept through her like a tidal wave, burying everything in its path: guilt, pain, anger. All she could feel was an almost desperate need for the man holding her in his arms.

Phineas, too, seemed desperate, his hands rough and possessive, giving voice to the very sentiment he had spoken of before. His kiss did not allow for objection, not that she truly intended to voice any, and he held her with such insistence as though she was already his.

And in that moment, Louisa wanted to be. It was a weak moment, far from thought, and she allowed herself to feel it all. This was what she had always wanted, was it not? A moment of freedom. A moment to forget. Was that not why she had gone to the masquerade that night? But she had not found freedom or peace that night, not even for a moment, not the way she felt it now.

In his arms.

Why was it always him? Why did he make her feel all these things? Why could it not be someone who treated her kindly and with respect? Why did it have to be Phineas?

Dimly, Louisa took note of all the voices once more piping up in the back of her head. His kiss had silenced them before, but now they were reawakening, reminding her that he was not good for her, that he would never be able to stop teasing her, that a mere look at him sufficed to make her once again feel inferior and insignificant and worthless. Because of what had happened—even if he had not meant what he had said—these emotions were now irrevocably tied to him.

Steeling herself, Louisa whispered a silent goodbye to the beautiful emotions currently coursing through her. Indeed, his kiss felt wonderful; unfortunately, it could not make up for all the harsh words he had said to her. They were imprinted on her mind, and she could not imagine a time without them tormenting her. For a second, she wondered what would have happened if she had not overheard his words, if he had at some point simply addressed her and they had slowly gotten to know one another. What would have happened then?

Breaking their kiss, Louisa struggled for some distance between them. She struggled against him as much as herself, for a part of her still urged her to yield. Indeed, there had been something beautiful in this moment, and she could not help but cherish it. Nevertheless, it was but one moment, and it could not change what was.

"Let go of me," she demanded, looking up at him, trying not to feel regret.

His arms remained around her as he slowly shook his head. "We need to talk."

"We did talk." Again, she shoved against his chest.

Again, he would not release her. "There is more to say, and you know it."

Louisa shook her head. "No matter what you say, it will not change anything. When I look at you, I will forever remember that moment." She inhaled a slow breath, dimly realizing that she was looking at him now, and although she did remember that moment, it was not the only thing on her mind.

Contrition came to his face. "I'm deeply sorry for wounding you thus," he whispered, his dark gaze upon hers, wide and open and honest. "I never for a second believed what I said."

Louisa swallowed, feeling the usual sense of shame and disappointment drift into her heart. "And yet, you were right. I cannot fault your observation."

"I observed nothing of the kind!" he all but snarled, a hint of anger in his voice as his hands tightened upon her. "I said those words because I knew they were the opposite of what he was looking for in a woman. That is it! That is the sole reason for saying what I said."

Indeed, the words did feel soothing, but they failed to correct the fault in her stars. "Still, it does not change that...your words were true." She inhaled a lungful of fresh air, wishing it could somehow wash away this lingering regret. "Are true."

His gaze became contemplative, and she could all but see his thoughts turning toward her failure of learning something any child learned with ease. Before he could speak, though, Louisa swung down her arms, her elbows connecting with his, finally breaking his hold on her.

Quickly, Louisa took a step back and then another, determined to keep away from him. She knew there was a weakness within her, a weakness where he was concerned. A part of her wanted him close. A part of her longed for him. A part of her wished that things could be different. And yet, she needed to face reality.

Standing a few feet away from her, Phineas watched her most intently. She could almost feel his gaze sweeping over her features. "Does anyone else know?"

Louisa's jaw tensed. "That is none of your concern."

He took a step closer. "Why not?"

"That is not for you to know," she snapped, backing away as he approached.

Stopping in his tracks, Phineas heaved a deep sigh. "Why are you hiding yourself? Why does this frighten you so?"

For a long moment, Louisa simply stared at him, unable to believe her ears. "How can you ask that? After teasing me endlessly? After making fun of me wherever you could?"

Anger tensed his features. "I did not know," he replied in a dark voice. His shoulders drew back, and once again he took a step toward her. "I already told you that. Why is it that you cannot believe me? I never knew, and the way I spoke to you over the past two years had nothing to do with it. It couldn't have. I spoke to you the way I did because of the way you spoke to me."

Louisa scoffed, "Can you truly blame me? Can you truly expect me to speak to you politely after hearing you utter these words?"

Huffing out a deep breath, Phineas raked a hand through his hair. "Of course, I understand *now*. But I did not then. I did not know that you had overheard what I'd said. How was I to know...any of this?" His gaze seemed to darken as it burned into hers. "Whenever I spoke to you, you lashed out at me. Whenever I entered the room, you left." Staring at her, he shook his head. "What was I to do? Yes, I understood well that you hated me, but I had no idea why." He surged forward, and his hand closed over her wrist, pulling her closer against him. "And you never said a word."

Glaring up at him, Louisa jerked on her arm, trying to free herself. "What did you expect me to say? The way you spoke to me never failed to make it absolutely clear how little you thought of me."

Frown lines encroached upon his forehead. "What?" he demanded, utter surprise in his voice.

"You insulted me," Louisa told him with a scoff. "Don't act as though—!"

"How?" His hand still wrapped around her wrist almost felt hot to the touch. The pulse in his neck beat wildly, an echo of the blazing emotions only too visible in his dark gaze.

Louisa lifted her chin, forcing herself not to bow her head, but hold it high and look at him. "You called me Lulu."

His eyes widened. "That was not meant as an insult."

Louisa laughed, "It certainly felt like one."

"But it wasn't," he gritted out.

"Well, I did not like it, and you knew that I didn't. It could not have escaped your notice that I loathe that name. Why then did you continue to call me that if not to insult me? To see me squirm? To revel in the knowledge that your words could wound me so deeply?"

His breath came fast now, his chest rising and falling rapidly. His hand upon her wrist tightened, and the other reached out to grasp her around the waist, pulling her into his arms. He tilted his head downward to keep his eyes fixed on hers, and she could feel his breath against her lips. "I called you Lulu," he whispered almost menacingly, "because it kept you near me."

Louisa felt her brows draw down as she looked up at him in confusion.

"Whenever I drew close, you would all but run from me. Yet, when I teased you, when I called you Lulu, you did not. You remained and answered my challenge with one of your own." The hand on her waist moved and settled on the small of her back, his gaze briefly dropping from hers and touching upon her lips. "Your eyes would blaze with anger and passion. I could see the pulse thundering in your neck and knew that at least on some level I affected you as much as you affected me."

His words overwhelmed Louisa, stealing the breath from her throat and sending a shiver of temptation down her back.

"I enjoyed our heated back-and-forth," Phineas whispered, a bit of a playful smile coming to his face as he finally released her wrist, his hand rising to grasp her chin. "Still, I always hoped that one day your anger would drift away and leave behind only passion."

Louisa did not know what to think or feel. The meaning behind his words was unmistakably clear, or was it not? But was he being honest? Was he speaking the truth? Could she dare trust him?

Her heart urged her down that path, longing tugging her toward him. Her mind, however, cautioned her, remembering the many moments she had been hurt. Despite his explanations, she ought not believe him, ought she? Phineas Hawke was a man who said what he needed to say to get what he wanted, was he not? His reputation was far from clean, and more than once she had heard wicked rumors about his amorous activities. Had those simply been lies? Exaggerations?

"The day of your cousin's wedding," he whispered, something soft and almost vulnerable now in his voice, "was your wager the only reason you kissed me? Did you truly feel nothing?"

Afraid to reveal more than was wise, Louisa dropped her gaze, searching frantically for something to say.

A soft chuckle reached her ears before she felt his fingers upon her chin tighten, urging her to look up at him. "I daresay," he spoke, his lips closer to hers than was safe, "your reaction is quite telling."

The need to protect herself, to keep him away washed over her, and Louisa lifted her hands, one to his chest and the other to grasp the hand that still held her chin. "Release me," she demanded, her voice, though, was far from steady.

Slowly, his gaze never leaving hers, Phineas shook his head. "Do you feel something when I hold you? When I kiss you?" The pad of his thumb brushed over her lower lip.

Louisa trembled, cursing her treacherous body for revealing all that she felt.

The right corner of his mouth curled upward. Then, to her surprise, he released her. His hands fell away, and he took a step backward.

Louisa instantly missed the feel of him, his warmth, the temptation he presented. She longed to feel his skin against her own, his strong arms wrapped around her. But that was not wise, was it?

"I never meant to hurt you," Phineas told her, regret darkening his features, "I'm deeply sorry for doing so unknowingly. Nevertheless, nothing that happened changes what I want. The only question is, what do you want?"

Breathing hard, Louisa stared at him. It did not change what he wanted? What was it that he wanted? Had he said so and she had missed it?

His dark eyes looked deeply into hers. "I want you," he told her softly. "Perhaps I did not court you as I should have." He chuckled, "I admit, I made a mess of things by saying what I said. I put us on a path that could only have led to disaster. But I'm grateful that we finally talked."

Louisa barely heard the words that followed. All she *had* heard were the first three, and those three sent her heart into an uproar the moment they were spoken, *I want you.*

"Do you not believe me?" he asked, no doubt noting the disbelief upon her face. "Or is it simply that I am mistaken? That your emotions were never fueled by passion, but by anger alone?" He exhaled a slow breath. "Do you want me to go? Do you not want me to be here? With you? At Whickerton Grove?"

Indeed, Louisa had loathed the very sight of him. She had hated him for seeking her out here, at her home a place where she felt safe. She had wanted him to leave and never come back.

But she did no longer, did she? At least a part of her knew that his departure would bring sadness and regret. She would miss him. It was a shocking revelation, and for a moment, Louisa was too overwhelmed to form a clear thought.

It was that moment, however, that her heart seized its chance.

Without any thought at all, Louisa found herself stepping forward, closing the distance between them. His eyes flickered over hers as she reached up her hands to cup his face. Her toes pushed her closer, and she stretched up to capture his mouth with her own.

A low growl rumbled in his throat, and his hands seized her immediately, yanking her against him as he dove into their kiss.

Louisa felt him everywhere, his hands, his lips, his body. They were fused to one another, their heat mingling. She had felt echoes of this before when he had kissed her in the alcove as well as only moments ago. It felt familiar, and yet, still utterly intoxicating. In that instant, Louisa doubted she would ever be able to pull away, to break the connection that had so unexpectedly formed between them.

Phineas, too, appeared almost possessed. Gone was the softness and thoughtfulness, replaced by an almost desperate need.

I want you.

Indeed, his words seemed to be true, each touch, each kiss proving them right. He did want her, and truth be told, she wanted him as well. It was a beautiful thought, but it was quickly crowded by others. Even if he wanted her now, would he still want her tomorrow? Did he simply desire her? Or was it a deeper feeling he had for her?

As her rational mind once more took over, Louisa broke the kiss and stepped away, feeling his reluctance to let her go in the way he tried to hold onto her. "I need to think," she panted, seeing the desire in his eyes, an echo of what coursed through her own veins. She retreated another step, needing a bit of distance to clear her head. "I don't know if... I don't know how..." She shook her head. "I need to think."

Inhaling a deep breath, Phineas nodded. "Do so," he told her, a smirk coming to his face, "but don't for a second believe that you will be able to pretend with me a moment longer." In two long strides, he closed the distance between them, his head lowering to look down into her eyes. "Now that I've felt your passion, you won't ever be able to deny it again."

A small smile teased Louisa's lips. "You are incorrigible. I don't know why I bother."

Phineas grinned at her. "Then think on it," he urged her, a wicked gleam coming to his dark eyes. "Perhaps you'll discover the reason."

"Perhaps I will," Louisa replied, taken aback by this odd energy humming in the air around them. It no longer felt as it did before. Somehow it had changed.

"Come and find me once you do."

Granting him one last teasing smile, Louisa turned around and strode away. Her legs felt heavy and her feet moved with great reluctance. Indeed, she would have much rather liked to walk in the other direction, toward him instead of away from him. But she did need to think.

A lot had happened, and her mind was utterly confused. Who was Phineas Hawke? And how did she truly feel about him?

Two questions not easily answered.

Chapter Twenty-Seven

VISITORS

Over the next few days, Louisa did not dare venture into Phineas' presence alone. The mere sight of him alone made her feel dizzy and brought heat to her cheeks. She felt foolish, like a young girl, when she had not even felt like this when she had been one.

Cheerful voices echoed through the house as everyone ventured downstairs for breakfast. Anne and Tobias fit into their family perfectly. In truth, Anne had always been like another sister, and she and Tobias suddenly felt at home at Whickerton Grove.

Sitting together, they laughed and chatted across the table, food being passed around and comments exchanged about everything and nothing. No one held back. Everyone spoke their mind. It was as it had always been in their family.

Grandma Edie chuckled, "I admit I wagered a good deal of money on whether or not you two would ever tie the knot."

Tobias's jaw dropped, and he turned to look at his new wife. "Did you now?" Then his gaze rose to meet Grandma Edie's once again. "Did you win or lose?"

Across the table, Chris, Harriet and their friend Sarah giggled, exchanging amused looks and whispered words.

Again, their grandmother chuckled, "Now wouldn't you like to know that."

Everybody laughed. Even Leonora cracked a small smile, her eyes still downcast and her face just the smallest bit paler than usual. While she often took meals with everybody, mostly she seemed absent-minded, her replies to questions halfhearted at best.

Of course, her family had noticed. Their mother and father often exchanged worried glances, something meaningful passing between them. Louisa knew that their mother had tried her best to speak to Leonora, but it seemed for a reason Louisa could not understand her sister was determined to remain silent on the matter.

On what had happened the night of the masquerade.

Not even Grandma Edie was able to reach her. Though, she too had tried. Everyone had as it seemed, but Leonora remained stubborn.

Troy set down his teacup, nodded to their parents in quiet agree-ment and then cleared his throat to catch everyone else's attention. His pale blue eyes quickly swept over his family, lingering here and there, before he spoke. "I simply wish to take this opportunity to inform you all that I have invited my old friend Christopher Hurst, the Earl of Lockhart, as well as his sister Lady Hayward to stay with us for a fortnight. I believe, they shall be arriving sometime this afternoon." With that, her brother seemed finished, not an additional word leaving his lips as he pushed to his feet and then left the room.

"Lockhart?" Grandma Edie frowned. "Was that his childhood friend? The one who spent the last few years traveling the continent?"

Louisa nodded, but before she could say anything, her father spoke. "Indeed, he is. I believe he only recently returned to England."

A warm smile came to her mother's face, and she exchanged yet another one of those meaningful glances with her husband. "It surely will be good for them to see each other again. They were so close when they were young. I do believe Troy missed him dearly when he left." A slight frown came to her face. "His departure was rather abrupt, was it not? Do you recall why he left?"

Harriet laughed, "I assume to travel the continent." Chris and Sarah joined in.

Louisa rolled her eyes at her sister but could not quite keep a chuckle from leaving her lips. When she turned back, her gaze briefly met Phineas', and she felt her cheeks heat once more. Was this a sickness? For it certainly felt like one. Whenever he would look at her, Louisa could all but feel it like a touch. Did he feel the same? Or was it only her?

After breakfast, Louisa all but fled from the parlor. She knew she was acting cowardly, but she still had more thinking to do. Nothing seemed to be simple as her thoughts drifted everywhere and nowhere. Nothing made sense, and she could not bring herself to answer even the simplest questions. What was even more annoying was the fact that she could not stop thinking about Phineas, about their kiss, about what he had said to her. It made her feel wonderful, special and filled her heart with deep longing.

Oddly enough, Phineas seemed to understand that she needed time and space. He was never far away, their eyes meeting often, always sending a thrill of awareness through her. Still, he never approached her, but merely smiled in that infuriatingly tempting way of his as though he knew her thoughts better than she did.

Walking through the gardens one afternoon, Louisa heard hasty footsteps trying to catch up with her. She stopped in the middle of the path and turned around. Shockingly, her heart sank when she found Lady Hayward and not Phineas hastening after her.

"Is there anything I can help you with?" she asked the young woman, who had been a close friend long ago before life had pulled them apart.

Lady Hayward had been born the same year as Leonora. Strangely enough, her parents had named her Leonora as well. When they had met and realized they shared the same name, the two Leonoras had found a bit of an unusual solution.

They had agreed to share it.

In fact, they had cut it in half, each keeping one and relinquishing the other. Thus, Louisa's sister had been called Leo, henceforth, while Lady Hayward—before she had married and become Lady Hayward— had from then on been known as Nora.

A smile came to Louisa's face as she remembered their joyful childhood days. Not only Troy and Christopher, the new Earl of

Lockhart, had been close friends, but Nora, too, had been one of them.

A rushed breath escaped Nora's lungs, and she pressed a hand to her chest, breathing in deeply. "I admit I wish to speak to you." She glanced over her shoulder at her brother as well as Louisa's siblings nearby. "In private."

Louisa frowned, and her gaze swept over Chris, Harriet and Sarah —once again playing with Sir Lancelot—before it drifted to where Phineas, Tobias and Anne were walking among the rosebushes. "Is something wrong?"

For a moment, Nora simply looked at her, her dark brown eyes almost the same color as her mahogany hair. She looked lovely, her cheeks flushed from her short sprint, and her eyes aglow with something Louisa could not quite grasp. "In fact," she began rather quietly, casting another glance back at the house, "I do believe it is." She pulled Louisa's arm through hers, and they proceeded further down the path. "I believe something is very wrong with Leo, and I came to talk to you about her. Do you know what has happened? She's not acting like herself. I admit I have not seen her in a long, long time, but I cannot shake the feeling, that she is suffering." Nora's warm, dark eyes looked at Louisa, a friend's compassion clearly visible in them. "Is there anything I can do?"

Louisa swallowed, torn about what to do or say. "I do believe you're right," she finally said, feeling strangely at ease in Nora's presence despite her long absence. "Something happened that I am afraid I cannot speak about. I am not certain what it is. I've tried to speak to Leo, but she is shutting me out. She refuses to say anything." A deep sigh drifted from her lips. "I don't know what to do."

Nora stilled, her gaze strangely distant. "Do you think she would speak to me?" she asked, and her dark brown eyes once more returned to Louisa. "Sometimes, it might be easier to speak to someone outside of the family. I might be a friend, but we have not seen each other in years." She chuckled slightly, but it had a sad undertone to it. "Perhaps I would qualify as a stranger."

Doubting that Nora would have any more luck than Louisa had had herself, she smiled gently at the young woman who had once been an incredibly good friend. "You're welcome to try," she told her. "I urge you not to be disappointed though when you find that she will reply with nothing but excuses."

Nora nodded. Again, her gaze became distant before it suddenly cleared, lingered on something far beyond Louisa's shoulder and then dropped abruptly.

Louisa frowned at Nora's strange behavior. Still, something about the way she had just dropped her gaze echoed within Louisa's heart as though she ought to know what it meant. "Are you all right? You, too, look sad." She squeezed Nora's hand warmly. "How is your husband?"

Nora had been married quickly after her introduction into society. Four years had passed since, and the radiant, exuberant young woman Nora had once been seemed to have disappeared. She was still kind and caring, but she no longer smiled the way she used to. It was one of the first things Louisa had noticed upon Nora's arrival at Whickerton Grove a few days past.

Nora's features tightened, all emotion leaving her eyes. "He is well," she said in a hard voice. "At least as well as can be expected." She swallowed, then blinked, an apologetic smile coming to her face. "There is no need to speak of him. I'd much rather hear about you."

Louisa frowned, her heart tensing at the tortured look in Nora's eyes. "Is he not treating you kindly?" she asked, knowing that she was likely overstepping a line; but she simply could not help herself.

To her dismay, Nora did not object or try to explain away any shortcomings her husband might have. She simply drew to a halt, sadness clinging to her features.

"You're not happy, are you?"

Nora's lips thinned, and tears began to glisten in her eyes. "There is no point in lamenting what is, is there?"

Louisa tightened her grasp on Nora's hands, hoping to give at least a little comfort. "There might be comfort in speaking to a friend."

Nora sighed. "Perhaps you are right," she whispered. "Perhaps I have hidden away in the country for too long." Once again, she looked up at the house. "I believe Leo is doing the same. I know how much it crushes the soul to retreat from the world, to see no other way to deal with something that you cannot forget." Her gaze returned to Louisa. "You must find a way to help her...before she loses herself."

Gritting her teeth, Louisa nodded, cursing that helpless feeling deep in her chest that told her no matter what she did, nothing would make a difference. "And you?"

Nora cast her a sad smile. "I made one mistake, and I regret it to this day."

"What mistake?"

Nora sighed, then she turned and looked over her shoulder to where her brother and Troy were just then walking down the path toward the pond. Again, Nora sighed before she turned back to look at Louisa. "I married the wrong man." The words left her lips in a rush, and Louisa knew without a doubt that right here and right now it had been the first time for Nora to speak these words out loud. "I barely knew him, and I allowed myself to be fooled by smiles and charms." Again, she glanced over her shoulder to where Troy and her brother were striding past. "I wish I had made a different choice."

Louisa's gaze drifted from her old friend to her brother, who rather coincidentally glanced over at her in that very moment. Troy, however, was not seeing her. Louisa was certain of it. Instead, his gaze seemed to linger...upon Nora.

And from one second to the next, everything suddenly made sense. Only too well did Louisa remember the way her brother had drunk himself into a stupor the day of Nora's wedding. He had disappeared afterward for weeks as though the earth had swallowed him whole. Her parents had been frantic. They had looked for him all over Town. And then one day, he had turned up again, his composure back intact, but his eyes strangely dull.

Again, she recalled the conversation she had overheard between Troy and Lockhart the night of the masquerade. *I saw the way you looked at her*, Lockhart had said. *I know how you feel, but there is no point.* Had he spoken of his sister? Did he know how they felt about one another? For clearly, the feeling was mutual.

Louisa gently brushed her hand over Nora's arm, waiting patiently until the young woman turned to look at her again. "I had no idea," she whispered, casting Nora an encouraging smile.

To her surprise, Nora blushed, then dropped her gaze, her fingers fidgeting with the hem of her sleeve. "Neither did I," she whispered back, her eyes rising to look into Louisa's, "not until it was too late."

"Is there anything I can do?"

Sadly, Nora shook her head. "It is too late for me, but I pray it is not too late for Leo. Please, tell me if there's anything I can do."

Louisa nodded, wondering if there was anything any one of them could do. How did one recover from what had no doubt been a vicious attack? Louisa could only imagine what had happened; yet, the way Leonora had staggered toward them, her face pale and her dress torn had painted a disturbingly vivid picture.

Heaving a deep sigh, Louisa glanced at Phineas, wondering about the sadness that seemed to linger everywhere these days. Had something changed? Or had life always been thus? Perhaps as children, they had simply not been aware of it, of the harshness, the unfairness and the many disappointments suffered throughout a life lived.

Was there any way to turn it around?

Chapter Twenty-Eight

ANOTHER WAGER

Staying away from Louisa was torture!

Nevertheless, Phineas knew that she needed to be the one to seek him out. It had to be her decision, not his. He was done urging her, pressuring her, persuading her. If she wanted him—and by heavens, he hoped she did!—she needed to be the one to take a step toward him.

Days passed, and Phineas found that he lived from glance to glance and smile to smile. Whenever her deep green eyes looked into his—even if only for a moment—he felt it all the way to his bones. He felt unsettled, and yet, strangely at peace. Excitement coursed through him, and he longed to rush to her side, pull her into his arms and kiss her yet again. Oh, the way she had kissed him! Not a night passed that he did not relive these few precious moments they had shared, hoping for more to come.

Still, he needed to be patient.

"Are you all right? You seem distracted," Tobias remarked, as he eyed him carefully.

Phineas shook his head to clear it, trying to remember what they had been speaking about. "I'm perfectly fine, merely bored with this conversation."

Tobias chuckled, "Is that so? And here I thought you were still obsessed with my new cousin."

Phineas rolled his eyes at his brother, aware that he was failing miserably at maintaining any sort of composure. "You are enjoying this, aren't you?"

Tobias laughed, slapping him on the shoulder. "Do you even have to ask?"

Phineas refrained from answering, reminding himself that Tobias had every right to tease him, to mock him even. After all, he, Phineas, had been most entertained by his brother's attempts to woo Anne, and what had probably been worse, he had not even tried to hide his amusement.

Right now, right here, Tobias was getting even.

"Have you ever considered talking to her?" his brother asked mockingly. "Without insulting the poor girl, of course?"

"I did," Phineas replied, his jaw clenching with each word to leave his brother's mouth, "and I have."

Tobias stopped laughing, a bit of an incredulous look coming to his eyes as he stared at him. "You have?" His head moved, and he turned to look down the slope to where Louisa stood with Lady Hayward, deep in conversation. "And?"

"And what?"

Now, it was Tobias's turn to roll his eyes. "And what did she say? Does she care for you? Not that you could blame her if she didn't," he remarked with a bit of a chiding laugh. "Not after the way you have been treating her."

Phineas felt his insides burn. Indeed, he had not insulted her on purpose. Of course not! Yet, it seemed that he had, that she had understood every word from his lips as a way of trying to humiliate her. How had things gone so very wrong?

Rather gently, Phineas felt his brother's hand settle upon his shoulder. When he turned to look at him, the expression on Tobias' face was no longer one of mocking; in fact, a warm smile rested upon his face. "She cares for you," he said then, these words the last Phineas had expected to hear in that moment.

His shoulders tensed, and his heart seemed to pause in his chest. "How would you know?"

"I don't," Tobias admitted. "However, Anne believes it to be so."

Phineas dared meet his brother's eyes. "She does?"

Tobias nodded. "She does."

Phineas inhaled a slow breath, savoring the intoxicating thrill that coursed through him at the thought of Louisa, of her affections belonging to him and him alone. It was a thought that lingered and kept lingering until darkness fell that night, until the sun rose once again the next morning.

It was then, after breakfast, when everyone was leaving, eager to be off and seek out some new activity or entertainment that Louisa stepped past him in the hall. Her eyes rose to settle upon his, and she paused in her step for no more than a moment. Her lips parted, and she leaned closer before whispering, "Meet me in the clearing."

Then she rushed away.

For a moment, Phineas simply stood and stared after her, a part of him utterly convinced that he had merely imagined her. But then excitement began to bubble under his skin. His heart began to beat faster with anticipation, and his feet moved forward without conscious thought. He rushed out of the house and into the gardens, down the soft slope toward the grove. He stepped in-between the trees, here and there catching a glimpse of her emerald gown as she slipped ahead of him through the trees toward the clearing.

And then he stepped out into the sunshine, his eyes falling on her as she stood there the way she had the last time he had caught up to her.

Her golden tresses gleamed in the soft morning light. Her cheeks were rosy and warm, and her eyes shone brightly and full of eagerness. Still, the way she wrung her hands, her shoulders just a little bit stiff told him that this was far from easy for her.

"Admit it," he dared her with a daring grin, his feet slowly carrying him closer, "you like me."

Instantly, the tension left her face, and she laughed out loud, shaking her head at him in a most adorable way. "Never."

Coming to stand in front of her, Phineas felt all but entranced as those deep green eyes looked into his. Something wicked and teasing, something utterly bewitching twinkled in them, and he wondered in that moment if he would ever tire of simply looking at her. "At least, my kiss you like."

The warm rosy glow upon her cheeks seemed to deepen, but she held his gaze. "Perhaps," she conceded to his utter surprise, the corners of her mouth curling up into a temptingly sweet smile, one that was teasing and honest all at the same time.

Inevitably, it drew his attention down to her mouth, his gaze lingering until a soft chuckle drifted to his ears. "It seems you liked mine as well."

Meeting her eyes, Phineas wanted nothing more than to draw her into his arms and kiss her yet again. "You have no idea," he told her, his jaw clenched almost painfully against the impulse to feel her lips beneath his. He breathed in hard, reminding himself that passion was all well and good, but in the end, he wanted more.

He wanted her trust.

Her confidence.

Her heart.

Phineas could see that she too felt the temptation that seemed to swirl around them, drifting here and there on the soft morning breeze. And so, he cleared his throat, forcing his gaze away from her lips and asked, "Is there something you wish to speak to me about?"

Instantly, Louisa's gaze seemed to darken, clouded with something she would rather not dwell on. "I'm not certain," she admitted, doubt in her voice. "I thought a lot about what you told me last, about many other things, too." Her eyes lingered upon his face as she slowly shook her head as though seeing him for the first time, unable to align what she knew about him with the man before her. "Ever since..." The look in her eyes told him exactly which moment she was referring to. "I've seen you as my enemy, someone who threatened all I held dear. Every word from your mouth proved that for a reason I could not grasp you had made it your life's mission to make me feel...awful about myself, about who I was. Every time I looked at you, I felt reminded of all these emotions, and I hated you for it."

Hearing how he had made her feel, even unknowingly, unintentionally, made Phineas want to punch himself for having been such a fool, for having been so blind. Yes, she had always been angry with him and he had wondered about that, but here and there he had also seen a glimmer of pain in those deep green eyes, had he not? Yet, he had never wondered why it had been there. He ought to have! If he had, then perhaps they might have reached this point, right here, right now sooner.

"I heard what you said," Louisa continued, her gaze growing distant as she began to pace around him, the hem of her dress absorbing the early morning dew. "And I realize now that I judged you too fast, too harshly." She turned to look at him. "Still, when I look at you, I cannot help but feel as I did before."

Phineas nodded. "I understand, and I do not expect you to place your trust in me this instant. Things have gone horribly wrong for a long time, and it will take time again to right them." He stepped toward her, wishing to reach for her hands, but he did not, fearing that it might distract them from what they needed to speak about. "All I ask is that you give me a chance to prove to you that I have no ill intentions. I never did."

Her eyes searched his. "It feels strange to speak to you in this manner," Louisa said, a slight frown coming to her forehead. "We only ever argued and snapped at one another. To speak to you now in this way, it feels surreal, does it not?"

Phineas smiled at her. "You're not wrong. I admit I feel out of my element. When I see you, it is like an instinct to tease you, to look for your eyes blazing with fire, to see the pulse in your neck quickening with every word I say." He stepped closer, and this time his hand did reach out, the tips of his fingers slowly trailing down her arm. "Though, I always hoped for a different outcome: for you not to rush off in anger, for you to realize that what you felt was more than you thought."

The look upon her face whispered of surprise, disbelief. "You never said a word."

"Neither did you." His fingers trailed down her hand, feeling the warmth of her skin against his own. He watched her glance down before meeting his eyes once again, her chest rising and falling with a slow, slightly unsteady breath. "You thought I knew, and yet, when I asked, you never said a word. Why?"

Her teeth sank into her lower lip, and for the longest moment she remained silent. "I admit, I wondered if you truly knew or if you only suspected, if you had observed something, a moment that had made you suspicious. I wasn't certain, and so I never dared speak of it."

Phineas laced his fingers with hers. "Will you speak of it now?"

At his words, she tensed, her fingers curling around his. It sent a stab of regret through Phineas' heart, and yet, he knew that her reaction did not mean that she did not believe him, but instead that years had taught her to fear revealing her secret to another.

"I promise I shall not mock you or tease or laugh at you in any way," Phineas vowed, his gaze holding hers, willing her to see that he was sincere. "Neither shall I ever breathe a word of this to anyone without your permission. Trust me."

Again, her chest rose and fell with a slow breath before she nodded, her lips parting as she searched for words. "I don't know why," she began, something resembling relief slowly drifting onto her features. "I don't know how it happened, why I did not learn. My sisters and I, we had the same tutor, the same lessons, but they learned, and I didn't." Her eyes closed, and Phineas knew that her mind was drifting back to a time long ago. "At first, I did not notice. I was able to read passages from stories we had discussed. My eyes flew over the page, and my mouth formed the words. It was only later, at some point, when I suddenly realized that I wasn't truly reading, but remembering. I was always so quick to remember everything, poems, stories, almost word for word." Her eyes opened, once more settling upon his. "At first, I did not notice, and once I did, it was too late."

The embarrassment that stood upon her face broke Phineas' heart. He could only imagine how she had felt in these moments, too frightened, too humiliated to confide in anyone, even her sisters. "And no one else ever noticed?"

Tears blurred her eyes as she shrugged. "Of course, I cannot be certain. Perhaps every now and then, one of my sisters suspected something or thought my response was odd. However, they never said a word, never asked me."

Reaching out, Phineas gently cupped her cheek, the pad of his thumb brushing away the tear that had spilled over. "How?" It was only a single word, and yet, Louisa understood exactly what he was asking.

A dark chuckle left her lips, and she moved closer as though seeking comfort. "I'm not certain. Once I knew, I tried my best to hide it, to avoid situations that might reveal what I could not do. I've always been good at memorizing, and so I worked hard to remember everything anyone ever read to me. I would repeat the lines in my head, again and again, until I would hear them echoing in my dreams. I offered to read when I knew exactly what something was to say so that it would not seem so odd when I declined other times." She swallowed, and her head lowered. "Letters and notes always posed a problem, but I quickly thought up a number of excuses for any situation that might arise. I feigned disinterest, fatigue, preoccupation, anything I could think of. So far, it's always worked. Even if they frown at me, I don't think they ever questioned my ability to read."

Phineas slipped an arm around her shoulders and pulled her against his chest, breathing in deeply as she rested her head against his shoulder. "I always knew you to be quick-witted," he whispered against the top of her head, pride swinging in his voice. "Your mind always worked so fast, capable of anticipating twists and turns. I never for a second suspected anything." Once more, he grasped her chin, tilting her head up so she would look at him. "You are one of the most intelligent women I have ever met."

Looking up at him, Louisa blinked, hesitation in her eyes before it passed, and she tried to lower her head.

Phineas understood instantly. It was what he had feared. "You don't believe me, do you?"

Gritting her jaw, she pulled away, her hands all but pushing her away from him. "How can I? I know it to be a lie." She whirled around and stomped a few steps away from him, anger and frustration in the way she moved, whether directed at herself or him remained unclear.

Perhaps both.

Phineas forced himself to remain still, to not charge after her. Of course, that was not an easy feat for he had never been a patient man. "It is not a lie," he insisted, his gaze following her as she began to pace, her eyes now and then looking up, flashing in his direction. "Reading is a skill one can learn, but it does not speak to your intelligence. Believe me, there are countless shockingly dumb people who know how to read."

Louisa stopped in her tracks and looked up at him, the urge to laugh sparking in her eyes. She did not though. She merely looked at him, and Phineas understood that she wanted to believe him, but did not yet dare.

Her shoulders seemed to slump. "Then why did I not learn when my sisters did? They could do it, but I could not. Is that not proof enough?"

Her eyes held his, and Phineas got the distinct impression that she was waiting for him to contradict her.

For years now, she had locked herself away, keeping her secret from everyone around her. Never had she spoken about it to anyone. Never had anyone been able to counsel her. To tell her that she was wrong to assume she was lacking in intelligence simply because she could not read. "It is no proof at all," Phineas told her vehemently, his eyes never leaving hers as he strode toward her. "I don't know what prevented you from learning when you were a child, but whatever it was, it does not mean you cannot learn now. Perhaps you were simply distracted, your attention elsewhere. As you said yourself, you have an infallible memory; perhaps you were simply honing a different skill."

Listening, everything about her had stilled. Her eyes were wide, and yet, unblinking. The pulse in her neck jerked wildly, but it seemed as though she was holding her breath. "Learn now?"

Phineas nodded, reaching out his hands and grasping hers. They had been warm before, but now they felt chilled. "Of course. You cannot tell me that you do not wish to learn! I can see it in your eyes. You're not one to run from a challenge nor are you one to hide when you can stand and fight. You're a proud woman, and you know you want this."

A soft smile came to her lips, and he felt her hands tighten on his. "I have tried before," she whispered. "I could not do it though."

"Then I shall help you," Phineas stated, the corners of his mouth once more twisting upward into a playful smile. Of course, he did not mean to ridicule her, but it was simply who he was, who they were together. He hoped they would not lose that.

"You will help me?"

"Of course. I'd be delighted to."

Her gaze narrowed. Still, the soft smile remained where it was. "And you will not tease me?"

Phineas chuckled, "That, I cannot promise for I admit I do enjoy it. What I can promise you though is that I shall never ridicule or humiliate you or make you feel...as though you are inferior to anyone, least of all myself." Was that not what she had said? Had she not accused him of not thinking her worthy of his friend? "Can you believe that?"

For a long moment, she held his gaze. "I do want to, but a part of me cannot help but feel cautious. I suppose it's force of habit."

Phineas nodded. "Then we shall work on a new habit," he told her, rubbing his chin as he thought about how best to proceed.

Suddenly, she laughed, "You look like Leonora when you do that, so thoughtful and concentrating, the way she does when she starts working on a new project." The moment the last word left her lips, her eyes dimmed, and her smile vanished.

"Have you spoken to her?" Phineas asked, seeing with one glance that the night of the masquerade still stood between the two sisters.

"I have tried," Louisa replied, softly shaking her head. "She does not wish to speak to me though. She barely answers me, turning away the moment she sees me heading toward her."

Phineas sighed, "Perhaps...perhaps you should share your secret with her before asking her to share her own." Her gaze snapped up to meet his, and he could see naked fear in those deep, green pools. "She's your sister," Phineas told her determinedly, his hands tightening on hers lest she try to pull away. "She will not laugh at you or think less of you. If she were the one to tell you she could not read, what would you do? Yes, you would be surprised, but you would not laugh at her. You would offer your help. You would protect her and guard her and stand by her side, would you not?"

A muscle in her jaw twitched, but she held his gaze, then nodded slowly. "I would."

"As would she," Phineas told her. "I'm certain of it." A new thought sneaked into his head in that moment, and he could not help the smile that spread over his face.

"What is it?" Louisa asked, suspicion darkening her eyes.

Phineas chuckled. "Let us make a wager," he suggested, pulling her closer, his hand slipping from hers to wrap around her body. "If Leonora laughs at you, you get to punch me in the face."

Laughter burst from Louisa's lips, and her eyes widened. "Are you serious?"

"Deadly serious."

"Indeed, you must be." Her gaze became contemplative as she looked up at him. Then a smile teased her lips. "And if she does not?"

Phineas' hands moved to the small of her back, pulling her closer against him as he lowered his head to hers. "If she does not," he whispered, feeling the breath shudder from her lips, "I get to kiss you."

Her hands snaked up to reach around his neck as a slow smile spread over her face. "Sounds as though I cannot lose."

Phineas chuckled, "I'm glad you see it like that. Awfully glad indeed."

Chapter Twenty-Nine
FROM ONE SISTER TO ANOTHER

L ater that same day, Louisa went down into the gardens after spotting Leonora walk down the small gravel path toward the fountain. As expected, the moment Leonora saw her approach, she turned around, her steps quickening, and hurried around back, trying to slip away.

This time, however, Louisa was determined not to let her run off. She, too, quickened her steps, her hands grasping her skirts and lifting them a fraction so she could move faster. "You might as well stop," Louisa called, noting the way her sister flinched as her voice echoed across the lawns. "I'm sick and tired of you running away from me, and I will not let you escape any longer."

To Louisa's surprise, her sister did slow her steps. She all but hung her head as her feet proceeded onward, her gaze still fixed on something on the distant horizon. Step-by-step, she walked, on and on.

"Come with me," Louisa said as she linked her arm with Leonora's, pulling her along and toward the grove. They wove their way through the trees until they came to the old fort that had brightened many of their childhood days. "Up," Louisa instructed, pointing to the dangling rope ladder, half overgrown with vines.

Leonora turned to her, a deep frown upon her face. "Are you mad?

These ropes have been out here for years. They will not support our weight. They will rip, and we will fall and hurt ourselves."

"Then I'll go first," Louisa stated, her hands finding the rope ladder quickly. Without another thought, she began climbing up it, knowing she could not stop now. "Come."

To her utter relief, the ropes held.

As she pulled herself up onto the wooden platform, Louisa looked down, seeing her sister's doubtful face. "You've done this hundreds of times. Do not pretend you are genuinely worried. Come!"

Leonora heaved a deep sigh, then she stepped forward, her hands grasping the old ladder. Step-by-step, cautiously, she moved upward until she had almost reached the top. Then she grasped the hand Louisa offered her and allowed her sister to pull her up to sit beside her.

Together, they sat with their legs dangling over the edge, their eyes sweeping over the forest around them, bright sunlight filtering through the canopy overhead. "We need to talk," Louisa said, feeling her sister stiffen beside her.

"I will not say anything," Leonora replied, a darkness in her voice Louisa had never heard before. It worried her, frightened her, and a part of her wished she could simply turn and leave, ignoring that she had ever heard it.

But she did not. "Will you at least listen?"

Leonora glanced in her direction, a hint of surprise in her blue eyes. Then she nodded.

Louisa swallowed, then inhaled a deep breath, finding it harder than she had expected it to be to find the right words. To speak them. Out loud. Everything within her screamed out against it, and she had to fight down a wave of panic before the first words finally tumbled from her lips. "I cannot read."

Three little words, and Louisa's world turned upside down. Three little words that changed everything. Three little words, the hardest she had ever spoken.

Leonora turned to look at her, a frown slowly drawing down her brows. "What do you mean?"

Louisa forced herself to hold her sister's gaze. "I mean, I cannot read. I don't know how."

Leonora simply looked at her, her blue eyes holding confusion before they slowly widened as realization dawned. She looked aghast, shocked, completely taken aback. It was clear as day that she had never suspected this. Not for a second. "That cannot be true," she mumbled, her gaze alternately seeking Louisa's and then straying off into the distance. "I've seen you read. I've heard you read."

Louisa shook her head. "No, you haven't. You've heard me recite from memory, but not read."

Silence fell over the two sisters as they sat in their childhood fort, looking at one another with new eyes. The wind whistled overhead, and birds chirped nearby. A blackbird settled on a branch before flying off once again. And all the while, the two sisters looked at one another.

"How is this possible?" Leonora finally asked, her hands settling on Louisa's, holding them tightly within her own. Her eyes held tears, but they shone with warmth and compassion and love. As much as Louisa had feared to see disappointment and shame, she saw none of it now.

Her heart grew lighter, and holding onto her sister's hands, she told her everything. The words all but tumbled from her lips now, one tripping over the other in their rush to finally be released out into the world, to be heard by someone who would not judge her. On and on, she spoke, watching her sister's face first in confusion and then soften in compassion.

"Why did you never tell me?" Leonora asked as tears streamed down her face. "I would've helped you."

Louisa wiped her own eyes, her voice choked with emotion. "I was ashamed," she admitted, feeling a heavy weight lifted off her heart. "I was afraid of what you would think of me. I felt like a fool, especially compared to your intelligence."

Leonora scoffed. "Don't be foolish!" she chided. "Intelligence represents our ability to learn and grow, to understand the world, to ask questions and seek answers, to find connections between things that seem separate, but it is not represented by one single skill. Being able to read does not make you intelligent, and neither does not being able to read mean that you are not intelligent."

Louisa chuckled.

"What is it?" Leonora asked, her wide blue eyes searching Louisa's face.

"That is precisely what Phineas said."

Leonora's eyes widened. "Phineas? You mean Lord Barrington? Does he know? Did you tell him?" She frowned deeply. "I thought you hated him."

Again, Louisa chuckled, overwhelmed by all these many changing emotions. "So, did I," she admitted with a laugh. "However, it turns out that the reason why I hated him was nothing but a misunderstanding. A lot happened in the past few weeks that made me reconsider everything I thought I knew."

"Including how you feel about Lord Barrington?" A small smile teased her lips, the first in weeks. "I remember a ball we attended—perhaps two years ago. You were looking at him, and when I asked you, you acted with such dismissal that I felt certain you would come to care for him." Her eyes searched Louisa's face. "But then everything changed. You seemed to loathe the very sight of him. It didn't make sense to me, but I thought I had simply been mistaken."

Louisa shook her head. "No, you weren't mistaken. I think...I think I did care for him. Perhaps that was why it hurt me so much to hear what he said."

Leonora frowned, and Louisa then told her sister about the misunderstanding that had made them enemies for two years. "But he did not know," Louisa explained. "He said what he said because he wanted to dissuade his friend from pursuing me." Her heart skipped a beat at the thought, and a smile pushed onto her face.

Leonora squeezed her hand. "He seems to care for you very much."

Louisa stilled, looking into her sister's eyes. "I think so too, but sometimes I do not dare believe it."

Shaking her head, Leonora smiled. "I've never seen you so at odds, so vulnerable, so worried. Always have you been so brave and strong, facing whatever came your way head-on."

Louisa swallowed. "Except this. This secret has been with me for so long that the thought of letting it go feels utterly impossible."

"I'm glad you finally told me," Leonora assured her, her hand reaching out and brushing a curl back behind Louisa's ear that the wind had tugged loose. "It is not good for the soul to keep such things to oneself."

Louisa exhaled a deep breath. "No, it is not." She held her sister's gaze, waiting.

A long moment passed between them before Leonora dropped her gaze, her eyes closing. "I try not to think of it," she finally whispered, anguish in her voice. "Still, I cannot keep it out of my head. It is there when I close my eyes at night, and it is there when I open them in the morning."

Now, it was Louisa who gently took her sister's hands into her own, holding them tightly, promising that she would be here, that she would always be here by her side. "What happened that night?"

A sob tore from Leonora's lips, and she pressed them into a tight line to contain the ones that followed. Her hands squeezed Louisa's to an almost painful degree as she breathed in and out, trying to calm herself. "I watched you," she finally whispered, her eyes still closed. "I watched you dance and laugh, and although I was still worried, I felt myself beginning to relax. I looked around at all the masks and wondered at all the people beneath them." She exhaled a slow breath, then drew another one back in. "I watched them, and questions formed in my head, so I watched them some more. My feet began to move, and I began to wander around, trying to understand what made them behave in such a different fashion than they would otherwise."

Leonora's eyes blinked open, and the tears caught in the corners of her eyes spilled over. "I know it was foolish," she exclaimed suddenly, anger at herself evident in her voice. "I should've stayed with you." Again, her lips thinned, and she shook her head as though disappointed by her own thoughtlessness. "I didn't even realize that I was moving away or where I was going. I simply walked around, my notebook clutched to my chest, my fingers itching to take notes. I wondered about all these people, what had brought them here that night. I think..." She swallowed hard, and Louisa knew they were getting closer to the moment that had destroyed her sister's life. "I think I was walking down a corridor. I cannot say that I remember exactly, but then I stopped, and I found that the sounds had grown dimmer and only a few people were around, walking past me, hurrying back toward the ballroom. I turned around and intended to follow them when..."

Louisa's teeth gritted together painfully as she watched her sister relive her pain. Leonora's hands were like an iron vice, almost squeezing the life from Louisa's. "I never saw him coming," Leonora whispered, her fingernails digging into Louisa's hands. "I felt a hand grab my arm and then yank me sideways. I lost my balance and fell into his arms." Her lower lip trembled, and she could barely speak, her words shaking. "I think...I think he pulled me into an alcove. It was so very dark, and I thought I saw a curtain swing closed." Her mouth opened again, but no sound came out. Her breathing quickened as the panic of that night caught up with her.

"It's all right," Louisa whispered, pulling her sister into her arms. "I'm here! I'm here!" She held her tightly, perhaps too tightly for comfort, but Leonora clung to her with an almost desperate need. Choked sobs wracked her body, and she shook like a leaf as though it were winter and not summer, the cold creeping into every region of her body.

Suddenly, Leonora pulled away, her face tear-streaked, but her eyes narrowing with anger. "It's been weeks!" She huffed out on a breath as her hands balled into fists. "It's been weeks, and still I cannot put it behind me." She shook her head, dumbfounded, staring at Louisa as though hoping for an answer. "I was not injured. I don't even have a scratch. Even the marks upon my arms have faded..." Her voice lost a little strength when she realized she was speaking about something Louisa had not previously known.

Still, her hands trembled, the sinews standing out white as she clenched them together. "I can think of little else," she mumbled, all strength suddenly gone from her body, her voice sounding weak and defeated. "I used to be able to lose myself whenever I discovered something that interested me. It didn't matter what it was if it piqued my curiosity. I still feel echoes of that emotion now and then, but I can no longer drift into this other world where nothing else matters but to seek an elusive answer to a most pressing question." Her eyes closed as she slumped back, almost crumpling into herself. "I should simply forget what happened, but I can't. Even though nothing that happened has any bearing on my life now, I keep thinking about it, remembering it, reliving it." Her eyes opened, and she turned to Louisa, the look upon her face almost pleading. "What can I do? What can I do to make it go away? I should be able to, shouldn't I?"

Once again reaching out for her sister, Louisa rubbed her hands up and down Leonora's arms as she began to shiver. "What happened to you was awful," she said gently, aware that her sister was only a hair's breadth away from falling apart. "What happened might not have left scars upon your body, but it did leave them on your soul. Believe me, I know what it is like to carry something around with yourself that you simply cannot forget, that is tormenting you day and night, that you can't seem to shake. And my secret is nothing compared to what happened to you. You're strong for finding the will to get up in the morning, to continue on and try your best, to speak to me about it here, now." She looked deep into her sister's eyes, nodding to her encouragingly for there was little else she could do. "Perhaps you should speak to Mother. Or to Grandma Edie. They might be able to advise you better."

Tensing, Leonora shook her head. "I cannot. I'm not strong enough to go through this again." She swallowed, lowering her head, then glancing up at Louisa. "If anyone found out what happened, I'd be ruined. All of our sisters would suffer by association with me, their prospects reduced." Again, she shook her head, determination sparking in her blue eyes. "No, I cannot speak of this to anyone. Only you know, and you must promise me not to say a word to anyone else, not our parents, not Grandma Edie, not our sisters or our brother. No one must know. Promise me, Lou!"

Only too well did Louisa understand her sister's fears, for what she said was the truth. Society did not care what was wrong or right in the truest sense. All it cared about was that people adhered to its rules. "Phineas knows as well," she reminded Leonora.

Her sister looked up at her with mournful eyes. "Will you speak to him? Will you ask him to keep it to himself?"

Louisa nodded, unfathomably certain that Phineas would not breathe a word of what had happened that night without express permission. After all, weeks had passed since and he had not said a word. "Your secret is safe with me," she reassured her sister. "With us."

Sighing, Leonora leaned into Louisa, resting her head upon her sister's shoulder. For a long time, they simply sat there, arm in arm, and listened to the wind above. Then Leonora whispered, "Thank you." The words drifted away, mingling with the soft rustling of the leaves around them. Still, Louisa felt great relief that her sister had finally confided in her. Leonora was no longer alone. She still suffered, but now they could stand together, side-by-side, as always.

Chapter Thirty

NONSENSE TO READ

"**I** wrote you a letter."

Whirling around, Louisa stared up at Phineas. He had all but snuck up on her as she had been standing by the windows in the drawing room, her gaze fixed on the far horizon. "A letter?" she gasped, panic instantly flooding her heart as she looked up at him. Was he mocking her? Had all that he had told her been a lie after all?

"Do not look so worried," he chided her, the beginnings of an annoyingly amused grin coming to his face. "I understand things have changed between us and that change is always difficult to adjust to. Still, I demand that you stop looking at me with suspicion."

Louisa drew back, annoyed with his accusation. "I'm not looking at you with suspicion."

"Yes, you are." He leaned a little closer, his dark eyes watchful as they trailed over her face. "I can all but read your thoughts upon your face," he told her teasingly. "You are wondering if I'm making fun of you, are you not? You're worried that all I promised you was nothing but a lie, is that not so?"

Louisa swallowed, but drew herself up nonetheless, meeting his eyes without flinching. "It is not a far-fetched notion," she stated vehemently. "Given our history, can you honestly blame me for being cautious?"

Phineas chuckled. "Did you speak to Leonora?" he asked, catching her off guard.

Louisa flinched, unable to prevent it, hating the way his face lit up with glee at seeing her honest reaction. Crossing her arms over her chest, she glared at him. "Don't look so smug," she chided. "I assure you it does not become you."

Still grinning, Phineas moved even closer, until the hem of her skirts brushed over the tips of his shoes. "Then what does become me? Care to enlighten me?"

Louisa raised her chin. "Very little, I assure you."

Phineas laughed, "You did not answer my question. Did you or did you not?"

Louisa inhaled a slow breath, hating and loving the way he teased her. It riled her, and yet, excitement coursed through her body, making her feel more alive than any other situation she had thus far experienced. "I did," she conceded, but refrained from saying any more than that.

His grin widened, and he moved closer still until the tip of his nose almost touched hers. "And?"

Louisa could not deny that she too wished for another kiss. However, she would never surrender without a fight, and on some level, she was certain that he would not want her to. "You should not stand so close," she admonished him, putting a most haughty expression upon her face. "What if anyone should enter? Have you thought of that?"

He did not move. "The door is closed."

"Are you certain?"

"I closed it myself," he told her with more patience than she would have thought him capable of.

"But surely it is not locked. Thus, someone could simply open it." She arched her brows, daring him to contradict her. "And what of the windows?" she went on, allowing her gaze to drift to the side. "What if someone were to walk by and see us?"

A dark chuckle rumbled in Phineas' throat; yet, his wicked grin remained firmly in its place. "Are you afraid to kiss me?"

"Oh, I assure you I have no intention of kissing you." Yet, her gaze strayed to his lips, temptingly close to her own.

"Have you forgotten our wager?"

"I have not," she replied without hesitation. "Nevertheless, the wager stated that you would get to kiss me, not the other way around." Her lips curled up into a victorious smile when she saw his rather unsettled expression.

Phineas all but swayed toward her in that moment, his hands reaching out to settle upon her waist. His gaze remained fixed upon hers. His breath, though, suddenly appeared the slightest bit unsteady. "Now, do you get to slap me, or do I get to kiss you?"

For another heartbeat or two, Louisa remained quiet, torturing them both. Then she spoke. "You get to kiss me."

And without a second of hesitation, Phineas did.

The speed with which his lips claimed hers made Louisa utterly weak in the knees. A moment before, she had felt strong and in control, but now, all that was gone. She almost swayed into his arms, her hands clutching his shoulders as his settled more firmly upon her waist, urging her closer.

His fingers once more pinched her chin, gently, almost tenderly, before she felt his knuckles brush along the line of her jaw, teasing her skin. Then his hand slid into her hair above the back of her neck, holding her to him as he deepened their kiss.

Passion swirled around them, and Louisa completely forgot the world that still went about its normal pace not far away. She barely heard the distant voices of her sisters or felt the bright, warm sunshine drifting in through the windows. All she did feel was Phineas.

His hands upon her body. His lips teasing her own. His heart beating against her chest. He felt warm and alive and far from the hazy dream that had occasionally visited her in the night. The solid feel of him made Louisa wish it could always be so.

And then she heard the dim thump of Grandma Edie's walking stick on the marble floors just outside the door.

"Someone's coming," Louisa whispered breathlessly, looking up into his dark eyes that gleamed with daring intent.

In reply, Phineas merely grinned, his hands once more tightening upon her, as he leaned down for another kiss. "Whoever it is, they will walk past." His head swooped down, and his lips brushed against hers.

Louisa leaned back, trying to escape long enough to utter a reply. "Is that wishful thinking? Or can you suddenly see the future?"

Bowing his head, Phineas chuckled, "There is nothing I can say that will make you forget whoever is outside in the hall, is there?" Without waiting for an answer, he took a step back, his hands falling from her waist before he reached up and straightened his jacket.

Running her hands over her dress, Louisa ensured that neither one of them would be looking too obvious. "What you did was far from wise," she chided as the footsteps outside drew nearer.

"What *I* did?" Phineas demanded, open amusement in his voice. "I think you mean what *we* did."

"Well, I—" Louisa broke off when the door suddenly began to swing open, of course revealing none other than Grandma Edie. She hobbled into the room, leaning heavily upon her walking stick, her pale eyes wide awake and watchful as always.

Louisa swallowed, nonetheless grateful that it was not one of her parents, who had come upon them. "Grandma," she greeted her, stepping forward with a wide smile upon her face. "How wonderful to see you!"

Grandma Edie rolled her eyes at her. "Oh, don't act as though you have not just been doing something utterly scandalous!" A knowing chuckle rumbled in the old woman's throat.

Although Louisa had known her grandmother all her life, she could not help but feel at least a little bit shocked at the old woman's reaction. Phineas, on the other hand, appeared thoroughly amused, joining in Grandma Edie's laughter until tears appeared in the corners of his eyes. "You have impeccable timing, my lady," Phineas complimented her with a rather informal bow. "May I ask what brings you here? At least this time, I'm not here on your behest."

Louisa stared at Phineas before her gaze swiveled to her grandmother. Why she was surprised, she did not know. After all, she had known that Grandma Edie had sent Phineas to her more than once, leaving them alone together, inviting scandal with open eyes. Why then should this surprise her?

Crossing her arms, Louisa glared at both of them. "Is there anything I should know? Have the two of you made any plans concerning myself? If so, I believe I have a right to know."

Grandma Edie smiled at her as though they had just been conversing about the weather. "My dear, wait until you reach my age and find yourself watching your beloved grandchildren making a mess of things, then we will talk again." And with a nod at Phineas, she then turned on her heel—as fast as Grandma Edie possibly could—and headed toward the door, mumbling, "Proceed."

Rather dumbfounded, Louisa watched the door click shut behind her beloved grandmother. Then she turned to look at the man by her side, amusement still darkening his cheeks. "I love her dearly," she said with a shake of her head, "but that woman is insane."

Phineas scoffed, "You are only noticing this now?" He chuckled.

Sighing, Louisa brushed her hands over her eyes, wondering if the last few minutes had only been a dream. Still, her lips still tingled from the kiss they had shared. "I cannot help but think that..." She moved her fingers and peeked through them at Phineas. "I cannot help but think that she wishes for us to be together."

At her words, Phineas' gaze sobered, something intense and demanding sparking in those dark eyes of his. He turned toward her, but did not move, his arms crossing over his chest as he leaned back, one shoulder propped against the wall. "Would that be so bad?" he asked, his brows arching upward.

It was not the look in his eyes that sent goosebumps down her arms and legs. Neither was it the question he had so casually asked. Instead, it was the idea of sharing a life with him, something that only a few days ago would have sent her running for the hills, would have made steam come out of her ears, would have seemed utterly ludicrous. Now, however, Louisa could not deny that her skin hummed at the thought of him as her husband. But was it honestly what she wanted? And what about him? Was she merely a conquest for him? Was it the chase that drew him near? The challenge she presented?

"You're not answering me," he observed rather nonchalantly.

Giving herself a shake, Louisa squared her shoulders, determined to steer them back to something less terrifying. "You said you wrote me a letter," she exclaimed without thought, surprising herself. "Why? Why would you do that?"

Phineas chuckled, giving her a look that all but said, *I know exactly what you're doing.* "Why should I not?" he teased in that usual way of his. "I thought it might be sufficient temptation to inspire you to work with me."

Louisa frowned. "Work with you? What do you mean?"

Pushing off the wall, he stalked toward her, his dark gaze fixed upon hers. "You want to learn how to read, do you not?"

Confused, Louisa stared at him, uncertain what he was about. Was he teasing her again? Or was he serious?

Stopping in front of her, he reached out a hand, the backs of his fingers brushing against hers. Then he took another step closer and wrapped his large hand around hers, holding it gently. "Do you want to learn?" he asked, and this time there was no humor there, neither in his face nor in his voice.

Louisa swallowed, suddenly terrified by this seemingly insurmountable task. What if she tried and could not do it? What if it turned out that despite what Phineas and Leonora believed she simply was not intelligent enough for the task?

"Do you want to?" he asked, his dark gaze gentle and encouraging as he looked at her, his fingers brushing tenderly over her own.

Unable to speak, Louisa merely nodded as her heart thundered in her chest, terrified but also elated.

Phineas smiled at her, a kind, devoted, heartwarming smile. "Then I shall help you," he told her, "if you let me."

As the promise of redemption washed over her, Louisa found herself surge forward, her arms wrapping around his shoulders as she buried her head in the crook of his neck. "Thank you," she whispered repeatedly, wishing she could express how much his offer meant to her.

∿

An utterly bewitching frown came to Louisa's face, and Phineas felt the overwhelming desire to kiss it away. "The cat with the hat sat on the mat?" Louisa read from the small sheet of parchment he had set in front of her. Then she looked up at him, her frown deepening. "That is nonsense. Why would you give me nonsense to read?"

Phineas laughed, loving the way she always criticized his approach. "It is not nonsense," he insisted, unable to resist the urge to tug on the soft curl swinging from her right temple. "It is simple, yes, but it is not nonsense. It is merely a first step."

Still eying him with a doubtful expression upon her lovely face, Louisa pulled back, removing her golden curl from in-between his fingers. "Are you saying that we will continue like this?" Her gaze moved to the other sheets of parchment he had given her over the last few days. She gathered them together, her eyes sweeping over the words and sentences written there. "The pot on the cot is not worth a lot. The pen and the hen and eight men make ten," she read, then looked up at him. "Seriously?"

Phineas laughed, "What do you suggest we do?" he asked, fighting for breath as she tried to glare him into oblivion. "That we work our way from A to Z through the encyclopedia?"

If possible, Louisa's glare darkened even further. "Will you stop teasing me?" she snapped, her hand gesturing rather wildly at the parchments on the table. "This makes me feel like a child. I'd rather begin with words that...have more relevance to my life."

Inhaling a deep breath, Phineas tried his best to appear serious. "I understand your frustration, and believe me, I'm not laughing about you. I'm laughing because you are so very adorable."

"Adorable?" Her face scrunched up as though he had just hurled the most insulting insult of all insults at her face.

"Yes," Phineas insisted, reaching out to grasp her hands and pulling her to her feet. "The way you glare at me is adorable. The way you scrunch up your nose is adorable. The way you look thoroughly disgusted is adorable." He slipped his arms around her, ignoring her efforts to push him away—not that she was truly trying. "So, if you do not want me to call you adorable, then stop distracting me."

Louisa chuckled, "I'm distracting you? How on earth could I

possibly be distracting you?" She rolled her eyes at him. "We've been cooped up in this room for an hour and all you've giving me to read are sentences that are worse than nursery rhymes. Please, tell me how I am distracting you."

Grinning at her, Phineas simply bent his head and kissed her.

For a moment, Louisa seemed a bit taken aback, but then her arms rose, her hands moving up onto his shoulders, her fingers tracing the line of his neck. A soft moan escaped her lips as she returned his kiss, clearly not offended by the liberties he was taking.

"I asked you to tell me," she whispered against his lips, a playful note in her voice.

Phineas chuckled. "I've always been better at show than tell." And he kissed her again.

"Is this why you offered to help me?" Louisa demanded, pulling back before once more brushing her lips against his. "So, you can kiss me? Again, and again?"

Phineas saw no reason not to do what she accused him off. "A thoroughly thought-out plan," he mumbled between kisses, "if ever there was one."

Indeed, Phineas had to admit that things could not have worked out better if he had indeed planned for them. After two years of trying to figure out why Louisa loathed the very sight of him, two years of teasing her so she would not run off, two years of savoring each precious moment she granted him, Phineas felt like the luckiest man on earth.

Suddenly, she was right here. She was right here when he came down for breakfast in the morning. She was right here when he strode outdoors for a stroll through the countryside. She was right here when he headed to the stables for a head-long gallop across the fields.

She was here. Right here. In his arms. And if he wanted to, he could kiss her. And to his utter surprise, she did not stop him, did not argue or snap at him. Of course, she certainly teased him, but then again so did he. It was a game of sorts between the two of them, a game Phineas had always enjoyed. At least, *that* had not changed.

"You need to leave," Louisa mumbled against his lips as she pulled back. Her hand settled upon his chest, the force behind her push now more pronounced.

Phineas looked at her, surprised. "Are you serious? Why? I thought we were practicing."

Louisa chuckled, once more giving him a slight shove so that he had to take a step backward to keep his balance. "We certainly are practicing," she said, amusement in her voice. "The only question is, what is it we are practicing?" She wiggled her eyebrows at him, and Phineas laughed. "Now, you're the one distracting me," she accused with a smile, her arms rising once more to cross over her chest. "I insist you leave this instant so I may have peace of mind to look over these…" A deep frown came to her face as her gaze drifted back down to the words on the parchments. "These rather unusual sentences," she ended diplomatically.

Grateful not to see her disheartened, Phineas took a step back, nodding his head to her. "Very well, but only under protest."

Louisa grinned. "Duly noted."

Spinning on his heel, Phineas headed toward the door, but then stopped with his hand on the doorknob and glanced over his shoulder. "I shall see you later," he said, surprised to hear his voice rise ever so slightly as though he were asking a question. Was he?

Deep down, Phineas could not help but wonder if Louisa genuinely cared for him. Of course, one could argue that simply because he had learned of her secret by happenstance, she had had no choice but to accept that he knew. After all, had he not all but badgered her into accepting his help? Had she not rolled her eyes at his method from the very beginning? Did she truly dislike it, or did she rather enjoy the heated back-and-forth that had always existed between them?

Sometimes, Phineas was certain that something deep and meaningful lingered between them, still elusive, but there, nonetheless. Other times, he wondered if he was simply imagining things, seeing them in a certain light simply because he wished for them.

Closing the door behind him, Phineas rested his back against it and for a moment closed his eyes. If only he knew!

Chapter Thirty-One

WITH FAMILY

Leonora's sad eyes were the only cloud on the horizon as far as Louisa was concerned. For these days, life was good and beautiful and exceedingly invigorating. She woke every morning with a smile upon her face and went to bed each night with a happy giggle drifting from her lips.

Indeed, it would be safe to assume that her progress regarding the written word was at its root. Every word that no longer remained a mystery encouraged Louisa, brought a smile to her face and eagerness to her heart. Letters no longer appeared as random scribbles, but were part of a whole, a network that made sense and promised explanation if one only were to look closer.

Of course, like everything worthwhile, it took time and endurance and tenacity for her to claw her way closer to understanding. However, Louisa did not mind. It only made her want it more.

As the days passed, and summer slowly drew to its end, Louisa found that notes and letters no longer terrified her. Of course, she was far from being able to read them with anything even resembling fluency. Still, the veil was lifting, and Louisa eagerly gobbled up each word. She even strayed into the library and snatched books randomly off the shelves, her eyes scanning the titles, trying to make them out. It was a small step, but to her it was uplifting.

It felt so incredibly good to not be reliant on others in this matter. It felt free, utterly free.

"You look happy!"

At the sound of Anne's voice, Louisa spun around and the book in her hands slipped from her fingers, clattering to the ground. Her heart beat fast, almost painfully as she stared at her cousin. It had been a long time since she had been on her guard; now, here, she was deeply unprepared to have someone intrude upon her own little world.

Watching her most intently, Anne stepped forward, then bent down to pick up the book, handing it back to Louisa. "Is something wrong? You look tense."

Louisa inhaled a slow breath, her gaze lingering upon her cousin's face. More than once over the past few weeks, both Leonora and Phineas had separately urged her to share her secret with the rest of her family. Considering how well both had reacted, Louisa had been open to the thought. She had at length contemplated who to confide in next, however, to be now, so abruptly, so unexpectedly, faced with this decision was overwhelming...and utterly terrifying.

Anne barely moved, and Louisa felt oddly reminded of someone trying not to spook a deer. "Louisa?"

Shaking off her paralysis, Louisa swallowed, her fingers closing more tightly around the book. She did not even know what kind of book it was. If she had read the title, she could no longer recall it. Still, she clutched it to her chest, the movement reminding her of Leonora and her precious notebook. Unwittingly, a chuckle drifted from her lips.

Anne frowned. "Lou, what is going on?" Carefully, she took a step closer, her hand rising very slowly before it gently settled upon Louisa's shoulder. "Is there anything I can do?" Her blue eyes lingered, searching Louisa's, no doubt contemplating her rather odd behavior. "A moment ago, you looked utterly happy, and now, you seem worried. Did I do something? Did you wish to be alone?"

Louisa closed her eyes, then once more inhaled a deep breath and decided to take a leap of faith. "I was happy," she told Anne honestly, the book still clutched to her chest. "I was very happy."

A slow smile came to Anne's face. "Does your happiness by any chance have something to do with Phineas?" Her blue eyes sparkled, and Louisa could see the same hope in them that she herself had felt when she had worked tirelessly to bring Anne and Tobias together.

"It might have," Louisa admitted with a slight huff, feeling rather self-conscious to be at this end of the conversation.

Anne clapped her hands together and almost shrieked with joy. "You must tell me everything! I mean, I've seen the two of you together, and I could not help but think…" She shook her head, words failing her. "Tell me everything!"

Louisa laughed, delighted with her cousin's joyous reaction. "You will not tease me?" she asked, watching Anne skeptically.

Anne gave her an odd look. "Why would I tease you?"

"I teased you about Tobias, did I not?"

Anne shrugged. "That was a long time ago."

"Not a year has passed since," Louisa pointed out, unable to help herself.

Anne was about to reply when she suddenly paused, her eyes narrowing. "Are you stalling for time?" she asked, her right foot slowly tapping against the floor. "Or do you not want to answer me?"

Louisa grinned. "Perhaps a bit of both."

Anne's gaze became thoughtful. "What are you worried about? That he might not care for you? Because I assure you that he does."

Louisa's hands tensed upon the book. "How would you know? Did he say anything?"

Anne grinned. "For the same reason I know you care for him." She chuckled, "It is written all over your face. Was that not how you knew I cared for Tobias?"

Louisa hung her head. "I cannot believe it," she mumbled, a smile teasing her lips. "Bested by my own weapons." With a sigh, she looked back up at Anne…and then told her everything.

The words simply spilled forth, and Louisa barely had to think about how to phrase what she wanted to say. Her lips moved, and she spoke without thought. Her heart expressed everything that had happened with ease, and she could see in Anne's face that her cousin understood.

"Why did you never tell me?" Anne asked, tears misting her eyes as she looked at Louisa. "I would've helped you."

Louisa smiled. "Leonora said the same thing."

"Of course, she did."

Louisa laughed, "In retrospect, I should've known. Of course, I should've known." She shook her head, wondering how she could ever have believed that her family would not be there for her. "But before, I..."

Anne grasped her shoulders, her kind, blue eyes looking into Louisa's. "Fear makes us blind," Anne whispered knowingly. "Everybody knew that Tobias cared for me, but I did not see it. I feared it might not be true, and that fear made me blind." She offered Louisa a warm smile. "It was the same for you, was it not?"

Blinking back tears, Louisa nodded. "I suppose it was."

Anne grinned. "And then came Phineas."

Biting her lower lip, Louisa could not help but grin. She felt embarrassed, for the notion that Phineas might care for her, that she might care for him was still something to be ridiculed, was it not? "He is... infuriatingly stubborn," she whispered, and her heart danced in her chest. "He simply would not leave me alone. Whenever I turned around, he was there. No matter what I did or where I went, he always followed." She would have thrown up her hands had they not still been clutching the book. "He was relentless."

Anne grinned from ear to ear. "That sounds as though you are displeased."

"I was!"

"Was?" Anne inquired, mirth glittering in her eyes. "Am I right to assume that you are no longer?"

Turning around, Louisa finally loosened her grip on the book and gently sat it back down onto the shelf. She heaved a deep sigh, then leaned her head forward, her forehead coming to rest against the smooth wood. "I'm afraid so," she mumbled, unable to look at Anne.

Behind her, Anne laughed, "He is not the man you thought you would marry, is he?"

As though struck by lightning, Louisa whirled around, her jaw dropping. "Marry? No! No! No! I am quite ready to admit that he is not...as bad as I thought, however—"

Anne chuckled, "As bad as you thought? Unbelievable," she remarked, shaking her head. "You're worse than I am! Worse, you're worse than he is!"

Louisa did not know what she wanted Anne to say. Within her, a war was being waged. She could not even name the sides that struggled with one another, much less wish for an outcome. She did not dare.

"Trust me," Anne said gently, taking Louisa's hands in hers. "You care for him. I've watched you most closely over the past few weeks," Louisa's eyes widened, "and what I've observed is that you know what you want. You're simply afraid to admit it to yourself."

Louisa sighed, "Perhaps." It was all she was currently willing to concede.

One step at a time.

"If this experience taught you anything," Anne continued, giving Louisa's hands a gentle squeeze, "it should be that being afraid is never rewarded. Be brave, take a risk and people will surprise you." Her smile deepened. "You taught me that, and I'll be forever grateful to you. You helped me when I did not even know I needed help. Now, let me do the same for you."

Embracing her cousin, Louisa exhaled the breath she had been holding for a long, long time. All tension left her body, and she suddenly looked to the future with a carefree heart.

Autumn came and went, and Phineas still felt at peace. Never had he enjoyed a stay out in the country as he did now. Always had he felt restless and rather bored. Now, however, life was vastly different because of one woman.

Louisa.

Days passed with stolen kisses, whispered words and longing glances, but also with teasing notes and nonsensical riddles, for Louisa's mastery of the written word grew with each day. Pride shone in her dark green eyes, and her enthusiasm was all but infectious. Never had Phineas read as much as he did over the course of these few weeks. He read by himself, but also with her or for her. Always would they speak about choice of words, their impact as well as alternatives. Of course, they also spoke of spelling and grammar, and Phineas was rather dumbfounded to see that even such a dry topic could hold his interest.

In truth, it was not the dry, rather uninspiring topic that held his interest, but the woman glowing like a beacon in the night sky.

"I've made a decision," Louisa told him one day as they once more sneaked off to the library together. Glancing up and down the corridor, she quickly shut the door, then hurried over to him, grasping his hands as though they were an old married couple, and it came to her as naturally as breathing. "I will tell my family."

Phineas could not prevent his jaw from dropping, but he quickly recovered, afraid his reaction might change her mind. "Why? I mean, not that I'm arguing against it. But...I'm curious what made you change your mind."

Louisa shrugged. "I'm not sure," she mumbled, her gaze a little distant. "I'm not certain I actually changed my mind. Of course, for years I could not imagine telling them. But recently..." She shook her head unable to find the words. "I think all I needed was a little time to familiarize myself with the thought. I'm still worried about how they might look at me once they know." She cast him an apologetic grin. "I'm sorry. I can't help it."

Phineas squeezed her hands. "I understand."

Louisa smiled at him, one of those utterly endearing and intoxicating smiles that always made him feel weak in the knees. "Lately, I feel that it bothers me that they don't know, that there is a part of me they know nothing about." The look in her eyes dimmed. "When Leonora wouldn't speak to me, I realized how painful it was that someone I loved did not trust me enough to confide in me."

"It was never about trust," Phineas told her, his gaze searching hers. "You know this, do you not?"

Louisa nodded. "I know that she didn't tell me because she, too, realized that I had a secret that I wouldn't share with her. It was all extremely complicated, and we all believed something to be true that simply wasn't. That's what secrets do, is it not? They addle your mind and separate you from the people you love."

Phineas loved the passionate way she spoke about herself, her family, those she cared about, and he wondered if at least a small part of her thought of him in the same way. "How do you wish to do this? One after another? Or all at once?"

A slight tremor snaked down her arms, and Phineas' grip upon her hands tightened, hoping she would draw courage from his presence. "I've thought long and hard about this," Louisa told him, her breath quickening as the pulse in her neck began to gather speed. "I do not believe I have the strength to explain myself repeatedly. The mere thought of it makes me feel dizzy and lightheaded." She exhaled a slow breath, her hands tightening upon his. "No. I shall tell them all at once." Her eyes locked upon his. "Today. Now."

For a long moment, they simply looked at one another, Louisa's decision lingering in the air, its effect feeling like a deafening roar in absolute stillness. "Do you want me there?" Phineas asked, surprised at how nervous he himself suddenly felt.

"Of course! I need you there!" There was no hesitation in her reply, and her voice sounded strong and determined. Her eyes glowed with something Phineas could not quite make out, but he knew that it made him want to pull her into his arms and never let go.

Lately, that feeling had been sneaking up on him in a variety of moments. Always unexpected, but always forceful. It seemed to grow with each passing day, and rather abruptly, in a moment that held no meaning, Phineas had realized only recently that he thought of Louisa as his brother thought of Anne. Deep down, he knew what these emotions meant, what he wanted. What he also knew was that the right time had not yet come.

Hurrying through the house, Phineas gathered every Whickerton he could find while Louisa sat in the drawing room, waiting, no doubt terribly nervous.

"What is this about?" Troy asked as Phineas urged him to abandon whatever he had been working on in the study and head to the drawing room.

"You shall see," was all he replied, not wishing to reach ahead and say more than Louisa would want him to.

Lady Hayward had already returned home to her husband's country estate a few weeks back while her brother, Lord Lockhart, had traveled to London on some business. Tobias, Anne as well as Phineas himself had stayed on though, feeling quite at home at Whickerton Grove.

That left Louisa's parents, her grandmother—although Phineas wondered if the dowager might suspect something for, she frequently did—as well as her brother and sisters.

And Miss Mortensen.

As the drawing room slowly began to fill, Louisa's family taking seats here and there, exchanging glances of surprise and curiosity, Phineas moved closer to Louisa without thought. He felt that he should be at her side, that that was where he belonged. Still, he did not wish to encroach on this moment and so he kept a little back, just lingering near enough in case she should need him.

Everyone began to speak simultaneously, asking questions and voicing their surprise. The sound was almost deafening, and Phineas could see Louisa's hands tense. He was about to interfere when a loud knocking sound could be heard above the cacophony of voices. He glanced around and saw Grandma Edie, rapping her walking stick on the floor. "Silence, everyone!" she exclaimed, scowling at her family. "I cannot hear myself think."

When everyone had settled down and taken their seats, their lips finally sealed, their ears ready to listen, Grandma Edie turned to Louisa and said, "Now, dear, what is it you wish to speak to us about?" An encouraging smile shone upon the old woman's face, which convinced Phineas that she already knew.

Somehow Grandma Edie knew. She always knew. How? That was a good question. Phineas doubted that they would ever find out for she did not strike him as the kind to reveal her secrets. She liked them far too much.

Louisa cleared her throat, her green eyes rather wide as they swept over the many faces of her beloved family. Then her lips parted, and she said, "I cannot read."

Phineas held his breath as he waited for what might happen next.

Silence continued to linger as Louisa's family looked back at her, the look in their eyes speaking of confusion. He could see that they were all but waiting for her to continue, certain that there was more to whatever story she was trying to tell them.

Louisa's parents exchanged a confused look before her mother rose from her spot by the mantle and walked over, seating herself next to her daughter. "What are you trying to tell us?" she asked gently, her hands settling upon Louisa's.

Louisa inhaled a slow breath, her eyes never leaving her mother's. "I am trying to tell you that I cannot read. I don't know how."

While most of her family found themselves experiencing a rather severe shock at those words, Phineas saw Leonora smile gently at Louisa, relief upon her face that her sister had finally decided to share her secret with them. Anne and Tobias, too, were smiling, their hands linked.

Troy suddenly strode forward, a deep frown upon his face. "You cannot be serious!" he exclaimed, slowly shaking his head as he stared at his sister.

Ignoring her brother, Harriet rose to her feet, her face bearing a most similar expression. "But you always read to us," she objected, her hands gesturing wildly. "All those lovely poems. How...?" She shook her head. "How?"

Squeezing her mother's hands, Louisa turned to look at her youngest sister. "I did not read," she admitted. "I recited from memory."

More questions bubbled up and everyone in the room suddenly shot to their feet, asking and commenting, confusion and disbelief foremost on their minds. Phineas could see that Louisa was becoming overwhelmed, and yet again, it was a Grandma Edie's forceful interference that quieted the room. "If you wish to hear her answers," the dowager chided after once more using her walking stick, "then you need to give the poor girl a chance to talk."

Casting her grandmother a grateful smile, Louisa then began to tell them everything. She spoke of her childhood, getting confused with the letters and words and their meaning. She spoke of being ashamed, and thus not mentioning that she was falling behind, that she did not understand. She had tried her best to remember what was read to her, but memorizing could only help her to a certain extent. Some situations had always been difficult and terrifying.

Coming to sit beside his wife, Lord Whickerton placed a hand on his lady's shoulder while the other reached around and closed over Louisa's. His expression, too, spoke of disbelief, but also of sorrow and regret. "Why did you not tell us?" he asked gently. "We could've helped you. We *would* have helped you. Do you not know that?"

Tears were brimming in Louisa's eyes, and Phineas smiled, relieved that her family was reacting exactly how he had hoped, how she deserved. "I should've known," Louisa replied on a sob. "Perhaps somewhere deep down I did know. But I was afraid and ashamed, and I did not want you looking at me with pity in your eyes. I did not want you to be ashamed of me."

Her father's jaw hardened. "We would never!" he exclaimed, a tinge of anger in his voice. "You did nothing wrong. It is I who failed you."

Louisa frowned. "Father?"

Shaking his head, her father closed his eyes. "I should've noticed," he mumbled, then looked at his wife, who looked back at him nodding. "We should've noticed. I'm so deeply sorry, my girl."

"No, Father." Louisa squeezed his hand, her other wiping away the tears that still lingered upon her face. "Do not blame yourself. It was not your fault. It was—"

"It was no one's fault," Grandma Edie exclaimed, her voice surprisingly strong, for it silenced everyone else. All heads turned to look at her, and she paused for a moment to ensure she had everyone's attention. "The past is the past," she told them wisely, "and it is the future we need to concern ourselves with. Now, what do you suggest we do?"

"We help her," Christina mumbled, her voice rather quiet at first before certainty replaced confusion upon her face. A wide smile teased her lips, and she looked at Miss Mortensen and then at her sister warmly. "We shall help you. Of course, we shall."

Miss Mortensen nodded vigorously, answering her friend's smile with one of her own, mere seconds before Harriet shot to her feet. "We can teach you all we know," she chuckled, "which, I'm afraid, in my case is not that much."

Everybody laughed at that, and the tension that had been lingering upon the room was broken. Everything felt lighter suddenly, and Phineas stood back, allowing Louisa this moment with her family, and watched as they all came together to help her.

"I still have all my old books," Juliet threw in, a rather maternal smile upon her face as she looked at Louisa, "from when I first started to learn. We should leave you little notes and—"

"And riddles!" Harriet interjected, all but bouncing on her feet with excitement. "Oh, perhaps a scavenger hunt, where one note leads to the next and so on." She glanced around the room, quite obviously very eager to get started.

Christina nodded, also surging to her feet. "Oh, that will be so much fun!"

Troy cleared his throat in that moment. "Should we not hire a tutor?" he asked, looking around the room from one face to the next.

Immediately, his sisters protested loudly, and once again Grandma Edie was forced to silence them. "I believe Louisa should decide."

Lady Whickerton nodded as she looked from her mother-in-law to her daughter. "I quite agree," she stated brushing a tear from Louisa's cheek. "What do you want? How do you wish to proceed?"

Louisa inhaled a shaking breath, then her tear-filled eyes swept around the room, lingering upon every member of her beloved family. "I think, I like the idea of a scavenger hunt." She turned to look at her two younger sisters. "It does sound like a lot of fun!"

Christina and Harriet all but shrieked in delight.

"I hate to be a naysayer," Troy threw in, a bit of an apologetic look upon his face, "but to get started, I suppose, she ought to learn at least a few necessary words. Do you not agree?"

Indeed, his objection put a bit of a dampener on everyone's mood. At least, until Louisa exclaimed, "But I already know a few words. I have been practicing these past weeks."

Stunned faces turned back to look at her. "How did you learn?" Juliet asked, looking deeply surprised.

And for the first time since they had stepped into the room, Louisa turned to look at Phineas. Her eyes still shone with tears, but he could not help but think that the moment they fell on him, they grew warmer and shone more deeply than before. "Phineas has been helping me, teaching me."

Instantly, all eyes turned to him, and Phineas swallowed, a chuckle drifting from his lips. "And she's been criticizing me the whole time."

Everybody laughed, even Louisa. "You've made up nonsensical sentences," she accused him before her gaze turned back to her family. "He's made up nonsensical sentences."

Smiling warmly, Juliet shrugged. "What does it matter? If they help you learn, and you have a bit of fun along the way." Her gaze shifted back and forth between Louisa and him, and something contemplative came to her green eyes. "And you do look as though you've had fun."

Louisa's gaze returned to him, a deeply affectionate smile coming to her face. "I did," she whispered, her eyes never leaving his. "I did have fun. Thank you."

And it was in this very moment that Phineas realized that he was in love with Louisa and had been for a good, long while.

Chapter Thirty-Two

A SCAVENGER HUNT

Never in his life had Phineas seen Louisa this happy or this carefree. She seemed to wake every morning, eager to begin the day, and head to bed every night, regretting that it had ended.

"What does this mean?" A deep frown came to her face, and she heaved a deep sigh as though she could feel it linger like a heavy weight upon her chest as she peered at the small note in her hands. "*Pat it and prick it.*" Still frowning, she looked up at Phineas. "What on earth does this mean?"

Phineas could not help but smile at her for she had not even paid attention to *reading* the note but had jumped right away to trying to understand it. "It might be a clue," he said with a shrug.

Standing by the drawing room windows, Louisa gazed out at the wind whipping through the trees, gathering up leaves and tossing them about. The skies were gray, and heavy clouds lingered over Whickerton Grove, promising a downpour soon. "A clue to what?"

Leaning against the wall, Phineas chuckled. "Well, I suppose if it were too obvious, where would be the fun in that?"

Lifting her gaze off the parchment, Louisa glared at him. "You're not helping," she chided, tapping the tip of her forefinger against the corner of her mouth. Her gaze became distant as she continued to stare out the window, her thoughts racing in her head.

Phineas would not have been surprised if steam had been coming out of her ears. "Anything?"

"You could help," she grumbled, annoyance slowly sneaking onto her face. "Instead of simply standing there, doing nothing."

Fighting to suppress a grin, Phineas crossed his arms. "I'm not doing nothing. I am...giving you the opportunity to...exercise your... formidable intelligence."

Louisa rolled her eyes at him. "Oh, Phin, that is the worst thing you've ever said. How do you come up with these things?"

This time, Phineas did laugh, "That, I cannot say." Again, he watched her as she poured over the little note. "Anything?"

"You know, if you don't contribute anything," Louisa remarked with a snap, "you might as well leave."

Grinning, Phineas pushed off the wall and walked over to her. He came to stand behind her, his hands settling upon her shoulders before they slowly slid down her arms. He could feel her inhale a soft breath before she leaned back into his embrace. "Do you truly want me to go?" he could not help but ask, longing to hear her contradict him.

A soft laugh drifted from her lips, but she did not say anything, at least not something in answer to his question. "My sisters have been sending me countless notes," Louisa mused, thinking out loud. "Most of which held some sort of reference to a book or a poem I'm familiar with. One or two were even about old nursery rhymes that our governess used to teach us." For a heartbeat or two, she remained silent before Phineas suddenly felt her stiffen.

"Is something wrong?" he asked, a bit alarmed.

Louisa whirled around to face him, her eyes wide and a hint of triumph upon her features. "It's from a nursery rhyme," she exclaimed, her hands gesturing wildly as she tried to contain her excitement.

"Which one?" Phineas asked, trying to peek at the parchment.

Louisa rolled her eyes at him as though the answer should be obvious. "From Patty Cake, of course!" she exclaimed, her lips once more parting to recite the rhyme.

. . .

"Patty Cake, Patty Cake,
    Baker's Man.
    That I will Master,
    As fast as I can.
    Pat it and prick it,
    And mark it with a T,
    And there will be enough for Tommy and me."

"Very well," Phineas said, once more crossing his arms over his chest as he regarded her. "What does it mean?"

Again, Louisa frowned, her gaze moving back and forth between him and the small note. "Well, considering this is a scavenger hunt, I suppose this note is telling us where to go. Now, where could this nursery rhyme tell us to go?" She grinned at him, and he knew that she knew the answer.

Indeed, it was rather obvious. Still, he loved the way she was teasing him, and thus pretended to be utterly ignorant. "I do not have the faintest inkling."

"The kitchen, of course!" Louisa threw up her hands. "Where else would you bake a cake?" Then she grabbed his arm and pulled him along as she hastened out of the room.

As expected, they found another little note in the kitchen, set down carefully upon a bag of flour. Louisa unfolded it rather impatiently and began to read, her eyes flying over the small scrap of parchment. Phineas was amazed at how quickly she was able to make out the words and assign the meaning. Indeed, she had come a long way, and perhaps distracting her with a scavenger hunt, letting her read without focusing on reading, was the perfect way to help her along.

And on they went, from room to room, finding note after note. Some were simple and straightforward while others required some thought. Most stemmed from nursery rhymes or short, little poems the girls had loved as children. Now and then, Phineas thought to see tears glistening in the corners of Louisa's eyes as she read through yet another one, most likely one very dear to her heart.

Her brow furrowed though as they stood in the library, her head bent over yet another note. "Hmm?" she mumbled, then looked up and showed him the note. "What do you think? Do we need to dance? Without shoes? But how does that help?"

"*She will dance without her shoe,*" Phineas read, the line echoing in his head, sounding oddly familiar. However, for a moment, he was stumped. "I'm certain I've heard it before, but I don't know where. Do you think it's a nursery rhyme as well?"

The next instance, her jaw dropped, and her hand shot out, grasping his arm, her fingers squeezing him rather tightly. "It *is* a nursery rhyme!" She exclaimed, her voice sounding a little hoarse. Then she recited from memory:

Cock a doodle do!
　What is my dame to do?
　Till master's found his fiddling stick,
　She'll dance without her shoe.

Phineas grinned, slapping his forehead. "Yes, that's the one."

"But where do we go?" Turning, Louisa looked out the window where soft raindrops had begun to come down. Then she glanced at the door behind him. "The ballroom? We've already been there. The music room? We've been there as well." Her gaze once more dropped to the parchment, but then rose when she did not find the line, she was looking for there.

Phineas watched as she closed her eyes, her lips parting and then moving as she quietly recited the nursery rhyme once more. A moment later, her eyes flew open. "The barn!"

Now, it was Phineas' turn to frown. "Why the barn?"

Before answering him, Louisa once more grabbed his arm and pulled him along. Phineas had no choice but to follow, not that he minded. "Where else would you find a rooster?"

Phineas laughed as they hurried along, running as though time mattered. Out of the corner of his eye, he thought to spy one of the Whickerton sisters, probably Harriet, judging from the soft reddish glow of her hair. Were they spying on them? Or were they simply too curious to stay away? Whatever it was, Phineas could not help but smile.

Rushing to slip into their coats, they headed outside where a harsh wind blew into their faces. Phineas blinked, and glanced up at the sky. "There are even snowflakes among the raindrops," he observed, pulling his coat tighter around himself as another gust of wind found its way to his skin, chilling him to the bone.

Running ahead, Louisa laughed. "It is winter, is it not?"

Phineas hurried to catch up with her. "Still, I've never cared for snow." Again, he glanced up at the dark sky. "I hope this will not get worse."

"Don't be such a spoilsport," Louisa chided as she pushed open the barn door and slipped inside.

Rushing to get out of the cold, Phineas breathed in deeply as he stepped into the stables. The scent of hay tickled his nose, and he blinked his eyes at the dim light inside. A striped cat slunk around his legs, brushing up against him and purring. "Lou?"

"Over here!"

Trying to step around the cat, Phineas moved along toward the back of the stables. Two large sheets seemed to have been fixed to the upper beams and then crossed before their other ends were attached to the floor. "What is this?" Phineas mumbled as he came to stand beside Louisa.

A rosy glow shone on her cheeks, and she was nibbling on her bottom lip. "I think this is it," she whispered almost reverently.

Phineas frowned. "This is it? How do you figure?"

She turned to look at him, a wide smile upon her face. "Well, this is an X, is it not?" she said, one arm lifted, pointing at the two sheets strung from top to bottom, crossing one another diagonally.

Taking a step back, Phineas nodded, suddenly seeing something that had eluded him before. "Now that you mentioned it," he mumbled, then turned to look at her. "Do you suppose there is treasure buried here?"

Louisa laughed, "Perhaps not buried," she replied, then ducked under the crossed sheets and stepped onto the straw-covered floor behind it. "Or at least not buried in the ground." She bent down to push aside the straw. "Help me!"

Somewhat reluctant at first, Phineas joined her, leaning down to push aside the straw. In the dim light in the barn, he could barely see anything, but rather felt his way around. "What do you think we are looking for?"

"I haven't a clue." She rummaged around in the straw somewhere to his right, shoving and pushing, now and then even lifting armfuls of straw and dumping it elsewhere.

On his head, for example.

Phineas tensed as the load came down upon him, the straws scratching his skin. "Lulu!" His voice rang with warning, using the nickname she had once hated. He wondered if she still did. Shooting to his feet, Phineas rushed to brush the straw off himself. He glared at her, by now utterly annoyed with the scavenger hunt. He was cold and tired and now dirty.

Louisa, however, was still in excellent spirits, for she stood no more than a few arms' lengths away from him, a hand covering her mouth as she tried not to laugh. Still, even in the limited light in the barn, her green eyes glowed with mirth and exuberance. "You should see yourself," she laughed, finally giving in and no longer trying to hide it. "You look ridiculous. It suits you!"

For a moment, annoyance surged through Phineas. Still, it vanished as quickly as it had appeared. Instead, laughter bubbled up in his own throat, and he found himself reaching for the straw by his feet, clutching a handful and tossing it at Louisa. "Perhaps straw will improve your appearance as well."

Louisa shrieked and tried to dash away. Soon, they were both dancing around in the small space, launching armfuls of straw at one another, laughing so hard that their sides began to ache. Phineas could not remember the last time he had had that much fun.

Childlike fun.

Something utterly useless and without purpose.

"Wait!" Louisa exclaimed suddenly, holding up a hand to halt his next attack.

Phineas chuckled, "Don't for a second believe I will show you mercy!"

"No, I found something!" Crouching down in the straw, Louisa once more used her hands to dig a little hole, soon revealing the lid of the wooden chest. "It's a treasure chest."

Phineas slapped his knee and laughed, "I don't believe it!" Then he knelt beside her. "Is it locked?"

"I don't think so." Louisa ran her hands over the smooth wood before she flipped back the small metal slab that held the lid closed. Then she slowly opened the chest, her teeth sunk into her lower lip as she all but held her breath.

"I'm not expecting gold or jewels," Phineas remarked with a grin as he watched her. "Any ideas what could be in there?"

Louisa did not answer. Her eyes were all but glued to the growing gap, slowly revealing what lay inside the treasure chest they had found.

And then the chest lay open before them, the fading light in the barn unable to illuminate the contents within. "What is this?" Phineas asked, carefully reaching out a hand.

Louisa was faster, though. "Notebooks," she replied before she had even pulled the first one out and slowly turned it in her hands, her eyes running almost lovingly over the leather binding.

"Notebooks?" Phineas frowned. "I must admit, notebooks I would've expected as a treasure for Leonora, but for you? Do you hold any secret ambitions of becoming a scientist?"

Louisa laughed at the playful note in his voice, "Don't be absurd." Then she sighed, a faraway look coming to her eyes as she reached for yet another notebook.

Phineas watched her curiously. "This means something to you," he observed.

Louisa nodded. "When we were little," she began with a sigh, "our mother gave these to us, saying that the world of the written word opened up new possibilities for us. She told us to fill these notebooks with whatever held our hearts. She said it did not matter what it was as long as we cared about it enough to keep it close, to make a note of it, to remember it in the years to come." She looked up at him, and he could see tears brimming in her eyes. "Jules filled hers with musings, thoughts that simply came to her throughout the day. Leonora, of course, noted down all kinds of observations about the world around her, posing questions to herself she wished to be able to answer one day." Her hands moved to yet another notebook, opening it gently. "Chris wrote stories about fairies and elves and dragons, and Harry wrote about her animals." A deep sigh left her lips.

"And you?" Phineas prompted, wondering how Louisa had solved the problem of being unable to write down anything important to her. How had she filled a notebook without being able to read and write thoughts of her own?

Louisa shrugged, and a tear ran down her cheek. "I simply copied poems Jules used to read to us, claiming they held a special meaning for me." Regret and shame darkened her voice, but she lifted her chin and met his gaze without flinching. "I did what I could."

Phineas nodded, reaching out a hand to cover hers. "I know you did." His gaze swept over the open chest and the many notebooks inside. "Why do you think they left these for you?"

A smile slowly spread over Louisa's face as she opened yet another notebook, the one she had been holding in her hands. "They left a new one for me," she whispered, her voice choked with emotions. "So, I can begin again."

Phineas returned her smile, glad to see her spirits lifted. "What will you write in it?"

Louisa shrugged. "I don't know...yet." A hint of a smile came to her face as she contemplated all the possibilities opening to her. If she continued down this path, she would soon be able to express anything she wanted.

"Will you ever write *me* a note?" Phineas asked grinning. "After all the little notes you've received this week, I assume everyone would be delighted to receive some in return. I know I would be."

Louisa groaned in mock exhaustion, slapping a hand to her forehead. "Oh, all the work! If only I had known, I would have never wanted to learn. Now, I suddenly must write notes?" she chuckled, carefully settling the notebooks back into the small chest.

Phineas heaved a deep sigh, suddenly feeling utterly content for the thought of exchanging notes with Louisa was one most—

Stilling, Phineas felt all blood drain from his face. The air around them no longer felt warm and soothing, but utterly chilling as his thoughts were drawn back to a night months ago.

A night at a ball when a footman had brought him a note. A note asking him to come to the library. A note he had assumed had been from Louisa.

Only once there, it had not been Louisa who had awaited him, but Miss Mortensen instead. She, too, had received such a note, the words written in the same hand, signed by nothing more but the letter L.

Who on earth had written these notes? Had Miss Mortensen done so to lure him there? Had she meant to trap him into marriage? It was not a practice unheard of. In fact, Phineas remembered that soon upon entering the library, footsteps had echoed outside in the hall, coming closer. To save them both, Phineas had disappeared through the window.

Had it been her? Or someone else? But who? And why?

Indeed, Phineas could not shake the feeling that Miss Mortensen did not possess the daring nor the kind of calculating mind required to set such a plan in motion. Indeed, she had seemed utterly dumb-founded herself.

Who then?

Chapter Thirty-Three
RETURN TO WINDMERE PARK

Christmas was drawing near, and the Archibald Christmas Ball once more loomed on the horizon. Anne and Tobias could not wait to attend as their own happily-ever-after had begun at that very event a year before.

Louisa enjoyed the expectant thrill that seemed to linger upon Whickerton Grove these days. Everyone was counting the days until their departure for this year; all the Whickertons intended to attend.

All but one.

"You cannot stay behind on your own," Louisa counseled Leonora as they walked arm in arm across the snow-covered grounds. "Everyone is going. You will be utterly bored. Also, people might talk if you remained here all by yourself."

Leonora exhaled a slow breath, its small cloud drifting away upon the icy breeze chilling their skin. "I know," she mumbled, a look of deepest turmoil upon her face. "I know." She stopped in her tracks and turned to look at Louisa. "What am I to do? I cannot imagine attending and...and...and..." Utter panic stood upon her snow-white face.

Louisa grasped her sister's hands tightly. "You will not be alone," she promised her, her green eyes looking deeply into her sister's blue ones. "I promise I shall not leave your side. Nothing will happen. Trust me." She could see plain as day that the thought of once again mingling within society terrified her sister more than anything else ever had. It was the night of the masquerade that still lingered in her thoughts as well as the question of who her masked attacker had been. What if they crossed paths again at a societal event? Would she recognize him? Or would she converse with him, never knowing that it had been him?

Inhaling a deep breath, Leonora nodded. "I know I cannot shut myself away for the rest of my life," she said, her jaw tensing as she forced more strength into her words. "And I do not want to." She shook her head, a dark scoff leaving her lips. "This is silly! Of course, nothing bad will happen. Nothing bad ever happened before. Not at a ball. Not with my parents, my grandmother, my family around." She swallowed hard. "Nothing will happen."

"So, you will come?" Louisa asked, once more squeezing her sister's hands reassuringly.

With her lips pressed into a thin line, Leonora nodded. Still, the look of panic upon her face had not waned, and Louisa worried how her sister might fare at a crowded house party with dozens of people around. She could only hope it might bring back old joys and prove to her that she was indeed safe with her family at her side. After all, Leonora needed to take that first step back into life. Louisa did not dare imagine what would happen to her sister if she never found the courage to do so.

And so, after weeks of planning and packing and chatting and laughing, all the Whickertons set out for Windmere Park. They were accompanied by Anne, Tobias and Phineas as well as by Sarah and her mother, Lady Hartmore, who had arrived only a sennight before their departure.

Snow lay in a thin layer upon the ground, allowing their carriages to reach Lord Archibald's estate without much delay. Fluffy snowflakes drifted to the ground here and there, occasionally whipped about by an icy wind. The evergreen bushes and trees planted strategically along the drive as well as in the gardens glittered from the frost as though decorated with diamonds.

The general mood was cheerful and expectant. Harriet, Chris and

Sarah never ceased speaking, discussing all they were hoping for this Christmas season. Of course, they had heard the story of Anne's disastrous mistletoe kiss and were wondering if this year they could claim one of their own.

Of course, not a disastrous one.

As the carriage pulled to a halt in front of the large front stoop leading up to the tall oak doors, Grandma Edie was jarred awake, her eyes blinking furiously as she pushed herself into a more seated position. "Have we finally arrived?" she asked, stifling a yawn. "It certainly took long enough."

Beside her, Louisa felt Leonora tense, and she immediately reached out a hand to her sister, pulling her close and patting her hand. "All will be well," she whispered. "I'm here."

Leonora cast her a fearful look but nodded. Then they disembarked from the carriage, followed by Jules and Grandma Edie.

As always, their grandmother all but hugged Jules to her side, clinging to her as though she were incapable of walking on her own. Of course, she had her walking stick, which in this moment she chose to ignore. More than once, Louisa wondered about her grandmother's insistence on keeping Jules by her side at all times, especially whenever they ventured out into society. It seemed rather unnecessary considering Grandma Edie's rather resolute nature. Still, Jules never fought their grandmother and tended to give in without an argument.

After settling into their assigned rooms, most of the Whickertons returned downstairs to greet the other guests and speak to someone new, someone they had not seen in the last few months. Harriet, Chris and Sarah were soon nowhere to be seen, exploring the house as well as its grounds. Grandma Edie settled into an armchair by the fire in the drawing room, Jules, of course, by her side, alternately fetching her warm tea and biscuits. While their parents were soon engulfed in a conversation with Lord and Lady Archibald as well as a few other close friends, Troy simply stood by the window, gazing outside, the somewhat slumped appearance of his shoulders suggesting that he was far from in a good mood.

Under normal circumstances, Louisa would have addressed him, asking what was on his mind. Unfortunately, Leonora still clung to her arm, her eyes wide as she looked around the room. "Are you all right?"

In answer, Leonora's hands tensed upon Louisa's arm. "I...I hardly know."

Louisa continued their walk around the room, ensuring they never ventured too close to other guests. She was hoping that Leonora would slowly get used to being around other people once more. It seemed, though, that it would take a lot of time.

As the afternoon progressed, Louisa decided to follow her younger sisters' example. She urged Leonora into the front hall where they slipped into their warm winter coats and drew on fur-lined boots. Then they hurried outdoors, enjoying the warm sunlight upon their faces as they walked across the frost-covered ground. "Better?"

With a tentative smile, Leonora nodded. "I can hardly explain it," she replied, shrugging her shoulders. "Everything is as it always has been. It is me. Only me."

"Do not blame yourself," Louisa insisted as they turned down into the gardens, spotting Harriet, Chris and Sarah engaged in a snowball fight. "After what happened to you, your reaction is most natural. It will take time to heal. Do not expect too much of yourself and be patient."

Leonora cast her a warm smile, then rested her head against Louisa's shoulder as they stood side-by-side, looking down at the not-quite frozen lake nearby. "Do you think they will be able to skate again this year?" she asked with a chuckle, no doubt remembering Louisa's break-neck stunt from the previous year as she had done what she had to in order to save Anne from Lord Gillingham's advances.

"Not unless it grows colder," Louisa replied as her gaze swept over the grounds and the many guests strolling across the green lawns, here and there powdered with snow. "Do you think he's here again this year? Lord Gillingham?"

Lifting her head off Louisa's shoulder, Leonora, too, looked around. "I do not see him." Her gaze moved to where Anne and Tobias were strolling along the entrance to the maze where only the year before he had asked for her hand. "I admit, I hope he is not, for it would be most difficult for him to see Anne with Tobias, would it not? Do you think he genuinely cared for her?"

Louisa shrugged. "That I cannot say." A strange shiver suddenly danced down her spine, and she turned, not surprised in the least, to see Phineas walking toward them. A wide smile came to his face the moment their eyes met, and Louisa could not deny that she had missed him over the course of the long carriage ride. Indeed, her earlier hatred of him had completely disappeared, replaced by something warm and intoxicating. Did he feel it, too?

"Who is that?" Leonora asked, an odd, breathless flutter in her voice.

Louisa blinked, and saw a tall, dark man walking next to Phineas. How she had not noticed him before she could not say. Although both men shared certain outward similarities, their dark hair and tall stature, Phineas had a cheerful and at times wicked look about him. The man by his side did not. His face looked most serious, and Louisa could not help but wonder if he even knew the meaning of a smile. "I do not know," she replied, a frown drawing down her brows as she watched the two men most closely. "I cannot say that I have ever seen him before."

Headed their way, the men approached with slow steps, words passing between them. Still, Phineas' eyes rarely strayed from hers, and she felt the effect of it in every fiber of her being. "Good day, my ladies," Phineas greeted them with the usual mischievous twinkle in his dark eyes. "I hope you're well and have not suffered overly much over the course of our journey, which unfortunately deprived you of my charming presence."

"I cannot say that we have," Louisa replied with a chuckle. "Although Grandma Edie's snoring became a tad irritating after a while."

Phineas laughed, "So did the meaningful looks exchanged between Anne and Tobias. Perhaps on our way back we can make other arrangements."

Louisa was about to agree when Phineas' friend cleared his throat rather loudly, a displeased look coming to his face.

"I apologize," Phineas exclaimed, turning to look at his companion.

"Ladies, may I introduce you to an old friend from Eton, Drake Shaw, Marquess of Pemberton. Pemberton, these are Lady Louisa and Lady Leonora."

The marquess offered them a formal bow, his dark gray eyes glittering with something unspoken. "A pleasure, my ladies."

Louisa and Leonora returned his greeting. "My lord," Louisa exclaimed, wondering about this man she had never seen before at Phineas' side. "I admit, I am most surprised to make your acquaintance. I cannot say that...Lord Barrington has ever mentioned you before."

Phineas grinned at her directness. "To be quite truthful—"

"Which you rarely are," Louisa interrupted with a teasing chuckle.

Phineas cast her a mocking glare. "To be quite truthful, we have not seen each other in many, many years. I admit we were not the closest of friends at Eton. However, Pemberton has always been a man who despite our many, many differences has earned my respect." He grinned at his friend, who all but ignored him, his face rather impassive.

"And you've come across each other here by chance this Christmas season?" Louisa asked as she looked from one to the other.

Beside her, Leonora remained perfectly still, neither saying a word nor moving in the slightest.

An odd look came to Phineas' face. "Not quite," he replied, once more exchanging a look Louisa could not quite determine with the man by his side. "In fact, I asked him here."

"Why?" Louisa asked, unable to shake the sinking feeling that somehow it had something to do with her. Perhaps it was the look upon Phineas' face. There was guilt there, etched into his dark eyes. But why?

Inhaling a deep breath, Phineas stepped toward her, his hands reaching out to hold the one not currently clasped by Leonora. "Please, hear me out." He glanced over his shoulder at his friend, who shifted rather uncomfortably on his feet. The stone-like expression upon his face, however, remained the same.

Louisa tensed. "Say it then."

Phineas swallowed, and she could feel his hand tightening its grip upon hers as though afraid that she would slip away any moment. It was that sensation more than any other that sent a cold chill down Louisa's back. "I reached out to him," Phineas began, "because I thought he might be able to help you."

Although Phineas' hands were warm, Louisa felt her own fingers grow chilled. "What do you mean?" she asked, hearing the warning in her voice loud and clear. She could only hope Phineas heard it as well.

For a long moment, his dark gaze remained locked on hers, and she could see that he did understand her. "I apologize for not consulting you beforehand," Phineas told her, no hint of teasing in his voice now. He shook his head and scoffed, "In retrospect, of course, I should have. Still, all I can say is that it did not occur to me at the time. I'm sorry."

Louisa's teeth gritted together as she stared at him. "Sorry for what?" He didn't...! He couldn't have...! Thoughts ran rampant through her head, jerking her this way and that, not allowing her to finish any one of them. Confusion settled in, mingling with disappointment and regret. "Sorry for what?" she pressed when Phineas looked utterly contrite.

Behind him, Lord Pemberton linked his hands behind his back, his chin rising slightly, the look in his dark gray eyes one of disapproval. Still, he did not speak, but remained as still as an ice sculpture.

"What you told me," Phineas finally said, the look in his dark eyes telling her full well that he knew that his next words would infuriate her, "made me think of an old friend. I wondered, replaying old conversations and events in my mind, and in the end, I decided to simply speak to him. I did what I did because I want to help you. Perhaps I did not go about it the right way, but I urge you to believe me that I never meant you any harm." The look in his eyes was almost pleading, and a part of Louisa wanted to forgive him more than anything. Still, old emotions welled up, rose to the surface and buried everything tender and forgiving under a layer of shame.

As much as Louisa had expected her old anger to return, it did not. Instead, it was something cold that crept through her body, robbing her of every bit of strength she had left. Her muscles grew weak, and her arms all but dropped to her sides, hanging limply. She felt Leonora's hands fall from hers as a cold—one much colder than that of the icy wind around them—drifted into her bones. "You didn't," she mumbled, her voice no more but a faint whisper. Her feet stumbled backwards as she shook her head, staring at Phineas, dumbfounded. "You didn't. I trusted you." Shaking her head, Louisa continued to stare at him as her feet moved her backwards, increasing the distance between them. "I never should have. I was wrong to think that you—"

Suddenly becoming aware that they were not alone, that they indeed had an audience, Louisa clamped her lips shut. She glared at Phineas one last time, her eyes blurring with tears, and in that moment, she hated him for attacking her in such a way in front of others. Then she spun on her heel and rushed off, cursing her own weak heart for daring to believe that he could genuinely care for her.

Oh, how wrong she had been!

Chapter Thirty-Four

FIGHT OR FLIGHT

The shock and disappointment on her face felt like a dagger to his heart, and Phineas knew that he had acted most unwisely. In truth, the only reason he had not spoken to her beforehand was that he had not been certain.

After she had spoken to him about learning to read, about the difficulties she had faced, her words had echoed in his mind, tickling old memories, drawing him back to his days at Eton. It had been years since he had thought about those times, about the people he had met there, about those he had not seen since.

Still, after a while, his memories had become clearer and he had remembered an old friend, sitting at his desk, trying hard to make out words on the page. Phineas once again remembered his jaw set in determination, his eyes all but staring as though he simply needed to look hard enough to understand. He remembered frustration, but also an iron will to continue and not be deterred by the obstacles in his path.

He had finally remembered Drake Shaw, Marquess of Pemberton.

Long years had passed since they had last seen each other. Never had they been much alike. Where Phineas had always been one to seek the company of his friends, to spend time with others and share in their laughter and cheerfulness, Pemberton had always been one to keep to himself, rarely saying a word, his dark gray eyes always observant.

Cursing under his breath, Phineas called a quick apology over his shoulder to his friend as well as Lady Leonora. Then he immediately set off in pursuit of Louisa, knowing he could not let her think that he had betrayed her, that she could not trust him. Never would he have shared her secret with a person who would think ill of her. Indeed, Pemberton was one of only a few people Phineas knew to be beyond reproach.

Long strides carried him after her as she rushed back into the house. Phineas all but burst through the door only a few steps behind. "Louisa, wait!" he hissed under his breath, unwilling to draw too much attention.

Still, she kept going, barely glancing over her shoulder as she handed her coat to a footman. The look in her green eyes told him that she was not thinking clearly, that she did not choose her way with thought. She was merely putting one step in front of the other, trying to get away from him and the shame he had caused her.

Phineas' heart burned with regret as he followed her down the corridor and around the next corner. He was about to call out to her once more when she suddenly turned right and stumbled through open doors into a large drawing room.

A fire roared in the grate, its flames dancing cheerfully as it cast a warm light about the room. Evergreen garlands were hung everywhere, decorated with red ribbons and golden stars, and in the corner near the pianoforte, Phineas once more glanced a sprig of mistletoe.

Unfortunately, the room was far from deserted.

As her eyes fell on the assembled guests, Louisa pulled to a sudden halt and Phineas barely managed to still his own feet in time.

Many eyes turned in their direction, and Louisa drew in a deep breath as she faced them without flinching. Still, her hands balled into fists before she hid them behind her back, her whole body tense.

Phineas wanted nothing more but to get her out of there and find a quiet corner to explain and apologize. However, before he could speak a single word, Lady Hartmore bustled in behind him.

She stood tall with sharp eyes and a pointed nose that was raised in a haughty way. She held what looked like a letter in her hands, and a bit of a disconcerting smile came to her face when her gaze fell on Louisa. "Oh, my dearest Louisa, there you are," the lady exclaimed, a hint of deepest joy in her voice. Still, Phineas could not help but think that there was something dishonest about her. "I've received a letter from my eldest."

Lady Hartmore swept over to Louisa, looped her arm through hers and pulled her farther into the room. Then her eyes swept over the assembled guests, their attention caught by the sudden developments, and said for all to hear, "She married an earl a few years back, captured his heart in a single season." She beamed at everyone, clearly enjoying being the center of attention before she turned to Louisa. "I know, you used to be the dearest of friends and so I thought you would very much enjoy reading her letter." Smiling at Louisa in that odd, calculated way, the lady held out the letter to her. "Would you mind reading to us all?"

Louisa's face went frighteningly pale, and Phineas could feel his own heart come to a halt. He was torn about what to do as he watched Louisa slowly reach out her hand to take the proffered letter. Was he to interfere? Certainly, it would cause a scene. What did Louisa want him to do? Still, she would not look at him, and the thought that she no longer saw him as an ally, a confidant, a friend to whom she could turn pained him greatly.

"Of course," Louisa replied in a croak, her hands trembling as she unfolded the parchment. "It is my pleasure, Lady Hartmore." A distant, almost unseeing look lingered in Louisa's eyes, and Phineas wondered if she might think herself lost in a dream...or rather a nightmare.

As far as she had told him, Louisa had always been one to think quickly, to conjure explanations and excuses with the naturalness that had never raised any suspicions. Why did she not use such an excuse now? Why was she unfolding the letter? Did she honestly intend to read it?

Phineas felt as though he were about to explode. He felt like a caged tiger, the need to pace once more shooting down his legs. At the same time, he wished to plant his fist in Lady Hartmore's face, the notion surprising him for he had never experienced the desire to harm a woman. Still, the devious look in the lady's eyes made him wonder if she might have uttered this request for a specific reason. Could it be that she knew Louisa could not read?

Had Miss Mortensen shared Louisa's secret with her mother?

Louisa swallowed hard as her eyes fell onto the parchment. Then she began to read. "D-Dearest M-Mother." Her voice was unsteady, and Phineas was certain that not only he could hear how she carefully sounded out the words.

Frowns appeared on many faces as people turned to one another, exchanging confused glances. Still, no one said a word.

Not one.

And Louisa kept reading. Word for word. Slowly. Excruciatingly slowly. "I am w-well as is my h-hus-b-band. We w-would both like to see you and F-Father a-g-gain soon and were won-d-dering if..."

Phineas felt an almost desperate desire to rush to her side and snatch the parchment from her hands. Still, the moment his gaze moved away from the guests surrounding her to Louisa herself, all his anger vanished.

As though he had never seen her before, Phineas stared at her. He stared at the determined set of her jaw, at the strength glowing in her eyes, at the iron will that made her read on and on, ignoring the hushed whispers that now rose from the assembled guests.

And Phineas felt proud. Utterly and overwhelmingly proud.

A moment ago, she had seemed so vulnerable and near collapse, shaken by the mere thought that another knew her secret. And now, here, she stood, holding her head high as she faced her greatest fear, refusing to be intimidated any longer.

And so, Phineas simply stood there and watched and listened, a proud smile upon his face as Louisa read.

When she had all but reached the end, voices began echoing from down the corridor, and Phineas knew that her youngest sisters were heading their way. Their voices suddenly stilled, though, when they stepped over the threshold, their eyes drawn to Louisa, standing amidst a small crowd, reading.

Christina's eyes grew round, and she grasped Harriet's arm. Her younger sister, too, looked around the room, shocked. She recovered quickly, though, casting a warm and reassuring smile at her sister as well as her friend, who had entered with them.

Indeed, it was Miss Mortensen, and she grew utterly pale. She stared at the spectacle until Louisa finally lowered the letter. Then she suddenly rushed forward and grasped Lady Hartmore's arm, pulling her aside. "Mother, what is this?" she demanded in a hushed voice. "Did you do this?"

Phineas stared as the mother hissed a few words, then shook off her daughter, a displeased frown upon her face, and stepped forward to retrieve her letter. "Thank you, Lady Louisa. That was most...informative."

Louisa smiled at her, no hint of embarrassment upon her face. "It was my pleasure." Then she nodded to the assembled guests, turned around and left the room, not even glancing in Phineas' direction.

Phineas, however, had another matter on his mind in that moment. Instead of hurrying after Louisa once more, he walked down the corridor after Miss Mortensen, who had slunk out of the room the moment her mother had turned away from her.

With his gaze fixed upon the young woman, Phineas moved onward, keeping his distance until they reached a more deserted part of the house. Then he quickened his steps until he reached her, grasped her arm and pulled her aside. "Did you do this?" he demanded as he pushed her through a door into what looked like the conservatory.

Most walls were made of glass, allowing a magnificent view of the surrounding grounds, glistening as snowflakes slowly descended upon them. Bits of green still peeked out from under the soft layer of snow, whispering of what lay hidden underneath the white blanket.

As she turned around, Phineas could see the tears glistened in the young woman's eyes. "I had no idea she would do this," Miss Mortensen sobbed. "When she arrived at Whickerton Grove, she was most curious about my time there. I did not mean to tell her, but she has a way...a way of finding out everything. She promised me she would keep it to herself." She wrung her hands, her eyes pleading. "Please, believe me. The Whickerton sisters are like a second family to me. I would never betray them."

Phineas felt his anger subside at the sight of her honest turmoil. "What about that note?" he asked, remembering the night they had been almost found in a compromising situation. "Did you send it? Because we both know Louisa did not."

"No, I didn't. Of course, I didn't." She shook her head frantically, her mouth opening and closing, words tumbling from her lips, assuring him that she knew nothing.

"But then who—?" Phineas broke off when the young woman's face suddenly turned dangerously pale. "What?"

All but staring through him, Miss Mortensen whispered, "It was Mother." She blinked, and her blue eyes settled on him. "She and Father were the ones to come upon me that night, and the way she looked at me, the way she looked around the room, I..." She shook her head in disbelief. "It was Mother."

As though on cue, footsteps once more echoed closer, and Phineas felt reminded of that night months ago. His blood ran cold as he gazed around for another way out. However, before he could move, the door behind them was flung open and a group of guests filed in, led by none other but Lady Hartmore, a triumphant smile flashing over her haughty face before she quickly feigned confusion. "What is this? Sarah? Lord Barrington?" She looked from her daughter to him, clearly expecting him to do the honorable thing.

Phineas inhaled a deep breath, fighting the urge to yet again hit the lady square in the face. If she thought she had cornered him, she was very mistaken!

Chapter Thirty-Five

A BIT OF A BIND

Louisa knew not how she felt, nor did she know where she was going. Her eyes blinked, and she looked around, finding herself in the entrance hall, in that moment unable to recall how exactly she had found her way here.

Inhaling a deep breath, Louisa tried to calm down. Her blood pulsed wildly in her veins as the aftermath of what had just happened sank in. Indeed, after being so fearful for years and years on end, she had just now revealed her most shameful secret to the whole world.

And she had done so with pride in her heart, had she not?

A smile teased the corners of Louisa's mouth upward, and she felt a bit of the trembling that still lingered in her muscles subside. Yes, now, they all knew that she could not read...well.

And, no, the world had not ended.

Certainly, there would be those who would now whisper behind her back and snigger whenever she walked past. But why should Louisa care? In fact, she did not. Even in the very moment when she had read from Lady Hartmore's letter, she had not cared. The revelation had been shocking, yes, but ultimately Louisa knew she had never placed much stock in what other people thought. In truth, what had always held her back had been what she herself had thought.

And somehow, that had changed.

Unbidden, Phineas' face appeared before her eyes, that teasing gleam in his dark gaze and an equally teasing smile upon his lips. She could already hear him comment in his usual way about what she had done, about what others would now say. She could see him laugh and smirk and tease her, and it made her smile.

It made her miss him.

Still, the thought of him brought back a most unpleasant feeling. Why had he betrayed her secret? Why had he told his friend without asking her permission first?

"Pardon me?"

Startled out of her reverie, Louisa turned to find herself looking at a young woman about her own age. Brown curls danced down her temples, and her wide eyes shone in a startling blue. "I'm sorry to bother you, Lady Louisa," the young woman said, her voice no more than a whisper as she glanced over her shoulder as though looking to see if anyone was nearby. "I was wondering if I could ask you a favor."

Confused, Louisa nodded. "Certainly..."

A tinge of red came to the young woman's face. "I'm sorry. I'm Lady Agnes, Lord Whitmore's daughter."

Louisa smiled at her, wondering what this could possibly be about. Indeed, the look upon Lady Agnes's face did not speak of malice. It seemed unlikely that she had sought Louisa out to laugh in her face or poke fun at her in some way. "It's a pleasure to make your acquaintance. What can I do for you?"

Lady Agnes pressed her lips together, her hands trembling as her fingers played with the hem of her sleeve. "I...I heard you read Lady Hartmore's letter," she said carefully, her wide eyes watchful as though she was expecting Louisa to burst into flames.

"And?" Louisa prompted when the young woman remained quiet.

Lady Agnes swallowed hard, looking all but ready to faint. Fortunately, she did not. She opened her mouth and said, "I...I was wondering if you could help me. You see..." Her mouth opened and closed a couple of times before she once more spoke with an audible voice. "I, too, find...reading to be a challenge I...cannot quite seem...to master." Her eyes dropped from Louisa's face for a long moment before she once more dared to raise her gaze.

Thunderstruck, Louisa stared at Lady Agnes. Whatever she had expected, it had not been this. Of course, there was no reason to assume that she was the only one who had had trouble with the written word. Still, Louisa had always strangely assumed that no one else faced the same problem.

"I'm sorry," Lady Agnes stammered, slowly backing away. "I did not mean to bother you."

"No," Louisa called out before the young woman could slink away. She shook her head and inhaled a deep breath, then stepped forward. "I'm sorry, too. To be quite honest, you surprised me with your request. Yet, it is not unwelcome. Although I still find myself struggling, I am more than happy to assist you in any way I can."

Lady Agnes beamed at her. "Truly?"

Louisa nodded, feeling strangely light and unburdened. "Truly."

"Louisa!"

At the call of her name, Louisa turned around and spotted her two younger sisters rushing toward her. Alarm stood on their faces, their eyes wide and full of urgency. "Louisa, you must come! Quickly!" Harry exclaimed, not even glancing at Lady Agnes. Then she seized Louisa's hand and began dragging her away, Chris by her side. "Come quickly!"

Louisa frowned, looking from one sister to the other. "What is this about? What did you do?"

Chris shook her head, and her golden curls danced wildly through the air. "We did nothing," she assured her, the look upon her face suggesting something most alarming, nonetheless. "But it seems Sarah and Phineas have gotten themselves into a bit of a bind."

A jolt went through Louisa's heart. "Phineas?" Her steps quickened. "What happened?"

By now, they were all but running down the corridor, the distant sound of voices drifting to their ears. "I insist that you marry her," Louisa heard Lady Hartmore's rather shrill voice as they pulled to a halt outside the conservatory.

Many guests were assembled in the doorway, blocking their view, and it took some time to wind their way through the crowd.

"I will not," Phineas said in a dark voice the moment Louisa and her sisters managed to fight their way through. "Nothing happened. We merely had...something to discuss."

At that, Sarah nodded, her tear-streaked face unusually pale. "He speaks the truth, Mother," she replied, the tone in her voice strangely accusatory. "We only talked. Nothing else happened."

Lady Hartmore scoffed, "I find that hard to believe," she replied, her eyes sweeping over the assembled guests, most of whom were whispering most intently amongst themselves. "I came here with the sole intention of showing this beautiful conservatory to my dear friends, and what do I find here? My darling daughter alone with a most disreputable rake." She shook her head in disapproval. "Indeed, what mother would not insist they marry? My dear, you have your reputation to consider." She turned hard eyes on Phineas. "As do you, Lord Barrington. I suggest you think long and hard before you answer."

Louisa stared at the scene in bewilderment. She could see anger in Phineas' eyes, not guilt. How on earth had this happened?

Clearly refusing to be intimidated, Phineas drew himself up to his full height as he glared down at Lady Hartmore. "Perhaps you ought to do the same," he said in a menacing tone, his dark eyes appearing almost black. "Do you think so little of your daughter that you feel the need to trap her into marriage?"

More whispers arose from behind Louisa, but she tried her best to ignore them, her gaze fixed on Lady Hartmore's face. "I feel nothing of the kind," she exclaimed heartily. "Why would you ask such a thing? Especially after you've already kissed her? Do you deny it? That you kissed my daughter in this very house only a year ago?"

To Louisa's utter shock, Phineas gritted his teeth and said, "I do not. However—"

"Then why would you refuse to do the right thing? Are you not a gentleman?"

Phineas' words hit her like a punch to her midsection. She almost groaned in pain, her knees growing weak. Was this true? Of course, it was. After all, Phineas had just admitted to it. Had he truly kissed Sarah while chasing after her, Louisa? Had she misunderstood him?

Had whatever had been between them been nothing more than a flirtation? Could she have been so utterly wrong?

Overwhelmed, Louisa longed for solitude. She was about to whirl around and fight her way out of the room when a familiar wrinkled hand settled upon her arm. "You need to hear this, my dear," Grandma Edie whispered beside her, her grip strangely strong for such an old woman.

Blinking, Louisa looked down at her, wondering where she had come from and how long she had already been standing there. "Grandma?"

Giving her a warm smile, Grandma Edie patted her hand. "Listen."

Reluctantly, Louisa turned back to look upon Phineas, her grandmother's iron grip giving her the strength she needed to remain where she was and listen.

As though he could feel her eyes upon him, Phineas looked up in that moment and saw her. He tensed, a muscle in his jaw twitching, and his teeth ground together. Wild emotions stood in his dark eyes, and for a moment, she thought he might stride forward and seize her. He had done so before in these kinds of moments, moments that thudded wildly in his veins as much as in hers. But he remained still, his gaze shifting back to Lady Hartmore. "I kissed your daughter under a sprig of mistletoe," Phineas clarified, "which I assume you know." His brows rose, daring her to contradict him.

Displeasure flickered over the lady's face, but she quickly recovered. "That does not matter," she stated simply. "The facts remain. You compromised my daughter and are thus required to do the honorable thing."

Anger emanated from Phineas, and he took a menacing step closer to Lady Hartmore.

The woman flinched and almost took a step back. "Was it not you, who sent my daughter a note asking her to meet him in the library only a few months back?"

Sarah gasped in shock, her eyes wide as she stared at her mother. "How do you know this?" she demanded breathlessly. "I never told you about the note I'd received. I never told anyone, and I burned the note. How do you know?"

Phineas chuckled darkly, "I assume she knows because she was the one who wrote it. Is that not true?" he demanded, rounding on Lady Hartmore. "It is what you wanted, is it not? For your daughter to be compromised? To be forced into marriage?" He shook his head, disgust turning his lips into a snarl. "Do you honestly believe you have the right to manipulate everyone around you as you see fit? Is that not the most dishonorable way of treating one's family and friends?" He turned to look at Sarah, and the look in his eyes softened. "She's your daughter, and you've treated her without respect. I have no doubt that one day a most fortunate man will call her his wife." His eyes moved to settle upon Louisa. "But I am not that man."

Louisa felt a shuddering breath leave her lips as she stared across the small space at Phineas. The whispers in her back receded, and she was barely aware of her grandmother still holding on tightly to her arm.

All she could see was him.

Phineas.

And then Louisa heard her grandmother bring down her walking stick hard upon the marble floors. "Well, I suppose all has been said," she exclaimed, releasing Louisa's arm and turning toward the crowd. "Out you go! Out!" And swinging her walking stick in a rather uncoordinated fashion, Grandma Edie managed to clear the room of people in record time.

"I assure you I did nothing of the kind," Lady Hartmore hissed under her breath, indignation in her voice. Still, her cheeks blazed red-hot, marking her a liar before she turned and fled the room.

Louisa blinked as Sarah suddenly appeared before her. "I'm so very sorry," her sister's dearest friend exclaimed, large tears glistening in her eyes. "I had no idea. Never would I trick a man into marrying me. I could never be happy, knowing that his heart was not mine." She glanced over her shoulder at Phineas, then looked back at Louisa. "And his heart clearly belongs to you."

Louisa blinked, afraid to believe her ears. Then she looked up and found Phineas standing beside Sarah. "She's right, you know."

"Come, dear girl," Grandma Edie said gently, ushering Sarah toward the door. "You two as well." Reluctantly, Chris and Harry followed, and then the door closed behind them.

Once again, her grandmother was leaving her alone with Phineas Hawke.

Louisa could not help but smile. Perhaps her grandmother had been right all along. Who would have thought?

Chapter Thirty-Six

ONE DOWN

Phineas inhaled a deep, steadying breath as the room slowly cleared of people. The last one to leave was Louisa's grandmother, and as she walked past him, her watchful eyes looking up into his, she whispered, "One down. Five more to go." Then she chuckled and left the room, closing the door behind her.

Phineas grinned after the dowager, who had once more succeeded in locking him and Louisa in a room—alone. In truth, he would not be surprised if she had indeed *locked* the door.

"You received a note?" Louisa asked unexpectedly, her blue eyes settling on his. He saw uncertainty there as well as the need for reassurance.

Phineas nodded, stepping toward her. "I did. It was months ago."

A deep frown came to her face. "And you went to meet her?"

Reaching for her hands, Phineas held them tightly within his own. "I thought the note was from you," he told her slowly, needing her to hear him, to believe him. "It was only a few words, signed with an L. I didn't think for a moment that it could be from anyone else."

Louisa remained still, her eyes drifting left and right as she thought, mulling all he had said over in her head. "It must've been before you found out that..." She lifted her gaze to look up at him.

Phineas nodded. "I did not know then, and when I found out, I no longer thought of the note." He moved closer, slipping his hands around her middle. "I had other things on my mind by then."

The hint of a blush came to her cheeks at his suggestive words, telling him that she understood quite well what he was referring to. "Is that so?" she asked, a hint of the familiar banter back in her voice.

"It is."

For a long moment, they merely looked at one another, all that had just passed lingering in the air around them. "Are you all right?" Phineas finally asked, still feeling a slight tremble in her frame.

Louisa heaved a deep sigh. "That, I cannot say. Suddenly, this question seems much more complicated than it once did." Her hands moved up his arms and then drew down over his chest, her fingers curling into his lapels. She gave him a slight tug, her eyes snapping up to look into his. "Tell me everything. Now."

And Phineas did, leaving nothing out. "I never meant to go behind your back," he assured her. "Or keep anything from you. I only meant to help. I thought if you knew that you were not the only one who struggled with this…If you knew that there were others…"

"And the kiss?" she demanded, her green eyes blazing with something that resembled jealousy.

Phineas could not deny that he liked the way she looked at him, a possessive twinkle in her eyes. He laughed, pulling her closer, "Jealous?"

"Yes!" Louisa replied, surprising them both.

For a heartbeat or two, they remained still, utterly unmoving, breathing the same air, their eyes locked. Then Phineas said, "Good" and pulled her into a kiss.

And Louisa reciprocated in kind. She did not pull away or resist in any way. No, to Phineas' delight, she sank into his arms with the same desperate urgency he felt pulse in his own veins.

Only a few moments ago, all had seemed lost. Although Phineas had never had the intention of *doing the right thing* and marrying Miss Mortensen, Louisa could not have known it. And he, on the other hand, had feared that she might not be able to see past his thoughtless betrayal of her secret.

All had been uncertain only a few moments ago. And now?

Wrenching his lips away, Phineas stared at her. "I need to ask you something," he gasped breathlessly, delighting in the small noise of discontent she made when he broke their kiss.

"Then ask it quickly," Louisa ordered before she pushed herself up onto her toes and reclaimed his lips.

Kissing her back, Phineas felt passion flared to life, overruling all rational thought. Need burnt in his veins, only tampered by the deep emotions warming his heart. "You're a fierce one, are you not?" he chuckled against her lips.

"Don't act surprised." Louisa pulled back, her green eyes dark as she smiled up at him. "What did you want to ask me?"

Without another thought, Phineas blurted out, "Marry me!"

Louisa stilled, her eyes going wide as she stared at him. "That's not a question," was all she said, looking utterly stunned.

Phineas, too, had to admit that he could have phrased his request differently. "I'm sorry." He swallowed, feeling an oddly vulnerable smile coming to his lips. "Will you marry me, Lulu?"

For an agonizingly long second, Phineas thought she would refuse him. Indeed, it had been a poor choice to use the nickname she loathed above all others in this very moment. Still, that nickname held a different meaning for him!

"You know you deserve a slap for that, don't you?" she asked him instead of answering his question. Still, the corners of her lips strained upward, and soon she grinned at him from ear to ear, her eyes aglow in the dim light streaming in through the windows.

"Is that a *yes*?" Phineas dared to ask, tightening his hold on her as he dipped his head, his nose brushing against hers.

Louisa inhaled a bit of a fluttering breath. "Are you certain? I've just made a bit of a fool of myself, revealing to all that—"

"Yes!" Phineas replied, not feeling the slightest hint of doubt in his heart. "I want you. It doesn't matter what anyone says or thinks; I want you. You!"

Tears suddenly misted in her eyes. "Good!" she replied as he had before, pulling him into another life-changing kiss.

"My own reputation is not sparkling like gold, either," Phineas warned her as they came up for air. "Perhaps you should consider how a connection to me might impact your life."

Panting, Louisa clung to him. "It might not be wise," she mumbled, kissing him again, "but it feels right."

"Is that a *yes?*" Phineas asked again, reluctant to break their kiss, but equally determined to have his answer.

"Yes!" Louisa finally said, but then added, "Under one condition."

Phineas nodded, holding his breath.

"No more lies," Louisa stated, a strange severity lingering in her green eyes. "No more secrets. No more *protecting*. No more *good intentions*."

"I'm not allowed to protect you?" Phineas teased, wondering if he would ever tire of doing so. He rather doubted it.

Louisa rolled her eyes at him, and Phineas knew he would not tire of that, either. "You know what I mean," she rebuked him. "People always find excuses for justifying something they know they should not do." She shook her head. "Let's not be like them. I want you to trust that I'm strong enough to bear whatever comes our way. Do you not want the same? For me to see you as my equal, a man I can always count on, a man I trust without hesitation, a man I can lean on whenever I need to."

Phineas knew she would slap him. Still, he could not resist and said, "Of course, I see you as an equal." He fought hard to maintain a straight face. "However, I might have some difficulties seeing you as a *man* I can always count on, a *man* I trust without h—"

As expected, a dark glare came to Louisa's eyes before her open hand connected rather painfully with his upper arm. Indeed, the woman was not one to hold back, and he loved that about her. "Can you not ever be serious?" she demanded, annoyance in her voice. "How will I ever know when and if you mean what you say?" She was about to say more, but then stilled, the playful spark that had been in her eyes despite the glare she had directed at him slowly extinguishing. Her face became thoughtful, and her eyes distant, her mind no doubt lingering upon something else.

Gently, Phineas placed a hand on her shoulder. "What is it?"

Louisa blinked, and her green eyes returned to him. "Why did you tell Lord Pemberton about me? Why did you not ask me before you spoke to him?" Taking a step back, she crossed her arms over her chest, then lifted her chin. There was vulnerability in the way she looked at him. Still, her posture spoke of someone determined not to bow her head but to stand tall no matter what.

"As I said before, I only wanted to help," Phineas said honestly, knowing that the truth was exactly what Louisa had just demanded of him. "After what you told me about the difficulties you faced, I felt reminded of him, of my old friend from Eton." He shrugged, looking at her with all the sincerity he could. "I admit, I did not think. Yes, it was wrong of me to talk to him without consulting you first. But I meant no harm, I assure you. I simply did not wish to give you hope when I could not be certain that he would agree to lend his assistance, to speak to you and to reveal how he himself struggled with this." He reached out to grasp her hands once more, relieved when she allowed him. "Will you forgive me for being a thoughtless fool?"

Her gaze softened, and he could see that she was trying hard not to smile. Still, after a heartbeat or two, she lost the battle, and the corners of her mouth drew upward. "I will this time," she told him, her forefinger raised in warning. "Nevertheless, this is the one and only time I will allow you to get away with such a lame excuse. Next time, there will be severe repercussions." A devilish smile came to her face.

Phineas laughed "I must say I rather like this wicked side of you," he whispered to her, pulling her closer into his embrace. "I hope to see it more often." As she lifted her face to his, Phineas lowered his head in turn, determined to pick up where they had left off.

Unfortunately, before he could reclaim her lips, Louisa jerked backward out of his arms, her eyes wide and a hint of horror coming to her face. "Oh, no!"

A cold shiver ran down Phineas' back. "What is it? What happened?"

"Oh, no! No! No! No!" Backing away, Louisa shook her head from side to side, her gaze still distant and unseeing. Then she spun around, and pulling open the door, made to rush out.

Phineas barely managed to grasp her arm, pulling her back. "Will you tell me what's going on?" His pulse started hammering wildly in his veins, and he felt a sense of fear and terror he had never experienced before. His hands closed more tightly around her upper arms as his dark gaze searched her face. "What's wrong? Tell me!"

Swallowing, Louisa stared up at him, the look upon her face still sending chills through his body. "I left her alone," she stammered, still shaking her head. "I promised her I wouldn't. I told her she would be safe with me." Her breathing came quickly now. "I left her alone!" Again, she tried to jerk out of his arms, but Phineas held her tight.

"Are you speaking of Leonora?" he asked, trying to understand why Louisa was looking so horrified. "Why can you not leave her alone? Perhaps she is still outside with—" The words died on his lips as Phineas finally realized why Louisa looked so horrified. "He would never hurt her! I've known him forever, and he is the most decent man I have ever come across in all my years. I give you my word!"

Louisa swallowed hard. "I never for a second thought he would," she replied, still straining away from him, her feet eager to leave. "It is not about him, but about her. She feels...afraid around any man right now. It does not matter who he is. The thought to be alone with some-one, anyone frightens her. She didn't even want to come here. She only agreed because I promised her I would not leave her side." And with that, she broke free from his hold and dashed out of the conservatory.

Phineas could only hope that Louisa would find a way to help her sister because living in fear was no life at all. And Leonora deserved better.

Chapter Thirty-Seven

A TRUE GENTLEMAN

Louisa cursed herself for having been so caught up in her own drama that she had all but forgotten about her sister. The thought of what Leonora had to have gone through pained her. After everything that had happened to her, she deserved to feel safe now. How could she, Louisa, have been so careless?

After slipping into her coat, Louisa rushed back outside to the last spot where she had seen Leonora. Would she still be there? Or had she escaped Lord Pemberton's presence right after Louisa had fled the scene? Where could she be?

Leaving fresh prints in the thin layer of snow covering the lawns, Louisa headed back out into the gardens. The light was dimming, gray clouds drifting overhead, whispering of rain or snow. A chilling wind blew into her face, cooling her heated cheeks after the emotional moment she had just experienced. "I'm betrothed," Louisa whispered suddenly, shocking herself as the significance of that simple moment only a few minutes ago sank in. "I'm getting married. I'm going to marry...Phineas Hawke." As outlandish as the thought felt, it still brought a wide smile to her face and sent utter happiness to her heart.

Her smile quickly disappeared, though, when her gaze swept over the small slope where she had last seen her sister. Unfortunately,

Leonora was nowhere to be seen. Neither was Lord Pemberton. "Where could she be?" Louisa mumbled, craning her neck, hoping to spot her sister's slender figure and bright blue eyes somewhere in the gardens.

"Louisa!"

At the sound of her sister's voice, Louisa whirled around.

To her utter surprise, Leonora looked neither terrified nor angry. The look upon her face held mild nervousness; a far cry from the full-on terror Louisa had seen there before.

Especially, considering that Lord Pemberton was standing only an arm's length or two away from her.

Louisa frowned, momentarily wondering what had happened since she had rushed off. Then she inhaled a deep breath, willed a smile onto her face and approached. Curiously, she looked back and forth between her sister and her fiancé's—that still felt odd!—old friend. "Is everything all right?" she asked, her gaze seeking Leonora's.

Her sister nodded. "Everything's fine," she told Louisa before her gaze moved back to Lord Pemberton, something oddly intimate in her blue eyes.

Still rather stoic, Lord Pemberton inclined his head to her in answer or reassurance; Louisa did not know. His gray eyes were watchful, but kind, and he kept sweeping his gaze over their surroundings as though expecting an attack at any moment. There was something tense in his shoulders, and Louisa could not help but think that he looked angry...although he did hide it well.

What was most odd was the fact that Leonora did not seem terrified at all. Under the circumstances, Louisa would have expected her to have bolted long before now. After all, Lord Pemberton appeared far from harmless. Indeed, something rather dangerous lingered in his gray eyes, enhancing the threat of his towering stature and broad-shouldered appearance. Why was Leonora still here? What had happened between them? Had they spoken to each other?

After another sweep of their surroundings, Lord Pemberton once more turned to look at Leonora. "I bid you good day, my lady." Again, he inclined his head to her most respectfully, then took a step back, turned and strode away.

A small smile played over Leonora's face as she watched him leave. Then she inhaled a deep breath, and her blue gaze flickered back to Louisa. "Did Phineas catch up with you?" she asked, slipping her arm through Louisa's and pulling her along back up toward the house.

Confused by her sister's increasingly odd behavior, Louisa found herself stopping every few steps of the way, turning to look at Leonora's face. "He did."

"And? Did you let him explain?"

Louisa frowned. "Let him explain?" She stopped for good, her hands settling on her hips as she looked at her sister. "Whose side are you on?"

A warm smile came to Leonora's face. "The side that will see you two married soon." She laughed, and Louisa could do little else but stare at her. "Is something wrong?" Leonora asked, a slight frown drawing down her brows as she looked at her sister. "Please, don't tell me that you refused him. It is so obvious that he cares for you. You must believe him that he only spoke to Lord Pemberton to help you."

Louisa shook her head, trying to clear it. "I know that," she replied, a bit of an annoyed note in her voice. "How do *you* know? How could you possibly...?" Her gaze shifted back to the spot where they had all stood together not long ago before it returned to Leonora. "You spoke to Lord Pemberton, did you not?"

Leonora nodded. "Of course, I did. Why is that such a surprise to you?"

"Because... Because..." Louisa stared at her sister, torn between a feeling of deepest guilt and one of slowly growing annoyance. "Because I promised to remain by your side," she finally exclaimed, confused and admittedly a bit concerned by Leonora's strange behavior. "I promised, and I broke that promise. I did not mean to, but when Phineas..." She shook her head, momentarily too overwhelmed to find the right words.

Leonora's hand settled upon her shoulder, a warm smile coming to her face. "I'm not angry," her sister assured her. "I saw your face, and I know that you were afraid and overwhelmed. I understand."

Louisa exhaled a breath of relief. "And you are all right?"

A faint shadow crossed over Leonora's face. "I admit for a moment

I was terrified." A faraway look came to her eyes, and no more words tumbled from her lips.

Louisa reached for her sister's hand, squeezing it gently. "What happened?"

Leonora blinked, and that warm smile slowly reclaimed her face. "I'm fine," was all she said.

Louisa frowned. "You need to tell me more than that."

Laughing, Leonora shook her head, "For now, I'm afraid I cannot."

"Why?" A cold feeling settled in Louisa's belly. "Do you not trust me?"

"Oh, that is not it!" Leonora assured her instantly. "It is simply that I...need some time to understand it myself." The hint of a question lingered in her voice as though she honestly did not know what to make of the moment she had spent alone with Lord Pemberton.

Searching her sister's face, Louisa wasn't quite ready to drop the subject. In fact, she was far, far from it. "What did he do?" she demanded, feeling a sudden urge to strangle the man despite not knowing what exactly he *had* done.

If anything at all.

Leonora inhaled a slow breath before releasing it once more, her eyes clear and no longer overshadowed as they had been for so long. Indeed, something *had* changed. "He did nothing untoward," Leonora finally said. "I can see what you're thinking, and I assure you that Lord Pemberton behaved as a perfect gentleman should."

"Then why won't you tell me what happened?" Louisa asked, wishing she could understand the sudden change in her sister. What could Lord Pemberton have possibly said or done that could have reassured Leonora in such a profound way that she suddenly almost seemed like her old self again?

"I cannot explain what I do not understand," Leonora replied in her gentle way. "I need time to analyze everything that happened, to make sense of it and to understand how one thing is connected to another. I hope you can understand that."

Far from satisfied with her sister's answer, Louisa nodded, nonetheless. After all, Leonora had always been thus. Always observing. Always assessing. Always taking her time before making up her mind.

She was a scientist, and she knew not how to be anyone else. It was who she was, and perhaps it would help her find her way back to her old self.

Indeed, listening to Leonora prattle on about another project she sought to undertake felt deeply reassuring. The worry that had lingered upon Louisa's soul since the night of the masquerade lifted and drifted off, hopefully never to be seen again.

Walking with her sister arm in arm back to the house, Louisa smiled. "I'm glad to see that you are still capable of confusing me in that usual way of yours," she chuckled.

Leonora gave her one of her usual looks. "You do know that I don't do it intentionally, don't you?"

Louisa nodded, grinning. "That doesn't make it any less confusing." She patted her sister's hand as they stepped back across the threshold into the warm house. "But I'm glad to see you did not lose that side of you."

For a moment, Leonora's gaze held hers. "As am I," she whispered then, a slight catch in her voice. "I'm still me. I...I simply need to find a way to...to reclaim myself." A brave smile teased her lips. "I'll manage. Don't worry. It might take some time, but now...now I know that it can be done."

Footmen took their coats. "And you did not know so before?" Louisa asked in a hushed tone before they strode away across the foyer. "Before speaking to Lord Pemberton?"

Her sister shrugged. "I cannot explain it." She looked at Louisa. "I'm sorry, but I need some time to think everything through." She inhaled another deep breath. "But, yes, he...he helped me."

Staring at her sister, Louisa shook her head. "I admit I'm a bit jealous that he managed to help you where I could not. Not that I'm saying I regret that he did! I'm glad you feel..." Her voice trailed off, not certain if *better* was an appropriate word for she could still see that fearful spark lurking in the depth of Leonora's blue eyes. Would it ever vanish completely? Or would she carry it for the rest of her life?

Footsteps echoed closer, saving Louisa from finding a fitting word. She turned and saw her new fiancé walking toward them, a smile fighting to claim his face as his gaze fell on hers. Still, he held back, and his gaze drifted to Leonora, caution in his dark eyes. "There you are," he said, glancing from one sister to the other.

Louisa offered him a reassuring smile. "Were you looking for us?"

Understanding her silent reply to his equally silent question, Phineas nodded, that smile finally fighting through to the surface. "Indeed, I was." He glanced at Leonora, another question on his face. "I've gathered our families in the blue salon. Will you join us?"

Louisa grinned, her heart skipping a beat, while Leonora frowned, looking from Phineas to her. "The blue salon? Why?" She grasped Louisa's hand tightly, her eyes opening wide. "What happened?" Her gaze darted to Phineas. "Are you—?"

The grin upon Phineas' face was unmistakable, and Louisa found her own head bobbing up and down rather vehemently, a wide grin upon her face, as Leonora's eyes returned to her.

"Truly?" her sister asked, utter joy barely held in check clearly visible upon her face.

"Truly," Louisa replied before Leonora threw herself into her arms, hugging her with a strength Louisa would not have expected.

Phineas chuckled, "I'm glad you approve," he said to his future sister-in-law. "I confess I did not procure your father's blessing before asking Louisa." He looked at her, a deeply meaningful look in his eyes that Louisa felt all the way to her toes. "It was a rather overwhelming moment."

"Oh, do not worry," Leonora assured him cheerfully. "Father will take one look at her, see how she is glowing and welcome you into the family without further ado." And with that, she grasped one of their hands each and pulled them ahead toward the blue salon.

Chapter Thirty-Eight

A NEW CHAPTER

Fortunately for Phineas, Leonora ended up being right. She dragged him and Louisa into the blue salon where not only her parents, grandmother and brother and sisters were waiting, but also Tobias and Anne. All their faces held expectant looks, and Phineas guessed that at least half of them were assuming quite accurately why he had summoned them here.

"Will you finally tell us why we're here?" Harriet complained, a bit of a bored expression upon her face as she kept glancing out the window. "I admit I'd rather be out there than in here."

"Patience," their mother chided gently, a knowing smile upon her face as she walked by her daughter and patted her shoulder before seating herself next to her.

Troy eyed Phineas with a rather tense expression, suggesting that he, too, guessed what they were about to reveal to their families. Anne and Tobias grinned widely, exchanging meaningful glances with one another. "Well," Phineas finally said as Leonora stepped away and joined her family, leaving him and Louisa side by side.

"Well," Louisa repeated, catching his eye, a joyous smile coming to her face as she sidled closer, slipping her hand through the crook of his arm.

Phineas felt like the luckiest man in the world and would have easily forgotten the other people in the room if the dowager countess had not cleared her throat rather loudly. "No one's getting any younger," she chided with a chuckle. "I, for one, would like to hear the good news before my heart gives out."

Phineas laughed and pulled Louisa into his arms, his gaze moving to look at the dowager countess, remembering what she had said to him after clearing the room so he could speak to Louisa. "I suspect nothing that happens ever truly comes as a surprise to you, does it?"

The old woman laughed but did not say a word.

It was Louisa's father, who stepped forward, his watchful gaze lingering upon his daughter, a warm smile on his face. "I assume congratulations are in order, my dear," he said, stepping toward her and holding out his hands.

Leaving Phineas' embrace, Louisa grasped her father's hands. "Yes, Father."

His smile widened. "You're happy," he observed, squeezing her hands.

Louisa nodded, and Phineas was overwhelmed to see tears mist her eyes. Indeed, he had known that she cared for him, that she even loved him. Still, the strength he had always seen in her had never allowed him to see her as one of those women who could be brought to tears by words of affection, by moments of love. And it touched him that she showed her happiness so openly.

"We're betrothed," Louisa finally said loud and clear for all to hear. "I'm going to marry him."

Joyful cheers erupted throughout the room, and they were pulled into many warm hugs as Anne and Tobias surged forward, closely followed by Louisa's brother and sisters. "You sound rather surprised," Chris remarked with a smirk as she finally released Louisa, stepping back and looking at the two of them.

Harriet nodded. "Indeed, you look more surprised than the rest of us. How is that possible?" She glanced at her sister. "Of course, we have every right to be surprised for you always made it quite clear that you —how can I put it nicely?—that you rather loathed Phineas Hawke."

She said the word *loathed* carefully and with an apologetic look cast in his direction.

Louisa laughed, hugging her mother and then her grandmother. "Oh, believe me, for the longest time I was convinced that I did."

"Then what changed your mind?" Juliet inquired, assisting their grandmother back into her armchair. Phineas could not help but doubt that the old lady required it and wondered what she was up to; for clearly the dowager always had a plan...for everything. Had it not been her who had somehow maneuvered them, Louisa and him, together again and again?

"It was not one isolated moment," Louisa told her family, her eyes moving to meet his, the look in them whispering of the many challenges they had faced over the course of the past few months. "It was..." She shrugged, unable to find the words.

Moving to her side, Phineas pulled her back into his arms where she belonged. "It was everything and nothing. It was the good and the bad and everything in-between."

"It usually is, is it not?" Louisa's mother remarked as she looked up at her husband, and Phineas noticed for the first time that the way Louisa's parents looked at one another echoed within himself. Was it the same way he now looked at Louisa? The same way she now looked at him? Did love always feel the same? But in truth it did not matter, did it?

"Indeed, Lord Archibald's Christmas house party is proving utterly life-changing for our families, is it not?" Anne chuckled, snuggling closer into her husband's arms as she looked around at her family. "This is the second marriage proposal here." She looked around the sisters. "Perhaps not the last one."

Everyone laughed. "Does that mean you intend to return next year?" their father asked, a wide grin upon his face as he hugged his wife closer, his gaze sweeping over his assembled children. "At the risk of finding yourself betrothed before you know it?"

Harry frowned. "As though we do not always attend even in lieu of this additional reason."

"When you say *risk*, it sounds very dire," Chris remarked with a small smile upon her face. "Perhaps it's simply our family's good fortune."

Anne nodded in agreement. "Perhaps there is something magical at work here and it will see yet another one of us happily married next year." Her gaze drifted to Juliet, who as the eldest sister ought to have married first. The look upon Juliet's face, however, betrayed that she doubted she would be the next one to tie the knot.

Or even at all.

"I would certainly like to attend again next year," Tobias replied diplomatically before he smiled warmly at his young wife. "It is a wonderful reminder of the beautiful start of our lives together." Anne sank into his arms.

"I quite agree," Phineas whispered to Louisa as everyone began talking at once, planning future visits and speculating if indeed one of the sisters would find herself proposed to next time around.

"You need to tell me more about your old friend from Eton," Louisa said suddenly as they moved a bit farther away from the cacophony of voices.

Phineas felt a twinge of guilt. "I'm truly sorry about—"

Louisa shook her head. "Not because of me, but because of Leonora."

"Leonora?" Phineas frowned. "What do you mean?"

After glancing over his shoulder—no doubt at Leonora—Louisa then leaned closer and whispered, "I mean that something happened between the two of them."

"What do you mean *happened*? You mean...?" His brows rose meaningfully.

"No, not like that."

"Then what do you mean?"

A hint of exasperation came to her eyes. "I don't know."

"She didn't tell you?" Phineas asked, concerned that some underlying resentment still lingered in Leonora's heart after Louisa had taken so long to confide in her about her inability to read.

Louisa did not seem pained, though. "She said she didn't know. She said she needed time to...analyze everything." Her nose scrunched up a bit.

"But something happened," she insisted, her green eyes blazing with certainty as she looked up at him. "When they met, they were strangers, and when I came upon them again, they...were not." She shook her head, not finding better words to explain the feeling that had settled in her heart.

"Very well," Phineas replied, seeking to calm her. "I'll speak to him, and we'll keep an eye on them. If she needs time, then give her time. It was what you needed as well, was it not?"

Begrudgingly, Louisa nodded. "I'm not good at waiting." A huffed breath drifted from her lips.

Phineas chuckled, "That, I know." He pulled her into his arms again, resting his chin on top of her head. "Neither am I." He inhaled a slow breath, enjoying the feel of her so close. "We have a wedding to plan."

A moment of silence passed, and Phineas wished he could see Louisa's face. When she spoke, a hint of amusement lingered in her voice. "You don't want to wait?"

"Heck, no!"

Louisa laughed, muffling the sound by burying her face against his shoulder. "Neither do I."

"Do you think your father would object to a special license?"

Lifting her head, Louisa looked up at him, her eyes shimmering in a dark green. "He won't deny me anything that'll make me happy."

"That is good to know." Phineas' hands settled upon her waist, pulling her closer. "I'm a rather impatient man myself."

"We are a perfect match in that regard."

He quirked an eyebrow. "And in all the others?"

Louisa smiled at him, a teasing gleam in her eyes. "We shall see. I suppose only time and practice will tell."

"That sounds most promising," Phineas agreed, growing more impatient by the minute to finally begin this new life that awaited him. Marriage had always rather seemed like the end to his carefree and exciting days. Now, however, it seemed the most exciting adventure was only about to begin.

Epilogue

January 1802, London

A Fortnight Later

T he New Year had barely begun, and yet, Louisa's life had changed so completely that she still experienced moments of utter disbelief.

Truthfully, she had only been married for about an hour, but every time she looked at her new husband, seated next to her at their wedding breakfast in her family's London townhouse, Louisa felt as though she had strayed into a dream.

She had married Phineas Hawke! Phineas Hawke, her nemesis! The man she had loathed for the past two years! But had she truly? Loathed him, that is?

That question had occupied her mind as of late, and Louisa had begun to wonder if her hatred would have been so overwhelmingly complete if she had not in truth cared for him. Would he have been able to wound her in such a profound way if her heart had not opened to him?

She rather doubted it.

"You're frowning," Phineas commented in a hushed whisper as he leaned in, his gaze quizzical. "What did I do?" They were standing in the drawing room now, the voices of their friends and family echoing around them as everyone chatted and laughed, enjoying their special day.

Snow glistened outside the tall windows, reflecting the sun and brightening their day. Despite the chill, spring seemed to already linger nearby as though only waiting for the cold to retreat before reawakening the sleeping world under its snowy blanket.

Louisa laughed, slapping his shoulder, wondering if anyone would notice if she were to pull him into a kiss. "Don't worry," she told him, sliding her hand up his chest as she moved closer. "You're safe."

His breathing paused as his gaze drifted down to her exploratory hand upon his chest. "I'm glad," he muttered, then lifted his gaze to meet hers. "Then tell me which unfortunate creature managed to get onto your bad side."

Biting her lower lip, Louisa marveled at the tingling sensations chasing each other down her back as her husband's hands settled upon her waist, his dark gaze speaking of other things than his words suggested. "You," she finally whispered, savoring the slight frown that came to his face.

"You confuse me," Phineas replied with a grin, clearly not bothered by her contradictory comments at all.

Nodding her head at an acquaintance across the room, Louisa turned her attention back to her husband. "I was merely thinking of *that moment* two years ago," she told him honestly, noting the slight tension that came to his shoulders as he nodded in understanding. "Perhaps I never did hate you. Perhaps I was merely furious with you for wounding me." Her fingers curled into his lapels as she pushed closer still, his head lowering to hers. "Don't ever do it again!" Her eyes held his, and despite her instinct to hide her every weakness, Louisa allowed him to see how much she depended upon him for her happiness.

"I can be a fool sometimes," Phineas told her earnestly, his fingers grasping her chin, his gaze never veering from her, "but I'm not suicidal. I'll never risk what we have. I'll tease you and irritate you to see your eyes light up, but I'll never break your heart. I promise."

Touched by his words, Louisa pushed onto her toes and kissed him. To hell with anyone who might disapprove!

Phineas responded instantly, his hands pulling her against him until their hearts beat against one another. Still, she could feel his restraint, which, of course, was advisable since they had an audience. An audience, which in the next moment, erupted in loud applause!

Pulling back, Louisa felt her cheeks flush and found an equally self-conscious look come to her new husband's face as well. Still, after an acknowledging nod to the small crowd, Phineas once more leaned down to her. "Tonight," he whispered, the look in his dark gaze stealing her breath.

Unable to form proper words, Louisa merely nodded.

"I shall take my leave."

Turning around, Louisa found Lord Pemberton had approached rather soundlessly, his face once again not betraying even the slightest emotion. In fact, the man seemed continually bored or at least rather unimpressed by life in general. "So soon?" she asked, slipping her arm through Phineas' and leaning into him in a hopefully inconspicuous way.

Lord Pemberton nodded. "I have an appointment I was unable to postpone."

Louisa frowned, wondering if she had truly detected a hint of disapproval in his voice for their rather impromptu wedding. Indeed, even she had had to cancel a prior engagement with a friend to marry Phineas this very day!

"I'm glad you were able to come today," Phineas told his old friend, gently placing a hand upon Louisa's as he spoke, the pad of his thumb drawing lazy circles over her skin. "What a coincidence to find you the Whickertons' new neighbor!"

Lord Pemberton nodded once again, not another word passing his lips before he turned and walked away.

"He is rather tight-lipped, is he not?" Louisa remarked, not certain if she liked the fact that Lord Pemberton had been the one to purchase the townhouse next door, Sarah's old home.

Phineas nodded, a chuckle passing his lips. "I believe I can count the words he spoke during our time at Eton on one hand."

"But you found him to be of decent character?" Louisa asked for it had not escaped her attention that Leonora had taken an odd interest in their new neighbor ever since their first encounter at Windmere Park a mere fortnight ago. Unfortunately, after today, Louisa would no longer be around daily to keep an eye on her sister.

Perhaps she ought not have rushed their wedding after all! Still, one look into her new husband's dark, smoldering gaze convinced her differently. Indeed, they had wasted enough time bickering!

"A good heart does not need words," Phineas told her. "He might seem dark and forbidding at times, but I have no doubt that your sister will be safe with him."

Whirling around, Louisa stared up at him. "What? How do you know I've been worried th—?"

Smiling down at her, Phineas once more pinched her chin. "Your concern for Leonora has been written all over your face ever since..." His voice trailed off, and a shadow passed over his face. He, too, still felt regret and anger whenever that fateful night resurfaced in their conversation.

Louisa sighed.

"Additionally," Phineas added with a smirk, his gaze straying to the window and coming to rest on something beyond her shoulder, "I can see her sneaking away this very second." He nodded his head in the very direction that had caught his gaze. "That is her, is it not?"

Once more whirling around, Louisa stared out the window at the lone, cloaked figure, carefully picking her way through the snow toward the hedge growing on the property line to the neighboring townhouse. In years past, Chris and Harriet had often sneaked through a gap in the green to visit with Sarah. Or Sarah had ventured over here.

"Oh, no, she wouldn't!" Louisa muttered as she stood with her hands pressed to the cool windowpane, watching her sister glance over her shoulder before squeezing through the gap in the evergreen hedge.

"Seems to me that she would," Phineas remarked chuckling.

"This is serious!" Louisa exclaimed, looking back and forth between her new husband and the spot where Leonora had been standing only a moment ago. Now, however, it lay deserted. "Why would she sneak over to his place?" Her gaze narrowed as it swerved back to Phineas. "Do you know anything?"

In a show of innocence, he lifted his hands. "I'm as ignorant as you in this matter, I swear. I know no more than you do."

Again, Louisa turned to the gardens, her hands settling back onto the glass as though she could summon her sister back by sheer willpower alone. "Why would she seek him out? Why would she risk her reputation?" She spun to face him. "What if she is discovered there? We have to do something!" She was about to rush off, but Phineas caught her arm and pulled her back.

For a moment, they stood silently, nodding to a few guests, who had looked up at Louisa's outburst. "We need to do something," she hissed under her breath, holding onto her smile until most eyes turned from them.

Phineas held on tightly to her hands, his gaze seeking hers. "Have you ever known Leonora to make a rash decision?" he asked, a cautionary tone in his voice.

Louisa swallowed. "No."

"Then trust her now," he urged her, his gaze gentle as his fingers once more grasped her chin, the pad of his thumb brushing over her skin in a soothing gesture. "Speak to her, but do not interfere. We may not know the reason for—"

"—this lunacy?" Louisa could not help but throw in.

Phineas chuckled, "But whatever it is, it has to be a very good one for her to do this, don't you agree?"

Reluctantly, Louisa nodded, knowing that Phineas was right. Never had she known Leonora to act rashly or without thought. Indeed, every step was generally well thought-out...except for the one that had led her to the masquerade that night! "Still, I cannot help but wonder why she would...speak to him and not to me."

"Don't be jealous," Phineas told her gently, a warm smile upon his face as he pulled her into his arms, settling her head against his shoulder. "She'll speak to you when she is ready. Give her time."

"I will," Louisa mumbled, closing her eyes and inhaling a deep breath, enjoying the comforting warmth of her husband's embrace. "But it will not be easy. I'm not a very patient person."

Phineas smiled—she could all but feel it in his voice when he spoke. "I could distract you," he whispered, the tone in his voice temptingly suggestive. "I already have something in mind."

Intrigued, Louisa looked up at him. "Do you now? Tell me more."

"Tonight," Phineas whispered, that mischievous grin back on his face. Once, it had riled her. Now, she couldn't imagine living without it.

Craning her neck, Louisa huffed out an annoyed breath when she saw that only half an hour had passed since she had last checked the time. "It seems we have more waiting to do."

"It'll pass quickly."

She frowned at him. "Do you promise?"

"I'll promise." His grin deepened. "If not, I'll make it up to you."

"I'll hold you to that."

"I certainly hope so," Phineas laughed, and Louisa once more glanced at the tall grandfather clock in the corner, impatience humming in her blood.

Another two minutes had passed.

In that moment, Louisa was utterly glad that she had not postponed her wedding, for she would certainly not have been able to be patient much longer.

THE END

Thank you for reading *Once Upon a Devilishly Enchanting Kiss*!

Be on the lookout for **Drake and Leo**'s story!
Get your copy of *Once Upon a Temptingly Ruinous Kiss* now!

Also by Bree Wolf

THE WHICKERTONS IN LOVE

LOVE'S SECOND CHANCE SERIES: TALES OF LORDS & LADIES

LOVE'S SECOND CHANCE SERIES: TALES OF DAMSELS & KNIGHTS

About Bree

USA Today bestselling and award-winning author, Bree Wolf has always been a language enthusiast (though not a grammarian!) and is rarely found without a book in her hand or her fingers glued to a keyboard. Trying to find her way, she has taught English as a second language, traveled abroad and worked at a translation agency as well as a law firm in Ireland. She also spent loooong years obtaining a BA in English and Education and an MA in Specialized Translation while wishing she could simply be a writer. Although there is nothing simple about being a writer, her dreams have finally come true.

"A big thanks to my fairy godmother!"

Currently, Bree has found her new home in the historical romance genre, writing Regency novels and novellas. Enjoying the mix of fact and fiction, she occasionally feels like a puppet master (or mistress? Although that sounds weird!), forcing her characters into ever-new situations that will put their strength, their beliefs, their love to the test, hoping that in the end they will triumph and get the happily-ever-after we are all looking for.

If you're an avid reader, sign up for Bree's newsletter on www. breewolf.com as she has the tendency to simply give books away. Find out about freebies, giveaways as well as occasional advance reader copies and read before the book is even on the shelves!

Connect with Bree and stay up-to-date on new releases:

Printed in Great Britain
by Amazon

28419563R00165